BAD LOON
RISING

Other great stories from Warhammer Age of Sigmar

BAD LOON
RISING

A ZOGRAT & SKROG NOVEL

ANDY CLARK

BLACK LIBRARY

A BLACK LIBRARY PUBLICATION

First published in 2023.
This edition published in Great Britain in 2023 by
Black Library, Games Workshop Ltd., Willow Road,
Nottingham, NG7 2WS, UK.

Represented by: Games Workshop Limited – Irish branch,
Unit 3, Lower Liffey Street, Dublin 1,
D01 K199, Ireland.

10 9 8 7 6 5 4 3 2 1

Produced by Games Workshop in Nottingham.
Cover illustration by Henrik Rosenborg.
Internal illustrations by Nuala Kinrade.

A CIP record for this book is available from the British Library.

ISBN 13: 978-1-80407-341-4

See Black Library on the internet at

blacklibrary.com

Find out more about Games Workshop
and the worlds of Warhammer at

games-workshop.com

Printed and bound in the UK.

*For Mrs T-C, in anticipation of once again being asked
'what is wrong with you?'*

The Mortal Realms have been despoiled. Ravaged by the followers of the Chaos Gods, they stand on the brink of utter destruction.

The fortress-cities of Sigmar are islands of light in a sea of darkness. Constantly besieged, their walls are assailed by maniacal hordes and monstrous beasts. The bones of good men are littered thick outside the gates. These bulwarks of Order are embattled within as well as without, for the lure of Chaos beguiles the citizens with promises of power.

Still the champions of Order fight on. At the break of dawn, the Crusader's Bell rings and a new expedition departs. Storm-forged knights march shoulder to shoulder with resolute militia, stoic duardin and slender aelves. Bedecked in the splendour of war, the Dawnbringer Crusades venture out to found civilisations anew. These grim pioneers take with them the fires of hope. Yet they go forth into a hellish wasteland.

Out in the wilds, hardy colonists restore order to a crumbling world. Haunted eyes scan the horizon for tyrannical reavers as they build upon the bones of ancient empires, eking out a meagre existence from cursed soil and ice-cold seas. By their valour, the fate of the Mortal Realms will be decided.

The ravening terrors that prey upon these settlers take a thousand forms. Cannibal barbarians and deranged murderers crawl from hidden lairs. Martial hosts clad in black steel march from skull-strewn castles. The savage hordes of Destruction batter the frontier towns until no stone stands atop another. In the dead of night come howling throngs of the undead, hungry to feast upon the living.

Against such foes, courage is the truest defence and the most effective weapon. It is something that Sigmar's chosen do not lack. But they are not always strong enough to prevail, and even in victory, each new battle saps their souls a little more.

This is the time of turmoil. This is the era of war.

This is the Age of Sigmar.

PROLOGUE

Badwater Drop

In a dank cavern on the outskirts of Badwater Drop, Zograt the runt shovelled squig droppings. It was a dangerous and thankless task. He had to stretch through the crudely built fence of the squigs' paddock to reach their leavings, not helped by his twisted leg or scrawny stature. The grot's rudimentary shovel was little better than a stick topped with a tough flange of fungus. Zograt thrust it hurriedly into the mounds of ordure, scooping as much dung as he could before hastily withdrawing. Each time he cringed, anticipating a squig snapping its mantrap jaws shut on his arms.

'Keep dat jingler goin', Driggzy,' Zograt panted as he nerved himself up for another lunge. Driggz glanced down from his perch atop a tall bloatcap fungus, whose broad brim jutted over the paddock.

'Yoo jus' keep shovellin',' called Driggz. 'An' hurry up. Skram's takin' da ladz out soon. We don't want 'im to find us still doin' dis. Yoo know wot 'e gets like before a raid.'

Though also a runt, Driggz was slightly bigger and stronger than Zograt. Accordingly, he had bullied his way into the job of distracting the squigs instead of having to do the shovelling. Not that this was a much safer task, since it involved balancing precariously atop a 'shroom while dangling a cluster of bells over the squigs on the end of a long pole. The snarling, spheroid beasts jostled one another to leap and snap at the bells. Zograt reckoned all it would take was one moment's inattention by Driggz for the squigs to bite down on bells or pole and haul him screaming into the pen.

Still, it was a safer job than shovelling, and Zograt cursed himself for winding up on dung-duty. He was normally quick-witted enough to trick Driggz into thinking his suggestions were Driggz's own bright ideas, but today he had been too distracted by his nerves. It had been a while since their Loonboss, Skram Badstabba, had taken the ladz out on a raid. He was bound to subject Zograt to a beating if he stumbled across him before setting off. Such a display of bullying would impress Skram's ladz – for every self-respecting grot enjoyed watching those weaker than them being picked on. Zograt had nothing but contempt for Skram, who was stupid enough that many of his ladz wondered if he wasn't part orruk. He also feared him. The Loonboss was taller and thicker-set than Zograt by far. He had been the one to give him not only his twisted leg but also his crooked, thrice-broken nose. Just the thought of receiving yet another beating at Skram's hands made Zograt's own shake a little more.

'It'll go fasta if we swap, Driggzy,' he suggested. 'Yoo'z stronger dan me. Ya got longer arms.'

'Yeah, an' I wanna keep 'em, so keep shovellin' and I'll keep jinglin',' replied Driggz.

Zograt scowled, then lunged through the fence and scooped another pile of dung. He cursed his treacherous body as his shaking caused squig droppings to spill from his shovel. Zograt tipped what remained onto the stinking heap of dung and refuse that loomed over him. He gritted his cracked teeth in frustration. This entire task was pointless, he thought. Even an idiot like Skram must be able to see that. The dung and rubbish just heaped up and up until eventually it toppled, often straight back into the pens. Zograt could think of half a dozen ways the foul heap could be disposed of, or even used to fertilise the tribe's fungus crops.

'Skram ain't smart enuff to fink of stuff like dat though, is he?' he muttered to himself. 'And he wouldn't lissen to a runt like yoo. No-grot does. So jus' keep shovellin' and get out of 'ere before–'

'Oh zog it, he's 'ere,' hissed Driggz.

Zograt went cold. His gaze darted frantically about as he sought for a hiding place. His shaking became a convulsion that saw the shovel spill from his hands and spatter dung across his shins and the ragged hem of his black robe.

Nowhere to go, he thought. Backed up with the squig pen on one side and the dungheap on the other, he was cornered.

'Oi, runt!' Skram's shout froze Zograt in place. He had a deep voice for a grot, and there was no mistaking the glee in his tone. 'Yoo'z meant to be shovellin' dung, not rollin' in it!'

Skram's words were greeted with massed cackling. Zograt forced himself to turn and face the Loonboss and the crowd of toadies trailing in his wake.

'Oh zog me, dat's 'alf da tribe,' muttered Driggz, sounding dismayed.

For a moment, Zograt seriously contemplated scrambling through the bars of the squig pen and fleeing for its far side. He despised himself for the thought at once, however; it wasn't just cowardly, it was also stupid. He didn't doubt that Skram was about to hurt him, maybe badly, but the squigs would kill him for certain.

Skram loomed over him, a hulking mass of stringy muscle and ragged scars with a big cleaver hanging from his belt. The loonstone amulet hanging about Skram's neck glowed with sickly light. His small, deep-set eyes glimmered like embers of spite in the dark shadow thrown by his cowl.

'Told yooz to get dat job done,' snarled Skram. His tone was surly, but his features were twisted into a leer of delight. Dozens of grots pressed in behind him, their expressions eager. Zograt noted that many were decked out for a raid, festooned with quivers of black-fletched arrows or lugging shields, pokin' spears or dented brass gongs.

Zograt tried to reply. He was furious with himself when all that came from his tightened throat was a strangled wheeze. Skram, however, appeared delighted.

'Wossat, runt, yoo ferget 'ow to speak? Or is yoo too stoopid?' Skram advanced on him, knuckles bunched, and Zograt took an involuntary step back. He bumped against the paddock fence. From behind him came a scrambling and snarling. Zograt realised to his horror that he couldn't hear Driggz's bells and that, while watching the spectacle playing out below, the bigger runt must have forgotten to jangle them.

Fear of the squigs' jaws eclipsed all else. Driven by instinct, Zograt lunged away from the fence. From behind him came a jarring thump and the splintering sounds of huge fangs sinking deep into rotten wood. Zograt barely heard it, for in throwing himself clear of one danger he had literally run straight into another. He rebounded from the solid bulk of Skram's chest and landed on his backside in scattered squig dung with his heart racing and his head swimming from the impact. Skram loomed over him.

'Daft zogger nearly got hisself eaten!' crowed Skram. Most of his ladz jeered and hooted with laughter. A few just chuckled dutifully, or else looked bored and a bit disgusted by the entire spectacle. One of these stepped up to Skram's side. Zograt recognised Nuffgunk Manstrangle, Skram's second-in-command.

'Boss, we gotta get da ladz movin',' he said. 'Dunno 'ow long da Twitchleggz will be away for. Don't wanna miss our chance to raid 'em while yoo is wastin' time on dis runt.'

Skram's expression became petulant, the look of a cruel child forced to stop tormenting an insect. He snarled at Nuffgunk, then back down at Zograt.

'Fine, but I told dis runt to get a job done, an' he ain't done it. No-grot gets away wiv dat in Badwater Drop!'

Skram took double handfuls of Zograt's threadbare robe and hauled him up so they were almost nose to nose.

'Yoo wanna roll about in squig shit instead o' shovellin' it? Fine, I'll stick yoo where da dung goes,' Skram growled. For one horrible moment Zograt's mind became a blank scream of panic as he envisioned the Loonboss hefting him up and throwing him into the squig paddock.

Instead, Skram kicked Zograt hard in his twisted leg, causing an explosion of pain to rocket up the limb and cramp Zograt's guts with its severity. Skram punched Zograt in the stomach, doubling him over and driving a thin spray of air and spittle from between his lips. Then, even while Zograt still retched, he felt himself spun around and pushed face first into the teetering dungheap.

His mouth and nostrils filled with ordure and festering food waste. His gorge rose, and only the terror that he might choke prevented him from vomiting. Instinct drove Zograt to recoil. He was prevented by the weight of one of Skram's hobnailed boots, which landed none too gently on the back of Zograt's neck and shoved him deeper into the dungheap. Something wet and wriggling squirmed up one nostril and made him gag again. He could hear the muffled sound of grots laughing uproariously, over the nauseating squelch of muck and the roaring of his own blood in his ears. The fear came to Zograt that he was going to end his short and miserable existence drowning in squig droppings, and he scrabbled to gain purchase on something and force his head up for a breath.

Skram shoved back, harder. The laughter redoubled. Suddenly Zograt felt angrier than he had ever been in his life. The pain he was used to, could bear with weary resignation as simply being his lot as a runt. But the mockery of creatures so much more stupid than him enraged Zograt beyond words. What he could do, if he had even half their strength, or even if he simply hadn't had the horrible misfortune to be the smallest and weakest of his tribe.

He wasn't sure if it was anger, lack of oxygen or perhaps discarded scraps of hallucinogenic fungi forced down his throat, but Zograt's mind filled suddenly with lurid visions of the horrors he would unleash on Skram if he had the chance. And not just Skram either, but his whole stupid tribe, and all the uncaring realms that had left him so completely to this ignominious fate.

The visions lent Zograt the strength to heave himself back out of the filth long enough to spit out a mouthful of muck and drag in a shrieking breath. Then he heard Skram snarl with outrage and was shoved back down again.

'Mucky little runt!' roared Skram. 'Stay in da filth where ya belong!'

Zograt's lungs burned in his thin chest. His maimed leg throbbed in time to his labouring heartbeat. Dimly, he heard a voice that might have been Nuffgunk's, but the words no longer made sense to him. Colours swam across Zograt's vision and he felt a tickling sensation like the feather-light scrabble of insect legs against his skin. The moist darkness of the dungheap seemed to seep through his robes, through his flesh, into the very heart of him, and Zograt lost himself to it.

* * *

Deep in the Shudderwood, a few days later

Skram Badstabba crept through the Shudderwood, hoping not to meet a monster. The Loonboss was an imposing figure, bulky for a Moonclan grot with scars to prove his toughness. The tall cowl of his black robes was pierced with the bones of ex-rivals. His cleaver had been torn from the grasp of a dying orruk and was festooned with hidden slittas. Skram believed the talisman about his neck, a Bad Moon hewn from loonstone by his tribe's shaman, protected him from danger, though as he had quickly bored of the aged shaman's explanation, he was hazy on the details.

The point was, Skram thought as he took stock of his leaderly assets, he was a tough Loonboss with blades aplenty and the magic of the Bad Moon to protect him. Yet none of this staved off the crawling unease bred by his surroundings.

The trees of the Shudderwood crowded in. Their translucent trunks twitched with insectile movement within. Overhead, their branches meshed conspiratorially. Leaves like black satin whispered against pale fronds glimmering with bioluminescence, while many-legged things scuttled everywhere. Tree roots had torn up the ground. Skram had to watch his step to avoid his foot plunging down some hidden hole. Liar's Grass grew underfoot, each blade night black on one side and ghostly white on the other. It stirred fitfully as though moved by a breeze Skram couldn't feel, creating a dizzying carpet of darkness and light.

Mist rolled between the trees and gathered so thick in dells and ditches it appeared solid. It glowed faintly, its sickly yellow-white light seeming to dance just ahead, or off to one side, or through the next thicket. Rumour had it that if a grot stared too long into those lights, they would wander away never to be seen again.

Dwelling on those rumours reminded Skram to check on his ladz.

'Don't wanna be out 'ere alone,' he muttered to himself as he glanced back at the skulkmobs trailing him. Nervous grots hastened on Skram's heels, red eyes darting beneath their cowls. The dented gongs they had bashed so enthusiastically during their raid on the Twitchleggz tribe were smothered with dirty rags lest an inadvertent clang alert something dreadful to the grots' passing. Even their usual bickering was muted.

At the head of the skulkmobs walked Nuffgunk. His long face wore a perpetual scowl even at the best of times. Right now, Skram thought the grot boss looked as though he'd just eaten a bitterspurt 'shroom. Nuffgunk held his pokin' spear tight and ready to stab.

'Wot yoo jumpy for, Nuffgunk? 'Fraid of da monsters?' Skram spoke as loud as he dared with mocking bravado. Nuffgunk cringed. Skram's courage was bolstered as the closest grots cackled. In Skram's experience there were few things a Moonclan grot liked better than bullying, except perhaps a shiny bottle or wicked blade. A pleasant memory came back to him of giving that runt Zograt a good beating just before they had left Badwater Drop. He wondered briefly if the little git had survived his dive in the dungheap. If so, Skram thought, he was going to be in for a repeat performance when the raiding party got home.

Skram had stopped walking, unable to pick a path across the treacherous ground and engage in ridicule at the same time. Nuffgunk stalked past, baring his back to Skram defiantly.

'Know wot dey sez, boss,' he hissed. 'Monsters always takes da noisy ones, or dem wot falls be'ind.'

Skram hastened to overtake Nuffgunk, ignoring the nasty chuckles from his ladz.

'You *is* scared of da monsters!' Skram crowed. His lieutenant looked incredulous.

'Course I is, boss,' Nuffgunk whispered. 'Yoo 'eard da stories, ain't ya? Snikkersnak jawz, slithaquick clawz, an' all dat.'

The grots told tales of the Gob-hole monster, which stayed still so long the moss grew over it until some curious grot decided to explore the dripping cavern that turned out to be a mouth. Then there were the Ganglers, swaying through the trees on spindle limbs, lantern eyes watching for stragglers, cavernous ears alive for loud voices. There were the Snatchers, said to squirm from the soil and wrap wormy fingers around the necks of grots who lingered above ground, and the Glintygrab, who tracked down wasteful grots by the trails of discarded shinies they left behind.

Skram realised he'd slowed, lost in ghastly contemplation. Nuff-gunk had pulled ahead again. Skram sped up, jostling his lieutenant as he passed. He wouldn't shiv an underling as useful as Nuffgunk, who did a lot of the hard work of being in charge, but Skram wasn't above using his brawn to remind the grot boss of his place.

'*I* ain't afraid of monsters! Dey's afraid o' me,' bragged Skram. 'I just gave dem Twitchleggz a zoggin' good kickin'!'

Nuffgunk spat a gobbet of phlegm into a bush. 'Right, boss. Yeah.'

Skram's hand strayed towards the handle of a concealed slitta as he wondered whether maybe he *should* shiv Nuffgunk, just to make an example. To his alarm, his loonstone pendant glowed sickly yellow. Skram stuffed it inside his robes lest it shine like a lantern between the trees.

'Wot yoo mean?' he demanded.

Nuffgunk gave him a look of weary disgust. As the two of them scrambled up a muddy rise over coiling roots, Skram felt an unac-customed twinge of self-doubt. It *had* been a good raid, hadn't it?

'We didn't 'zactly bring da Everdank, did we, boss?' said Nuffgunk.

'We gave da Twitchleggz a good kickin',' Skram insisted. 'Half o' Funnelsnare Pit woz on fire by da time we got done wiv 'em!'

'Only cos Raznut dropped 'is torch when dat spider bit 'is legs off,' Nuffgunk retorted. 'Right before da Twitchleggz grabbed all 'is ladz and dragged 'em off ta feed Arghabigskuttla. Told yoo we shouldn't 'ave wasted time kickin' da runt about.'

Now that Skram thought about it, the living spider god of the Twitchleggz probably had dined well today.

'Raznut an' his ladz woz a useless bunch o' gitz,' said Skram, waving the point aside. 'We pushed over dat big spider statchoo, stabbed up a bunch of dere ladz, an' nicked a load o' dere spider eggz to feed to da squigs!'

'You know dey can just stand dat statchoo up again?' Nuffgunk asked. 'An' I reckon dey cut up as many of our ladz as we did deres.'

'Still got da eggz!' Skram insisted.

He looked back to where Spruggit's ladz carried bags full of lumpy white egg sacs. He cackled as he saw several of the grots were tangled in the sticky wisps of web that fronded the eggs. Others bore purple swellings where infant arachnids had bitten their kidnappers. These luckless grots staggered, eyes glassy, lips flecked with foam.

'*Might* be good, if we can get 'em back to Badwater Drop wivout our ladz gettin' eaten alive,' replied Nuffgunk. 'All I'm sayin' is…' His voice trailed off as he crested the rise and looked down into the dell beyond.

'Oh zog,' he said.

Skram thought this seemed an odd conclusion to Nuffgunk's point, until he too reached the top of the rise. The tunnel leading down to Badwater Drop was across the dell, a few hundred yards further through a dripping tangle of boulders and rotting trees. Between the grots and sanctuary squatted a hulking thing of chitin, luminescent eyestalks and grot-sized claws, so huge that it filled the dell.

It struck Skram belatedly that scouts might have been useful.

'Er,' he croaked. A dozen bulbous eyes swivelled in his direction. The monster rose on segmented legs, antennae quivering with a sound like wind through dry reeds.

He looked at Nuffgunk.

Nuffgunk looked at him.

They both glanced back down the slope to the grots staggering under their spidery burdens.

'Leg it,' shrieked Skram.

He and Nuffgunk dashed in opposite directions. Behind Skram, the screaming began. He kept running. In his opinion, a grot who couldn't escape a monster attack didn't deserve a place in his skrap anyway.

By the time Skram made it to the entrance to Badwater Drop, he was gasping for breath. The cave was a diagonal slash of darkness, like a maw opening amidst slimy stone and rotting vegetation. Most sane beings of the realms would have viewed such an entrance with fear. Skram plunged gratefully into its promised safety, ducking to avoid a curtain of stragglenekk fungus that hung like sweaty meat. The fungus would strangle unwary victims, drinking their juices once the squirming stopped.

Cool shadows welcomed Skram back like old cronies. He felt safer without open space above him, at least until a roar from the direction of the dell sent him scurrying deeper. The cave narrowed into a dank tunnel that wormed its way into the deeps. Thick mycelium straggled along the walls and ceiling, sprouting outcroppings of thumb-sized mushrooms that gave off a pallid glow.

Moisture dripped.

Insects squirmed and scuttled.

Skram took a moment to compose himself. He pulled his hood back into place and gulped deep breaths as he leant against the wall. Fungal fronds fumbled at him with idiot curiosity. Skram batted them away before any could prick his skin and seed him with spores. A fat millipede trundled from a crevice to investigate Skram's hand and he snatched it gratefully, biting the insect in half and sucking down its bitter juices. The back end of the insect flopped about, little legs kicking. Skram exhaled slowly.

'Well, *dat* woz zoggin' 'orrible,' said a voice behind him. Skram jumped and squashed the other half of his snack. He turned to see Nuffgunk slinking down the tunnel, a score or so of grots behind him.

'Yeah,' replied Skram. He fixed his lieutenant with a beady eye.

'Wouldn't want to get blamed fer dat mess,' said Nuffgunk.

'Da monster must've 'eard them squigwitz staggerin' about wiv da egg sacs. So dey's to blame, right?' Skram drew himself up so the peak of his hood scraped the tunnel ceiling.

In the foetid 'shroomlight, he saw the swift calculus of self-preservation behind Nuffgunk's eyes. Could the grot boss take Skram in a straight fight at such close quarters? Did he have the guts to try? A tingle shot through Skram's body, part anticipation, part millipede poison. The glow of his loonstone pendant showed through the threadbare fabric of his robes like a blessing from the Bad Moon.

Nuffgunk's shoulders sagged.

'Yeah, boss, musta been dem gitz wiv da eggz,' he said, eyes downcast.

Skram grunted his satisfaction before baring his back to Nuffgunk. He licked insect juices from his palm, then set off down the passage, allowing himself a leer as he heard his ladz following.

The route down to Badwater Drop was long and tortuous. The grots passed through slime-slick caverns where water plopped into stagnant pools and pallid worms writhed. They scrambled over the remains of ancient statues long disfigured by time and mineral accretions. They squirmed through claustrophobic tunnels and between rocks like jagged fangs, picked their way through glowing thickets of bulbous fungi, and balanced over boulders jutting from pools teeming with leech-beetles.

By the time they reached his tribe's lurklair, Skram had convinced himself anew of his raid's success. Like every raid he ever led, he told himself, it had been glorious. So convincing a job had he done of lying to himself that he entered Badwater Drop with the swagger of a conquering hero.

Skram's confidence soared as he passed under the ancient arch that was a last remnant of some other, long-ago fastness, now defaced by fungi and crude trophies. The feeling held as he entered the outer slinkhole and found its ramshackle barricade abandoned but for scurrying insects.

His good mood faltered as he followed the tunnel from the slinkhole towards the main lair and found himself crunching over a carpet of bugs. Badwater Drop had its fair share of creepy-crawlies, but Skram thought this infestation was unusual. The walls and roof of the tunnel churned with movement. He swatted away scrabbling things as they dropped onto his shoulders or tried to swarm up his shins. Skram did his best to ignore the nervous muttering of his ladz as he pressed on, determined to find out where all these bugs had come from.

It was only as he emerged into Da Big Cave, where the more important grots of his tribe had their huts, that Skram's self-assuredness took a serious knock. He halted so suddenly that Nuffgunk, hurrying to extricate himself from the infested tunnel, walked into his back.

'Wot da zog 'appened 'ere, boss?'

For the second time that day, Skram could manage only a bewildered 'Er...'

Da Big Cave had been so named because it was the widest open space in the lurklair, albeit still possessing a reassuringly low ceiling carpeted with glowing fungi, and plenty of stalagmites and stalactites to sneak between. When Skram had herded his skrap out of Da Big Cave a few days ago, it had boasted boss-huts thrown together from the shiniest scrap and best bits of rock the tribe could gather. Some had been built against stalagmites for solidity. Others had been studded with eye-catching shiny glass and stolen trinkets. A few were intermingled with the pipes and burners of alchemical stills or thickets of rare fungi, marking them out as the dwellings of the tribe's Gobbapalooza.

Almost all the structures had now been demolished as thoroughly as though boom-squigs had detonated within them. Skram saw the ruins of his own hut, formerly the most impressive in the cave, now reduced to a slumped shell.

Insects swarmed everywhere. Now Skram could see them properly he felt his confidence wither. He had lived all his days in the underdanks, but had never seen bugs as strange as these. There were segmapedes longer than his leg, their carapaces inky black and furred with white mycelial tendrils. Arachnid things lurched through the wreckage on odd numbers of legs, their bloated bodies covered in tiny 'shrooms, their heads fanged moon-crescents. Myriad beetles scrabbled over one another in drifts, their mouthfuls of grot-like fangs visible in the 'shroomlight.

Only now did Skram register the pitiful corpses of fallen grots, half-buried in bugs. Skram realised that every one of them was distorted and bloated. Rancid-looking fungi protruded from eye sockets, yawning mouths and ruptured flesh. This horrid revelation was followed by another – he could hear terrified shrieks echoing from the tunnel mouths that led deeper into Badwater Drop. Skram realised that whatever had happened here, it was still happening.

'Wot d'we do, boss?' asked Nuffgunk. He sounded bewildered and dismayed. Skram considered simply legging it. He could find a new lair, he thought, get a new tribe together. Badwater Drop was cramped for a grot of his ambitions, now that he thought about it, and as for that thing that lived in Da Soggy Cave…

It was the looks on his ladz's faces that stopped him. Skram realised that if he were to turn tail and run so soon after that business with the monster, his time as Loonboss would be at an end.

Preferring the vague threat of the unknown to the absolute certainty of half a dozen slittas in his back, Skram squared his shoulders. He donned his most ferocious scowl.

'We find out wot da zog is goin' on, and we stab up whoever made all dis mess!' he said. Hefting his cleaver Skram waded through the insects towards his hut.

By the time he reached the wrecked structure, Skram had been bitten and stung many times. Fortunately for him, no Moonclan grot grew to maturity without building up a powerful resistance to the cocktail of toxins, poisons and spores inherent to their ecosystem. All the same, Skram's head was swimming badly enough that it took him a moment to recognise the figure cowering in the ruins of his hut.

'Hoi, Stragwit, dat yoo?' he asked.

Stragwit Skrab was a portly grot with a bulbous nose and deep-sunk eyes, currently perching atop a pile of Skram's favourite shiny rocks. The wreckage of a wood-and-leather harness clung to Stragwit's shoulders, and he clutched a dented cauldron the size of his head which he was using to bludgeon insects as they climbed his rock pile. Stragwit served the tribe as its Brewgit, foremost purveyor of potions and augmentative unguents. Right now, Skram thought Stragwit just looked like a scared runt. The sight brought out his overdeveloped bullying instinct.

'Stragwit, ya daft zogger, wot's goin' on? Where'd all da bugs come from?'

'Zograt!' screeched Stragwit hysterically. 'It's Zograt, he's got da Clammy Hand on 'im!'

Skram blinked, scowled, then cursed as something bit him on the backside. By the time he had performed a swift dance of cursing and swatting at his robes, he had processed Stragwit's words. They still made no sense.

'Zograt don't 'ave no Clammy Hand, he's a wonky-nosed little scrut covered in squig muck,' said Skram. 'Wot really 'appened?'

Stragwit clubbed at the encroaching insects with feverish intensity. Shrill screams issued from deeper into the lurklair, echoing flatly from the cavern's low ceiling. Bugs seethed on every surface. Their massed rasp and chitter filled Skram's ears. Growing panic fed his anger and he waded up to Stragwit, grabbing the Brewgit by the scruff of his robes.

'Asked yoo a question,' Skram snarled.

'An' I toldya!' Stragwit replied. 'Somefin' 'appened to da runt while yoo woz off raidin'. Da Bad Moon blessed 'im, and if yoo knows wot's good for ya, boss, you'll do a runner before 'im and dat troggoth of his finds ya!'

'Da Bad Moon blessed dat little freak?' Skram released Stragwit then, belatedly, wondering aloud. 'Wot troggoth? Zograt ain't got a troggoth.'

This couldn't be right, he thought. The Brewgit must have been bitten one too many times and was delirious. Zograt was a reedy-voiced little creep too weak to go raiding or wrangle squigs, and who Skram despised. He hated Zograt's crooked nose and his weakling limp, and never mind that Skram had inflicted both upon the smaller grot with repeated beatings. There was just something about Zograt that got under Skram's skin and infused him with the need to brutalise and embarrass the runt over and again.

'Boss, wot if he's tellin' da troof?'

Skram brushed bugs angrily from his robes as he rounded on Nuffgunk.

'Yoo reckon da Bad Moon would bless dat little turd over any of yooz lot?' he demanded. 'Over yoo, Nuffgunk? Zog it, over me, da Loonboss? Wot for? Wot's dat limpin' little sneak got dat I don't?'

But Skram knew, down in the deepest grotto of his rancid little soul, what Zograt had. Zograt had brains. He *thought* about things in a manner that Skram found both unsettling and offensive. It was his own deficiency in that regard that had always lain at the heart of Skram's hatred towards Zograt, even if the Loonboss only dimly understood his own motivations.

An icy tendril of fear broke through the armour of Skram's indignation.

What if Stragwit *was* telling the truth? he thought. If Zograt had somehow secured the blessings of the Bad Moon, had gained the power to do all this, then how would he treat Skram now that the shiv was in the other back? And what had Stragwit said about a troggoth...?

'Lissen, maybe we betta–'

Skram was interrupted by a sing-song voice from outside the hut. It had the reedy tone he hated so instinctively, the nasal burr that made him want to black an eye or snap a bone. Yet now it was underlaid by something resonant and deep, as though another voice echoed out from unimaginable gulfs to entwine its words with Zograt's.

'Welcome back, boss... Yoo like wot I done wiv da place?'

Skram turned slowly, almost against his will. Wriggling things crunched and popped underfoot with every step. He didn't want to look, but he had to.

There was the runt, standing outside the hut in his threadbare robes, barely tall enough to come up to Skram's shoulder. Skram took in the fungi that had sprouted in glowing tendrils from Zograt's scalp. He saw the insects that teemed through the runt's robes, skittered across his skin and swirled about his feet. He stared into Zograt's bulging eyes and saw motes of poisonous green power drifting through them like spores. Skram's gaze travelled past Zograt to take in the huge Dankhold troggoth looming at the runt's back. The beast's head and shoulders weren't visible from this angle, but what Skram could see of it was enough to do involuntary things to his bowel control.

'Wot's da matter, *boss?*' asked Zograt, his tone mock-cheerful, his words squirming between gritted fangs. 'Don't like da mess I made? Gunna give me anuvver *kickin'?*'

Skram glanced over his shoulder in the hopes that, against all odds, Nuffgunk and his ladz would be there to back him up. Surely, they too saw the wrongness of this bewildering apparition, would fight against this perversion of what Skram saw as the natural order of things?

He was in time to see the last few stragglers fighting one another to scramble out of the ruined hut, black robes trailing as they fled.

Skram looked back at Zograt, who favoured him with a grin of infinite malice. Stragwit, still stranded atop his rocks, whimpered.

'Nah,' said Skram, then ran for his life.

CHAPTER ONE

Badwater Drop

Zograt would forever savour the expression on Skram's face in the instant before the Loonboss turned and fled. He knew he would recall again and again that look of dawning comprehension, of ignorant belligerence melting away to expose the panic of a hunted animal. He suspected it would bring him the same surge of pleasure every time. It felt almost as good as the magic that flowed through his body, churning his guts and tingling his fingers and scrabbling like spiders' legs behind his eyes.

As Skram vanished through a rent in the side of the hut, Zograt fixed Stragwit with a beady eye.

'Yoo scared o' me, Brewgit?'

Stragwit nodded vigorously.

'Rememb'rin' all dem times yoo made me carry scaldin' 'ot potions and gave me beatings when I dropped 'em?' Zograt asked, enjoying the new rumble that lent menace to his reedy voice. 'Finkin' about dem names wot yoo called me, dem nasty brews wot yoo tested on me?'

Zograt twiddled his fingers, experimentally flexing his new-found powers. The insects surrounding Stragwit shrilled and seethed in response. The Brewgit screeched. He tried to pull his extremities in further as the many-legged tide flowed upward, but only succeeded in overbalancing.

The Brewgit toppled with a forlorn wail and was immediately buried in insects. Zograt giggled at the sight of Stragwit's flailing, the sound of his shrieks turning to choking as insects wriggled into his mouth.

Then the question struck Zograt of where the tribe would get their potions, if not from Stragwit. He heaved a put-upon sigh and looked up at the Dankhold troggoth towering over him. The creature was tall enough that his head scraped Da Big Cave's ceiling. His warty hide was mottled pale purple, encrusted with fungi and waxy-looking mineral accretions. Near as many insects scurried and squirmed across him as nestled in Zograt's robes. The troggoth's boulder-like knuckles dragged along the ground.

'Wot ya reckon, Skrog? Dunno 'ow to brew potions meself.'

Skrog returned Zograt's stare with all the comprehension of a granite slab. A scutterbug clambered from the troggoth's ear, waved its antennae fussily, and set off down his neck for points south.

Zograt nodded. 'Yer right, lad. We need 'im.'

Zograt wiggled his fingers again and the insects scuttled back to leave Stragwit in a ring of clear space. The Brewgit struggled to his feet, retching up a throatful of squirming things. He wiped a bug-bitten hand across his mouth.

'Don't kill me,' Stragwit croaked.

'Not gunna,' Zograt replied, exhilarated at the sense of holding another creature's life in his claws. His tribe had only ever looked at him with contempt. The terror and hope now warring on Stragwit's face gave him a sense of power like nothing he'd ever known.

'Not gunna?' echoed Stragwit.

'Not if yoo does wot I tells ya,' replied Zograt.

'Wot, like yoo'z da boss?' Stragwit cringed at his own incredulous tone, his eyes flicking to the circle of insects surrounding him.

'Stragwit, ya daft zogger, I *is* da boss now,' said Zograt.

'Yoo'z da boss?' That tone again. Zograt twitched one finger. Several hundred insects took a collective step closer to Stragwit.

'Yoo'z da boss! Yoo'z da boss!' screeched Stragwit.

'I'm da boss,' said Zograt. The realisation left him light-headed. He steadied himself against one of Skrog's pillar-like legs.

Zograt.

Not the runt.

Not the tribe's punching bag.

Not face down in a mountain of squig dung.

The boss, by the say-so of the Bad Moon itself!

Zograt couldn't hold back a mad cackle that bubbled up and echoed around Da Big Cave. Something in his new-found magics amplified the sound so that it boomed fit to shake the cavern. Stragwit cringed, hands over his ears.

As the echoes of Zograt's laughter died away, the chitter of insects and the distant cries of terrified grots could be heard again. Stragwit ventured to speak.

'Boss, if yoo'z da boss now, wot about... da boss? You gunna let 'im leg it?'

'Course I ain't,' replied Zograt.

'But ain't 'e gettin' away?'

'Nice fing about Da Big Cave, Stragwit, is it's big,' said Zograt. 'Takes a while t'get across it through all dese bugs.'

Zograt limped past Stragwit, insects flowing in his wake as though caught in a tidal pull, forcing the Brewgit to scurry alongside him or be buried again. They both looked out through the tumbled hut wall. In the wavering 'shroomlight, Skram could be seen wading through biting insects, shooting fearful glances over his shoulder, making for the tunnel that promised escape. Zograt saw Nuffgunk leading the fleeing remnants of the raiding party in flight. He realised he had taken too long tormenting Stragwit, that Nuffgunk was within a few yards of reaching the tunnel.

'Can't be 'avin' dat,' Zograt said. He reached for the power within. It responded eagerly, flowing at his command. A detached part of Zograt marvelled at that. Old Spurk, the tribe's decrepit shaman, always made a literal song and dance over conjuring his powers. Even then, half the time they just gave him a nosebleed or made somegrot's head go bang. Yet Zograt's power felt as though it were part of him, a reservoir he could tap into as instinctively as breathing. If that wasn't proof of the Bad Moon's favour, he didn't know what was.

Now he drew deep upon that power and sent it coursing into the bedrock of Da Big Cave. It raced beneath the feet of the fleeing grots to the tunnel beyond. He heard Stragwit gasp as a mass of insects spilled from the tunnel mouth, causing Nuffgunk and the others to falter. Bulky shapes swelled in the darkness, then a mass of multicoloured fungi ballooned outward to block it. Zograt watched Nuffgunk turn and flee back into Da Big Cave. A couple of his ladz weren't so quick-thinking. One got a leg trapped under a grotesquely swelling mass of stinkcranny fungus, which rolled over him and crushed him flat. Another grot was pierced by swaying tendrils and lifted off the ground, limbs thrashing as his body bulged and tore through his robes. Taut skin split, blood drizzling onto the bugs below as a forest of glowing 'shrooms erupted from the luckless grot.

'Oh, zog me,' whimpered Stragwit. Zograt watched with satisfaction as his victims performed a scrabbling about-turn and fled deeper into the cavern. Skram pulled up short, looked frantically around for an escape route, then dashed off after his fleeing ladz.

'Dat's better, off to Da Soggy Cave dey goes,' he said.

'But boss… dere's uvver tunnels down dere, uvver ways out,' said Stragwit.

'Wot makes you fink I didn't 'shroom dem up too?' Zograt shot a toothy grin at Stragwit before limping off in pursuit of Skram. 'Come on, Skrog,' he called. Behind him, Zograt heard the troggoth grunt, followed by a series of rending, crashing sounds as he ploughed through the remains of Skram's hut.

As Zograt limped down the wide, slanting tunnel that led to Da Soggy Cave, Stragwit caught up to him.

'Boss?'

'Wot?'

Stragwit's jaw worked as though he were fishing for the right words. They picked their way down the tunnel between stalactites, and across overlapping slabs of stone between which foetid streamlets gurgled.

'Boss, 'ow come ya got da Clammy Hand? Wotchoo do?'

Zograt had known the question was coming, but wasn't sure how to answer because really, what *had* he done? His memory of the events leading up to his sudden apotheosis were hazy…

Zograt recalled being thrust face down into the dungheap until he must have lost consciousness, because the next thing he recalled was Driggz hauling him out of the filth. He had been surprised that the other grot had dragged him to safety instead of rifling his pockets, until it occurred to him that he had nothing worth Driggz's while to steal. Zograt suspected Driggz maintained their shaky alliance mostly because, with Zograt around to pick on, he himself was spared the worst of the bigger grots' attentions. Ergo, Zograt was worth more to him alive than drowned in squig turds.

It was about here that Zograt's memory grew hazy, yellowing in his mind's eye as though his thoughts had become mildewed. He remembered shrugging Driggz off, limping through the caves to his hidey-hole, the cramped grotto where he went to skulk and lick his wounds after each beating. His mind had been boiling with thoughts of vengeance, the desire to drive a shiv into Skram's back even if it killed him. The crawl to get to his grotto through a narrow fissure was hard on Zograt's bad leg and bruised ribs, but it was worth it. He was the only one of his tribe small enough to reach the hidey-hole. It was the one place where he could feel safe for a few precious hours.

Only, had there been something different about his grotto this time? Was that what curdled his thoughts? Zograt wondered. Was that what sent glowing mycelia burrowing through his recollections and rummaging through his brain until they burst from his scalp as malformed fungal braids? Zograt dimly remembered a leprous light washing over him. A bitter taste danced on his tongue, his saliva burning as he felt again a sponginess yielding between his teeth.

A sense of delirium followed. Zograt recalled nonsensical images tumbling over one another like a river of insects. He shuddered as his memory brushed against something vast and foul that stirred amidst darkness and stared with yellow eyes as wide as craters.

Zograt's next clear memory involved limping along one of the lurklair's outermost tunnels and feeling powerful in a way he never had before. He had registered the scrabble of insects infesting his robes and welcomed it, known it for the blessing it surely was. He had felt the potential squirming through him and watched in amazement as fungi bloomed from the tunnel walls in answer to a wiggle of his fingertips. A glance over his shoulder had caused Zograt to halt in surprise as he saw the hulking troggoth that followed him. Zograt had looked the huge beast up and down, felt it sizing him up in return. He had observed the infestation of insects scampering over its body just as they did his own. Zograt had known in that moment that he should have been fleeing for his life, for he had never seen this troggoth before and as far as he knew the huge creature fancied him for a snack. Instead, he had felt a sense of rightness in that moment. There had come a sensation that it took Zograt long moments to identify, so alien was it to him. This beast made him feel as though his hiding grotto had somehow come alive in troggoth form.

To his frank amazement, he felt safe.

'You wiv me?' he had asked. The troggoth had appeared to consider this question for so long that Zograt wondered if it understood. It had held one huge hand outstretched, patiently waiting for a fat-bodied spider to descend on a strand of silk then scuttle away across the tunnel floor. At last, the troggoth had jerked its head and given a grunt that sounded to Zograt like 'Skrog'.

'Skrog, is it? I ain't got a zoggin' clue wot's 'appened to me, and I dunno where yoo came from, but zog it, I can feel da Clammy Hand on me!'

The troggoth had stared down at him. Moisture beaded on the end of its nose like water on a stalactite and dripped to the floor.

'Glad yoo agree,' he had said at last, realising that he had more pressing matters than holding a one-sided conversation with a troggoth. It had dawned on Zograt that he needed to find his way back to Da Big Cave. He had been blessed with strange new powers, and he couldn't think of a more deserving bunch of gitz to practise them on.

'Skram Badstabba, yoo'z about to 'ave a zoggin' 'orrible day...' he had chuckled to himself as he set off...

'Boss?'

Zograt came back to himself. Stragwit was staring at him in confusion while he stood muttering under his breath. Zograt glanced up at Skrog, who had halted a few steps behind and was ponderously licking moisture from the wall. The troggoth seemed to feel his gaze and turned to regard him with glacial patience. Zograt felt again that inexplicable sense of safety in the beast's presence.

'I got da Clammy Hand cos I deserves it more dan da rest o' yooz,' said Zograt. 'I'm smarter an' meaner, an da Bad Moon knows just 'ow bad I want to stick some shivs in some backs. Don't worry 'bout what I did, Stragwit. Worry 'bout wot I'm *gunna* do.'

He set off down the tunnel again, Brewgit, troggoth and a chittering sea of insects following in his wake.

Da Soggy Cave was named for the lake whose dark waters took up much of its floorspace. Moisture dripped from stubby stalactites festooning its ceiling, causing the lake's surface to ripple and dance.

A monster inhabited Da Soggy Cave. The tribe called it Da Lurk, and regularly threw captives, trussed squigs and other assorted rubbish into the waters in the hopes of appeasing it. Zograt had narrowly avoided being served up to Da Lurk several times. Da Soggy Cave was where the tribe's lowliest members built their hovels from whatever rubbish was to hand, the structures huddled against the walls as though recoiling from the lake. This did not put them outside the reach of Da Lurk on the rare occasions it chose to surface. Nor did it stop the monster from dragging screaming grots into the depths, tangled amidst the pitiful wreckage of their homes.

The tribe usually hastened through Da Soggy Cave as quickly as they could, making for the tunnels that led off to Da Wonky Cave, Da Shouty Cave, Da 'Shroomcave or the squig pens. Today, however, Skram had rallied them on the lakeshore, presumably to fight back against Zograt and his bugs.

'Yoo ferget 'bout Da Lurk, Skram?' wondered Zograt aloud. 'Or is yoo hopin' a ruckus'll bring it up 'ere and maybe it'll get me after all?'

He surveyed the skulkmobs Skram had evidently bullied into

position. The intimidating effect of such a massed horde was somewhat spoiled in Zograt's opinion by their ongoing efforts to trample the insects that bedevilled them mercilessly. The front of the ragged formation bristled with leering-moon shields and pokin' spears, Nuffgunk right at their centre. Further back, Zograt spotted Ogbrot's ladz readying their bows. There was Old Spurk, leaning on his gnarled fungus stave and squinting through one eye at Zograt, and there were a couple more of the Gobbapalooza, too: Skutbad Da Leg with his basket of poisons and his wicked-looking stikka, and Wabber Spakklegit, his eyes swirling with weird colours beneath a pointy blue hood.

'Boss, dat's a lot of ladz,' said Stragwit, halting in his tracks.

'Yeah, but I only give a zog about one of dem,' replied Zograt. His eyes settled on Skram, perched on a rock in the tribe's midst with his hood jutting skyward and his cleaver in hand. Zograt locked eyes with his nemesis and felt a surge of satisfaction as Skram quailed.

Zograt drew in a deep breath and wiggled his fingers, amplifying his voice to an ensorcelled rumble.

'Skram ain't boss no more, an' yooz lot don't 'ave to do nuffin' 'e sez,' he said. His voice boomed around the cavern. On the lakeshore, grots flinched and squealed. The shield wall shuffled backwards. Vicious rows broke out as grots trampled one another's feet, or tripped over each other's weapons in their fear.

'Boss… you'll wake up Da Lurk!' moaned Stragwit. He backed towards the mouth of the tunnel but was forced to stop when he bumped into Skrog's shins.

'If I do, I'll clobber 'im an' all,' replied Zograt, giddy with power. He realised belatedly that his voice was still an amplified boom, and that the grots below were now peering up at him in confusion. That wouldn't do, he chided himself. These new-found powers needed some work.

'I am still da boss!' yelled Skram. After the boom of Zograt's pronouncements, his voice was the one that sounded reedy.

'Yoo'z da boss?' roared Zograt, limping forward. 'Can yoo do dis?' He had recognised Lunkit, Graggs and Murkk amongst the front row of spear-grots, three of Skram's favoured bully boys. With a wiggle of his fingers Zograt caused masses of stragglenekk fungus to burst from the ground at their feet. The grots howled in terror as the fungus surged over them, coiling about their limbs and snapping their bones. Eyes bulging, tongues lolling, the three grots were crushed in seconds.

'And 'ow about dis?'

Zograt had spotted the handful of grots Skram had hidden behind a hovel to his left, no doubt the Loonboss' idea of a cunning backstab. He summoned gangle-legged git-grabbers from amidst the cracks in the cavern roof. The arachnids descended silently upon silken strands, enfolding the ambushers' heads and shoulders with their hairy limbs and sinking fangs deep.

Skram's ambushers ran about screeching with huge spiders wrapped around their heads. The main mass of the tribe backed away from Zograt with increasing haste. He limped relentlessly towards them, bugs churning around him and Skrog looming just behind.

'Come on, Skram, if yoo'z still boss, wot yoo gunna do?'

'Arrerz, stikk 'im!' shouted Skram. The answering volley was desultory, owing to most of Ogbrot's ladz being halfway around the lake and running for the nearest tunnel. Zograt eyed the handful of shafts as they arced through the air towards him. He swept one arm across his body. In response, a wave of insects surged up to meet the arrows. Chitin shattered. Fluids splattered. A couple of shafts punched through the mass of bugs, but clattered harmlessly to the ground, thrown far off target.

As the insects rained back to the ground amidst broken shafts,

Skrog gave a rumble of profound displeasure. Zograt glanced back at him.

'Sorry, lad, yoo really don't like anyone 'urtin' your little mates, eh?'

The troggoth tore a huge stalagmite out of the ground and hurled it, spinning end over end, into Skram's grots. The resultant carnage was the final straw. The tribe fled in terror.

Zograt saw Skram turn to join them and felt a surge of hate grip him. He used the feeling, channelled it into the boulder under Skram's feet and caused glowing ropes of fungus to burst from the rock and wind about the Loonboss. Skram howled as he was hauled aloft. His treasured cleaver tumbled from his grip and sploshed into the lake. The talisman around his neck blazed bright as a beacon, but whatever magical properties it possessed, it did nothing to save the Loonboss from Zograt's fungal grip.

'Da Lurk ain't gunna save yoo, and da ladz ain't gunna either,' Zograt called to Skram as he limped closer. Writhing and spitting, eyes wild, Skram was lowered to the ground by the fungal mass and held there against the rock. As Zograt faced his nemesis, he noted that not all the grots had fled. Some of the boldest, Nuffgunk amongst them, had halted at a distance to see what would happen.

Good, Zograt thought, let them see who's really boss. As though he heard the thought, Skram spat.

'Yoo ain't no boss, runt. Yoo'z a scrut an' a runt an' yoo ain't never goin' to be nuffin' else.'

'Found yer guts now ya can't run away?' asked Zograt. 'Shame yoo never 'ad no brainz to go wiv 'em. Look wot I can do now, Skram. Bad Moon'z marked me. I got da Clammy Hand on me shoulder.'

'Yoo ain't,' whined Skram. ''Ow can ya? Yoo'z just a runt!'

'Just a runt who'z da boss now,' replied Zograt. 'But dat's not da question, Skram. Question is, wot do I do wiv yoo? I ain't just gunna give yoo a kickin', or I ain't no smarter dan yoo.'

'Let me outta dese 'shrooms an' I'll give *yoo* da kickin' of yer runty life,' raged Skram. 'I'll stab yoo up good, feed ya to Da Lurk.'

Zograt couldn't restrain a malicious giggle.

'Feed ya to Da Lurk,' he repeated, in the tone of one who has just been offered the most marvellous suggestion. 'Maybe I woz wrong, Skram. Yoo does 'ave a good idea once in a while!'

Skram's eyes widened in horror as the fungal ropes hoisted him into the air.

'Nah, 'ang on, we can sort dis!'

'We is sortin' dis,' Zograt replied. 'We'z findin' a use for ya, Skram, first one yoo ever 'ad. Yoo'z gunna keep Da Lurk 'appy so it don't eat no grots wot are actually worth keepin' around!'

Zograt expected more pleading, or perhaps a last, defiant tirade. It took him a moment to interpret the wet ripping sound he heard instead, the spatter and thump. He turned as he remembered, belatedly, the wicked shivs Skram kept secreted about his person. Zograt reached for his powers, but years of instinct forced him to cringe as the vengeful Loonboss charged him, slittas in hand.

Skrog's fist came down on Skram like a boulder plummeting from the cavern roof. Zograt tasted bitter blood as the Loonboss' juices splattered him from head to toe. He blinked bits of Skram from his eyes and looked at what remained of his lifelong tormentor, the mass of pulverised flesh and metal.

Zograt stared up at Skrog.

'Cheers, lad,' he said, voice shaky. Skrog's gaze was fixed on the insects Skram had crushed underfoot as he dropped from the severed tendrils, the trail of them the Loonboss had squashed as he charged. The troggoth lifted his gore-splattered fist and, gaze wandering to the middle distance, began to lick bits of Skram from it.

'Right... Don't tread on yer little mates,' said Zograt, wondering what distinguished those dead bugs from all the others the grots had trampled in the last few minutes. Perhaps they had just been the last straw for the troggoth's patience? Perhaps it took that long for Skrog to formulate his response? Maybe the mind of a troggoth made no sense at all?

Whatever the case, as the boldest of his tribe slunk back around the lake to stare at the gory remains of their Loonboss, Zograt banished the insect masses to their crannies and crevices, keeping only the bugs that squirmed through his robes.

No sense taking chances, he thought.

It took a while for the tribe to creep from their hidey-holes. By the time the last of them sloped in from the shadows, Zograt had limped up to Da Big Cave. The tribe followed him. He felt their eyes on him as he clambered with Skrog's help onto the heaped wreckage of Skram's hut. Dozens of wary stares almost pinned him in place. The runt threatened to resurface and send him cowering and fleeing, to cede power to Nuffgunk or some other more obvious successor.

Instead, Zograt wrapped one hand tightly around Skram's pendant, which now hung glowing around his own neck. He glared at the assembled grots, doing his best to look menacing and boss-like. At a spot near the back, he spotted the slope-shouldered Driggz, who gave him a wary grin. Nearer to hand, their backs shown defiantly to the crowd, stood Nuffgunk, Old Spurk and the bruised and battered Gobbapalooza. All watched Zograt carefully, seeming afraid he would set his pet troggoth loose on them.

It wasn't that the idea didn't tempt him – in return for the kicks and jeers, for their complicity in Skram's idiotic rule and endless beatings. But Zograt was cleverer than that, cleverer by far than Skram had been. He recognised his potential rivals, but he also guessed they could be useful if he kept them obedient.

The Bad Moon had chosen him. Zograt had become certain of this as he limped up the tunnel with the tribe at his back, as he replayed in his mind the moment Skrog saved his life. The Bad Moon had blessed him with powers, and with a big, strong, loyal protector. The Bad Moon didn't do that sort of thing just for a laugh. Zograt had become certain that he had a destiny. He was meant for Big Things!

He just hoped, as he glared out at the mob of duplicitous, self-centred, spiteful little back-stabbers surrounding him, that he could figure out what those Big Things entailed before his tribe worked up the courage to put a blade in his back.

'Lissen up, yooz lot!' he said, and his echoing voice silenced their chattering and arguments. 'I'm da boss now. Skram woz a small-time idiot, a no-brainz squigwit. I ain't dat, and fings is gunna be different around 'ere from now on!'

CHAPTER TWO

Taremb

Shadows surround her. They are forest boughs, whipping at a rider who gallops through the night. They are a river in flood that will sweep her helpless onto unseen rocks; a faceless crowd that whispers and pleads in voices she might understand if only she would lean close enough for them to reach; they are soil packed tight about the wrongfully buried, filling nostrils and mouth against one last attempted scream. They are menace, danger, false refuge. They are whatever they sense might break her.

She knows the shadows, knows what they want. She knows they long to snatch away her companions as their price for permitting passage. Knows they will take her too if they can.

She grits her teeth and focuses her will. The shadows recoil like burned fingers. She sees light bloom ahead. She steps into the light, drawing her companions with her.

Wilhomelda Borchase, Magister Princep of the Coven Unseen, stepped from the shadows and into the town square of Taremb.

She felt whorled flagstones of an earlier age beneath her feet, reassuringly solid. Wilhomelda released the breath she always held while performing a shadow-step. She glanced around to reorient herself with the real.

A marble column rose at the square's centre, the roost of a winged stone figure so eroded they were barely recognisable as Stormcast. Beneath its blinded gaze, the square was ringed by squat buildings in the gloomy hues of local stone. A few elements of much older architecture stood out, easily recognised by their superior craftsmanship and paler hue. Wilhomelda reflected it was fitting for the buildings of Liminus' only major settlement to flow from old into new, light into dark. Such was the nature of the region. They complemented the low ceiling of gunmetal clouds that broke and re-formed overhead. Shafts of bright light speared through gaps to dance over Taremb's rooftops and bathe its streets before vanishing again as the jealous clouds choked them off.

The square boasted two taverns, a smithy, a coppery-scented butchers and an establishment that might have been an alchemist's, a herbalist's or a scam; Wilhomelda had yet to work out which despite having repeatedly passed its colourful window display. She suspected the latter. There were more businesses mundane enough to be beneath her notice, as well as a scattering of stalls and barrows whose presence proclaimed market day. Each business, large or small, thronged with locals. All had stopped to stare.

The people of Taremb were always staring, always mistrustful of the sorcerous outsiders come lately into their world. Wilhomelda knew she must look strange, a tall and slender figure in robes of silver-grey, her long white hair braided tightly, an ensorcelled locket glimmering at her throat, her eyes dark in a pale face weathered by battle, hardship and the first inroads of old age. Doubtless she presented a mysterious and alien figure to such simple folk.

When she realised that most of them were staring past, not at her, Wilhomelda couldn't help a self-deprecating snort. She glanced back at the portal of whirling shadows she had just stepped from.

'Ah yes...' she said.

Lanette Ezocheen stepped out after her. The Magister Secundi was a woman of medium height whose flowing robes did not conceal her muscular frame. Her hair was flame red, chopped short. Her irises were the colour of firelight through rubies. A complex spiral of tattoos climbed one side of Lanette's neck and jaw, where it clashed headlong with a knot of old battle-scars. A blade sat at Lanette's hip with a glowing ruby set into its pommel, while her hard, watchful expression completed the look of a veteran warrior-mage.

Wilhomelda still thought Lanette beautiful, even after all that had transpired between them. She discarded the thought as unhelpful.

'I bloody hate doing that,' said Lanette.

'I know you do,' replied Wilhomelda.

'The locals don't seem keen on it either,' said Lanette, scanning the wary crowd.

'It is time they became acclimated,' Wilhomelda told her.

'It scares them,' Lanette said, and Wilhomelda heard reproach. She pressed down a surge of irritation.

'We mean them no harm. We provide soldiery and mages to fortify their defences. And it is a far quicker means by which to travel between Muttering Peak and Taremb than hiking up and down that dratted pass.'

'Still scares them,' replied Lanette. Wilhomelda blew out a breath.

'Well then they will have to make peace with their disquiet, Magister Secundi. Matters are accelerating. I do not have the time to coddle fearful farmers.'

She set off across the square. She glanced back to see the portal ripple again and disgorge a dozen Freeguild swordsmen garbed in the silver-grey and half-masks of the coven's soldiery. At a gesture from Lanette, the honour guard hastened to catch up to their Magister Princep. Lanette herself took a few jogging steps and fell into stride with Wilhomelda.

'Just going to leave that there?' Lanette asked.

'It might do them good to get used to its presence,' Wilhomelda replied.

'Or it might help to turn the townsfolk irrevocably against us,' said Lanette. Wilhomelda sensed another argument creeping up on them. She wasn't sure she had the energy to avert it.

'It is not our duty to pander to ignorance, Magister Secundi.'

Lanette looked back at the portal, then around at the locals scattering from their path or gathered into glowering knots. She lowered her voice.

'Wil, what if a child falls into it?' Wilhomelda's annoyance swelled, fed by guilt. She had been picturing pompous shopkeepers and officious militiamen forced to give the portal a wide berth. She'd imagined them learning a little more respect. The thought of endangering an inquisitive child hadn't occurred.

She gestured with her left hand while clutching her locket with her right, and hissed a string of arcane syllables. The portal collapsed with a sound like an indrawn breath. It sent a gust of icy wind rippling across the square.

'You are right, of course,' she said, striving for a conciliatory tone. She received a grunt in response, long years telling her that was the best she would get.

They strode from the square and onto Whisperer's Way. From here they could pick a path through the streets until they reached Old Taremb at the heart of the settlement. The ancient stonework and domed roof of the Listener's Court jutted above the surrounding buildings, making for the surest landmark in town.

Columns of bright daylight flitted across their path. Each seemed only to accentuate the gloom it left in its wake.

Wilhomelda could feel unspoken words between herself and Lanette, like the pressure of a gathering thunderstorm.

They rounded a corner, followed a stone stairway down between hunched houses and entered another square where more malformed statues clung doggedly to their plinths. One side of the square consisted of a sprawling Myth-age ruin whose propped arches led onto torchlit tunnels sloping down and out of sight. Wilhomelda didn't need the rich scent of soil that wafted from those tunnels to tell her Taremb's mushroom farms lay below. Locals in mud-stained aprons halted their barrows in the tunnel mouths to glare at the outsiders as they passed.

To the opposite side of the square the ground dropped away, stone stairways descending between jostling rooftops over which Wilhomelda was afforded a clear view north. She couldn't help slowing and staring out over the buildings and streets of Taremb to where a mountain loomed dark and distant.

Taremb sat at the neck of a headland jutting out into the Umbralic Sea, on the north coast of Liminus. The headland was largely impassable, a nightmare of jagged rock formations and sharp-lipped chasms wreathed in coiling mist and shadow. Yet between them ran a pass measuring precisely two miles in length. Its walls were glassy-smooth, and its paved course arrow-straight, marking it as ancient artifice of the Age of Myth.

Taremb, or rather the fastness amidst whose ruins Taremb had grown, had been sited in the southern end of that pass.

At its northern end, visible from this distance as a shadowy mass thrusting into the clouds, was Muttering Peak. Wilhomelda's gaze was held by the jagged stone. She found herself straining to hear faint whispers. She frowned and felt as though she might catch words if she only concentrated a little harder.

Lanette's hand thumped down on her shoulder and made her jump. Wilhomelda pulled away, surprise making the gesture more abrupt than she had intended. She caught a flash of something that might have been hurt in Lanette's eyes, suppressed as swiftly as it came.

'You were doing it again,' Lanette said quietly. Wilhomelda realised her guards had taken position around her, shields up and hands on the hilts of their swords. The locals had retreated into their mushroom farms. She wondered how long she had stood staring at the mountain.

Flustered, she frowned at Lanette.

'It?'

'Glazed. Muttering. Wil…'

More unspoken words, congesting the air between them, thunderheads building. Wilhomelda turned for the Listener's Court again.

'Guards, afford us some privacy,' she said.

Lanette shot her soldiers quick hand gestures that saw half of them jog on to take up position a hundred yards ahead, while the others dropped back to act as rearguards. Lanette stayed at Wilhomelda's side.

'Not concerned for our safety amidst this hotbed of hostile locals?' Wilhomelda asked.

Lanette snorted. 'Aye, two trained battle wizards in danger from a mob of bloody yokels.'

Wilhomelda couldn't help smiling. 'Then why bring guards at all?'

Lanette chuckled. 'Gives them something to do. Makes them feel useful.'

Wilhomelda welcomed the familiar banter. It wouldn't last, but it was more precious for it.

'You are too good to them, Magister Secundi.'

'Got to keep up morale, Magister Princep. Can't have the soldiers feeling useless.' They walked for a moment in companiable silence and Wilhomelda wondered if perhaps she had been imagining the build-up of tension. Then she saw Lanette's shoulders square, her jaw jut, and she knew with a sinking feeling that she had not. Part of Wilhomelda wanted to beg her companion to simply walk with her as though they were back in the streets of Azyrheim, to maintain the fiction that things were as they had been.

Before things went awry.

Before Leontium.

Instead, she waited.

'This place is bad for you, Wil. Bad for all of us,' Lanette said.

'*Bad* for us?' Wilhomelda fought to keep the scorn out of her tone.

'You know what I mean,' said Lanette. She made a frustrated gesture. 'It's bad for you. You aren't yourself.'

'I have already accepted that you were correct with regard to the portal, it was an unworthy impulse driven by irritation,' said Wilhomelda. 'But I expect better from my Magister Secundi than superstitious peasants' talk.'

'Why the market square?' asked Lanette. 'Wouldn't the Listener's Court have made more sense?'

'You would prefer that I demonstrate to Jocundas ParTaremb our ability to manifest directly within his seat of power?' asked Wilhomelda. 'I know you think it impolitic to frighten the locals with our arrival, but how much worse would matters be were I to prove to the Listener his lamentable vulnerability in the face of our magic? Do you not think that he might feel moved to act, lest his people ask why their Listener had not foreheard that particular utterance?'

'There are side streets.'

'I will be sure to take your geographical preferences into account on the next occasion that I magically transport you and our entire

bodyguard through a shadowy nether realm single-handedly.'
Wilhomelda felt petty at once. Lanette's expression hardened.
Wilhomelda saw the first flickers of lightning amidst the storm.

'You know why I submit to that awful experience, Wil?'

'I would have thought the expediency of such swift travel was
its own justification. Moreover, I am the Magister Princep of the
coven. Why would I need to ruminate upon whether my followers remain loyal to my commands?'

She was hedging now, hoping to reach the Listener's Court and
find shelter there. She knew it was hopeless.

'I do it because I trust you.' There, the lightning bolt that burned
through her bluster. 'We've done so much good together in Sigmar's
name, fought through Azyr only knows what, and I've always trusted
you.'

'And by leading you to Muttering Peak I have somehow broken
that trust? Am I no longer worthy of it?' Wilhomelda knew emotional blackmail was beneath her, but she was stung by Lanette's
implications.

'Don't,' replied Lanette. 'Don't try to make me feel guilty. You've
always listened, even when I was the novice and you the mentor.
We're still a team. More than that. But I don't know what we're
doing here, Wil!'

The frustration in Lanette's voice was sudden and raw, and it
shocked Wilhomelda. She remained tight-lipped as her companion
pressed on.

'I don't know why you replaced Avarni, or Osamalwe or Kven
with bastards like Borster and Ulke and all their bloody machines.
I don't know what this ritual you're planning is supposed to
achieve. You won't even tell me what our orders are!'

'I have told you,' said Wilhomelda. 'There is a power within that
mountain. Bound within the crystal pillar at its heart lies an entity–'

'An entity with power that we aim to bind,' Lanette finished.

'Yes, Wil, you've told me that much. But that isn't everything, is it? I don't know why you're holding back, but I don't like it.'

'Have I to explain myself to you now, Lanette? Have my every decision ratified? After all we've shared? Wilhomelda the Aged, Wilhomelda Silverhair, perhaps her judgement is declining as her years advance?'

Lanette scowled. 'Not what I'm saying. You have one of the sharpest minds in the Collegiate Arcane. You fight for Sigmar's cause with twice the vigour of one half your age. I have always idolised you, even when you didn't deserve it. But you're not yourself, Wil. I feel like we're on the brink of something bad, and I'm afraid it's my fault.'

'Your fault?' snapped Wilhomelda. 'Do you imagine you have so much sway over my decisions, then?'

There was a shocked pause before Lanette replied.

'Despite it all, I still trust you, Wil. But do *you* trust *me*?'

Wilhomelda faltered. Her anger wilted, the storm blowing out as quickly as it had broken. When had she started keeping secrets from Lanette? Another gradual decline, one she regretted deeply.

But Lanette was conservative, direct, loyal, perhaps to a fault.

She would not understand.

Not yet.

'Lanette, I trust you. I ask you to keep faith for just a little longer. We are close now. If I am right, we will soon be able to save more than mere cities. And we cannot have another Leontium.'

They mounted the stone steps up to the Listener's Court. Wilhomelda saw their advance guard waiting for them at the top of the stairs, Tarembites giving them a wide berth. The rearguard were hastening to catch up. The chance for talk was done. Wilhomelda despised herself for feeling relieved.

'I'm going to need more than that, Wil,' murmured Lanette as they neared the top of the stairs.

Then they were amongst their guards, with the columned mass of the Listener's Court looming and the eyes of Tarembite militiamen upon them.

'I shall proceed within and seek audience with Jocundas the Listener,' Wilhomelda said. 'Lanette, remain without and keep watch for anything untoward. Doubtless I will be quite safe in the company of our gracious host.'

With that she swept away, avoiding Lanette's gaze as she went.

Wilhomelda believed the Listener's Court had once been a temple. Its marble columns, wide corridors, rune-engraved archways and high, domed ceilings offered that impression. There were alcoves that could conceivably have held shrines to minor deities, or idols of the same.

Hundreds of years of Tarembite occupation had transformed the building into something more prosaic. Rich carpets and beast-fur rugs covered the floors. Woven tapestries and the portraits of the many former Listeners festooned the walls between beastmen skulls, orruk blades and other trophies claimed in battle. Robed Sigmarite clergy rubbed shoulders with Tarembite militiamen and local guild officials in its halls and chambers.

Each time she passed through the building, Wilhomelda felt there persisted a sense of parasitism, of lesser primitives crouching uncomprehending in the ruin of greater times. She felt the Tarembites' every effort to mark their territory had only emphasised the inadequacy of the attempt.

She kept such thoughts to herself as she was escorted towards the Listener's Seat by several surly-looking militia. They didn't like admitting her to their lord's presence, she knew, or indeed doing anything she asked them. Yet they feared her too much to refuse.

Wilhomelda and her escorts strode along a hallway, more luxuriantly appointed than the rest. The portraits here were newer, their colours vibrant. She let her eye rove over them as she passed. Some of the subjects looked young, others old. Some were formidable individuals who scowled from the canvas, surrounded by warrior trophies. Some were wizened, or delicate-looking. Had she been asked to guess at what similarity bound such disparate folk across the years, Wilhomelda might have suggested a common bloodline. Indeed, three family names did repeat time and again on the brass plaques beneath each portrait: VashTaremb; JalTaremb; ParTaremb.

Yet Wilhomelda knew the real bond between the Listeners, and blood was only part of it. There was an ability they alone possessed that helped them to shepherd their people safely through the years.

'Wait here,' said one of the militia, rapping his knuckles on the stone door of the Listener's Seat.

'The Listener is in audience,' came an officious voice from the other side. The militiaman turned back to Wilhomelda and was about to speak when the muffled sound of another voice came from behind the door, too distant to make out. The door swung inward, gliding on invisible hinges. The effect was only slightly spoiled as it snagged on the thick carpeting of the room beyond.

'The Listener admits Magister Princep Wilhomelda Borchase, and begs her indulgence while he completes his business,' said an elderly man in the overly elaborate robes of a seneschal. Wilhomelda saw the usual look of wonderment on the faces of the militia at the Listener's apparent feat of forehearing. She inclined her head.

'Gracious conduct must be answered in kind,' she said, before gliding regally past the aged seneschal.

The Listener's Seat had served Taremb's leaders as a throne room for centuries. Even here Wilhomelda couldn't shake her sense of the impermanent cluttering the ancient and enduring. The room was grand enough, opulently furnished with a domed

ceiling rich with frescoes of human warriors battling bestial horrors. At one end, arched windows allowed light to flood in over
a gilded throne atop what might once have been a plinth for an
altar. A hearth was set into one wall, well-upholstered chairs
huddling around it, one of several islands of comfortable furnishings that dotted the room. Opposite the throne was an archway
leading onto a spiral of upward steps that Wilhomelda knew
led to the Listener's Sanctum. The Listener himself stood beside
a large stone table that dominated the centre of the room and
seemed, in her experience, permanently festooned with maps
and parchment.

Surrounded by advisors and militia officers, still Jocundas Par-
Taremb eclipsed them all. He was tall and broad-shouldered, his
craggy good looks augmented by the streaks of silver in his hair
and beard. Jocundas' eyes were a piercing blue, and though he
affected the belted robes of a scholar there could be no mistaking
that he carried himself like a soldier. If pressed to ascribe a single
word to the man, Wilhomelda would have been forced to choose
'noble'.

Jocundas offered her a half-bow and a warm smile, before
returning to his discussion. Wilhomelda drifted to the chairs
by the hearth. Not listening to the conversation at her back, she
glanced about and spotted a cut crystal decanter and several
glasses on a small table nearby. She poured herself a generous
measure of the crimson liquid from the decanter, before leaning
back and sipping. Her demeanour was calculated to demonstrate
her ease in a place of power, her right as Jocundas' equal to take
a drink without asking.

It had also already been a very long day, she admitted to herself, and the stiff drink soothed her tension.

The Listener made her wait another ten minutes before finally
dismissing his advisors. She heard him shoo his seneschal from

the room, along with a couple of militiamen determined to hover. Only when the door shut with a thump did he acknowledge her presence again.

'That is a very rare and expensive vintage, brought all the way from Barak-Nar,' he said. Some of the warmth had leached from his voice now they were alone.

'It is a credit to your palate, Lord Listener,' she said, toasting him then inclining her head towards the decanter in a gesture that asked *do you want one?*

He barked a laugh. 'Offering me my own wine now, Wilhomelda?'

'Manners cost nothing, Lord Listener.'

Jocundas took the seat opposite hers, taking up the decanter and pouring his own drink. He swirled the liquid in its glass as he appraised her. She returned his stare.

'To what do I owe the pleasure?' Jocundas asked. Wilhomelda sipped her drink and eyed him over the rim of the glass.

'Your informants continue to earn their keep, bearing word of my impending arrival to you so swiftly,' she said with a conspiratorial smile. '*Their* whispers, at least, appear reliable.'

Jocundas' manner cooled another few degrees. He swigged before replying.

'When you first came to me, we agreed upon matters that would not be discussed. I am the ruler of Taremb, Wilhomelda, and I am busy. What do you want?'

'Only to maintain the cordial nature of our ongoing alliance and to further the spirit of mutual and open communication into which it was entered, Lord Listener.'

'I do not call arriving unannounced, undermining me in front of my advisors, or frightening my people with your sorcery "cordial",' said Jocundas. He set his empty glass back down with a clink.

Wilhomelda followed suit then leaned forward, fixing him with a hard stare.

'A real Listener would have had militia in place around the square to meet us and escort us in. A real Listener would have foreheard.'

Her eyes strayed meaningfully to the archway that led up to the Listener's Sanctum.

'You should have a care, Magister Princep,' snapped Jocundas.

'Should I, Lord Listener? For hundreds of years the people of Taremb have endured the hardships of Liminus because their Listeners could hear the whispers that issued from within Muttering Peak and tease the strands of truth from amidst the mountain's lies. What is life in Ulgu but that? Divining truth from falsehood. But your truth, Jocundas ParTaremb... it is an uncomfortable one. Imagine a Listener *who cannot listen.*'

Jocundas surged to his feet. Wilhomelda thought he might try to strike her. Instinct took over and she reached for her powers, one hand whipping up to the locket she wore about her neck. Instead, the Listener turned away and stalked across the room to lean on the stone table, shoulders hunched.

'I have allowed you and your coven to occupy the mountain, though Sigmar knows why you would do such a thing. I have left you to your sorcery, quelled the mutterings of my people. I do what you ask. Why then do you vex me?'

Wilhomelda took her hand from her locket and stood, casting a wistful glance at the decanter. It really was very good wine.

'Do not claim you act out of magnanimity, Lord Listener. Before my arrival your position was tenuous. Informants are only so loyal, even bound as they are to you by blood. They see and hear only so much. How much longer do you think informed guesswork would have kept your people in the dark and your backside upon that throne? Do you know the fate of those few ever to be found out as false Listeners?'

Jocundas' shoulders sagged. He laughed bitterly.

'You know I do, Wilhomelda. Public humiliation. Summary execution. Shame upon their bloodline for seven generations. The fate I have feared every day since I took the throne, but honestly, who else was there? The VashTaremb brat, too young to do aught but bawl? Evandine JalTaremb, meek as wool and by her own admission utterly whisperdeaf? Her obstreperous sister? Do you know how many orruks roam the plains to the south-west, how many horrors lurk in the Shudderwood to the south-east? Without a descendant of Tarembus upon the throne, my people would have lost heart. At least I had youth, and a strong sword arm, and the courage to try.'

'I do not doubt that, over the years, you have found countless ways to justify your deceptions to yourself, Lord Listener. I am not here to hear them. If you prefer it, I could withdraw the coven sorcerers and Freeguild soldiery who help to guard your walls? We would all be safe within the mountain from the peril that casts its shadows across your town. Would you? Would your beloved subjects?'

'What peril?' He turned, caught between alarm and suspicion. Wilhomelda didn't enjoy pressing her advantage over this man or endangering his people. She had a sense his deception really had been founded on duty, at least to begin with. But her goal was too important. A man like this would never grasp the scale of what she sought to do, the good that could be done with such power. She couldn't allow sentiment or sympathy to impede her passage and so she left his question unanswered. Let him wonder and fear. Let him remember that of the two of them, only she could discern the voice of Muttering Peak or take heed of its warnings.

'My plans gather pace, Lord Listener. My coven and I will be occupied within the mountain now, possibly for some days. In the meantime, I believe it possible that a threat will strike at your walls. Already my mages are reinforcing your outer defences, and my soldiers stand ready to repel whatever may come, but I need to know that you stand firm in our defence.'

He gave a hollow laugh and shook his head. 'How is it that you hear what I cannot? You are not of the blood.'

Wilhomelda kept her expression neutral. No sense in letting on that she knew no more than he did of this matter. It was one of many questions she hoped soon to have answers to.

'Can I rely upon your support, Lord Listener?'

'You speak as though I have a choice.'

She inclined her head. Yet Wilhomelda sensed that she had applied enough of the rod. Some sweetgrass, now, to complement it.

'Come,' she said, gliding across to the windows behind Jocundas' throne. He came to stand at her shoulder. Together they looked south over Old Taremb to where the inner and outer walls stretched across the mouth of the pass. The inner wall was a high, stone-built affair that owed much of its strength to Myth-age builders. Its outer counterpart was a staked wooden stockade, its origins in the Shudderwood clear from its disturbing translucence. From this vantage point Wilhomelda could see her and Jocundas' soldiers patrolling the fire steps behind both walls. She could also see coven wizards moving slowly across the fallow fields nestled between the outer and inner walls. Every few paces they crouched, bending low until they could almost have kissed the soil, remaining hunched over for long moments before rising once more.

'What are they doing?' asked Jocundas.

'They seed your fields with lies, whispered to soil and stone,' she replied. Seeing his sour glance, she added, 'They are bolstering your southern defences. Trust me, it will aid you.'

'Trust you,' he repeated. Wilhomelda was reminded uncomfortably of her recent exchange with Lanette.

'Yes, trust me. I can tell you also that two of the chambers within your fungus farms will collapse within the week unless they are inspected and shored. I can tell you that the proprietor of the Spitted Gor is plotting to burn down the Listener's Head so as to end the rivalry between the two inns. I can tell you that your seneschal is concealing a case of rattlestones out of fear that he will be dismissed from his position, and if not treated the man will be dead before the season is out. I can tell you all this, Lord Listener. It is up to you whether you choose to live up to your title.'

A little more than an hour after she had entered the Listener's Court, Wilhomelda strode back out of its arched entrance. She rejoined Lanette and their entourage, casting a glance at the darkening sky. The clouds had grown thicker and now boiled like smoke from a bonfire, any memory of the former brightness gone. As daylight faded, so the ensorcelled lanterns that lined Taremb's streets glowed to life. Their light was strong but cold, stark fact to drive back falsehoods. It did nothing to dispel the bleak sense of foreboding that had settled in Wilhomelda's heart.

'Night falls, and Liminus prepares another of its plentiful storms,' she said. 'We must repair to the mountain and make ready. Duty awaits and we shall not shy from it.'

Lanette cast her a doubtful glance but kept her peace. Wilhomelda told herself that soon her companion would know and understand. Soon they could embrace the power together.

Soon they would be strong.

Soon they would be safe.

'We'll be shadow-stepping again,' said Lanette. It wasn't a question.

'Perhaps somewhere a little less alarming to the locals though,' said Wilhomelda. As they set off down the steps, she shot another look at the lowering sky, and fought to hold on to her courage.

CHAPTER THREE

Badwater Drop

'We should go give da Flashbanditz a kickin'!'

It was the third time Naffs Gabrot, the tribe's Scaremonger, had shouted this. He was big for a grot and well used to yelling, the better to scare errant grots into obedience. His voice carried above the tribe's chattering, even muffled by his oversized Glareface Frazzlegit mask. Naffs threw in a few arm-waving gestures Zograt supposed were meant to look intimidating. Playing the role of the Moonclan bogeyman had doubtless given Naffs the idea everyone was scared of him.

Zograt glared down at the Scaremonger from atop the throne he'd had built from the wreckage of Skram's hut. Naffs paused, cocked his head, then tried a few more speculative arm waves. Zograt continued to glare. The Scaremonger subsided.

Zograt's throne had been raised in the middle of Da Big Cave. A few bits of Skram himself festooned the rusty metal spikes jutting over Zograt's seat, alongside glowy 'shrooms, fancy bottles on chains donated by the now obsequious Stragwit Skrab, and other shiny odds and ends rooted from dank corners by those hoping to curry favour. Skrog loomed protectively to one side of the throne. From time to time the troggoth uttered what Zograt took to be reassuring grunts.

He had gathered his lieutenants for a council of war. Zograt had hoped for some useful insights that he could then pass off as his own. He hadn't expected more than half the tribe to show up along with his supposed counsellors, surrounding Zograt with arguing grots who seemed not to have a good idea between them.

'Yooz only want to go after dem Flashbanditz to nick da Spanglestikk,' shouted Zograt. 'None o' yooz Gobbapalooza is allowed to say nuffin' about da Flashbanditz again.'

The five members of the Gobbapalooza had shoved their way to the foot of Zograt's throne: Naffs the Scaremonger, imposing even without the ritual Boingob skull he rode to battle; Stragwit the Brewgit, with his hastily repaired still strapped to his back; Wabber Spakklegit, the tribe's Boggleye, who Zograt had banned from looking directly at him for fear of his hypnotic powers and who now glared resentfully at the floor; the disturbing semi-arachnid form of Skutbad Da Leg, the tribe's Spiker; and in their midst, gazing dreamily into the middle distance while a flock of tiny winged fungi fluttered round his head, the Shroomancer known as Da Fung.

'But boss, dey fink dey's better dan us,' wheedled Stragwit.

'Yooz lot want da Spanglestikk cos it's big magik, an' yooz reckon yooz can push me around cos all yoo see is a runt,' said Zograt. 'We ain't goin' after da Flashbanditz. Dey'll scrag us like dey did last time, an' if dat daft git don't stop wavin' 'is arms at me I'll 'ave 'em chopped off.'

Naffs lowered his arms and took a careful sidestep behind the rest of the Gobbapalooza.

'Den wot do yoo reckon we should do?' asked Nuffgunk. He

leaned on his pokin' spear amidst a knot of his best ladz. Zograt didn't like the knowing expression on his long face. Skrog gave a low growl at the grot boss' tone, and Nuffgunk glared warily back at the huge troggoth.

'Bet yoo'd like to know me cunnin' plan, wouldn't ya?' Zograt replied.

'Yeah. Dat's why I asked.'

Zograt opened his mouth and shut it again, realising Nuffgunk had him there.

Zograt cast his eye over the crowd of expectant green faces. He ignored the grots who had started brawling near the back, and the gang who had lost interest and were gambling shards of shiny glass on the results of a deffcap eating contest. His gaze settled on Driggz, who had acquired a dented helmet with a spike on top from somewhere. To show he rewarded loyalty, Zograt had promoted Driggz to boss of the tribe's Boingrot Bounderz, the prestigious squig-riding lance-boyz. Several of them stood slouch-shouldered around their new leader, expressions as sour as Nuffgunk's.

It occurred to Zograt that a solid suggestion from Driggz would serve the dual purpose of reinforcing both his and Zograt's own position.

'Oi, Driggzy, wotcha got?' he shouted, struck by sudden inspiration. 'I been waiting t'see which one of dis lot can pass me test, figger out wot da plan is before I 'as to tell 'em, but none of 'em got a clue. An' dey calls demselves wisegrots! Bet yoo know, dontcha?' The babble diminished as the glare of the mob turned from Zograt to Driggz. Zograt's heart fell as Driggz's beady eyes widened and his mouth twisted into an alarmed scowl. Driggz wasn't stupid, but it occurred to Zograt belatedly that his old mate might not do well under such unaccustomed scrutiny.

'Er…' began Driggz. He coughed and spat a wad of green phlegm before trying again. 'Er, I reckon, boss, wot we should do is…' His expression brightened. 'Wot we should do is go an' give Ploddit's Karavan a kickin'! Big Limpy should be comin' through soon, shouldn't 'e?'

Zograt fought the urge to groan. Boss Ploddit ruled a procession of scrap-iron wagons, pulled by giant mugger beetles, that followed in the wake of Big Limpy's Troggherd. His skrap was more than a match for the Badwater Boyz.

'Ploddit an' his ladz ain't natural!' wheezed Old Spurk. 'Dey lives on da surface where Frazzlegit can see 'em! Ain't right!'

'Dey do well enough, don't dey? Rich gitz, and dem wagunz is all covered in spikes and shinies,' said Nuffgunk.

'Dey get da pick of wot Big Limpy an' his troggs trample,' put in one of Nuffgunk's ladz. 'Worth wearin' extra robes an' goggles an' livin' under awnings all da time.'

Big Limpy was a creature of legend amongst the local greenskins. A humungous Dankhold troggoth with a gammy leg, his tendency was to lean somewhat to the right. As Zograt understood it, this had caused him and his lumbering herd of troggoths to wander in a hundred-mile-or-so loop ever since anygrot could remember, seemingly with no greater destination in mind nor inclination to halt. The herd only wandered through the same region once every few seasons, giving just enough time for new victims to settle in their path with scant idea of the danger they were placing themselves in. Following close in the troggs' wake, Ploddit's ladz scavenged each settlement, merchant caravan or doomed band of marauding adventurers that got bulldozed.

'If we can't scrag da Flashbanditz, we can't scrag Ploddit's lot either,' said Naffs, half raising his arms then seeming to think better of it. 'Yoo'z a stoopid git.'

Driggz looked mortified. Zograt ground his splintered fangs in frustration and toyed with the idea of telling Skrog to go and slap the smug looks from a few faces.

'Wot's wrong wiv yooz lot?' he said, glaring about. 'Dis is small-time rubbish. It's just wot Skram would 'ave done!'

'We thought yoo sed yoo 'ad a better plan,' pressed Nuffgunk, who Zograt was rapidly realising had been more than just Skram's right-hand bully boy. It struck him that he had underestimated the intelligence of some of his new underlings. It had been a miscalculation trying to trick them into providing him with a plan.

A fist cracked into a jaw amidst the brawling ladz. A bloodied grot reeled into Driggz, knocking him down amidst a chorus of cackling. A cheer went up from the deffcap eating game as one unlucky grot vomited a stream of foam, blood and half-digested 'shroom before collapsing.

'Wot about dem Flashbanditz, though?' croaked Old Spurk, shaking his shaman's stick so the bones on it rattled. 'We could go give dem a kickin'?'

'Zog me!' snarled Zograt. With an angry gesture, he summoned glowing mycelia from the cavern floor to entangle the brawling and gambling grots both, trapping them amidst masses of fast-swelling fungus. Shrieks rang out as several grots were squashed until bones broke and blood spurted. The rest of the tribe subsided, eyeing Zograt warily. Skrog stirred and balled his huge fists, casting a jaundiced eye over the more mutinous-looking grots.

'No wonder we'z da worst tribe round 'ere!' Zograt shouted. 'Yoo squigwitz deserved Skram! I can't finish my plan wiv all dis racket, and yoo don't deserve to 'ear it yet if yoo can't even start figgerin' out wot it is. I'm goin' to me sacred grotto an' I'm gunna 'ave a word wiv da Bad Moon. When I gets done moonin'…' He glared around at them, wiggling his fingers in what he hoped was a suitably magical and ominous fashion. 'Big. Fings!'

CHAPTER FOUR

Muttering Peak

Wilhomelda was relieved to return to Muttering Peak. Stepping from her portal, she released her breath and felt an unexpected sense of being sheltered. The chamber was typical of Muttering Peak, its surfaces rounded and whorled in a way that evoked the shells of deep-sea creatures. Silvery veins branched through the dark stone, pulsing with a rhythmic glow. Wilhomelda felt there was something synaesthetic about the light. Each pulse conjured a heartbeat that was not there.

When she had first set foot within Muttering Peak, Wilhomelda had felt she entered the body of some titanic beast, long fossilised yet haunted by the ghost of life. The thought had unsettled her to begin with, but her disquiet had lessened over time. As Lanette stepped from the portal, her expression of disgust suggested Wilhomelda was alone in this.

'Be about your duties,' Lanette told the guards. They saluted then filed from the chamber.

'Shall we?' asked Wilhomelda.

'No sense putting it off,' replied Lanette.

On impulse, Wilhomelda placed a hand on Lanette's arm, stopping her before she could leave the chamber.

'I am sorry for the way things have been,' she said, holding Lanette's gaze.

'I appreciate you saying so,' Lanette replied at last, her words placed as carefully as footfalls on a crumbling ledge.

'I know what I am doing,' said Wilhomelda. 'We are going to help many people. We are going to keep them safe.'

Lanette's hand rose to brush Wilhomelda's.

'If I asked you to, would you stop? Just set this aside and return to Azyrheim together?'

Wilhomelda paused. She did not wish to offer untrue assurances, lest she be expected to act upon them. Her heart sank as Lanette's ruby eyes hardened. They had known each other too long. Neither had to speak aloud for the other to hear.

Lanette removed Wilhomelda's hand from her arm, gentle but firm.

'As I said, Magister Princep, no sense putting it off.'

Wilhomelda sighed. 'As you say, Magister Secundi.'

She led the way into the gently curving passage outside the chamber. All the passages within Muttering Peak curved. All were roughly circular, though their width varied from cavernous to claustrophobic. Slender archways of ice-white marble were spaced along them every thirty-three feet and inscribed with complex runes that none of Wilhomelda's coven could read.

Who or what had installed the arches was a mystery, but it was from them that the networks of silver veins spread out through walls, ceilings and floors to fill the tunnels with their glimmer. In places, some archways had cracked or collapsed. There the veins had died and darkness had gathered in their wake. Those who entered such darkened tunnels had not emerged. The only clues to their fate had been the low rumble of stone and cries of alarm cut off mid-scream.

Wilhomelda felt those lives upon her conscience. She remembered the crumbling pages of the ancient tome that had led her here, found in a time-worn vault in Azyrheim's oldest library. She remembered the words she had deciphered.

...the dark'nd tunn'ls deth be...

Yet after so long, how could she have been sure that the power within the mountain was still perilous? Wilhomelda asked herself. She could not have warned her comrades without revealing the extent of her foreknowledge, which in turn would have led to difficult questions. She had simply hoped, as the first soldiers crept into the dark, checking for peril before allowing the mages to put their own lives at risk.

Then had come the grinding of stone, and the screams.

A soldier's duty, Wilhomelda told herself bracingly, and better a few unexceptional sword-arms lost than the precious mind of a mage.

After several failed exploration attempts, Lanette had urged Wilhomelda to place all darkened areas of the mountain off limits. Though loath to leave a secret uncovered Wilhomelda had seen the sense of Lanette's urgings. It had been half a season now since the darkened tunnels had been branded malevolent. No more lives had been lost. Yet the secrets that might lie within the shadows frustrated Wilhomelda.

Questions to which she would soon have answers, she told herself.

In the meantime, no one went anywhere in Muttering Peak without a Radiant as escort. The precaution frustrated Wilhomelda, for without risking more lives they had no way of knowing if it even worked. The theory was that enough magical light might serve to hold back the darkness long enough to allow escape.

Two novitiate mages, designated Radiants, waited outside the chamber to accompany Wilhomelda and Lanette. The Radiants were festooned with magical light sources, from glimmerstones set into headbands and cuffs to crystal beacons yoked across their shoulders.

'The pillar chamber,' said Lanette. The two novices fell into step, one walking ahead, the other behind as they set off up the curving passageway. This was one of the arterial routes that coiled through the mountain, spur passages splitting off from it and winding away towards distant chambers or concealed windows set into the mountain's slopes. If they had turned the other way and strode downhill, they would have reached the mountain's main gate.

Wilhomelda reflected that she felt no desire to leave Muttering Peak. Neither in this moment, nor in general. Her path lay ahead and above, from where the mountain's hidden power whispered to her.

'It will be good when we no longer require our novitiates to carry these burdens,' said Wilhomelda. Lanette didn't reply. Wilhomelda lapsed back into silence. She tried not to feel resentful towards Lanette as they ascended, here and there passing robed mages, knots of patrolling soldiers or harried-looking Ironweld Engineers. These latter always seemed in a hurry, always loaded down with too many scrolls or bags of tools and components, and usually with a train of apprentices and labourers similarly burdened.

'Borster keeps them hard at it,' she commented as another sweating band of engineers passed. Again, Lanette didn't reply. Wilhomelda was irritated at how these one-sided exchanges must look to the Radiants. She felt suddenly absurd and resolved to make no further effort to mollify Lanette. The Magister Secundi would come around soon enough once she saw the full truth.

Wilhomelda had come to know the mountain's layout almost

instinctively. She wondered whether it was to do with the illusive nature of the magic she practised, some innate empathy helping her to navigate tunnels that wound and split, doubled back on themselves, and felt as though they shifted subtly when unobserved. She took the opportunity to reassert her authority as the Radiants faltered at several junctions.

'You require the leftmost fork. The right will take you to Master Ulke's alchemical laboratory, while the central route becomes malevolent after the next fork.'

'Straight up here, novice. That way leads only to a guard chamber and thence the eastern slopes.'

'No. That tunnel leads to the artefact vault. You have not earned the right to look upon the warded arcana we keep there, and you know not the warding magics to keep you safe. The right upward fork, please.'

Though all the tunnels were rounded and smooth, not all were featureless. Sometimes they passed darkly pearlescent alcoves. Within stood lumps of black onyx which might once have been graven figures. Here, Wilhomelda picked out a smooth face with a wide slit for a mouth and blank stone where her mind expected eyes. There, she saw something hunching menacingly, the vaguest suggestion of humanoid limbs straining against a pupa of glossy black stone.

Like so much about the mountain, none of her coven had been able to determine what these worn idols represented, or to date how ancient they were. Some had expressed fears these figures bore the taint of the Dark Gods, and that this in turn suggested whatever power lurked in Muttering Peak was similarly corrupt. Lanette had vocally supported this theory.

Wilhomelda scorned their fears, viewing them as superstitious. Thanks to her followers' suspicions, however, she had been forced to play down her ability to hear the mountain's whispers, lest they think her tainted by association. One secret always spawned two more, she reflected.

After a half hour's walk, they at last entered a perfectly round and smooth tunnel where the arches came every sixteen feet and the webwork of silvery capillaries thickened to pulsing arteries.

'Steel yourselves,' said Lanette. They passed under the final arch and emerged into the pillar chamber. Even Wilhomelda stumbled as her mind attempted to make sense of her surroundings. One of the Radiants would have fallen, had Lanette not grasped his elbow.

The pillar chamber was perfectly spherical, with a diameter of three hundred and thirty-three feet. Circular tunnel entrances opened into it seemingly at random, but no matter where one entered, all who visited would experience disorientation as they stepped through a doorway and then tilted ninety degrees from horizontal to vertical to stand upon the inner face of the sphere. It was entirely possible for one coven member to stand directly above another across the chamber's diameter, and for each to believe that their colleague stood impossibly upon the chamber's ceiling.

The silver threads grew thickest here. Their diffuse radiance only heightened the sense of disorientation. So bewildering was the pillar chamber that it was possible to become lost within it, visitors rapidly forgetting which tunnel they had emerged from or which way they had started out believing was up. Ulke and his alchemists had tried to ameliorate the effect by using acids to scorch paths into the walls, and numbers beside each entrance. Even their strongest solutions had proven ineffective. Several alchemists had been injured as the dangerous liquid ran in rivulets around the spherical chamber.

The only landmark by which one could orientate remained the pillar at the chamber's centre. It was formed from the same white marble as the archways, thicker across than Wilhomelda was tall, and looked as though it had been driven down through the chamber's ceiling and deep into the floor. Runes covered the pillar's surface, and a circular stair wound around it, up to a wide platform that ran around its circumference near the top.

The pillar offered at least the illusion of orientation yet was almost universally loathed by Wilhomelda's followers. Many described a feeling of being watched by something within the crystal column every time they approached it. Sometimes a faint darkness had been observed within it, as though the silhouette of something huge and diffuse was stirring.

It was Wilhomelda's desire to understand, and to harness, the power lurking within the pillar that had brought the Magister Princep and her coven to the mountain. The evidence of their efforts was visible in the clusters of brass machinery dotting the chamber. Copper wires snaked from one obscure device to the next, converging at the base of the pillar before coiling up it like a braided metal serpent. They vanished into the body of a blocky brass engine which had been set upon the platform at the pillar's top.

It was nauseating walking around the chamber, passing knots of engineers and wizards bent over the whirring machines, yet all the while moving perpendicular to the pillar. The effect was worsened by several of her inner circle walking down the winding stair to meet her, seemingly askew from her perception of the world. In Wilhomelda's peripheral vision they appeared to rotate slowly from the horizontal to the vertical as she and they approached the pillar's base.

'I bloody hate doing this,' grunted Lanette.

Wilhomelda raised a hand to the figures stepping from the stairway. By this point, she and they stood at the same angle, or as close as was possible upon the curving floor.

'Gentlemen,' said Wilhomelda.

'Magister Princep,' replied Vikram Borster, largest of the three.

Borster wore the blend of robes and leather overalls that marked him as an Ironweld Engineer. The fine quality of his tools and the arrogant set of his features marked the big man as high-ranking. Everything about Borster was large, from his elaborately curled whiskers and tattooed forearms to his broad shoulders, thrusting gut and booted feet. Even his temper was infamously larger than life. Wilhomelda knew the man considered his own belligerence an asset. She had her doubts about his bullying tendencies, but none about his abilities as an engineer. The combination had pushed him into her employ after he had offended several clients of more delicate sensibility.

The other two members of the trio could not have contrasted more with Borster. Aberthwhaite Gillighasp was amongst the senior magi of the coven. Ganglingly tall, painfully skinny and with an irritatingly obsequious nature, Gillighasp attracted unkind nicknames. Wilhomelda saw past the man's peculiarities, however, to the talented Gold wizard and unprincipled social climber behind them. Gillighasp's talents and lack of ethics made him useful. She tolerated the man even as Lanette radiated loathing for him.

Then there was the alchemist, Daedal Ulke. From his tatty wisps of beard to the perpetual moistness of his grey eyes, the oddly sour smell of the man to his habit of endlessly dabbing his lips with a stained kerchief, Wilhomelda found Ulke singularly unsavoury. If it had not been for his prodigious alchemical talents and the moral laxity of his scientific curiosity, she would not have allowed him within a dozen paces.

But then, she thought, what was one more unpleasant compromise? It would all be worth it in the end.

'I had hoped to find you here,' she said. Borster snorted. Ulke dabbed at his lips and stared. Gillighasp offered a deep bow.

'Where else would we be, Magister Princep, with the ritual

drawing nigh? You find us performing our final inspections of our devices just as you ordered.'

'And?' asked Wilhomelda.

'*My* devices are functioning as they should,' Borster replied, drawing himself up as though squaring for a fight. 'Took some doing, boring the augur rod into the pillar. Stubborn as a duardin is that crystal. But we got it done.'

'Thanks in no small part to the application of the correct solutions to weaken the surface,' put in Ulke. Borster waved the amendment away.

'All the resonators have been checked and rechecked,' the engineer continued. 'The verification filters are all in working order, and we've had your soothsayers check every sigil etched into them. Engineering and sorcery working in harmony. Just as I planned.'

'And alchemy,' put in Ulke. Borster continued as though he hadn't heard.

'All that remains is to perform the ritual, Magister Princep. So long as your lot hold up your end, mine'll do just fine.'

'What about the entity?' asked Lanette.

'What about it?' replied Borster.

'Do we know anything more about it? Have we determined its nature?'

Wilhomelda heard Lanette's real question: *Is it tainted?*

'Those enquiries are, uh, ongoing,' said Gillighasp. 'Whoever wrought the wards of binding throughout this mountain possessed knowledge and craft whose power and complexity were beyond anything we here possess. Their works continue to interfere with our own efforts. Whatever the nature of the being trapped within the pillar, whatever power of prophecy it possesses and how that power is transmitted to the Listeners of Taremb...' He shrugged and spread his hands in a 'who knows' gesture.

'And yet we intend to press on regardless?' asked Lanette.

'The ritual will reveal the precise nature of what is bound within the pillar,' said Wilhomelda. 'I maintain my belief that this entity is not daemonic. But if it transpires that the opposite is the case–'

'But how can you possibly know that?' interrupted Lanette.

'*If* it transpires that the opposite is the case then we will banish the creature and leave this place,' Wilhomelda finished. 'But that will not happen. Instead, we will bind a powerful source of prophetic insight for use in Sigmar's wars.'

'And is that all you seek, Magister Princep?' asked Lanette.

'We will not have this discussion again,' replied Wilhomelda. 'I have asked you to trust me, that my sources of information are sound and my conclusions well informed.'

Deep down, Wilhomelda suspected that if Lanette walked away, her own courage would falter and she would follow.

She couldn't allow that.

'Magister Secundi, if our master has told us all she deems mete, then surely we all must be content to abide by that judgement?' Gillighasp's tone was unctuous.

'You can't even say what's bound within that pillar,' replied Lanette. 'Not all of us are as comfortable as you are languishing in ignorance, Gillighasp.'

'We don't know for sure there's anything in there at all, and without this ritual we won't,' said Borster.

Lanette stepped up to the pillar and rapped the ruby pommel of her sword against it. Ripples of light radiated from the point of impact. The unpleasant sense of watchfulness intensified. Ulke flinched, dabbing at his lips.

'Even you're not that obtuse, Borster,' said Lanette. 'There is something in here, something that's been whispering to the Listeners for centuries.'

'And do *they* seem tainted?' asked Gillighasp, seizing on Lanette's words. 'You admit that whatever haunts this mountain has communed with and advised the Tarembites. In all that time there is no evidence of it having corrupted them. Indeed, I would be forced to call its assistance altruistic, for what has it ever asked for in return?'

'Chaos is insidious. Its schemes may play out over countless mortal lives,' replied Lanette. 'Anyway, if you are all so certain of this endeavour, if I'm the only one here with concerns, why the secrecy? Why are we doing this alone?'

Ulke shot a sideways look at Borster, who glowered at Lanette but remained silent.

'Our many victories have earned us a little freedom to manoeuvre,' said Wilhomelda. 'If my theories are correct then we will return to Azyrheim with a power to rival those of the gods.'

'The only god we need is Sigmar,' said Lanette.

'You were at Leontium. How did Sigmar's aid avail us that day?' For a moment, Wilhomelda heard again the groans of the dead, saw corpse lights burning in cavernous sockets, felt the heat sear her skin as the comet-strike fell.

'Choose your words carefully, Magister Princep,' said Lanette, and Wilhomelda heard something more than anger in her companion's voice. She thought perhaps it was fear.

'I mean only that the God-King expects us to find our own means of fighting his wars, and of defending ourselves against... even the darkest powers.'

Wilhomelda held Lanette's gaze. She found herself wondering what it would take for her companion to turn away from her entirely, to run back to Azyrheim and report them to the Order of Azyr. She loathed herself for even thinking it, but nor could she ignore the possibility. Even if Lanette's loyalty held, could she know for sure that no one else amongst her coven or their soldiery was suffering doubts?

She looked away first and found herself staring at the glimmering crystal pillar. Whispers brushed at the edges of her thoughts. Could she even stave off her own fears and doubts for much longer? In that instant Wilhomelda came to a decision.

'Borster, Ulke, Gillighasp, are you all in agreement that we are ready?'

'Aye,' said Borster.

'I believe so, Magister Princep,' said Gillighasp.

Ulke nodded and dabbed.

'Then we will delay no longer. Magister Secundi, I appreciate your counsel, but we can waste no more time. Every hour spent mired in caution is another in which our comrades in arms fall upon battlefields across the realms. Now is the hour for courage. Now is the time for action. Are we all in agreement?'

Again, the three men chorused their assent. Lanette shook her head and looked away.

'I trust you,' she said, in a tone that opened hairline cracks in Wilhomelda's heart.

'Then let us gather the coven and proceed,' said Wilhomelda. She felt mingled trepidation and excitement. Soon she would assert her mastery over the entity within the pillar and earn vindication in the eyes of her oldest friend. Soon she and her coven would possess the power to rival the gods that walked the realms and slew mortals on a whim. They would be forewarned. They would be safe.

That was worth the risk, she told herself.

It took time to gather the coven from their tasks throughout the mountain. Wilhomelda was kept busy with final preparations, directing her followers to their appointed places, running through the incantations over and over although she already knew them by heart. She insisted on performing final checks on the devices yet again, with Ulke and the clearly exasperated Borster in tow.

At last, all was in readiness. The wizards of the coven formed a line around the circumference of the chamber, the pillar rising through their midst like the spindle of a wheel. Even the Radiants had set aside their lanterns to join the circle. Wilhomelda would have preferred they stand close enough to hold hands and thus form an unbroken ring, but the chamber's size defeated that notion. Instead, a spool of copper wire had been passed around the circle, each mage winding it once about their left wrist before passing it on to the next in line so that it bound the coven as one. Wilhomelda held both ends of the spool where they braided and ran down into one of Borster's machines.

Lanette stood to her right in the circle.

'We're doing this?' she asked.

'No sense putting it off,' Wilhomelda replied, and was rewarded with the ghost of a smile.

'Just promise me if you sense any malevolence, you'll cut the connection,' said Lanette.

'There is no such malignancy there to sense,' replied Wilhomelda, wondering whether she was trying to reassure Lanette or herself.

'Wil...'

'I promise,' Wilhomelda replied, privately reserving judgement. Lanette nodded then fixed her eyes upon the glimmering pillar.

'Gentlemen, engage your machines,' commanded Wilhomelda. Borster, who had donned a heavy pair of reflective goggles, shot her a salute and barked orders at his engineers. Levers were thrown, dials turned, and the whine of arcane devices rose through the room.

Wilhomelda's chest was tight. Her heart thumped. She had to run her tongue around her dry mouth and swallow before she could speak. She would lead the chant, and, through the combined power of the Coven Unseen, they would pierce the ancient wards upon the pillar and set their own in place. If all worked as it should then the entity's whispers would be funnelled through the receptor of the augur spike and into Borster's device up on the platform above. Veracity filters and runes of compulsion would sift lie from truth, and Wilhomelda Borchase would become the mistress of her very own infallible oracle.

What better way to counter the powers of the gods, she thought, than to trammel a godbeast of her own?

'Ready, Magister Princep!' shouted Borster over the clatter of his machines. Arcs of cerulean energy danced over the wires wound about the pillar and leapt along the spool that bound the circle of magi. Wilhomelda felt the metal grow warm about her wrist.

She shot a last glance at Lanette, who nodded. Now that danger threatened, that gesture said, all doubts were set aside. Lanette would protect Wilhomelda with her life as she always had. The thought made Wilhomelda feel simultaneously guilty and glad, and filled her with fresh determination. When she began the incantation, her voice rang out firm and loud.

'*Luminus liminiaris,*
Occlusus penumbraii verifarium vo.
Umbracalis, umbrasestus, umbrathae.
Oublis electum vo.'

The first recitation was Wilhomelda's alone. As she began a second time, the rest of the coven joined her. Their intertwined voices rang through the chamber.

'*Luminus liminiaris,*
Occlusus penumbraii verifarium vo.
Umbracalis, umbrasestus, umbrathae.
Oublis electum vo.
Luminus liminiaris,
Occlusus penumbraii verifarium vo.
Umbracalis, umbrasestus, umbrathae.
Oublis electum vo.'

Sorcerous energies raced along the binding wire, causing Wilhomelda's skin to tingle. The arcane machines whined louder, bells jangling from some, whistles shrilling steam from others. Pressure filled the chamber, the air becoming greasy with magic. The silvery veins in the walls glowed in sympathetic response, and Wilhomelda felt resistance to their rite. Sweat beaded her forehead. She tasted copper and salt.

'Luminus liminiaris,
Occlusus penumbraii verifarium vo.
Umbracalis, umbrasestus, umbrathae.
Oublis electum vo.'

Wilhomelda pushed against the resistance and felt her comrades doing the same. Her eyes widened as she saw a dark shape writhe within the pillar, a vague impression of something brushing against the bars of its prison then receding into the depths.

'Luminus liminiaris,
Occlusus penumbraii verifarium vo.
Umbracalis, umbrasestus, umbrathae.
Oublis electum vo.'

Triumph kindled in Wilhomelda's breast as the resistance to their magic faltered. Her heart raced. The wire about her wrist burned. She sensed their sorcery overmastering some barrier, widening a crack like a fissure in a rock face and raising a supporting scaffold of good Sigmarite wards to keep the rent open. A memory flashed through her mind of the long-ago siege of Ghuldark, of she and Lanette leading the attack that captured the gatehouse and offered a way into the fortress proper.

The chamber shuddered. Then came a series of sharp cracks, ringing out over the chanting and the din of machinery. Light pulsed wild and urgent through the crystal pillar, revealing again the numinous shadow-form writhing within.

Then came the flicker of something amiss. Wilhomelda felt the shockwave build in the air around her then surge out from the pillar and into the Ironweld device atop the winding stair. The machine emitted a screech of grinding cogwork, then exploded.

Wilhomelda saw silver fire race down the wires coiled around the pillar, then speed like a burning fuse to first one then the next of Borster's devices. Each detonated like a bomb. Engineers cried in agony. Blood sprayed. The chant faltered.

'Do not waver!' bellowed Wilhomelda, but she knew it was already too late. Silver flames raced along copper wire with hungry speed and Wilhomelda realised they were coming straight for her coven.

'Untether!' roared Lanette.

Wilhomelda fumbled with the wire about her wrist. Panic made her clumsy. A nearby device exploded, shards of brass flying like shrapnel. A piece cut her cheek and made her gasp. The wire burned her fingers and slithered through them.

She cursed as she snatched at it.

The wire slipped again, constricting around her wrist.

As though it were fighting her.

As though it wanted her dead.

A horrific vision filled Wilhomelda's mind, of the fire speeding around the circle, setting her and her followers ablaze as surely as though they had been cast onto the pyre by witch hunters. Guilt paralysed her mind at the realisation she had brought them all to this.

Steel flashed. The wire parted a foot in front of Wilhomelda. An instant later the silver flames reached the severed end at her feet and jetted a furious spray of sparks. Wilhomelda danced back with a cry of alarm.

The coil of wire about her wrist loosened like a dead serpent and slipped to the floor.

The air was full of smoke from broken and burning machinery, and the groans of injured engineers. Wilhomelda panted with shock, blinking rapidly, trying to make sense of what had happened. She looked to Lanette and saw her Magister Secundi had her sword in a double-handed grip where she had sliced through the wire. The ruby in its pommel glowed fiercely.

'Thank you,' panted Wilhomelda.

There was something in Lanette's eyes that forced her to look away.

'I'll see to the wounded,' said Lanette, sheathing her sword with a hiss of steel on leather.

Wilhomelda stared around the smoky chamber. Figures swam through the murk, some hurrying to fight fires or aid the wounded, some collapsed to their knees, evidently as shocked as she. The unnatural curvature of the chamber made the already horrible scene disturbingly surreal.

Adrenaline and shock caused Wilhomelda to shake. She took a deep breath. She was the Magister Princep, she reminded herself. She needed to act like it. Lanette was doing her duty, after all, and Wilhomelda could do no less. But then, she thought, Lanette had expected this to go wrong, hadn't she? There had been grim vindication in her companion's eyes, she was sure of it. Worse, there had been something like pity.

'Did she expect the ritual to fail? Or did she cause it?'

Wilhomelda froze. Her breath caught in her throat. Had that been her own thought, or something from without? Her gaze was drawn back to the pillar, half-seen through the smoke. She remembered the gunshot cracks at the height of the ritual, the dark shape writhing at the pillar's heart. Wilhomelda thought she should have been alarmed, but instead all she felt was a slow bloom of realisation.

Perhaps the ritual had not been entirely a failure, after all…

CHAPTER FIVE

Somewhere really horrid...

Zograt was a mushroom.

He was a soggy runtcap, glowing feebly amidst an outcropping of fungi emerging from a dungheap behind the biggest squig pens he had ever seen. Fashioned from lurid purple and acid-green wood, the pens rambled away forever under a rocky roof that swam from hues of bilious blue and blood red to eye-searing yellow. The squigs within the pens were all gnashing teeth, squirming flesh and piggy little eyes filled with dumb ferocity.

They frightened Zograt. He was a mushroom, helpless and tiny and all too edible.

The taste of strange fungi fizzed on Zograt's tongue, but how could he have a tongue when he was a mushroom? A memory flitted through his mind of squirming into a claustrophobic little grotto where he felt safe, and of biting into a handful of fungus so that he could do something important. He blinked his impossible mushroom eyes and tried to look around, wondering how he could have eaten 'shrooms when he *was* a 'shroom.

How trapped he felt, and how powerless!

Zograt realised the mushrooms around him were looking back at him with eyes they also could not have, and he felt terribly afraid. The mushrooms swelled, growing swiftly even as he remained the same stunted and drippy little stalk. They crowded in around him, glowered down at him, choked off the light until he had nothing but his own sad glimmer to show him their fatted stalks, tighter and tighter.

Zograt tried to scream, but it was hard to do without a mouth. And how could a mushroom have a mouth?

But he wasn't a mushroom, he realised. Some part of Zograt knew it, and asked itself what it needed in that moment. Answers skipped across his mind like skimming-squigs over a pond: a better lair; a bigger tribe; a proper crown; the plan he'd claimed already to have. He wasn't a mushroom at all, Zograt remembered briefly, but then the hallucinogens billowed in his mind and once again he was. Yet now he was a mushroom with a purpose, and a part of him knew he wasn't a victim any more, but instead he was the boss! That part of Zograt forced open impossible jaws, split the fungal vision-flesh of his little glowing hallucination-self and thrust out wicked fangs to fill the new-formed maw.

The other fungi around him recoiled. As they did, his roots left the dungheap and he floated free, tumbling into a purple-and-yellow whirlpool of light. As they tumbled, so he bit, and gnashed, and chomped at the other mushrooms like an angry squig. The other fungi writhed in pain as he took great chunks out of their flesh. As he ate he grew, sending out mycelial tendrils that swelled into arms and legs and fingers and toes.

Zograt was a grot again, but as the whirlpool became a grotto with a lake at its centre he saw his reflection in the mirror-dark waters and realised he wasn't himself. Skram Badstabba glared up at him from the depths with the brutish malice Zograt loathed. He recoiled from the reflection and hated himself for doing it.

The grotto squirmed around him and again Zograt remembered that he was supposed to be formulating a plan. They were all waiting for it, and if he didn't have one soon…

Zograt realised that with every step he took away from the reflection in the pool, so the rocky walls ground together like troggoths' teeth and closed in around him. Suddenly terrified he would be crushed, Zograt lunged into the still waters with a splash.

Down he plunged into shocking cold and absolute darkness. With him went the Skram from his reflection, fingers lengthening into wicked talons as they wrapped around his throat. Zograt gave a bubbling scream as Skram's fangs elongated until they forced his jaws apart, until they tore Skram's face into a grotesque Bad Moon leer. That mantrap maw yawned and bubbles of air billowed out, vanishing upward in a trail that became insects that wriggled as they drowned.

Suddenly Zograt was angrier than he had ever been. As fangs closed about him and talons squeezed his neck, Zograt plunged arms like fungal tendrils down Skram's cavernous gullet. He gripped something wet and thumping. He pulled with all his might, and as he tore Skram Badstabba's heart out and dragged it up the monster's throat, he turned both his old boss and himself inside out.

Shock paralysed Zograt. He floated bodiless and bewildered in the void. He was nothing now. He had no sense of where he was or how to escape from this terrifying nothingness. Voices came to him, echoing from some impossible abyss.

'Wot we doin'? Wot yoo doin'?'

'Thought yoo 'ad a plan?'

'Ain't nuffin', is ya?'

'Stoopid as Skram, not worth nuffin'!'

His anger surged anew. Zograt drew upon the powers the Bad Moon had given him. He hurled them outward with the wild desperation of one trapped in a hallucinogenic state they could neither control nor bring to an end, but instead must simply ride out until normality returned. Suddenly he was a coiling mass of glowing mycelia that pulsated and grew to fill the void. High above him he saw the faintest dot of light, and with a surge of joy he swam towards it.

When Zograt broke the surface, he was himself again, fully formed and as twisted as ever, with fungal tendrils sprouting from his scalp and flying in the breeze as he shot up into the night sky. Yet he knew this was not real, not yet. For one thing, his fingers were wrapped around a pair of stubby orange horns. Zograt realised that he was riding atop the biggest squig he'd ever seen. The colossal ball of rubbery flesh had to be as big as the entirety of Badwater Drop.

Up and up the squig's leap carried them and the dot of light swelled into the unmistakable shape of the Bad Moon. Sickly yellow-green light spilled from it. Cavernous craters glared at Zograt like malevolent eyes. A jagged chasm like a fanged maw split the Bad Moon's surface, and Zograt saw the seething suggestion of countless insect bodies writhing within it.

'We'z gunna do it!' squealed a voice from below him.

'We'z gunna eat da moon!' yelled another.

'Driggz?' he asked, looking down. Where the squig's vast face had been, now he saw the entangled bodies and limbs of his tribe. Green faces were contorted with exultant glee or religious terror. Grubby digits twitched amidst the compacted mass of grots.

'Yooz ain't s'posed to eat da moon, it's da roolz!' wailed Old Spurk's face from beneath another grot's armpit. He heaved and vomited out the top half of Nuffgunk.

'Da roolz! It's da roolz!' Nuffgunk howled, dangling like some impossibly engorged tongue from Spurk's distended jaws.

The intertwined grots panicked. Zograt yelled in alarm as his tribe disentangled themselves, bodies and limbs tearing like fungus as they yanked wildly. He felt his steed disintegrating beneath him. He saw the Bad Moon's mouth open wide to consume them all.

Zograt closed his eyes and wailed, desperate for this horrible fantasy to be over. Echoing wails came back to him, accompanied by a shrilling chorus. He opened his eyes and blinked in confusion.

Zograt was a mushroom again, but a huge one this time. He sat alone in the middle of a cavern whose walls, floor and ceiling pulsed through nauseating waves of orange and green. Nuffgunk, Driggz, Old Spurk and all the Gobbapalooza were there, dancing in a circle around him. Each wore a heavy pair of clogs fashioned from fungi, and a preposterous fungal hat. As they danced, they waved their arms over their heads. Around them swarmed thousands of insects, also dancing, also waving their gangling limbs as they trilled their bizarre song in time to that of the grots.

'Er...?' said Zograt.

Silver fire tore through the cavern like a bomb blast. Hallucinatory rock and dancing grots and singing bugs were scoured away, leaving Zograt standing alone before the flames. He screamed but could not hear his own voice amidst the draconic roar of the firestorm.

In the next instant the flames were gone and Zograt felt himself racing northwards, flying through solid rock and up onto the surface, to where the lights of a settlement glimmered in the mouth of a rocky pass. Zograt swept over the town and on into the shadow of the mountain looming over it. The sight of the jagged peak impaling the clouds enthralled him. He felt a yearning for the dark tunnels he sensed running through its innards like maggot-holes. Then a sickly light limned the mountain and behind it rose the leering mass of the Bad Moon. The clouds fled its touch. The rocks of the mountain shuddered and splintered.

Zograt was entranced. This was the destiny the Bad Moon had in store for him. As he envisioned it, so the mountain changed before his eyes into a colossal loonshrine the like of which no grot had ever ruled. The titanic carved effigy of the Bad Moon eclipsed the stars, its chiselled eyes formed from huge boulders of glowing loonstone. Its fangs were battlements. Its tunnels teemed with grots.

Zograt reached a tentative hand up to his scalp and there, sure enough, he felt a crown.

'It's bootiful…' he breathed.

At the sound of Zograt's voice, something deep within the mountain stirred. He had a sense of eyes focusing on him, and of terrible malice. In that instant Zograt wanted that power more than he had ever desired anything in his life.

He realised with a shock that whatever it was, it could see him. The mountain shook as though something was trying to smash its way free from within. Zograt squealed with terror as another thunderous boom sounded and the mountain's slopes shuddered again. Peaks of stone snapped like broken fangs and crashed down the mountainsides. Cracks erupted across the slopes as though the mountain were a colossal hatching egg.

The cracks in the mountain's flanks widened and now the light of the Bad Moon was dying away amidst flowing shadow. From within the deepest chasm, a staring eye fixed upon him with insane intensity.

He scrambled backwards. He panted and shrieked, writhed in his efforts to escape the flowing shadows, and then he was falling onto his backside and banging his head against a jutting spur of rock.

Zograt blinked and took ragged breaths. He felt damp stone and crushed fungus under his palms. He tasted vomit and chewed 'shroom. His skull thumped with a pain that was at once unpleasant and tremendously reassuring.

'Just a 'shroom-seein'. Finally back in me grotto,' he gasped. The cramped space was so familiar that Zograt almost wept. He watched a seven-legged rockroach scuttle over the back of his hand and vanish up his sleeve. The squirming of insects across his skin was a comfort, reminding him of the strange new powers he possessed. The big glowy fungus protruding from the rocks near to hand, with a huge bite taken out of it, recalled to him precisely why he had been having visions in the first place.

And what visions, he thought. Now that he was calming, Zograt knew he had received a message from the Bad Moon. He was awed, infused with purpose. He knew what he had to do, and the power that would be his as reward.

'If dat ain't da Clammy Hand, I dunno wot is,' he exclaimed, scrambling to his feet.

'Oh, I dunno, 'ow about dese clammy 'ands?' croaked a voice behind him. Zograt spun then screamed as the fanged Skram-thing with the Bad Moon leer erupted from a fissure in the rock.

Zograt landed on his bottom once again. His breath came in shrieking gasps. His eyes darted wildly. Damp stone and fungus under his palms. Heart thumping. Head pounding. Bitten mushroom still growing where it should be. And no sign of the apparition that had followed him up from his vision.

Zograt's breathing took longer to slow this time. His gaze flicked nervously between the bitten mushroom and the fissures in the rock.

'Not eatin' one o' dem again in an 'urry,' he promised himself.

Zograt flinched at the sound of voices. He glanced around the cracks in the wet stone before realising that he could hear Nuffgunk and Driggz yelling for him in what sounded like panic.

'Zog me, wot now?' he muttered, before hauling his aching body out of the grotto and crawling to meet his frantic underlings.

* * *

Zograt emerged from the tunnel to be met by a gaggle of grots, shoving and jabbering over one another. Skrog stood before them, his menace enough to keep Zograt's subjects at bay. Zograt patted the troggoth's leg and took a breath. The creature uttered a sub-sonic rumble in return, the sound surprisingly comforting to Zograt. Flickers of his visions still danced through his mind, but before he could announce his grand plan, he recognised that he first needed to deal with whatever this was.

'Shuttit!' he screeched to little effect. Their voices tumbled over one another like a Squigalanche in full bound.

'...bapalooza just went all weird, boss, an' dey...'

'...dunno wot 'appened but da bugs woz all runnin' in circles and...'

'...broke out of da squig pens an' just went proppa bonkerz, bitin'...'

'...come up outta da lake, an' it smashed up Muggit's hut an' ate Big Squibb, den it...'

'Hoi, one at a time!' yelled Zograt, again to no avail. He scowled up at Skrog, who let out an ear-splitting roar. Grots dived to the floor and flung their arms over their heads. A few took off up the tunnel as though a Shudderwood monster were chasing them. The rest subsided into saliva-spattered silence, eyes wide. The scent of fresh grot faeces wafted over the gathering and made Zograt wrinkle his nose.

'Right. Wot's goin' on? Driggz?'

Driggz gaped at Zograt like one of the glowy fish that lived in the deep-cave pools. Evidently, fear of Skrog had stolen what little wits the scrawny grot possessed. A thick globule of troggoth-spit collected at the end of his nose and plopped to the floor.

Zograt turned to Nuffgunk.

'Yoo den. Wot's 'appened?'

'I dunno, boss, dat's wot I been tryin' to say! Everyfing started shakin', den da bugs all went funny and a bunch o' squigs went loony and smashed dere way outta da pens. An' dat's when da Gobbapalooza all starts jabberin' about a mountin and frowin' up all dis green goo.'

'A mountin, eh?' asked Zograt.

'Den Old Spurk made dis funny noise,' croaked Driggz. 'An' 'e spun round in a circle, den his eyes popped out, den his head 'sploded!'

'Got brainz all over me best bottle!' shouted a grot.

'Yeah, an' he bent me fork!' another complained.

'Oh, an' den Da Lurk popped up an' started smashin' stuff up an' eatin' grots!' added Nuffgunk.

Zograt blinked. Had all this been caused by the same blast of magic that had invaded his 'shroom-seeing? Just what was this incredible source of power to the north, he wondered, that it could reach all the way down to Badwater Drop and cause mayhem? Whatever it was, Zograt wanted it more than ever now.

He realised the grots were staring at him, having seemingly exhausted their immediate list of grievances. Nuffgunk was watching Zograt closely, a look of contempt on his mean features.

The grot boss was clearly waiting for him to make a mistake, or to abdicate responsibility as Skram would have done and leave Nuffgunk himself to pick up the pieces.

'Right,' said Zograt, as much to make a decisive noise as because he had any immediate answers. He paused, then shoved his way through the grots and limped off up the tunnel towards the main caverns of the lurklair. He found the expression of surprise on Nuffgunk's face gratifying.

'Right,' he repeated as they trailed after him, Skrog plodding in their midst. 'First fing, is Da Lurk still on da rampage? Cos if it is, we gotta get rid of it.'

'Can't 'ear no screams,' said Driggz.

'No crashin' neither,' added another grot.

'Me fork's still bent though, innit?' came a rebellious mutter from somewhere near the back.

'Sounds like it's zogged off into da lake again, don't it?' said Zograt. 'Driggz, take Mugrot, Widgit, an'… er… yoo dere, wotever yer name is, and sort out Da Soggy Cave. If Da Lurk comes back up, let me know. We'll see 'ow it likes a nice big bolt o' Bad Moon magik to da gob.'

'Right, boss,' said Driggz, saluting with a clank of his fist against scavenged helm. He didn't sound enthusiastic about his new assignment, but he led the grots off along a side tunnel towards Da Soggy Cave nonetheless. Zograt reflected that Driggz might make a half-useful underling yet.

'Wot about da squigs?' asked Nuffgunk.

'And me fork?' came the voice from the back again.

'We'z goin' to deal wiv da squigs now,' Zograt replied. 'An' if anyone mentions forks again, I'll get Skrog to pull dere 'ead off. Don't need a fork if yoo ain't got a gob, does ya?'

'Right den, boss,' replied Nuffgunk, in a tone of grudging respect.

Zograt led the way until ahead he began to hear the snarls, shrieks, wet thuds and crashing that hinted at squigs letting off steam. He realised they must be almost at the pens.

He would get this place straightened up, Zograt thought determinedly. Then, once he really had everyone's attention, he would reveal his grand plan. Zograt would march his tribe up to that mountain, blast his way inside with his new-found powers, and claim the destiny that the Bad Moon had set before him. A few rampaging squigs weren't about to get in his way. The Badwater Boyz were going to war.

CHAPTER SIX

The Shudderwood Eaves

'Dat's a lot o' open ground,' said Nuffgunk.

'Big sky above it,' added Stragwit.

'Glareface Frazzlegit be's always watchin' from da sky!' said Naffs Gabrot, voice muffled by his mask.

'It's night,' replied Zograt. 'Everygrot knows when it's night, Gorkamorka sticks a big glinty rock on top of da sky. Dat's why it goes dark, an' all dem shiny bitz is up dere glintin'. Glareface can't see past da rock, can he, ya zogwitz?'

He, Nuffgunk, Driggz and the Gobbapalooza were crouching amidst dense underbrush on the edge of the Shudderwood. Skrog stood nearby, having allowed Zograt to position him carefully behind the trunk of a large tree for concealment.

They were peering north, across an expanse of scrubland and rocky outcroppings to where lights marked the outskirts of the human town. The mountain was lost in the darkness beyond. Zograt could feel its presence, nonetheless. A vivid recollection came to him of an eye staring from a dark rent in the mountainside. Instinctively, he glanced back over his shoulder.

All he saw were his tribe, lurking the way he'd told them to further back amidst the treeline. Or rather, he saw, some were lurking. Some were too busy trying to keep the squigs corralled with proddas and sticks. Others appeared to have forgotten his orders already and were needling one another, dawdling about or gobbling down meagre rations. Zograt wondered, not for the first time, whether he had been wise to bring the entire tribe on this raid. Skram had always left the runts behind as useless, though, and he wasn't going to be like Skram. Besides, they had a town to sack and a mountain to reach. The more bodies he could fling into the fight, the better.

He returned his gaze to the open ground they would have to cross before the attack could begin. Despite his confident tone, Zograt was no keener on running around in the open than his lieutenants. He gripped the gnarled magic stick he had looted from Old Spurk's corpse and narrowed his eyes.

'Gotta be done,' he muttered.

'Wossat, boss?' asked Driggz. Despite the continued loathing and bullying of the Boingrot Bounderz, Driggz had been trying his best to play the part of aspiring grot boss since they had left Badwater Drop. It was a shame, Zograt reflected, that his best appeared to be rubbish.

'Nuffin', Driggzy, talkin' to da Bad Moon,' Zograt replied. 'Now lissen, yooz lot. I already told yoo wot we gotta do, an' why we gotta do it.'

'Cos da Bad Moon has given yoo a destiny,' said Nuffgunk, in a sceptical tone.

'Dat's right!' said Zograt, pointing north with a hand that squirmed with little segmapedes. 'Da Bad Moon wants me ta blast me way through dat rubbish humie town and nab da power in da mountin. When I do, it'll make me da Loonking!'

Silence greeted this pronouncement. Zograt's followers gaped at him, eyes wide.

'I'nt dere already a Loonking…?' asked Da Fung in a dreamy voice. Zograt glared at him, but the diminutive Shroomancer was sitting on his backside conjuring spider-legged mushrooms that danced about him in the grass. He gave no sign of noticing Zograt's displeasure.

'Can't dere be more'n one Loonking?' asked Driggz.

'Stoopid zoggin' question,' spat Nuffgunk, though Zograt noticed that he looked uncertain of its actual answer.

Driggz's shoulders slumped.

'Bosses change, Nuffgunk,' said Zograt. 'Loonkingz can too.'

'Yeah, bosses *do* change, speshully daft zoggers wiv loony plans,' Nuffgunk replied. Zograt ignored him. He didn't have time for petty rebellions at the moment. He had a battle to plan.

Zograt wasn't sure how long it had taken them to march all the way north to the edge of the Shudderwood. He dimly recalled a few sleeps between marches before the tunnels had petered out and forced them up onto the surface, then a few more after that. Now he thought about it, he had never really spent long outside the lurklair before this. It was all alarmingly unfamiliar territory to him. Part of Zograt, the limping runt that had cowered from each kick, was terrified that at any moment the sky would lighten as Glareface Frazzlegit smashed through Gorkamorka's sky rock, or a Shudderwood monster would lurch from the trees to eat him.

He had been surprised to find, however, that a bigger part of him was excited. Being the boss certainly helped, as did his new-found magical might. Yet Zograt imagined he would have felt this way regardless. He had spent his life being afraid, after all. He wondered if he had built up a tolerance, the way shamans ate steadily bigger portions of redcap 'shrooms until they could gain all the benefits of their magical properties while lessening the risk of sudden and horrible death. At the very least, if he was going to be surrounded by scary things, they might as well be new and exciting.

Besides, Zograt reminded himself, he had a destiny. However long it had taken to get here, however alarming it all might be now he saw it in person, he doubted the Bad Moon would wait patiently for him to acclimatise.

'We'z got work to do,' he said.

'So, wot *is* da plan?' asked Stragwit, wincing as he shifted his heavy still on his shoulders. Zograt didn't know why the Brewgit insisted on wearing the bulky contraption everywhere, but since it had been repaired Stragwit had refused to remove it even when he slept.

'Yeah, go on, wot's da plan?' asked Nuffgunk.

Feeling their eyes boring into him, Zograt experienced a moment of self-doubt. It wasn't as though he had ever even been in a battle, let alone commanded one. He glanced about, hoping for some sign from the Bad Moon to give him inspiration. All he got was the sight of Skrog, rooting industriously about in one cavernous nostril with a finger thicker than a grot's arm.

Zograt ground his fangs, thought hard, then spoke.

'No point hangin' about. It's too dark an' da town's too far away fer us ta see exactly wot dey got like walls an' guards an' dat. But if we can't see dem, dey can't see us neither, right? Means we can sneak up to da walls like we woz invisible.'

The Gobbapalooza looked impressed at this reasoning. Nuffgunk frowned as though attempting to work it out for himself. Driggz just nodded with a sycophantic grin. Encouraged, Zograt pressed on.

'Nuffgunk, yoo lead da ladz, get da skulkmobz ready to charge through da gates once we knocks 'em down. Driggz, yoo'z in charge o' all da squigs. Get 'em pointed da right way an' make sure dey don't get stuck in before dey're meant to.'

'And who's goin' to knock da gates down?' asked Nuffgunk.

'Who d'yoo fink?' replied Zograt with what he hoped was a confident grin. He wiggled his fingers so that sparks of green energy leaped between them. He felt the dozens of insects within his robes wriggle in sympathy with the gesture.

'Wot about us?' asked Skutbad Da Leg. The Spiker brandished his stinger-tipped stave as though keen to jab someone with it.

'Well, yooz lot do wot yoo do, dontcha?' said Zograt. In truth he had no idea what to do with the grots of his Gobbapalooza, beyond a vague notion that once the fighting started, they would all prove useful somehow. He glared around at them, pointedly avoiding the hypnotic gaze of Wabber Spakklegit.

'An' wot 'appens when da humies fight back?' asked Nuffgunk.

'We clobber 'em, don't we?' replied Zograt in a tone of withering contempt. 'Dey's only humies, not proper filthy green gitz like us. Now, no more time fer questions or Gorkamorka's gunna take 'is rock back an' den we'd 'ave to 'ide under da trees all day. Yooz know da plan, go get da ladz ready!'

Nuffgunk still looked mutinous but sloped away to do as he was told. Driggz saluted with a clank then hurried off, tripping over his ratty old scabbard as his helmet slipped over his eyes. The Gobbapalooza drifted away, Skutbad Da Leg tugging on Da Fung's arm to coax him along. Soon only Zograt remained, along with Skrog, who continued to pick his nose as he stared vaguely into the middle distance. Zograt took a steadying breath then hefted Spurk's staff and gave the troggoth a firm whack on the leg.

'Come on, lad, let's go 'ave a crack at dat mountin,' he said.

Wilhomelda had requisitioned a chamber high on the mountain's north slopes. She had chosen it partly because of the circular stone door that could be easily rolled into place across its entrance on a set of marble runners, affording her privacy largely lacking throughout Muttering Peak. The choice had also been influenced by the wide window in the rock face that admitted natural daylight while offering a view over the restless waters of the Umbralic Sea. Though it was night, still she stood at that glassless window, listening to the sigh and boom of waves she could not see. A wine glass sat on the stone sill, close to hand though currently empty.

'It has been five days since that farce in the pillar chamber,' said Borster from behind her. His voice jarred with the murmur of the waves and spoiled their calming effect. Wilhomelda turned to face him. Her chambers were sparsely furnished, boasting a handful of furniture items she had brought from Azyrheim: a simple but well-crafted sleeping pallet; a brass basin-stand for bathing; an antique dhaurwood drinks cabinet, whose stocks were running low; a finely wrought brass-and-cogwork orrery; a bookcase stuffed with tomes, and a locked and warded chest in which she kept more hazardous volumes; a large table that dominated the room and would have looked more at home in some Freeguild general's field tent.

Borster hovered by the table, having refused both the chair and the wine she had offered him.

'I am all too aware of the time's passing, Borster,' Wilhomelda replied. She strode across and snatched a bottle from the table, feeling a twitch of annoyance as she tipped nothing but dregs into her glass.

'How much longer before someone in authority wonders where we've gone, what we're up to?' asked Borster.

'We are already pressing our luck,' said Wilhomelda. 'But that is not my only concern. People are talking, Borster. People were injured. Two killed. There are doubts about what we are doing here, about whether it is possible.'

'The Magister Secundi,' he said with a scowl.

'Not her alone,' replied Wilhomelda. 'But she has been vocal since the ritual went awry.'

She drank her wine at a gulp and set the glass down. She wanted to forget the arguments she and Lanette had had in the days since the failed ritual. They haunted her regardless. Wilhomelda felt as though something had fractured between them, cracking as the pillar had cracked. She didn't know how to mend it.

Well, that wasn't true, she thought sourly. She knew how the repairs might begin, but they would require abandoning her endeavours and she could not do that. Not after Leontium. She wished sincerely that Lanette could understand all Wilhomelda wanted was to keep her and everyone else safe. It saddened her to realise she had come to trust in Borster's unapologetic lust for renown over the intentions of her oldest and closest comrade.

'Do you think she would rat us out?' he asked.

'Lanette is loyal. I trust her.' Borster's grunted response was non-committal, but he didn't press the matter further. Good, thought Wilhomelda. She wanted him focused on the task at hand, not entertaining paranoid fantasies about Lanette.

'It is not paranoia if it is true.'

Wilhomelda closed her eyes and dug the nails of her left hand into her palm, feeling again the wire burning her wrist. The risk of detection was not the only reason haste was required, she thought. Since the ritual, the voice whispering into her mind had become louder and more insistent by the day. Wilhomelda was not fool enough to believe its invasive suggestions her own, or to trust them. She believed that she knew what it belonged to.

But by Sigmar those sibilant mutterings had some power behind them, she thought. Just that morning, they had guided her steps almost to the pillar chamber before she realised the impulse she followed was not her own. Wilhomelda had the unnerving feeling of having unlocked a door behind which something terrible lurked, something that would force the door wide and escape if she did not bind it soon.

'Borster, we have tampered with the cage of a godbeast. Do you understand what that means?'

'I'm not a fool,' he replied, eyes flashing.

'Then stop whittering about my Magister Secundi and tell me what progress you have made.'

Borster reached into a satchel at his hip and unrolled several parchments on the tabletop, pinning their corners with weights.

'This was your idea. I know the quality of my craftsmanship but… you tell me.'

Wilhomelda circled the table to stand at Borster's side. As she tried to focus on his blueprints, she silently cursed herself for drinking too much. It helped her to keep the whispers at bay, but not to concentrate.

Had helped, she amended, at least for a day or two. And she was under a lot of pressure, could be excused for–

Wilhomelda dug her nails into her palms again and forced herself to focus. There was her concept laid out in a mixture of engineers' designs, magical formulae and alchemists' notations.

'A circlet, linked not by crude wires but through binding magics woven direct to the focusing awl driven into the pillar,' she said.

'You see there, the inlaid wards precisely as you described them,' he said, pointing to the designs. Borster's voice became brisk and eager now that he was dealing with an engineering problem. 'And there, the blood channels and alchemical philtre lines, all sealed and ritually warded after the work is complete.'

'And these?' she asked, pointing to a pair of needle-like protrusions angling down from the front of the circlet to describe equidistant curves of pointed brass. Borster shifted and harrumphed. When he spoke again, he sounded almost apologetic.

'The most efficacious means by which to allow direct informational flow and achieve the necessary contact with your vital humours.'

She let out a shaky breath.

'Of course, they pierce the corners of my eyes. Here and here?' She tapped two fingers against the bridge of her nose, close to her tear ducts.

'It was that or a trephinial barb, which would be even worse.' He sounded defensive. 'You requested absolute certainty of direct mind-to-mind contact. The pillar already has its awl.'

'And I will require mine,' she said, offering what she hoped was a firm and confident smile. 'You have no need to explain further, Vikram. We can take no more risks, not when dealing with an entity of such power. I will not place the burden upon others. I will not have them face the dangers in my stead. If this works then whatever pain or… disfigurement may result will be worthwhile. Think of the lives we will save.'

'Who else knows?' he asked.

'We two, Ulke, and Gillighasp,' she replied. 'By this method we ought to be able to channel the creature's energies directly into my mind, and employ blood magic to bind its will to my own. I will use my own subtle sorceries to bypass its defences, and to obfuscate our purpose from it until it is too late for resistance. The success or failure of the next ritual will be my burden alone to bear.'

And, she thought guiltily, there would be no need to tell Lanette what she was doing until it was too late for her to stop it. The voice had whispered more than once in the past days of danger circling, growing closer, of another who coveted the power she sought and would seek to foil her plans. Wilhomelda was a veteran wizard of countless wars. She believed that she had endured sufficient dealings with dark entities to resist the godbeast's attempts at instilling paranoia.

If it could first fashion a crack of its own within her mind as she had within its prison, then she suspected it could prise apart her willpower and use her as its puppet. Doubtless one of lesser sorcerous power and mental fortitude would have long ago fallen under its sway. She wondered if perhaps it had long hoped to achieve such an end with the Listeners of Taremb, but until now had been too soundly trapped to succeed.

The theory made some sense, she reflected. The godbeast might have spent centuries feeding the Listeners fragments of prophecy, enough for them to think of it as benevolent, keeping them alive and forewarned in the hopes of one day using one of them as the puppet that would free it. There again, perhaps a mortal attempting to understand the motivations of an imprisoned godbeast was nothing but foolishness, and it had done all that it had these many years for reasons that would forever remain ineffable.

'Gods offer no explanations for their deeds,' she murmured. Borster frowned at her. She shook her head. 'What whispers I hear now are unreliable, but that only makes me more determined to bind it. This entity *will* serve us, suffer at our whims, not the other way around.'

'Ulke, Gillighasp and I require privacy to work,' said Borster. 'Questions will be asked, otherwise. This'll not be quick or easy. You weren't lying when you said we'd work for our pay on this expedition.'

'And of course, the material and intellectual remuneration I am offering will be increased commensurate to the increasing challenges of your travails,' said Wilhomelda with a thin smile.

Borster grunted.

'You shall have a suite of chambers set aside, guarded night and day by my most obedient servants,' she continued. 'I will inform everyone that you three are engaged in refining devices that will ensure a second ritual succeeds, and that you are not to be disturbed.'

'Are you prepared for...?' He fished for the right words. 'Are you prepared for any challenges that arise?'

'Let me worry about such things,' she told him. 'You focus on getting this right. I don't wish to stab needles into my damned eyes only to find out your device doesn't work. And for the heavens' sakes, stow those drawings now, then lock them away in your chambers. It would not do for the wrong people to see them.'

'Ulke gave me a little something to help with that,' said Borster, though he began stowing the weights and blueprints. 'He's treated the parchments with an alchemical solution. Sigmar knows how this stuff tells the difference, but if anyone of ill or mistrustful intent handles my plans, we'll know about it.'

'Ill or mistrustful intent?' asked Wilhomelda, wondering how such a thing would work. 'You have made copies in case whatever Ulke has done proves... deleterious to the drawings?'

'Locked away in my chambers, I'm not an amateur,' Borster replied gruffly. 'And that's what the little creep said, word for word. I don't know, Borchase, I'm a bloody engineer not some 'browless bottle-boiler like–'

Wilhomelda held up a hand for silence. From outside the door came the sound of raised voices. She looked to the big engineer, who scrabbled up the last of his parchments and stuffed them into his satchel. Even as he did the stone door rolled aside and Lanette marched into the chamber. Wilhomelda caught a glimpse of the two soldiers set to guard her door, staring helplessly over the Magister Secundi's shoulder. As someone who had argued often with Lanette, she supposed she couldn't blame them for giving way.

Lanette stopped short, one hand on the ruby pommel of her blade. Wilhomelda suddenly recalled a time when, as a young woman, she had spent several months enjoying a relationship with a scullery maid well below her station. She had known discovery would lead at the least to her lover's dismissal, perhaps even to punishment, and that it would not matter that Wilhomelda, not the maid, had been the one to do most of the seducing. Each time they had been alone together, that danger had added a frisson of excitement while simultaneously seeming wholly unreal. Wilhomelda had believed herself far too clever to get caught. When at last the inevitable had occurred, the reality of panic and guilt had been almost suffocating. Seeing Lanette's brow crease now, watching her eyes jump from the flustered Borster to the hastily stowed parchments still jutting from his satchel, and then to Wilhomelda, resurrected all those feelings.

She saw the question in Lanette's eyes, and the hurt that spoke of a trust betrayed. A desperately inappropriate urge to laugh came upon her. She stamped down hard on it, again cursing herself for drinking too much.

'You guard your door against me now?' asked Lanette.

'I have guards upon my door, and I commanded that I was not to be disturbed. That is not at all the same thing,' said Wilhomelda.

'Except by him?' asked Lanette, pointing with her chin at Borster. 'And by whatever I have just walked into?'

'The, er, Magister Princep and I were just discussing some matters,' blustered Borster. Again, Wilhomelda silenced him with a raised hand.

'Why *have* you walked in?' she asked.

'The bells are tolling in Taremb, and they've sent runners up the pass,' said Lanette. 'The town is under attack. They require our aid. If you're not too busy?'

Embarrassment and alcohol sparked Wilhomelda's temper.

'You interrupt me in closed counsel to tell me that the local farmers are fighting off some bandits? I have already provided these bumpkins with soldiers and spellcraft! For Azyr's sakes, girl, can they not look after themselves?'

She knew immediately this last exclamation had been a step too far. Lanette's expression was a dropped portcullis, her eyes focused somewhere over Wilhomelda's shoulder.

'Magister Princep, there are greenskins assaulting Taremb's outer wall. It is our express duty as members of Sigmar's armies of reconquest and defence to lend them our aid. Lives are at stake. We do still save lives, do we not?'

'Borster,' snapped Wilhomelda. 'Ready your engineers and harness the dray beasts. It sounds as though we will require your arsenal.'

'At once, Magister Princep,' he said and hurried from the room. Lanette turned to leave herself.

'Lanette, wait, I'm–'

'What were the two of you discussing? What were those charts?'

Wilhomelda stood with one hand halfway raised towards Lanette. Indecision stole her voice. Frustration, guilt and fear closed her throat. Then the thought came unbidden of the failed ritual, of Lanette's apparent unsurprise, at her constant resistance to everything Wilhomelda was trying to do. She seemed suddenly a stranger.

'You are the one who counselled urgency. If Taremb is under attack, then other matters must wait.'

Lanette squared her shoulders like a fighter expecting a blow. When she replied, her voice was steady and cold.

'Then I shall see my duties done, Magister Princep.'

Lanette turned on her heel and left Wilhomelda alone in her chambers.

'Shit,' she breathed. She snatched up the wine bottle, hurling it across the room to smash against the wall. 'Shit!' she shouted, sweeping the glass away with the back of her hand. It too tumbled through the air and broke across the floor. Wilhomelda cast about wildly for something else to break and was halfway to reaching for an incantation before she got hold of her temper. She leaned on the table, shaking and taking deep breaths.

'Hurry, there is danger.'

'Shut up,' she moaned. She took another breath, straightened up and brushed down her robes, cast a critical eye over the smashed glass scattered across the floor. 'Just shut up,' she said, her voice firm and level again. Then she swept out of the chamber, all too glad of the chance for something to kill.

CHAPTER SEVEN

Taremb

The humans had built their stockade wall from Shudderwood trees. The translucent barrier glimmered faintly in the night's dark. Torches burned atop it, carried by patrolling guards and blindingly bright to Zograt's eyes. He had acclimatised to the hazy daylight of the Shudderwood since coming to the surface, but this vicious glare was something else.

The last hundred yards of scrub ground before the walls sloped upward, studded with outcroppings of porous stone. Fingers of the sentries' lights quested almost to the base of the rise. Zograt and his tribe were even now approaching that man-made boundary, crouched low, blades ready.

Moonclan grots were natural murderers. They could be silent as ghosts when creeping up to stab an enemy's back. Not so the tribe's squigs, who had strained and snarled all the way across the open ground, nor Skrog, whose thudding footfalls made Zograt wince. He was amazed they hadn't already been spotted by the wall guards and wondered why no grot had suggested they leave the noisy gitz in the treeline until the attack was underway.

'We'z makin' too much noise,' hissed Nuffgunk.

'I can 'ear,' Zograt whispered. 'Wotchoo want me ta do about it?' Nuffgunk shot him an exasperated glare.

'Can't ya do a magik or somefin'? In't dat why yoo'z boss?'

Zograt felt stupid. In his nervousness and exhilaration, his magical abilities had slipped his mind.

'Woz just waitin' until we woz close enuff,' he muttered.

Zograt clutched Old Spurk's magic stick tight and wiggled the fingers of his free hand. He felt sorcerous energies flow from the staff into his body and then out through his hand. He grinned despite himself. He was starting to get the hang of this.

At Zograt's bidding, the dark ground seethed. There came swiftly stifled squawks of alarm from amongst the advancing grots and Zograt saw several of the blinding torches halt in their progress along the wall top. Baring his fangs, he willed his spellcraft into being and hoped it would be enough.

The undulating shadows took shape. They rushed up the stony bank. They split, and solidified, and became a grotesquely weightless tidal wave of insects that swept over the wall guards and smothered their lights.

Zograt heard muffled screams as the humans were buried beneath thousands upon thousands of chitinous bodies.

'Get up dere, ladz,' he hissed as loud as he dared. 'Quick now, b'fore dey spots wot we done.'

'How d'we get over da wall, boss?' asked a grot, looking at him in bewilderment.

'Yeah, wot we doin'?' asked another.

Zograt felt irritation and panic. How *were* they getting over that wall? he asked himself. Why hadn't someone thought of that before they got to this point? An unpleasant suspicion was growing in his mind that that someone should have been him, but it was too late for self-recrimination now. Atop the walls he could see torch-lights bobbing, moving closer. The humans had noticed something was amiss and were coming to investigate. Panic threatened, and Zograt squashed it. He had a destiny. He wasn't about to let a crummy wooden wall prevent him from reaching it.

'Skrog, smash it down, lad!' He pointed at the wall for good measure. The troggoth peered at Zograt, then at the wall, then again at Zograt. Most of his tribe had scrambled up the bank and gathered in a confused mass at the wall's base. Others had halted and were staring at Zograt, awaiting orders. From nearby, he could hear the increasingly panicked sounds of grots attempting to keep angry squigs in line. Zograt stamped his foot in frustration.

'Skrog, ya great lump o' rocks, get up dere an' bash an 'ole in dat wall!'

Zograt felt a tug at his magical senses and realised the mass of insects he had conjured were spilling in all directions without his will to guide them. Some were feasting upon the corpses of the dead sentries. More had swarmed along the fire step behind the wall or started spilling off it. The tugs he was feeling came from little bodies bursting as alarmed grots swiped the bugs away and stamped on them.

This reached Skrog where Zograt's shouted commands had not. As insect squeals filled the air, the troggoth gave a tectonic growl and strode up the embankment. Grots scattered from his path. Skrog struck the wall a resounding blow with both boulder-like fists. Showers of insects were knocked loose. Translucent timbers splintered. Zograt heard human shouts from further along the wall and ground his teeth in frustration.

'Fink dey 'eard dat, boss,' said Nuffgunk, his tone withering.

'Zog it. Arrer boyz, give 'em a stikkin'!' shouted Zograt.

Even as Skrog's fists hammered the wall again, Ogbrot's ladz drew back their bowstrings and sent a ragged salvo of arrows whistling towards the lights on the wall top. Zograt refocused on his insects and sent them swarming out in both directions along the wall to spill over screaming sentries in a living tide.

A splintering crash announced that Skrog had succeeded in smashing an opening in the wall.

'Ladz, get in dere!' yelled Zograt.

'Form skulkmobz on da uvver side of da wall!' called Nuffgunk, who was scrambling up the bank towards the gap. 'No runnin' off! Get da gongz clangin'!'

Zograt scowled at Nuffgunk's presumption but reminded himself the scarred grot had been on a lot more raids than he had. He wondered if perhaps he should have asked Nuffgunk's advice before launching this one, but then pictured the sneering retorts this would have garnered.

Grunting with exertion, half a mind still on his insect swarms, Zograt struggled his way up the bank. Grots scrambled past him, able to move quicker than his twisted frame allowed. He heard Driggz give a whoop of mingled excitement and terror, and a volley of spheroid shapes sailed overhead to land beyond the wall. Zograt assumed they'd finally given up trying to restrain the squigs.

Ahead, his ladz were bunching up at the gap, yelling and pushing to get through the wall. Skrog stood by, and Zograt was glad that he'd thought to send the insects away from the breach; he didn't want to imagine the carnage if the troggoth had seen all those grots trampling bugs.

Zograt gasped as he neared the top of the rise. He cursed his frailties, and Skram for inflicting them upon him. Why couldn't he be big and strong like Nuffgunk? All this struggling made him look weak, he thought, and showing weakness to Moonclan grots was a sure way to invite a knife in the back.

He gasped as huge hands closed carefully around him and Skrog plucked Zograt from the grass with surprising gentleness before setting him on his broad shoulder.

Fighting off a moment's vertigo and struggling to regain his breath, Zograt grabbed on to one of Skrog's ears for purchase. The troggoth didn't seem to object, so Zograt hung on and pointed with Spurk's stick.

'Through da wall, Skrog.'

Skrog grunted and strode through the gap, grots staring up in awe at their boss. Zograt imagined the inspiring figure he must cut, fungal crest glowing, magic stick in hand and perched on the shoulder of a huge Dankhold steed. This was what a real Loonking ought to look like, he thought.

Zograt's elation faltered as Skrog passed through the hole in the wall and he took in the situation beyond.

'Dere's anuvver wall!' he exclaimed, outraged. 'Why didn't nobody check if dere woz anuvver wall?'

The next wall lay some distance ahead. The ground between the outer and inner walls was mostly churned-up dirt, with stringy human crops growing here and there. It looked every bit as unpromising to Zograt's eye as had the ground before the outer walls.

Zograt's shootas and his magic bugs had finished off the outerwall guards. A few of the humans had fled for the inner wall but had been caught by Driggz and his Boingrot Bounderz. In the gloom, Zograt could only make out flailing limbs, bouncing bodies and sprays of dark fluids as the luckless guards were torn apart.

His skulkmobs, meanwhile, had formed what looked to Zograt like an impressive battle line. He had honestly never realised what a formidable force his tribe could be, when Skram wasn't squandering their potential. Several big mobs of stikkas made up the core of the force, each with gong-bangers clanging away like loons at the front. The Gobbapalooza had spread out behind these massed units: Stragwit was doling out bubbling potions; Naffs Gabrot had mounted his squig-skull steed and been hefted aloft by his brawny and long-suffering lugger, Gobzit; Da Fung had hallucinated himself a nice big 'shroom to ride on, which was all hairy spider legs and gnashing fungal mouths.

Yes, thought Zograt, this was an army. This was *his* army, and with it he would seize his destiny, just as soon as he'd got through that second, much more formidable-looking wall. It was stone, he saw, not wood, dotted with tall watchtowers and boasting a sturdy gate at its centre. He could also dimly see more torches lining the top of the wall, human silhouettes moving around them.

Somewhere beyond the wall, bells were tolling the alarm. The sound bounced from rooftops and beat against the high rocky promontories that loomed to either side of the town.

'And beyond da town, da mountin,' Zograt breathed. He fancied he could just perceive its bulk, a deeper darkness to the north rising to blot out the stars. It would be his, he promised himself. He could almost taste the power already.

'We attackin' that lot den, boss?' Nuffgunk called to him. His expression told Zograt what he thought of the idea, but Zograt supposed he couldn't blame Nuffgunk for his worries. He had been led into fights by that idiot Skram, after all. A little pessimism was to be expected.

'We'z attackin'!' shouted Zograt, addressing his entire skrap. 'We go straight fer da big gate, smack it down, den zog da humies up good. Den it's shinies an' bottles for all!'

'An' a new fork?' came a hopeful shout from somewhere amidst the ranks.

'Dey got forks in dere da size o' proddas, and ain't none of 'em bent!' cried Zograt, eliciting wild whoops of excitement. 'Now come on, ya squig-fondlerz, let's get stuck in!'

Zograt gave Skrog's ear a tug and pointed at the gate with his stick. The troggoth set off at once, and the grots of Zograt's tribe followed, gongs clanging madly.

They crossed the churned fields at speed, Driggz and his ladz charging ahead. Zograt was impressed to see that the Bounderz were heading in the right direction, even if Driggz himself was bouncing along at the back with his helm askew.

The gate drew closer by the moment. Zograt wiggled his fingers and brought his tide of bugs flowing in around both flanks of his force. He had decided that what had worked once would doubtless work again, the insects pouring up the walls to keep the humans busy while Skrog took care of the gate. Then they would be inside, and nothing would stop them from reaching the mountain.

His plotting was interrupted by a crackle from atop the walls. Smoke billowed from the ramparts and the air was suddenly full of whizzing projectiles. Zograt saw some of Driggz's Bounderz knocked off their steeds in sprays of gore, their squigs bouncing wild. Something whipped past his ear close enough to make him cringe. He craned around and saw more grots falling, shot by humies on the walls.

'Bangstikks! Dey got bangstikks!' yelled Nuffgunk.

'Yeah, well I got da Clammy Hand!' cried Zograt, conjuring the full force of his powers. He jabbed Spurk's stick towards the walls and a lurid blast of green light leapt from it. The blast struck a section of rampart and exploded in a greasy fireball. Zograt saw humans tumbling and burning. A ragged cheer went up from his ladz, and Zograt aimed the stick again.

This time, his powers felt sluggish and hard to grasp. Straining, he sent a weak sputter of green sparks towards the walls.

'Wot da zog?'

He peered angrily towards the walls and realised more humies had appeared up there. They wore flowing robes a little like those of his tribe, and some carried staves topped with shiny crystals.

Zograt realised he was looking at wizards, an alarming number of them, and that not only had they quenched his magics with insulting ease, but they were now working spells of their own.

'Hang on, ladz, dey's doin' somefin' sneaky!' he shouted.

From beneath the grots' feet there arose whispering voices. Zograt strained to catch what was being said, but the susurration was too intermingled, a nonsense of whispered human words. What was the use of that? he wondered. Were the wizards trying to scare his tribe?

The first creature slithered up from the mud like some nightmare tree growing with impossible speed. The thing was vaguely humanoid but stretched and indistinct. It looked as though it were made of tattered cloth and shadows, one moment solid and dark, the next translucent. The whispers grew louder about the monstrous figure, which shot out tattered fingers and stabbed them deep into the front rank of Lugbog's ladz. Grots screamed and convulsed, black ectoplasm spilling from their eyes and ears before they collapsed.

Grots cried out in fear.

'Wot da zog is dat?'

'It's a Gangler!'

'Dere's more of 'em!'

Zograt saw that indeed, more of the indistinct things were billowing up from the soil to stab at his ladz. The whispering grew louder, and though he still couldn't make out a word, suddenly Zograt felt intense paranoia grip him. Nuffgunk was going to shiv him, he knew it, and Driggz, and maybe even that mask-bonced idiot Naffs Gabrot. They all wanted him dead. He had to get them before they got him!

Something felt wrong about these thoughts, though. Zograt had spent his life keeping one eye out for a knife in the back. To suddenly panic about the idea now made no sense.

'Oi! Get outta me 'ead!' he snarled. Skram's old loonstone pendant was glowing fiercely at his throat, and Zograt felt incensed at the creatures' attempt to drive him into paranoid madness. He levelled Spurk's stick and wiggled his fingers, blasting one of the nightmare things to tatters.

As Zograt looked around he realised that whatever these things were, they had done exactly what the humans wanted. Many of his ladz had succumbed to the whispering assault. His skulk-mobs had ground to a halt as grots turned on grots, sticking one another with shivs and screeching in boggle-eyed terror. Others were already fleeing towards the gap in the outer wall, several of the Gobbapalooza amongst them. Gunfire continued to rain down from the walls, taking a bloody toll. Zograt looked for Driggz and his Bounderz, and saw they had scattered, the squigs leaping off in all directions with their riders hanging on for dear life.

Zograt had felt angry and powerless many times in his life, but never like this. He had power now! He had the Clammy Hand! How could his army be falling apart before they had even broken into the human town? How could he be losing so badly when the Bad Moon had given him a destiny? Didn't these idiots realise that they were standing in the way of the Bad Moon's will?

'I ain't bein' bullied again!' he screeched, and fury boiled up within him until he felt he would burst like a prodded spattle-thwapper fungus.

Zograt half raised himself on Skrog's shoulder and jabbed Spurk's stick towards the walls. He gave an inarticulate yell of rage and poured every ounce of his anger into a colossal outpouring of sorcery. He felt the wizards try to tamp down his magics and cackled with manic glee as he overwhelmed their efforts. What exploded from the tip of Spurk's stick was something between an enormous squig made of green fire and a monstrous manifestation of the Bad Moon itself. The phantasm thundered away, eradicating several whisper-monsters as it went, then hit the humans' gate with tremendous force.

The explosion blinded Zograt. The shockwave almost knocked him off Skrog's shoulder. As his vision cleared, he gave a shout of glee. Nothing remained of the gate but burning wreckage. A great bite had been taken out of the wall for good measure. Human bodies were strewn everywhere, green fire dancing over their remains.

'Ladz, we got 'em now!' he cried. Yet a look back over his shoulder told him that precious few of his followers were still in the fight. Dozens of grots were running for the outer wall. Nuffgunk had vanished along with them. Zograt tried a headcount but gave up after running out of fingers on his free hand. Still, he told himself, the terrified-looking gaggle of grots clustering behind Skrog would have to be enough. Surely the humans couldn't have much fight in them after his display of magical power?

Zograt tugged Skrog's ear and got the troggoth lumbering towards the breach, zapping bolts of green light at the last few whisper-monsters for good measure. His ladz scurried after him, eyes wild beneath their cowls. He would lead them to victory, Zograt told himself, and then he would rub it in Nuffgunk's face to teach him a lesson for running away.

The sight that greeted Zograt beyond the ruined gate replaced his determination with dread. Lines of soldiers had been drawn up across a wide, cobbled square, all with swords and shields or guns at the ready. Intimidatingly large machines squatted between them on wheeled carriages, and it didn't take a mind of Zograt's calibre to recognise them as weapons. At the centre of the line, he saw another pair of human wizards, one tall and willowy with a face like thunder, the other shorter and broader with red hair and blade in hand.

'Don't stop now, ladz! Chaaarge!' Even as he yelled his battle cry, Zograt delved wildly into his reserves of magical power and hurled sorcerous bolts at his enemies. Insects seethed in swarms across the cobbles. Tendrils of glowing mycelia ripped their way through the ground, distorted fungi erupting behind them in profusion.

The two wizards reacted by chanting and waving their hands, and Zograt felt his magic blunted as though it had run headlong into a wall. Bugs squealed and burned. Glowing fungi withered. He screamed in fury and tried even harder, something hot and wet spilling over his lips as he strained to blast the wizards. Something in their defences faltered, just for a moment, and he hammered a bolt of raw force through the gap. Zograt saw the tall one stumble and fall, but his triumph was short-lived. The other, one hand still raised and surrounded with sigils of dancing light, pointed her blade and yelled an order.

The human guns roared. Their war engines spoke in voices of murderous thunder. Grot blood sprayed Zograt as he instinctively hurled his remaining power into a dense shield of fungus that shuddered and disintegrated under the barrage.

The next thing he knew, Skrog had grabbed him and cradled him to his chest. The troggoth lumbered away from the firestorm, grunting and jerking with bullet impacts.

'Oi, wotchoo doin'?' screamed Zograt. 'Turn round! Go back, ya zoggin' lump!' He could feel destiny slipping through his fingers, and his control went with it. Grots ran, tripped, screamed, burning and falling all around. Zograt flailed and kicked. He bit the troggoth's wrist with a crunch of splintering teeth. If Skrog felt it, he gave no sign. His ground-eating lope carried them back across the churned fields that danced with firelight glare.

Here and there, grots still wrestled one another over blades and dropped bottles, shadowy things swooping and stabbing above them. As the humans' barrage chased Skrog across the open ground even these maddened gaggles scattered, the grots' cowardice overcoming their bewitchment. Something screamed through the air and detonated so close to Skrog's heels that fire washed over the grunting troggoth, but Zograt didn't care. Exhausted, furious, defeated, he hung in Skrog's arms like a limp sack as he was carried back through the outer wall and off towards the treeline.

CHAPTER EIGHT

Taremb, an aftermath

'Thirty-seven men and women of the militia dead! My outer wall breached, the inner gate a ruin!'

Jocundas ParTaremb shook with anger. He had risen from his throne. His big hands clenched in fists, and a tendon stood out in his neck.

The Listener towered over Lanette Ezocheen, yet neither his physicality nor his obvious fury gave her pause. If anything, she found such obvious threats refreshing. She had spent weeks trapped by loyalty to Wilhomelda and the Coven Unseen yet held at arm's length, mired in half-truths, enduring arguments she did not want to have with one who should have trusted her. Azyr knew she expected shadows where Wilhomelda was concerned, but while such secrecy had always exasperated Lanette, she had at least always stood upon the right side of the wall. She'd always remained close to Wilhomelda, even after the passion between them had cooled to embers. She'd always been able to reach her, counsel her, protect her from herself.

Now, Lanette was the attacker in a siege she didn't know how to win. She had been wounded in ways she didn't know how to mend. Compared to all that, an honest argument with Jocundas ParTaremb was welcome.

Lanette did not shout, but her voice would have carried across a parade ground all the same.

'We answered your call. We put everything we had in the field and lost more than a score of our own for the privilege. Our liars' golems scattered the greenskins and our firepower culled them like vermin. In what capacity do you feel that we failed you last night, Listener?'

'Those... creatures... should never have reached our outer walls,' he spat, advancing upon her. Lanette stepped to meet him and glared up into his face.

'If only you had someone blessed with forehearing, Listener.'

His jaw worked.

'Your leader has that power,' he ground out. 'Why did she not warn us? You frighten my people, presume upon my hospitality, then when monsters from the Shudderwood attack my walls, you allow them to run rampant before finally deigning to drive them away. I have no masons who can repair the damage to the inner wall. You understand the precious nature of what they destroyed? The tower they toppled, the gate? Ancient. Irreplaceable. And now my people whisper that my reign is failing because I do not see the perils at our door.'

'A leader should not lie to their people,' Lanette spat. 'A leader should not keep those who trust them in the dark. They do not get to blame others for their own failings if they do.'

A sly look stole across Jocundas' features.

'She tells you no more than she does me, then?' he asked. Lanette had the sense of having thrust wide and left herself open. Yet she was not only a veteran soldier. One did not become Magister

Secundi of the Coven Unseen without some talent on the verbal battlefield.

'What my Magister Princep and I discuss when you are not present would turn your hair white and your mind to madness, Listener,' she said. 'The secrets she has whispered to me in the darkest watches of night would blast your soul to ashes. Should I speak them to you? Would you like to listen?'

Jocundas was not quick enough to conceal his spasm of fear. He took another pace back and bumped into his throne.

Lanette stepped back too, retreating from the dais entirely and offering him a slight bow. She had no desire to frighten Jocundas ParTaremb more than she had to. Besides, she too was angry with Wilhomelda for the events of the night before. She would not soon forget the panicked way Borster had shoved those parchments into his satchel, or the look of guilt on Wilhomelda's face. Perhaps, she thought, if her old friend had been less caught up in whatever she had been doing, or a touch more sober, she might indeed have heard some warning of the danger approaching Taremb's walls.

Behind this thought lurked another, that Wilhomelda had known and yet been too consumed with her own single-minded quest to care. Lanette thrust it away. She would not believe such things of the woman who had raised her up to greatness, who had taught her to fight for those who could not protect themselves, and how to temper her youthful anger with intellect and compassion.

Jocundas collapsed into his throne as though the air had gone out of him. He shook his head.

'My people talk,' he said. 'Their voices grow loud. They, at least, I hear well enough.'

'The grievances your people have with your rule are not the problems of the Coven Unseen,' said Lanette.

Jocundas gave a bleak laugh. 'You misunderstand. It is of your coven they speak, and not well. There have been signs. Ill omens.

They believe that my failure to forehear the attack last night is just the latest.'

'What omens?' asked Lanette. A chill of foreboding crept up her spine.

'The land is restless. Have you not felt it? For five days and nights, we have suffered tremors. There have been rock slips above the valleyside houses and a collapse in the mushroom caverns. Alwik Drend's cattle gave birth to… things… that had to be put from their misery before their first sup. My people besiege me with complaints of nightmares, about the mountain, about the things that it whispers to them in their dreams.'

Lanette swallowed. Five days and nights of disturbances. Five days and nights since the ritual. She had lived too long and seen too much to believe in coincidences, yet still she maintained an expression of neutral disinterest.

'And your people blame these occurrences upon the coven?'

'My advisors question whether your presence here is more bane than boon,' he replied. 'They ask what you have awoken within Muttering Peak.'

'And what about you, Listener?'

'For my part, I question more than ever why it is that Wilhomelda Borchase can hear the mountain when I cannot. I would have words with your Magister Princep, and not her messenger.'

Lanette paused. She too had wondered for weeks why it was that Wilhomelda heard the mountain's whispers when no other did. In the wake of the fighting, Wilhomelda had returned to Muttering Peak with all haste. She had ordered Lanette to deal with what she had termed the small matters of Taremb, and to return to the mountain only once Jocundas had been pacified. She had also left instructions that she, Borster, Ulke and Gillighasp were applying themselves to a project of the utmost secrecy and were not to be disturbed. That act of exclusion had hurt Lanette once again. Being denied the chance to press Wilhomelda for answers had been worse. Now, she cursed her old friend again for putting her in this position.

'The Magister Princep has better uses for her time than assuaging your fears or propping up your rule with borrowed prophecy,' she said.

'And what is it she spends her time doing that is so important?' he asked. Jocundas' expression told her that he heard the hollowness she had tried to keep from her words.

'I have warned you already about asking questions to which you do not desire answers,' Lanette replied. 'It is enough for you to know that our coven labours at a task that will benefit all worshippers of Sigmar.'

'I wonder,' he said, studying her shrewdly.

'If you doubt us so, why not send out messengers?' The words were out of her mouth before she knew it. 'Last I heard, the Howl Reach Realmgate was still in Sigmarite hands. Surely you have brave men and women who could make that ride across the plains, could take the gates to Sigmos or Astramar and ask about our presence here? Do you think they would bring back fresh troops to oust us from Muttering Peak? The Order of Azyr, perhaps?'

Lanette didn't know if she was daring the man to do it or willing him not to. Her uncertainty frightened her. How much easier all this would be, she thought, if he could absolve her of responsibility.

'I repeat my request to speak with your Magister Princep,' he said. Lanette had to admit grudging respect for the man; this time he managed to keep his expression and tone neutral. Still, a guilty part of her hoped she might have planted the seed of an idea in his mind.

'And I repeat my refusal,' she said, voice hard, leaving no room for doubt. 'If you do not wish us to reveal your inadequacies as Listener, you will not ask again.'

'So, it's blackmail?' he asked, bristling. 'At least you're more honest than her.'

Lanette couldn't let the man see how much that comment had stung. She turned, not waiting for him to dismiss her. As she crossed the room, she fired a parting shot.

'Be grateful for our aid, Jocundas ParTaremb. Your town would have been ruins this morning if not for us.'

It was raining when Lanette left the Listener's Court. She always found rain in Liminus a strange affair. With the restive tattering of the clouds, it did not fall uniformly but instead came down in patchy squalls that left some areas dry for minutes at a time while drenching others. Most peculiar was the constant need to watch for inverse showers when scrappy clouds swept over deep puddles and dragged them back up into the sky. On reflection, Lanette thought, as she hastened between unfriendly faces and wild rain-flurries, she really did not like Liminus.

As she picked her way through the streets, she gathered up some of the coven soldiers who had been left in Taremb to aid the locals. Most she found standing awkwardly in small knots, shunned by the people they were supposed to help. The sight made Lanette angry all over again, both at the parochial peasants' ingratitude towards those who had fought for them, and because things needn't have been this way.

'Storm's blood, Wil, why couldn't you have been a little more diplomatic?' she muttered to herself. She couldn't help a bleak laugh at her own words. Even before Leontium, even before the mountain, Wilhomelda Borchase had never been good with people. She wearied of their need for reassurance or explanations, or their inability to keep pace with her leaps of intuition and expansive knowledge. Lanette smiled ruefully. Even after everything, she had to admit she still all but idolised Wilhomelda.

Beneath the arch of the town's north wall gate, she met Captain Kasper Gulde. The Coven Unseen were accompanied by a large enough complement of soldiers that they maintained a trio of captains to command them, with Lanette acting in turn as their commanding officer. Their ultimate loyalty was, of course, to the Magister Princep, but in battle it was Lanette they looked to for orders.

'Mag'sec,' he said with a nod.

'Captain,' she replied.

Gulde was tall, a good decade older than Captains Rayth and VanJesp, and almost two more than Lanette herself. Rangy and hollow-cheeked, with shaggy grey hair and a brass leg from his right knee down, Gulde had more than earned a comfortable retirement in a modest suburb of some high-walled city. Lanette knew that the captain's deep personal faith kept him fighting. Gulde would not have done well languishing in safety while there were still wars to wage on behalf of his god. He refused the coven's signature half-mask, on the grounds that anything he did in Sigmar's name demanded pride and accountability, not anonymity.

The two of them fell into step as they left through the north wall gate, a score of Freeguild troops trudging in their wake. The unnaturally smooth stone of the pass was wet underfoot. The jagged slopes to either side rose to gore the underbellies of the clouds, while ahead the mountain was little more than a rainswept suggestion of light and shadow.

They had progressed halfway up the pass with only the slap of boots on wet stone and the rattle and clank of metal on metal before Gulde spoke. He pitched his voice low enough that only she could hear his words.

'Bad business last night, Mag'sec.'

'That it was, captain.'

'Presume the Listener was suitably grateful?' Lanette eyed Gulde and saw the glint of gallows humour in his grey eyes.

'He was... voluble,' she replied.

Gulde snorted. 'Far be it for a humble captain to speak ill of his superiors,' he said, and Lanette knew he did not refer only to Jocundas ParTaremb.

'She's getting worse, Kasper,' she said.

'Still not taking your counsel, Mag'sec?'

'She's shut me out entirely.' Lanette recounted the events of the night before, after a quick glance to ensure none of the coven soldiery were listening in. To her surprise, Lanette found herself giving Captain Gulde an account of her conversation with Jocundas, even down to her suggestion he send riders for aid. Gulde frowned, marching on in silence. Lanette waited patiently, knowing he was weighing all he had been told and would offer his thoughts once he had them properly marshalled.

'Do you want ParTaremb to send out riders?' he asked at last.

'No,' she replied without hesitation. 'I owe her better than that, Kasper. Besides, if he did, I've no way of knowing who would answer his summons. Order of Azyr? Stormcasts?'

'Trappers don't check which rats've got the rotbite,' said Gulde. 'They just bash all their little heads in and throw 'em in the sack to be on the safe side.'

'It won't come to that,' said Lanette, hoping it was true. She wondered guiltily if the Listener really would send riders, and if he did, how long it would take before her incautious words brought danger down on all their heads.

'They'll only punish trouble if there's trouble to punish, Mag'sec,' said Gulde.

'You're right, we need our house in order,' she said.

'And be careful who we talk to while we're at it,' said Gulde. The observation caused Lanette a pang of misery, at the thought she could no longer trust some within her own coven, Wilhomelda chief amongst them. Yet she also felt gratitude for the way Captain Gulde had so matter-of-factly affirmed his allegiance to her.

The rain fell more heavily. Ahead lay the mountain's formidable gatehouse, carved into the living rock of Muttering Peak and fitted with arches of glimmering marble. Lanette was impressed anew by the craftsmanship of whoever built the gatehouse, at its shielded firing slits and the towers worked into the slopes whose well-protected tops made perfect artillery platforms for Borster's big guns.

The crowning glories were the gates themselves. Set into an arch fifty feet high, they were graven from some metal Lanette couldn't identify but which bore bas-reliefs of great beasts and stylised warriors. At the pull of a lever within the gatehouse, those gates could be locked so firmly that she didn't believe an enraged gargant could break through them. When they were unlocked, they swung smoothly and silently open at the push of a hand. They were open now, their guards sheltering within from the downpour.

'We need a plan of action,' she said, feeling as though they were about to step into the monster's maw and certain they had to conclude their conversation before doing so.

'You mentioned Borster? His scrolls?' asked Gulde.

'If we could see what they're working on, we would at least know Wilhomelda's intent,' said Lanette.

'You said the Mag'prin and her cabal have secluded themselves, orders not to be disturbed?'

Lanette's mind raced at his implication. A tingle of adrenaline shot through her as she came to a decision.

'Have you two soldiers you trust, Kasper?'

'Machren and Solweyo,' he answered.

'They're to meet me straight away in the fourth-level guard-room and be ready to perform some light sentinel duties,' she said.

'Fourth-level guardroom puts you a few moments' walk from Engineer Borster's chambers,' observed Gulde, expression carefully blank. 'If they've sequestered themselves to work on their new project, won't they have the drawings with them, Mag'sec?'

'Borster might be a self-important arsehole, Kasper, but he's a thorough engineer.'

'Copies,' said Gulde as they approached the gates and a wizard hurried out to challenge them, robes clutched tight against the rain.

'I'd bet my life on it, captain,' she said.

'Let it not come to that, Mag'sec,' he replied sotto voce before switching to his clipped officer's bark. 'Magister Secundi and aid party returning to the mountain. Password is "obfuscate".'

'Halt and be seen,' replied the wizard, her tone making it clear this was a rigmarole she wanted to hurry through so she could get out of the rain. They stood and permitted her to sweep a crystal-topped staff before them each in turn, checking for glamours or supernatural imposters. As the wizard worked, Lanette steeled her courage. She worried she was rushing headlong into an impulsive plan, frustration making her impetuous. But who knew how long Wilhomelda and her allies would remain locked away? No, Lanette told herself, she could not afford to lose her chance to find out what was going on.

The wizard completed her sweeps and waved them through. Lanette stretched out her spine as she crossed the threshold into the mountain and offered Captain Gulde a salute, which he returned. She turned and hastened away, beckoning a Radiant to her as she went.

'Now or never,' she muttered to herself.

* * *

The two soldiers met her in the fourth-level guardroom as commanded. Machren and Solweyo were both known to her, solid fighters who had served the coven since it first contracted its Freeguild complement all those years before. They had been through Leontium. She knew she could count on them.

'Follow me,' she told them. 'You challenge anyone who approaches even if it's the Magister Princep herself.'

It was hard to read the soldiers' expressions behind their half-masks, but to their credit neither hesitated.

The walk to Borster's chambers was a short one, down one corridor then turning into another with their Radiant hurrying before them. His eyes had gone wide at Lanette's orders, but she had to hope he would have the sense not to do anything foolish if trouble occurred. She certainly wasn't about to risk discarding his shield of illumination. Muttering Peak had felt ever more malign to her in the days since the ritual, and hearing Jocundas' revelations about earth tremors and dark omens hadn't helped. Lanette felt like the mountain hated her and would see her dead if it had the chance.

It was not until Borster's chambers came into sight, arched doorway open and unguarded, that Lanette's nerves really gripped her. She had to consciously force the guilty hunch from her shoulders. She was doing nothing wrong, she told herself, merely investigating a suspicion regarding the safety of the coven. That was one of her principal duties, for Sigmar's sakes! And if Borster or, worse, Wilhomelda caught her in the act? Then she would simply confront them. It might be a relief to have it all out in the open, and the heavens knew one more unpleasant argument would be nothing new.

Yet as she approached the open doorway and gestured to her two soldiers to take up positions, still Lanette found her hands trembling at the thought of discovery. Her breaths came short and tight in her chest as she stepped into Borster's chambers and cast about. She felt the need for haste, the desire to have her business done and to escape before anyone should discover her. She glanced over her shoulder again and caught the Radiant staring at her with frank alarm. She would need to have a conversation with that one, she thought, make sure he understood that it was in everyone's best interests not to disclose what he had seen.

'But first,' she breathed, and her eyes darted around the suite of chambers that had been assigned to Vikram Borster. The richness of his furnishings did not surprise her, nor the profusion of half-built contraptions, parchment drawings, tools, viewing lenses and the like that covered every surface. It did cause her some quiet dismay, however; it was clear this would be no quick search. Worse, while Borster's work had been permitted to colonise every free space within his chambers, it was all arrayed with the neatness of a methodical and precise mind. Each area she searched, she would have to memorise the location of every object moved before setting it aside and ensure that she returned it to its proper place before proceeding. Borster would doubtless notice anything she left misaligned.

Unable to think of a better way to proceed, Lanette began her search. She performed a painstaking inspection of the drawings and gizmos covering the table in Borster's living chamber, but her hopes of a quick victory were dashed. Hoping she had put everything back as she found it, Lanette moved on to a nearby dresser, and then to the gryphdown armchair and its accompanying side table. Despite the presence of her guards, she tried to do everything as quietly as she could, building panic warring with the desire to be thorough and careful.

Lanette froze in the act of replacing a decanter as she heard Solweyo's voice in the corridor.

'No passage, Mag'sec's orders.' There was the sound of a reply, slightly too quiet for Lanette to hear. She realised she was holding her breath, hands balled into fists at the thought of discovery. 'That's right,' said Solweyo. 'You'll have to go around. Very well, thanks.'

Lanette allowed her breath to escape in a slow hiss, certain she hadn't felt this nervous since her last rite of passage within the Towers of the Eight Winds. She looked around, frustrated, feeling no closer to her prize.

'Stop and think,' she told herself in a whisper. 'You walked in on Wil and Borster. You saw what they were doing, and they saw you see. If you were Borster... Well, if I were Borster then I'd keep the damned drawings about my person and not leave them somewhere they could be found. But there's the copies.'

Lanette was sure a man as thorough and organised as Borster would have backups of all his blueprints. Workshops were, after all, hazardous places. The danger of plans being damaged was always present. She was also hopeful, if not certain, that a man of such towering ego would not conceive of someone daring to invade his personal chambers as she was doing. Borster was a bully who took other people's fear of him for granted. A man like that would be secure in the assumption no one would dare risk his wrath.

'So, a safe place, because Wil would have told him to, but nothing too out of the ordinary because really, who would dare break into the chambers of the great Vikram Borster?'

It took her less than a minute to find the squat metal strongbox, shoved beneath a side table in his sleeping chamber. Lanette cursed herself for seven kinds of fool that, in her nervous agitation, she hadn't thought more clearly and hunted for something like this to begin with.

The lock was solid but this, at least, Lanette had little trouble with. She had learned to pick locks many, many years ago, before the Collegiate Arcane, before Wilhomelda. The lessons of an ill-spent youth didn't fade. A carefully selected length of stiff metal wire from amongst Borster's engineering supplies, a minute or so of painstaking lock-picking, and the padlock clicked open.

Lanette eased the padlock gently off and set it aside. She glanced again at the archway that led out to Borster's main living chamber. She had not heard her guards speak again since that one interruption.

'Get it done,' she told herself.

Lanette eased the lid of the strongbox open, ears alive for the telltale click or snap that might indicate she had triggered some trap. Inside, she found carefully furled rolls of parchment tied off with waxed string. Her hands tremored in time with her thumping heart as she carefully extracted the rolls one at a time, delicately untied their bindings, inspected their contents, then retied and replaced them.

A device for filtering tainted water.

A three-barrelled cannon that looked as likely to kill its crew as the enemy.

Something she could make little sense of, but that had the words *Powered flight?* stencilled across the bottom of it.

Frustrated, painfully conscious of how long her search had taken, Lanette unfurled the next parchment. He eyes widened as she saw a device like a circlet, with curving needles descending from it. She saw the words *Crystal pillar* and something that might have been *Inflow.* Lanette was unable to tell for sure, as there came a sudden dry sizzling sound and her fingertips prickled where she held the parchment. She managed to smother her yelp of pain as the sensation caused her to drop the blueprint, but she could not entirely restrain the gasp of horror that followed. Before her eyes, the carefully inked designs bubbled and ran as though exposed to the rain outside. The sizzling sound continued, Lanette unable to tear her eyes away as the precious plans transformed into an illegible slick of smudged ink.

She didn't know how long she knelt there, aghast at the ruin of the plans, her thoughts tumbling. What had she seen? What was that device, and what was Wilhomelda going to do with it? What would happen when Borster returned and found his blueprints ruined? *Would* he check? Perhaps she could simply remove the ruined document, hope that either he would not look or, if he did, that the disappearance of one parchment roll would simply be a mystery he could not solve. She scolded herself for the useless hope of a guilty child who knows they have done something that will get them caught.

It was best, she decided, simply to bind the parchment again and return it to its place. She would have to hope that if Borster did check his strongbox, he would do no more than glance to see that all the parchments were present. Yet the ink had smudged to the very edges. Try as she might, Lanette could not entirely hide the marks of her guilt as she tied the parchment and set it back in its place.

For a mad moment she considered continuing her search. If he was going to see one parchment ruined and know what had occurred, why not all of them? Lanette had seen just enough to tantalise, to set her mind working, trying to draw connections between fragmented pieces of information. She had suspicions when she needed certainty, facts, evidence with which to confront Wilhomelda.

She rejected the thought. One spoiled parchment, Borster might miss. If she ransacked his strongbox, though, she might as well toss his chambers and tip over his table on the way out.

'Tempting,' she hissed, barely restraining a wild laugh.

A few minutes later, Lanette was out of the chambers and hurrying away down the corridor with her Radiant and soldiers in tow. The further she got from Borster's chambers, the further the sense of immediate danger receded, yet the knowledge of the spoiled parchment was like a splinter she couldn't work loose. And all the while her mind worried at the glimpses she'd had of that circlet, or crown, or whatever it was. The one Wilhomelda was working on right now, not more than ten minutes' walk from this very spot.

She might as well have been in another realm, for all that Lanette could reach her in that moment. As she walked away from the scene of her crime, the Magister Secundi could not help wondering what in the heavens' name she was supposed to do now.

CHAPTER NINE

A decidedly underwhelming cave

Zograt slumped against the back wall of a cave. Spurk's magic stick lay nearby. Insects scurried in and out of Zograt's singed robes and wandered over his face. He barely noticed them.

He ached, and felt as though he had inhaled a bonfire. He couldn't stop his fingers twitching. Sparks of magic sputtered from them each time they did. His head pounded fit to burst, and green-and-purple after-images persisted in his vision after he turned his head.

'Overdid da magik,' Zograt muttered, scowling. But what else could he have done after his tribe let him down so badly?

He couldn't see them from where he sat. The cave had a bend in it, around which Zograt had retreated. He could hear them though, muttering and squabbling. Zograt considered simply limping out there and blasting every last grot to smithereens. Right now, he didn't care if the extra exertion caused him to blow himself up. It might be worth it just to see the fear on their faces.

'Da Bad Moon chose me,' he muttered, gripping his shins and

rocking back and forth. 'It should've worked. I had da magik, I had da ladz, I had surprise on me side...'

An image rose in his mind of the whisper-monsters, then gave way to a memory of the two human wizards and their insurmountable battle line.

'Oo dey fink dey is?' Zograt exclaimed, thumping the cave wall. Didn't the stupid humans know he had a destiny? How dare they obstruct the Bad Moon's will?

From around the corner came a brief cackle, sounds of scuffling, then a wet crunch. The ladz subsided back into barely audible muttering.

'As fer yooz lot, why'd yooz all run away?' whispered Zograt venomously. 'We could've won if yoo'd not legged it.' Yet even as he spoke his bitter thoughts aloud, he felt doubt. Zograt wasn't confident with numbers above three, some or lots, but he knew there had been lots of humans defending that town. Once he considered the big walls, the magic and all the big fancy guns, Zograt admitted to himself that he'd led his tribe into a bad situation.

'Still don't mean dey all should've run off!' he exclaimed, not sure if he was addressing himself or the Bad Moon. Skram had always made excuses: half-arse the job then blame everyone else. Zograt groaned at the sick knowledge that the disaster of the night before had been, to whatever degree, his fault.

Zograt glared around the cave, battling despondency. It really was, he thought, a rubbish little cave. Dry walls, sandy floor, not enough headroom for a tall grot and not a 'shroom in sight. If he was going to wind up the boss of this dreadful little hole, he reflected, he might as well have stayed the boss of Badwater Drop. And hadn't he been the one to scorn that stunted ambition as unworthy?

'Yoo gunna sit in dis rubbish 'ole 'til one of yer ladz works up da guts to shiv ya?' he asked himself. 'Or yoo gunna live up to da Clammy Hand?'

Zograt grabbed Spurk's stick and levered himself upright.

'Gotta stop actin' like ya got squig turd fer brainz,' he told himself. 'Gotta fink like a proppa boss. First fing, dis *ain't* Spurk's stikk, it's *my* stikk!'

Leaning on *his* magic stick, Zograt hobbled out to face what remained of his tribe. Despite the revelations of the last few minutes, he hadn't forgiven them for running off, nor Skrog for turning tail and carrying him away like a helpless runt. That had hurt worst of all if he was honest with himself. Zograt had spent too long powerless. He couldn't bear anyone to make him feel that way again. His temper flared and he was glad of it. He wouldn't go back to them broken or apologetic, because Gorkamorka knew that was a sure way to get himself knifed. No, Zograt would return angry as a ravenous squig!

The feeling lasted until he rounded the corner and saw what awaited him. Zograt had assumed everyone had piled into the cave after him. After all, it wasn't in the nature of a frightened Moonclan grot to stay on the surface if there was a hole to hide in.

Instead, he realised the voices of his ladz were echoing from the overgrown dell outside the cave. The reason none of them had followed him inside, quite possibly the reason no one had come to stick a blade in him, was Skrog.

The massive troggoth squatted at an uncomfortable angle in the cave mouth, blocking it almost entirely. Zograt realised the ladz couldn't have got past the troggoth to knife him. He paused, bewildered by the notion that another living creature had stood guard to keep him from harm. Zograt didn't understand the emotions that thought stirred up, but as he hobbled towards the cave mouth he found his aches and pains hurt a little less.

Zograt now saw the extent of the wounds his protector had taken while carrying him to safety. Skrog's back was a torn mess, telltale scorching showing where the fiery blasts had stunted the usual troggoth talent for regeneration. The unfamiliar sensations within Zograt intensified. He felt both grateful and inexplicably cross.

'Zoggin' 'eck, lad, yoo took a kickin'.'

Skrog growled, reaching back with one huge hand. Zograt flinched, suddenly aware of the size and power of the troggoth. Yet all Skrog did was pat him heavily on the head before returning to his former position. Shaking his head to clear it after the hefty blows, Zograt laid a hand awkwardly on a patch of Skrog's unburned skin.

'All right, lad, we'll see if Stragwit's got a potion fer dem burns. Thanks fer savin' me, but don't leg it again unless I sez so.'

He bonked Skrog with his magic stick to reinforce the point. The troggoth gave a grunt that might have meant anything, then unfolded himself painfully from the cave mouth. Zograt winced at the burned mess of Skrog's right leg, thinking the troggoth would be limping for a while with that wound. He saw the survivors of his tribe, huddled under the tangled roof of bramble and vine that obscured the dell. They were glaring daggers at him.

''Ere we go,' he muttered, and hobbled into the green gloom of the dell.

Nuffgunk was first to speak, as Zograt had suspected he would be.

'Where yoo bin, hidin' from yer zog-ups?' Nuffgunk had a cut on his cheek. His hood was tattered and one of his protuberant ears had a scabbed hole in it. He looked angrier than Zograt had ever seen him, jabbing with his pokin' spear to emphasise his words. The surviving fighters clustered behind him, some emboldened enough to add their voices to Nuffgunk's.

'We got zogged up cos o' yoo!'

'Dat woz a mess!'

'Absolute squig's dinner, ya git!'

'Wiggit an' Splurk an' Spraggle is all dead, da monsters got 'em!'

'Never even saw no forks, never mind big as proddas!'

'Yoo'z a squigwit, Zograt!'

'Stoopid runt!'

'Shuttit!' yelled Zograt, using the trick he had learned to make his voice a menacing boom. The noise was enough to shut most of the tribe up. Some of the more rattled grots scrambled for cover amongst the thickets around the dell. Nuffgunk stood his ground. One by one, Naffs Gabrot, Skutbad Da Leg and Wabber Spakkle-git came to stand slightly behind him.

'He ain't wrong, Zograt. Yoo sed we woz gunna give da humies a kickin' but we woz da ones wot got kicked,' accused Skutbad.

'Yeah, why didn't yoo warn us 'bout da monsters an' da wall an' all dat?' asked Spakklegit, trying to lock eyes with Zograt. Avoiding the Boggleye's hypnotic stare, Zograt hobbled slowly forward. He took the moment to consider his answer. He knew the danger he was in, and that if they got their knives out for him, they might also drag down Skrog in his injured state. To Zograt's surprise, the thought of them shivving Skrog gave him the fire he needed.

'We got our teef kicked in cos yoo lot started stabbin' each uvver, den yooz all ran off!' he yelled, banging his stick against the ground. 'If yoo'd stuck to da plan, we'd be in dat mountin right now lordin' it up!'

Skutbad and Wabber looked uncertain. Zograt had a sudden intuition that both had run at the first sign of trouble.

Nuffgunk looked angrier than ever, though, and Zograt couldn't tell what was going on behind Naffs' huge mask.

'Yoo didn't have a plan!' screeched Nuffgunk. 'Yoo didn't know 'ow to sort da wall, yoo didn't tell us wot to do once we got stukk in, an' yoo didn't know 'bout dem monsters!'

'Nah, yer right, I didn't know 'bout dat stuff,' said Zograt. Nuff-gunk blinked in surprise.

'Why not?' demanded Naffs.

'Cos if it weren't a challenge, da Bad Moon wouldn't know we'z worthy, would it?' said Zograt. 'Yeah, we got taught a lessun last night. We zogged it up, but yoo don't get a destiny wivout takin' a few kicks.'

'Da boss is right!'

Zograt glanced around to see Driggz limping out of a thicket to lurk behind him. Driggz's helmet had a new dent in it, and he was covered in bruises. From the way he cowered, and the glares of the last few Boingrot Bounderz, Zograt guessed Driggz's wounds hadn't all been inflicted during battle.

Driggz simpered. Zograt rolled his eyes, suspecting that Driggz was doing his cause no good, then returned his attention to his challengers. Stragwit and Da Fung, he noticed, had not joined their fellow Gobbapaloozans. Instead, they lurked near the edge of the dell. Did that mean they were on his side, Zograt wondered, or on the fence? Or were they plotting something? He found himself glad of Skrog's reassuring bulk at his back.

'Boss,' spat Nuffgunk, sounding disgusted. 'Why we even callin' 'im dat? Cos he's crawlin' wiv bugs an' got 'shroomz growin' out of 'is 'ead?'

Zograt twitched a fingertip. The dozens of insects crawling across his body froze, then turned to stare at Nuffgunk. He was gratified to see Naffs, Skutbad and Wabber take careful sidesteps away from their spokesgrot.

'Dat's part of it,' said Zograt, keeping his voice dangerously calm. 'Dey's da signs of da Clammy Hand.'

'Is dey? We only got ya word fer dat, runt,' said Nuffgunk. Zograt couldn't help but be slightly impressed by the grot boss' guts.

'Yoo seen my magik,' said Zograt. 'Want anuvver look?'

'Wot would yoo do if ya skragged me?' Nuffgunk demanded. He gestured around the dell. ''Oo kept da ladz togevver when everyone legged it last night? Oo found dis place where we could lie low? Oo made sure everyone didn't get eaten by Ganglerz or Snatchyfingerz?'

Zograt doubted this last claim but couldn't argue the rest. He had been almost catatonic after the fight, but he remembered Nuffgunk's shrill shouts ringing amidst the trees as he stopped the rout becoming a catastrophe. Zograt saw many amongst the ladz nodding and muttering. He recognised he had come to a critical moment. Take a swing at Nuffgunk now, and it would all be over. The tribe would rush him. He would have to blast his way out, he and Skrog escaping into the forest and outrunning the angry remnants of his tribe. But Zograt wouldn't let his destiny end like that. The Bad Moon hadn't picked him because he was a thug and a bully, but because Zograt had cunning. He employed it now.

'Yoo fink I'm gunna kill ya?' he asked, feigning surprise.

'Well, ain't ya?' demanded Nuffgunk.

'Zog me, Nuffgunk, I ain't Skram,' said Zograt. He offered the tribe a wide grin. 'If I woz yoo'd be able to smell me from a lot further off.'

It was a weak joke but the sudden change in tone was enough to bamboozle some of his audience and elicit spiteful titters.

'Even Skram wouldn't 'ave led us into dat bad of a kickin,' said Nuffgunk.

Zograt blew out his cheeks and made a rude noise. 'Skram wouldn't 'ave led ya anywhere. Skram woz a know-nuffin' git who never would 'ave found out about da mountin in da furst place. Da Bad Moon didn't care 'bout Skram, so it didn't care 'bout dis tribe. We deserve betta, don't we, ladz?'

All Zograt got for his efforts were a few half-hearted grumbles of agreement, but he was encouraged nonetheless.

'We'd 'ave been safe in Badwater Drop wiv Skram in charge,' said Nuffgunk, arms folded.

'We'd 'ave still been in Badwater Drop,' agreed Zograt. As he spoke, he raised his arms and turned slowly to look at the assembled grots, intentionally turning his back on Nuffgunk as he did so. 'But we wouldn't 'ave been safe! 'Ow many raids did Skram drag yooz out on, eh? An' 'ow well did dey go?'

'I got bit by spiderz on da last one,' called somegrot from the back of the mob.

'Yeah, 'e got Bogzit's boyz and Skarpa's snufflaz killed by dem Beastie ladz on da one before dat, an' we never even seen all dem bottles 'e said dey had,' came another voice.

'Skram shoved me in front o' one o' dem Stormyboy chariot fings an' got me foot run over,' cried Driggz. Zograt had no memory of Driggz ever having been allowed out on a raid, nor any notion of how his old mate would have learned about 'Stormyboy chariot fings'. He was nonetheless grateful for another voice raised against Skram.

'Yoo got us skragged as bad as Skram always did,' said Nuffgunk.

'I got it wrong on me furst go,' said Zograt, turning back to him. 'But I ain't Skram. I ain't gunna blame it on everyone else.' As he said this, he hoped fervently that none of them would remember him vociferously doing that very thing several times. 'I know I got it wrong cos I did it Skram's way. But if 'e woz still boss, dis tribe would be stuck in da Drop, gettin' smaller an' smaller as 'e got us all killed off until it woz just Skram chewin' on yer bones. But not me, ladz. Da Bad Moon chose me! I got a plan!'

'Wot, like da plan last night?' Nuffgunk asked, but Zograt thought he sounded less sure of himself now. Nuffgunk looked puzzled, as though struggling to keep up with the thread of a conversation that had gone contrary to his expectations. The trio from the Gobbapalooza had lost themselves amidst the crowd. There was a reason none of those so-called 'wisegrots' would ever be boss, Zograt thought.

'Nah, not like dat plan,' said Zograt. 'Dat plan woz rubbish. I done it da way I'd 'eard about raids bein' done. But who ran all dem raids I 'eard about?'

A long and nonplussed silence followed. Grots gawped at him, most having long lost their place in all this complex reasoning. Skrog belched.

'Skram,' said Nuffgunk at last, shoulders slumping.

'Skram!' echoed Zograt, pointing his magic stick at Nuffgunk. 'An' last night is da last time dis tribe does fings Skram's way! Moonclan grots don't just fight gitz head-on. Dat's wot big lunks like orruks do. Us grots know betta, don't we, ladz? We know da best way to skrag an enemy is stab 'em in da back!'

This garnered real cheers, and a few wicked cackles.

'But 'ow do we stab 'em in da back when dey's so magiky an' that, boss?' asked Stragwit.

'An' wot 'bout all dem shootas and da big wall?' asked Nuffgunk.

'Wot if dey got more stuff we don't know about?' added a grot standing next to Wabber Spakklegit, who Zograt thought looked rather glazed. He glared at Wabber, who wore an innocent expression.

'Why are da uvver local tribes so scary to fight?' shouted Zograt. Again, he found himself the focus of many confused stares.

'Wot's dat got to do wiv anyfing?' asked Nuffgunk.

'It's 'orrid fightin' da Twitchleggz tribe, cos dey got all da big bitey spiderz and venoms an' dat, right?' asked Zograt.

'Yeah, an' dey can scuttle about an' sneak up on ya,' added a grot.

'Den dey feed ya to Arghabigskuttla,' said another, causing his fellows to shudder in fear.

'An' Ploddit's Karavan, dey's scary cos of dat big Troggherd dey follow, ain't dey?' asked Zograt. 'An' as fer da Flashbanditz–'

'Da Spanglestikk!' chorused several of the Gobbapalooza.

'Dat, an' all dere shamans,' said Zograt. 'But imagine we got all dat lot fightin' fer us, an' we scraped up all da local loonz on dere squigs, maybe even found us a gargant or two to join da fun. Dat many ladz, all doin' wot dey do, ain't no way dem stoopid humies could stop us!'

'But 'ow we gunna get 'em to fight fer us, boss?' asked Driggz.

'Yoo leave dat to me, Driggzy,' said Zograt. 'Da Bad Moon chose me. Wot proppa grot wouldn't wanna fight fer da Loonking?'

Zograt swept his arms wide, allowing flickers of magic to dance around him as his bugs chittered. The moment was only slightly punctured for him by the dreamy voice of Da Fung, floating across the dell.

'I'nt dere already a Loonking…?'

'Lissen, we ain't gunna kick over some fires den run away like wot Skram did,' cried Zograt. 'We'z gunna beat dem tribes one after anuvver an' lord it over dem, an' once we got a proper horde togevver we'z gunna go clobber da humies. It'll be such a good fight, da Bad Moon will come an' watch as we bash our way into dat mountin an' take it fer ourselves! We'll be da bosses, an' everyone will 'ave to do wot we say! Who's wiv me, ladz?'

The grots gave a ragged cheer, and if Nuffgunk and a few others didn't join them, then at least they didn't voice any more dissent. Zograt felt something loosen in his chest. It tightened up soon enough again, however, as it dawned on him he really was going to have to think up a clever way to trick, bully or beguile the local tribes into following him.

'One problem at a time,' he muttered, then, louder, 'Break out da fungus brew an' da squigmeat. Let's 'ave a bite an' a kip furst, den it's off to meet our destiny, ladz!'

CHAPTER TEN

Muttering Peak

Wilhomelda walked aimlessly. In one hand she carried a half-empty bottle, in the other a glass. She was vaguely aware her supply of both was running low. She was unaccompanied, had sent her Radiant scurrying away with her shouts echoing after him.

She felt guilty for that. Wilhomelda had needed to direct her anger somewhere; he had simply been the first available victim.

'Guilt again,' she muttered. 'Wonderful.'

Wilhomelda didn't care if the tunnels she walked were malevolent. She suspected that alone amongst the Coven Unseen she was safe in their shadows.

'How did we get here?' she demanded of the empty tunnel. 'This was supposed to be about protecting them! Allies become enemies, and all I can rely upon is–'

The sense of what she was trying to say eluded her. She took a gulp of wine, not that it helped any more. The being in the pillar insinuated itself into her thoughts with every passing hour, and whatever insulating powers alcohol might have had, they had long since failed her. It might just have been a placebo all along; she could no longer tell.

Wilhomelda spun with a sudden spasm of rage and cast the bottle away. It smashed against the tunnel wall, closer than she had expected. Wine spattered her. She snarled and hurled the glass down the passage, before scrubbing furiously at her face with the hem of her sleeve.

'Storms of the heavens and damnation curse it!' she swore. She was shocked to find herself on the verge of tears. 'This is all so frustrating, and bloody unfair, and difficult. You are allowed emotions, for Sigmar's sakes. Just… get a grip on them.'

Wilhomelda took a steadying breath and scrubbed distractedly at her robes. There was no way to hide red wine against pale grey, so instead she hastened away from the wreckage of what she was already guiltily considering her tantrum. It wouldn't do for anyone to see her like this. Morale was low enough already.

'You know the cause…'

'Shut up,' she hissed. Against her will, the argument of a few minutes before replayed in her mind. She saw again the guarded workshop cavern, the benches and tools and alchemical paraphernalia.

'I demand to know what you're going to do about this! You are the bloody Magister Princep, aren't you? They are your followers?'

That had been Borster, red-faced with anger, bulling into her personal space. It had taken all Wilhomelda's self-control to neither step back or reach for her locket and the power it promised.

'We do not know–'

'We bloody know exactly who did it!' he had exploded. 'Ezocheen! She's been into my quarters, into my strongbox!'

'Vikram, get a hold of yourself,' she had told him.

'Who else is working with her, eh?' he had demanded, banging his fist down on a workbench and making alembics rattle. 'You need to put your dog on a lead!'

Wilhomelda's hand had gone to her locket then, fury and disgust driving her. The lights in the chamber had dimmed and questing tendrils of shadow crawled along the walls. When she spoke, her voice had been accompanied by a susurrus of whispers.

'There are other engineers within this mountain to take your place if you cannot control yourself, Borster. We have been working on the circlet for days, yet it seems no nearer completion than when we began. Leave matters of the coven to me, and do not insult your betters. Concern yourself with your work. Lives depend upon it, your own amongst them.'

Borster had shrunk from her with an expression of shock and fear. Amongst her many sources of guilt, Wilhomelda couldn't bring herself to consider this another.

'We have, uh, been working every hour on this,' Gillighasp had said, striving for a conciliatory tone. 'Perhaps if we brought in a few more sharp minds to aid us?'

'No,' she had replied. 'Your combined efforts will be sufficient. Continue to work while I deal with this matter. I expect progress when I return.'

But Wilhomelda had not dealt with the matter. Instead, she had sought comfort in the bottle and then set to wandering the passages, telling herself she needed time to think. The worst of it was that, while he might be a misogynist boor, Borster was right about one thing. Wilhomelda couldn't forget Lanette's expression as the engineer had swept his parchments back into his bag. That moment would be etched on her mind forever and would elicit the same cringe of guilt and shame every time.

Wilhomelda had not yet sought out Lanette because she knew how the meeting would go. Recrimination then confrontation. If Wilhomelda wished to hold her course, Lanette would force her to cross lines she could never recant. Matters between them had grown more tenuous by the day, but she had not realised until now how close to adversarial they had become.

'*She plots...*' purred the voice in her mind. '*She is not alone...*'

'Shut up,' she said again, feeling besieged. Wilhomelda knew that the entity sought to manipulate her. She was no stranger to paranoia and manipulation. She had not told Borster and Ulke and Gillighasp, but much of her urgency was driven by the fear that the creature they sought to trammel was even now trying to overthrow her mind. Something had changed after their ritual. The entity's influence was growing. Wilhomelda feared that if they did not trap it soon, it would be beyond their ability to control.

None of which meant that it was wrong about Lanette.

Wilhomelda stumbled with sudden vertigo. She realised her feet had borne her all the way to the pillar chamber. A few engineers were scattered around the spherical space, and glanced up from the machines they were tending.

'Leave,' she told them with an imperious wave. Sharing glances, they obeyed, leaving Wilhomelda alone with the pillar and the nebulous shape just visible within.

She paced towards the crystal pillar, watching the entity stir fitfully. It reminded her of ink dropped into water. Not for the first time, she felt a strange sense of kinship with the shadowy form. Not for the first time she rejected the sensation, suspicious of it.

When she was no more than twenty paces from the base of the pillar, Wilhomelda gathered her robes and sat down facing it.

'This cannot continue,' she said. 'It was her, wasn't it? Who else would have the nerve? Who else in this godsforsaken place cares enough about me to cause me so much trouble?'

Wilhomelda shook her head as sadness, and affection, and anger and guilt all crowded in on her. She thought she might scream. Instead, she laughed bitterly.

'*Jealous...*' crooned the voice. '*Thief... She wants you gone... She wants the power...*'

Wilhomelda scoffed. 'If I'm right, then you are a godbeast. A *godbeast,* for Azyr's sakes. You'll have to try harder than that.'

Yet there had been moments in recent days when Wilhomelda had wondered at her companion's motivations. She couldn't believe Lanette wanted to supplant her. The woman had shown not the slightest interest in the power of the mountain, instead arguing vociferously against their being here at all. It seemed more likely to Wilhomelda that Lanette simply didn't have the breadth of courage and vision that she herself possessed. The Magister Secundi saw only needless peril, and another godlike being that could only pose a threat.

'She is trying to protect me,' she told herself. Yet even as she said it, Wilhomelda remembered again the battle in Taremb, and the way that greenskin shaman's wild sorcery had almost slain her. He had unleashed such raw power, and Lanette hadn't done anything to stop him. Wilhomelda had been hurt, might have been slain. Yet Lanette had simply carried on, the unruffled military commander, the beloved figurehead.

One of the soldiers.

The thing in the pillar stirred. Wilhomelda felt absurdly as though it offered encouragement while she reasoned things out. She couldn't believe that Lanette had purposely allowed the greenskin's attack upon her, could she?

'Did she seek to undermine me?' she wondered aloud. She wouldn't voice a worse suspicion lurking at the back of her mind. It felt as though naming it might make it real. But no, thought Wilhomelda, this was madness. Lanette was her oldest companion. What they had been through forged bonds to last a lifetime.

'*But you were always greater...*'

Wilhomelda felt her skin prickle at those words. It was one thing for the entity to whisper into her mind, another to feel as though it were prying into her deepest thoughts. She gripped her locket and muttered warding incantations.

'Stay out,' she warned it, voice quavering. 'Stay out or I will find a way to banish you, I swear it.'

It subsided, but the damage was done, the blow landed. Wilhomelda had always felt comfortably superior to Lanette: older, wiser, subtler and more cunning. If she were brutally honest with herself, she had manipulated the younger woman more than once over the years and had taken for granted Lanette's loyalty. Now her Magister Secundi was thinking for herself a little too much and had rejected Wilhomelda's commands more and more since coming to Muttering Peak.

'Or before...'

'The thing is, you muttering bastard, I think she might be right,' said Wilhomelda. Nor, she suspected, was she the only one who thought so. She had seen the doubtful glances amongst many in the coven these past days. Were they part of Lanette's faction? she wondered. How far did the rot spread? And since when had the Coven Unseen been factionalised at all?

Wilhomelda sprang to her feet. She swayed slightly, caught herself and paced angrily around the base of the pillar.

'Do they think I want to be here?' she demanded of the glowing crystal. 'Do they suppose I wouldn't rather be tucked away in the Constellum Library with a tome or two and a glass of red?' She uttered a bitter laugh. 'Of course, that's where all this started, isn't it?'

'Liar...'

Wilhomelda froze. She willed the entity to be silent, but it spoke again. It sounded in her mind as though it were smiling, cruel and cold.

'This started at Leontium. You commanded. They were your responsibility...'

'Stop,' she breathed.

'Nothing but a swarm of the mindless dead. A few mouldering conjurors herding them like livestock.'

Wilhomelda's words, echoing from a past she regretted more deeply than anything in her life. More deeply even than ruining things with Lanette.

'Stop, please,' she said, louder.

'Arrogance,' it crooned. *'Always easy. Always the heroine. Then came the Lord of Death.'*

'Be silent!' yelled Wilhomelda, snatching handfuls of her hair and shaking her head as though she could dislodge the whispering voice. It was too late. She was back there, on the field before the walls of Leontium, striding out with five thousand brave Sigmarite warriors at her back and the ranks of the reanimate dead withering before their fury. She had been so certain of victory, so convinced that her magics and her cunning would propel the counter-attack and catch the Necromancers by surprise. She had envisioned the entire army of reanimates collapsing like string-severed puppets.

'Months of pointless besiegement avoided...' it whispered, beating her down with her own words. *'Victory at a stroke...'*

Lanette had trusted her on that day, had come with her through the shadows, charged into battle alongside her; the wizards who were also warriors; the cunning coven proving what the Collegiate Arcane could do upon the battlefield when lesser minds gave them command.

She saw again the flaring realmgate, the tide of darkness spilling from it like vomit before that great dark shape had unfolded itself like a spider from a shadowed crack. She felt again the terror as she found herself in the presence of a malevolent god and saw her hubris laid bare.

'So many dead... then the rout, the starfire...'

Wilhomelda felt tears rolling down her cheeks. She fell to her hands and knees as memories bombarded her. She and Lanette had tried to lead a fighting retreat, but it had collapsed. Grasping hands had burst from the cracked ground to tear and strangle. Blazing lightning streaking the sky, bolts of vengeance falling from the heavens. Hope and elation blasted to ashes as the explosions erupted amongst her fleeing soldiery, and Stormcasts in ice-white armour cut a path through retreating soldiers and mages alike to reach the foe. She remembered, at their heart, a mighty figure whose feet never touched the ground and about whom miniature stars whirled.

She remembered the great hammer in the figure's hands ablaze with light.

She remembered her followers caught between god and demigod.

She remembered the feeling of powerlessness.

She remembered blood and sorrow.

The wine came up in a hot rush. It oozed across the curving floor, looking like frothing blood in the chamber's diffuse light. Revolted, Wilhomelda staggered to her feet. She swiped away tears and bile with the hem of one stained sleeve.

'Bastard,' she spat at the pillar. 'There was no need.'

'*So many dead…*'

'I don't need you to remind me,' Wilhomelda snarled. She shook as emotions long suppressed coursed through her like poison. Leontium had left her with enough guilt and anger to last a lifetime. It had shattered her faith in Sigmar and left her with a deep-seated resentment of all those beings that thought themselves gods. She, Lanette and barely a handful of their followers had made it back to the city gates, there to endure the months of besiegement she had thought to prevent. The divine combatants had carried their own fight back through the realmgate as though the entire matter of Leontium had been beneath their notice. Wilhomelda neither knew nor cared what had become of them.

'They aren't better than us. They have no right. *You* have no right.'

The thing in the pillar didn't respond. Wilhomelda hugged herself until her shuddering subsided and the feeling of wretchedness diminished. She shook her head, wiped a sleeve across her face again and forced herself to stand straight.

'Enough,' she told herself. 'Enough now. Stop feeling sorry for yourself. Act.'

Wilhomelda felt hollow but cleansed. Standing there in the pulsing light of the pillar chamber she knew what she had to do. There could not be another Leontium. She had to prevent it, and to do that she needed the power of this place. If that meant eliminating the threats to her one at a time, then she would do so.

'Lanette will have to wait until I am ready,' she muttered, turning her back on the pillar. 'I need to know more about her intentions, and who is working with her. But I know how to deal with the greenskin. He won't return to trouble me again.'

Wilhomelda had seen the creature carried to safety by its troggoth pet. She had fought greenskins many times in Sigmar's service, and if there was one thing she knew about them, it was that they were a weed which required pulling up by the roots. Matters were precarious enough without such an enemy lingering beyond the horizon, ready to return at some critical juncture and throw her plans into disarray. She would deal with the enemies without, before turning her attention to the potential enemies within. Feeling sober and composed, Wilhomelda strode from the pillar chamber without a backward glance.

Four Freeguild soldiers and a wizard guarded the archway leading into the artefact storage vault. When Wilhomelda marched up to them, their half-masks could not hide the guards' alarmed expressions. She realised belatedly that her robes were soiled and her hair in disarray. She dismissed such details as unimportant.

'Begone,' she told them.

'Magister Princep, are you quite all right?' asked the wizard. She thought the man's name was Remnus. Also unimportant, she thought.

'I have given you a command,' she said loftily.

Clearly uncertain but unwilling to disobey a direct order from their Magister Princep, Remnus and his guards filed past her and departed. Wilhomelda stepped through the arch into the large circular chamber beyond.

The Coven Unseen had spent long years exploring the Mortal Realms in Sigmar's name. While some had fought as battle wizards, others had been spies, assassins or questing adventurers in search of ancient secrets and weapons. Though she had lost some old and valued comrades at Leontium, many others had been abroad on such subtle missions and had survived to answer her summons in the conflict's wake. The coven had marshalled its remaining strength before coming to Muttering Peak. They had also pooled the artefacts of sorcerous power they had accumulated over the long years. These surrounded Wilhomelda now.

She passed racks of ensorcelled blades and suits of bewitched plate. An amber mirror rippled slightly at her passing. A jade cage rattled as something invisible to the eye sought in vain to break free. Some of the artefacts were considered safe enough to use, either in battle or during study, and were kept closest to the vault's entrance. Further back amidst the shadows lay those objects of arcana considered perilous. Some were only dimly understood and required further study. Others, like the device Wilhomelda sought, were all too clear in their purpose and had been deemed too dangerous or evil to employ.

Stepping over a line of warding charms, Wilhomelda ducked into a dark alcove to stand before a brass chest. Runes covered it, glowing with pale purple light. An intense aura of cold emanated from the trio of opals set into the chest's lid.

Wilhomelda steeled her nerve. It had been more than a decade since she had last been this close to the chest. Then, she and Lanette had been hunting the culprit of a series of grisly and seemingly impossible murders on behalf of the Collegiate Arcane. They had caught the chest's owner, a rogue mage banished from the Collegiate years before, and had extracted the secret of his sorcerous assassinations. In the process, the contents of the chest had almost slain them both.

Gripping her locket, Wilhomelda touched the middle three fingers of her left hand to the three opals. They burned cold to the touch. She muttered a string of jagged syllables.

The runes on the chest flared. Wilhomelda sprang back as the lid of the chest slammed open to reveal absolute darkness within.

First came the stench of wet rot and things left to fester in lightless places. There followed a series of glottal clicks and moist slithering sounds.

Fingers slipped one by one over the lip of the chest and gripped tight. They were corpse-pale and dirty, each tipped with a long black talon. Another hand appeared alongside the first, fingers crawling like the legs of a spider. More followed, gripping the rim of the chest. One by one their owners hauled themselves up from the depths so that their heads and shoulders rose proud of the dark void.

It took all Wilhomelda's considerable nerve to stand her ground. The entities were indistinct but humanoid in form, their pale bodies blurring and overlapping one another in a way that made them painful to focus upon. Where each one's face should have been there was only a dark pit of raw meat lined with concentric rows of needle fangs and fringed by ropes of lank black hair. They had no eyes, yet she felt their regard boring into her all the same.

'I have spoken the words,' she told them, voice firm. 'You are bound by my will. You will taste the spoor of sorcery and you will hunt.'

The beings swayed like serpents waiting to strike. They made wet and guttural sounds.

Wilhomelda focused on the memory of the greenskin shaman. She recalled all she could of his sorcery, how it had felt hammering against her magical defences, its crude but powerful patterns. Gathering her courage and grimacing in dismay, she stretched out her left hand towards the mouth-pit of the centremost being. Every instinct told her to pull back, to lock these awful creatures away and send soldiers and mages after the shaman. Yet she did not know who to trust. She needed reliable hunters, and she knew of none more deadly or tireless than these spirits of shadow and hunger.

Unable to restrain a low whine of horror, Wilhomelda slid her hand into the quivering pit of the closest thing's face. It gave a rattling exhalation that wreathed her in a stink like corpse gas and midden heaps. With obscene gentleness, the thing's mouth contracted until its rings of teeth pressed into the flesh of her hand. They tightened a little more, until a ripple of stinging pinpricks told her they had just barely punctured her skin.

Wilhomelda concentrated with all she had upon the feeling of the shaman's sorcery. She bade the memory flow into the beings before her, all the while fighting not to wrench her hand away in disgust. To do that would break the compact, and that would mean her death.

The teeth withdrew just when she was sure she could bear the creature's touch no longer. Wilhomelda snatched her hand away and moaned again at the rows of red-black puncture wounds ringing it. Reeking grey slime dripped from her fingers and smoked where it hit the floor.

As one, the predatory spirits rose from the chest in a tangle of half-seen limbs, scrambling obscenely over and through one another as they scuttled up the wall of the alcove and vanished through its ceiling.

'What in Sigmar's name have you done?'

Startled by Lanette's shout, Wilhomelda spun, cradling her bitten hand guiltily to her chest. There stood the Magister Secundi, expression aghast. She was flanked by Remnus, his guards and several other coven wizards, along with Captain Gulde. With the open chest yawning at her back and the mass of people blocking her way out of the alcove, Wilhomelda felt intolerably trapped.

'Clear my path!' she demanded. 'How dare you hem me in like this?' The guards and wizards stepped back, but Lanette and Gulde didn't move.

'Wilhomelda, what's happened to you?' demanded Lanette. 'In Azyr's name, you unleashed the Bleak Brood! Who have you sent them after?'

'The greenskin!' Wilhomelda exclaimed. She was dismayed to see a flicker of relief cross Lanette's face. 'Wait, did you think...?'

'They were not yours to set free! Those... things... It is forbidden! They were to be kept bound in perpetuity.'

'On my order,' snapped Wilhomelda. 'An order that is mine to rescind whenever I choose! Damnation, am I the Magister Princep of this coven or not?' She cringed inwardly to hear herself echoing Borster's words and tried to push her way out of the alcove. She could not bear the yawning gulf at her back, or the stares of her subordinates. To her shock, Lanette caught her by the arms.

'Wil, this has to stop. You're not yourself. I didn't want to do this in front of others, but you stink of wine and Sigmar knows what else. You look like a lunatic, and now I find you in here unleashing evil spirits? Is this your will, or something else?'

'Take your hands off me!' Wilhomelda screamed, ripping her arms from Lanette's grip and almost toppling backwards. For a horrible moment the gulf of the enchanted chest felt like a gullet ready to swallow her. Then Lanette caught her by the shoulder and pulled her back from the brink. They stood like that for a long moment, and as Wilhomelda looked down into Lanette's ruby eyes she saw more compassion and pity than she could bear.

'Magister Secundi, you will unhand me,' she said, striving for cold composure. She saw the dismissal hit home as she had known it would, saw Lanette's expression harden. She tried not to loathe herself for her vindictive pleasure at the sight.

'Only if you submit to Captain Gulde, to be placed under guard in one of the cell-chambers,' said Lanette.

'This is mutiny? A conspiracy revealed?' asked Wilhomelda. Bitterness and resentment welled within her.

'It's nothing of the sort, but you have betrayed my trust,' said Lanette. To Wilhomelda's ear the words rang hollow.

'An enemy unmasked,' she breathed. Lanette shook her head and scowled.

'Listen to yourself. This place has got into your head. It's poisoned your mind. I'm relieving you of authority until we can get you away from this damned mountain.'

Wilhomelda tensed, but the whispering voice slithered into her mind.

'Not yet... Bide...'

'Your locket,' said Lanette. Wilhomelda let her shoulders slump as though in defeat. She reached up and unclasped the chain from around her neck, then handed the locket over.

'Very well, I submit,' she said in a broken voice, and was pleased to see Lanette's expression soften.

'Weakness...'

'Thank you, Wil,' said Lanette. 'We'll get this all resolved. It will be all right.'

Wilhomelda nodded, keeping her eyes on the ground and a stumble in her step as Captain Gulde and his soldiers led her from the vault. All the while, her mind whirled as suspicions became certainties and anger overthrew guilt and shame.

'Soon...'

CHAPTER ELEVEN

Funnelsnare Pit

The brood slither and twine and twine and slither as they taste the tang of the sorcerous trail they slather and keen and knot about one another as they crawl through shadow and glimmer and real and not and all the time nearer and nearer they sense the one they desire...

'Dey ain't gunna lissen. Dey's just gunna kill ya,' said Nuffgunk.

'Blame Skram,' Zograt replied. The two of them crouched in a thicket of silver-grey underbrush, on the edge of a gloomy clearing. Beyond their hiding place the ground dropped away into a pit Zograt estimated to be as wide as Da Big Cave and Da Soggy Cave put together. Thick strands of web stretched between treetops around the clearing's edge to form a fibrous canopy. It shut out the daylight and swarmed with the incessant motion of uncountable spiders.

'Dey ain't gunna lissen,' repeated Nuffgunk. 'Why should dey? Dey got Bigg Leggzgit to do da shaman stuff, an' Chief Kreepzogga to tell 'em wot to do. Dey don't need some loon turnin' up tellin'' 'em to go fight humies just cos he finks da Bad Moon touched him on his clammy bitz.'

Zograt stared down into the sink. If he had to guess, he would have said Funnelsnare Pit had formed when the forest floor subsided. It was steep-sided, with ledges jutting from its walls where under-brush still grew, and crooked pillars of rock jutting up from its depths where the land hadn't given way. Dead trees protruded at angles from the walls of the pit, in places criss-crossing or spanning ledges and pillars. Webs festooned everything and formed bridges and tunnels leading into the depths. From his position of conceal-ment Zograt watched Twitchleggz Spider Riders patrolling the pit's upper reaches astride agile arachnid steeds.

'Dey got Arghabigskuttla to worship too,' he said.

'Dat's wot I'm sayin',' hissed Nuffgunk. He had to keep his voice down to avoid alerting the sentries, but his frustration was obvious. 'Even if we hadn't took a kickin' from da humies, we still wouldn't 'ave da ladz to lord it over da Twitchleggz. So why yoo fink dey's gunna do wot yoo sez?'

'Skram woz an idiot,' said Zograt.

'Yeah, and?' asked Nuffgunk.

'I ain't. We took a kickin'. We ain't gunna take anuvver one. I got a plan. But if it's gunna work, Nuffgunk, I gotta trust yoo.'

The grot boss furrowed his brow. 'Go on, wot yoo got dat's so clever?'

Zograt flicked away a lurid green spider that definitely wasn't one of *his* bugs, then launched into a description of his plan. When he had finished, he leaned back, wincing as his twisted leg cramped.

'Tell me why it's rubbish then, ya rotten git,' he said. Nuffgunk's expression was unreadable within the shadow of his hood.

'It ain't rubbish, boss. I don't like da risky bitz, but it ain't rub-bish.' Zograt felt surprise, then pleasure, then a stab of suspicion.

'Yoo gunna do it?'

'Yeah, reckon,' said Nuffgunk. Zograt was really alarmed now. He felt as though Nuffgunk had agreed too easily. He glanced about in search of an assassin. His mind spun and his bugs squirmed restlessly as he tried to see any angle by which this might be a trick. His amulet was glowing, and not for the first time Zograt wished he knew what that meant.

'Why?' he asked.

Nuffgunk rummaged a length of dried segmapede from a belt pouch and chewed on it. He crushed a bright orange spider with his thumb as it tried to scale his leg. Shrugging, he spat a gobbet of phlegm and insect legs into the bushes.

'Skram *woz* an idiot, an' I hated 'im. Never shivved 'im cos 'e woz too big, an' cos 'e knew dat I wanted to. Mighta seen it comin'. But den yoo, runt of da tribe, yoo go an' get all shamany an' yoo sayin' it's cos of da Bad Moon and yoo skrag Skram.'

'Yeah, I did,' said Zograt with a wistful chuckle.

'Den yoo start comin' out wiv plans an' all right, dey ain't gone right yet, but… I want shinies, an' a bigga, clammier cave, an' I want our tribe to put da boot into everyone dat ain't us, an' show 'em who's boss. Skram weren't never gunna do dat. I reckon yoo might. So all right, we'll give it a go, but if yoo louse it up, Zograt, I'm leavin' yoo down dat hole t'get et by spiderz.'

Nuffgunk receded into the shadow of his hood and chewed pensively as he watched the sentries scuttle back and forth.

'Show me yoo got da Gloomspite in ya, an' I'll keep me slitta outta yer back,' Zograt said at last. Nuffgunk scowled and jabbed a dirty talon at him.

'*Yoo* show *me*, maybe I won't murda ya,' he replied.

'Deal,' said Zograt with a wicked grin.

A short time later found Zograt lurking in a somewhat less spider-infested bush a hundred or so yards back into the forest. Skrog loomed behind him, as close as Zograt had permitted him to stay. Zograt had herded the troggoth behind a tree and given him some branches to hold, though between Skrog's size and the waft of burned meat still clinging to the wounded troggoth, he doubted it would conceal the creature well. It didn't matter, he told himself. His ladz only needed to hide long enough that the Twitchleggz sentries would run into their ambush.

He scoured the undergrowth. Skrog wasn't the only member of his tribe currently doing a poor job of hiding, and Zograt waved his stick menacingly at the most obvious grots. He felt satisfaction as they cringed and redoubled their efforts at concealment.

Driggz skulked in the bushes to Zograt's left. The weedy grot looked as though he was doing everything in his power to ignore the presence of his three surviving Boingrot Bounderz, clustered at his back and still glaring daggers. Zograt had ordered Driggz and his ladz to ditch the clankier bits of their armour and to switch their lances for stabbing blades. Their steeds had also been abandoned, herded into a nearby cave along with the rest of the tribe's surviving squigs and guarded by the last few herders.

To Zograt's right crouched Wabber Spakklegit and Skutbad Da Leg. Neither looked pleased to be there, but they had obeyed Zograt's orders without too much grumbling. He suspected this was because the Gobbapalooza hadn't been able to come up with a better plan than his. Skutbad looked odd without his basket of poisons strapped to his back, but Zograt had deemed it too cumbersome for the task they were to undertake. The Spiker had stuffed what bottles and vials he could into his pockets and belts, and now crouched on his four bandy legs with stikka in hand, looking more than half spider himself.

Nuffgunk had remained by Funnelsnare Pit, joined by a handful of his best grots. Skram's amulet glowed again as Zograt pondered

Nuffgunk's loyalties. He wondered idly whether the stone lit up whenever he was having a good think.

His train of thought was interrupted by a sudden commotion from the direction of the pit. Ululating cries echoed through the trees. Zograt cringed despite himself.

'Dat's da Twitchleggz war cry,' muttered Skutbad.

'Dey musta spotted Nuffgunk and his ladz,' Zograt replied. 'Spread da word t'be ready.'

Grot whispers rippled away through the underbrush. Zograt gripped his magic stick tight and patted Skrog's leg for luck.

There came the swish and crack of figures dashing through the underbrush, then Nuffgunk and his ladz appeared running full pelt. An instant later their pursuers hove into view. Having never been allowed out on a raid, Zograt had only heard tales of the Twitchleggz before this day. He had only glimpsed them from a distance while he was plotting with Nuffgunk. The sight of them up close caught him off guard. The grots were daubed with vivid patterns of bioluminescent paste. They wore armour made from spider chitin, carried long spears tipped with mandibles and stingers, and whooped like loons as they rode down Nuffgunk and his ladz. The spiders were even more alarming than their riders. Their bulbous bodies, gangling legs and dripping fangs were much larger than Zograt had realised.

His hesitation allowed the lead spider time to pounce. It bore the rearmost of Nuffgunk's grots to the ground and bit deep as he shrieked in terror. Within moments, the luckless grot's skin was swelling and turning bruise purple as he frothed at the mouth.

'Skrag 'em,' screeched Zograt. Black-fletched arrows whipped from the bushes and plucked two Twitchleggz from their saddles. Hurled pokin' spears brought another down, pinning him to his spider, which keened and kicked as slime spurted from its punctured abdomen. Skrog stepped over Zograt and brought a huge fist down to crush a grot and its spider. Ichor stung Zograt's skin where it spattered him.

A riderless spider snatched up another of Nuffgunk's grots and sank its fangs into him. Nuffgunk lunged, ramming his spear into the spider's underbelly and causing it to roll onto its back, legs curling in. The last couple of Twitchleggz sought to goad their steeds up into the trees. Zograt wiggled his fingers. A rain of bugs fell from the branches, pattering onto the Spider Riders like fat raindrops. Screeching and swatting at the biting insects, both grots fell from their steeds and thudded to the ground. More arrows knocked a spider out of the branches. The other scuttled away, boughs shaking beneath its weight as it fled.

Zograt shook with adrenaline. He looked about the glade at the dead grots and spiders as his ambushers emerged from their hiding places.

'We got 'em,' said Nuffgunk, sounding surprised, then, again and more fiercely, 'We got 'em!' Grots cheered and cackled. Several jabbed blades into the dead spiders, one getting a face-full of venom for his troubles as he popped something inadvisable.

'Dat's only da start,' said Zograt. 'Time fer da second bit, before somegrot wonders where dem sentries went.'

Nuffgunk started bullying the ladz into some semblance of order. Zograt turned to Skrog, who was licking mashed spider off his fist.

'Yoo keep an eye on dis lot, big lad. I'll see yoo in a bit!' Skrog blinked at him, uttered a somewhat reproachful-sounding grunt, and sucked a large arachnid gobbet from between his fingers. Hoping the troggoth had understood, Zograt turned and hastened through the trees with Driggz's ladz, Wabber and Skutbad following. He was surprised to find himself worried for Skrog in his wounded state. Zograt shook his head in disgust and forced himself to focus.

'Yooz lot got yer unstikkin' stuff?' he asked. A few mumbled agreements and some brandished bottles were his answer. Stragwit Skrab had long ago mastered the art of brewing a solution that when sprinkled onto spiders' webs, rendered them less sticky and made them traversable by a suitably cautious grot. This invention had allowed Skram to lead repeated raids into Funnelsnare Pit. Zograt considered it a damning indictment of his predecessor's stupidity that, even with such a cunning advantage, the best Skram had managed was property damage, theft and a few costly brawls.

Low on ingredients as he was, Skrab had only been able to provide a few vials of the precious solution. Zograt hoped it would be enough.

'Yoo know da plan?' he pressed his companions. They offered some more recalcitrant mumbling. Zograt stopped and turned on them with a thunderous scowl. He wiggled his fingers to stir up the unnatural insects infesting his robes. 'I asked do yooz lot know da plan? Dis is importunt!'

They watched him warily. Zograt's amulet glowed bright in that moment, which he felt added a nice touch of menace. It was Driggz who replied.

'Course we knows it, boss! We sneak down into da pit while Nuffgunk keeps dem Twitchleggz ladz bizzy.'

'And *where* is we sneakin' down?' asked Zograt. Driggz opened his mouth and closed it again, looking panicked. One of his ladz snorted. Driggz subsided into his cowl. Zograt's amulet glowed brighter still, and he wondered whether perhaps it did that when he got annoyed. Or maybe it was just broken?

'We'z sneakin' down near da wonky free-topped tree next to a boulder wot looks like an orruk's bonce, cos dat's da spot Muggit found last time dey woz raidin' da pit,' said Wabber Spakklegit impatiently. 'An' before yoo ask, we'z doin' dat cos dere's a cleft dere wot da Twitchleggz ain't webbed up much, an' leads down da back o' dere egg chambers. Is a good place t'sneak in. We ain't stoopid, Zograt. Can we get on wiv dis?'

'Come on den, an' no zoggin' it up!' warned Zograt.

'All right fer yoo, innit, your bit'z easy,' muttered Wabber. Zograt ignored him and forged on through the trees until he saw the one that divided into three halfway up its trunk. He had to admit that Muggit had been right: the boulder near the tree's base did indeed resemble the head of a very large and ugly orruk. He couldn't resist spitting in its face as he passed.

Slipping through the bushes, Zograt peered out at the pit. There was no sign of life, bar the tiny spiders that scurried over every surface. He hoped his own bugs would serve as a deterrent to these smaller, but doubtless venomous, arachnids.

Skutbad laid spindly fingers on Zograt's arm and pointed to the thickest web strands near the heart of the pit. They were vibrating.

'Someone's climbin' up t'see wot's wot,' said Skutbad.

'Den we need to move,' Zograt replied, gathering his courage and limping into the open. With every step he expected to see the hairy legs of some colossal spider emerge over the lip of the pit. Driggz pointed at a spot a little further along the rim.

'Dere, da... fing...!'

'Not so loud, ya git, want everygrot in da pit to 'ear ya?' hissed Zograt. Driggz cringed. 'An' it's called a *creviss*, not a fing. Zog me, lissen when I'm speakin'.'

Halting at the top of the crevice, Zograt looked doubtfully into the depths. A few feet wide and maybe twice that deep, the crack ran down the sloping wall of the pit to where a stone pillar had toppled against it and formed a cramped downward tunnel. It wasn't a sheer drop, but neither was it a gentle slope. Zograt wasn't sure whether the bits of rock and roots protruding from the crevice's sides would make the scramble easier or snag him and his ladz.

'Skram took 'em all down dis?' he muttered.

'Yeah, an' if we don't do da same, we'll get seen!' replied Skutbad, shoving past and clambering into the crevice.

'Yoo got four workin' legs, I got about one an' a half,' muttered Zograt, but he took Skutbad's point. Unwilling to allow anyone else to shove in front, he lowered himself into the crack.

Down Zograt scrambled, trying not to show panic as he sought hand and footholds. Nuffgunk must have known this climb would be murder for him and was probably having a nasty little chuckle at his expense right now. Zograt promised himself some harsh words with the conniving git if he got out of Funnelsnare Pit alive. As his knurled foot slid on a root and dislodged a scatter of dirt, Zograt wondered whether *this* had been Nuffgunk's plot: send Zograt down the pit on a climb that might kill him, then abandon him.

If Nuffgunk was going to double-cross him, Zograt would know about it soon. He cast a doubtful look back the way he had come, watching Driggz scrambling downward while trying to avoid the 'accidental' kicks and dislodged stones of his ladz.

That was when the clangour began above. Gongs crashed. Feet stamped. Reedy voices flung insults and battle cries.

'Oi, scuttlegitz, come get a kickin' from some proppa grots!'

'I skwashed yer little mates wiv me shoe!'

'Spiderzoggerz stink!'

'Gorkamorka sed yooz lot woz da worst grots 'e ever seen!'

'Spiderz is rubbish!'

Then came a bass roar that echoed through the pit and caused the barrage of insults to falter. Zograt grinned.

'Yoo tell 'em, lad,' he whispered proudly.

'Yeah, wot 'e sed!' came a shout from the lip of the pit, and the insults and banging returned with redoubled vehemence.

'Zograt, get movin'!' snarled Wabber from somewhere above.

'Look at da webz!' squeaked Driggz. Where before a handful of threads had thrummed with motion, now dozens danced wildly. Hoping Nuffgunk would remember the rest of the plan, Zograt half scrambled, half fell until he was hidden behind the toppled column.

Plunged now into almost total darkness, Zograt continued to descend, praying silently to the Bad Moon that he wouldn't slip and fall. Through cracks in the fallen pillar, he heard rushes of sinister movement interspersed with the whoops and shrieks of Twitchleggz grots.

'Webz down 'ere, puttin' some unstikka on 'em,' whispered Skutbad from below.

'All right,' grunted Zograt, trying not to show how physically exhausting the climb was becoming. He considered using his magic, whether to conjure mycelial strands to grab on to or perhaps to have his bugs support his weight. He decided he couldn't risk it in case he lacked sufficient control of his abilities. If he accidentally sent a mass of fungi exploding out through the wall of the pit, it would quickly ruin his plan.

And so he climbed, limbs aching, then burning like fire while the breath wheezed ragged in his chest. Once he almost lost his magic stick. He missed some strands of web in the darkness and cursed as they snagged under his chin. Panting and fumbling, Zograt managed to uncork his flask of unstikka and spatter some across the strands. They fizzled as their stickiness was neutralised.

Zograt was on the verge of chancing his magic, certain his other option was to slip and fall, when below him Skutbad reached the bottom of the crevice and stepped out of view. Gasping with relief, Zograt slithered the last few feet and hobbled to stand beside the Spiker, leaning heavily on his magic stick.

'Where da zog are we now?' he whispered. Zograt had a sense

of being in a hidden space at the bottom of the pit. To one side was the base of the toppled pillar. All around were walls of thick web, glowing faintly in places as though lit from behind.

'Last time we come through 'ere dere woz a thin bit in da webz,' said Skutbad, gesturing vaguely with his stikka.

'Well, ain't no thin bit now, is dere?' muttered Wabber as he joined them. Driggz and his ladz came behind the Boggleye, then halted and cast awkwardly about in the gloom for something to do.

Zograt felt faintly ridiculous. All his grand planning, and now here they were in a deep, dark hole with no idea where to go next. At least, he thought, there weren't the swarming masses of spiders he'd initially feared.

'Gunna 'ave to guess an' cut a way through,' said Skutbad conversationally.

'Well guess quick den. Our lot up dere ain't gunna be able to keep da skuttlerz bizzy fer too long,' snapped Zograt, who was getting his breath back. His arms and legs burned, his plan wasn't going to plan, and his temper was rising.

'Keep yer hood on,' muttered Skutbad. He squinted two of his three eyes shut, stuck his tongue out the corner of his mouth and sighted along one raised thumb. 'I reckon dat's da spot dere,' he said. 'After dat last raid dey musta webbed up any holes dey could find ta stop us gettin' back in.'

'Very 'elpful,' grumbled Zograt. 'Driggz, get dem stabbas out an' get cuttin'.'

Driggz hastily jabbed his blade into dense web only to have it stick fast. As the scrawny grot tugged at the blade to free it, only a glare from Zograt stopped one of his ladz from shoving their hated boss face first into the webs. Zograt uttered a put-upon sigh then stumped forward and sprinkled unstikka over the webbing.

'Zogwit,' he said as Driggz dragged his blade free and began sawing in earnest. The Bounderz grudgingly joined their boss, cutting through layer after layer of web. Snapped strands waved like seaweed in a current. The bioluminescence grew brighter as they carved a path into the web mass. Zograt blinked, spots dancing before his eyes.

He realised belatedly the black dots weren't anything to do with his eyesight when one of Driggz's ladz jabbed his stabba through a last screen of web and hundreds of tiny spiders spilled out. The Bounder staggered back, swatting at himself and screeching as he was bitten again and again.

'Zog me,' cursed Zograt, wiggling his fingers madly as he conjured up a swarm of moon-headed and gangle-legged insects. It was too late for the bitten grot, who collapsed with pink foam bubbling from his mouth while his melting eyes drooled down his cheeks. Driggz and his remaining two followers hopped back with yelps of alarm, making way as Zograt's insectile cavalry swarmed to their rescue.

So began a bizarre war in miniature as hundreds of mutant loonbugs clashed with the many-coloured, many-legged hatchlings of Arghabigskuttla. There were a lot of spiders, but where they acted on instinct Zograt's bugs were directed by a singular will. They swiftly drove the arachnids back, clearing a path for their master.

'Musta hit da eggzy bit,' commented Skutbad, stepping over the dead grot and through the rent in the web-wall.

'Musta,' replied Zograt with a sour glare.

Beyond the hole lay the hatchery. Its walls and ceiling were made of webbing, layered thick and stretched between rocky protrusions, dead tree trunks, and whatever else stuck out enough to make a good anchoring point. To Zograt's relief the floor, at least, was bare earth, presumably so that the Twitchleggz ladz could walk around without getting trapped by their own lair. There were egg sacs everywhere. They dangled in clusters amidst nets of webbing. They piled in drifts against the walls. The scene was lit by the bioluminescence of grotesque chitinous fungi that sprouted here and there from the ground and pulsated as they glowed.

'Don't touch nuffin' sticky,' said Skutbad, rather unnecessarily in Zograt's opinion.

'An' don't poke no eggz, dere's enough spiderz about,' he said, mostly to reassert that he was the one giving the orders. 'Skutbad, Driggz, yoo and yer ladz is up front. Wabber an' me will follow ya. Yoo knows where yoo'z goin', Skutbad?'

'Course I do, we just follow da web-tunnels to da middle of da pit.' The grots all paused at these words, exchanging anxious glances. They looked nervously to Zograt, who sensed their courage wavering. Gorkamorka knew his own heart was bouncing around in his chest like an uppity squig at the thought of it. But this was his plan. He knew he couldn't afford another failure.

'Come on den, ya zoggers, get movin'.'

Stepping over the vicious insect-versus-arachnid skirmishes still raging through the hatchery and trying not to touch the sticky strands of the walls, the grots crossed to the tunnel that led deeper into Funnelsnare Pit.

The minutes that followed frayed Zograt's nerves near to breaking point. Cowls pulled up and blades in hand, the Moonclan grots crept along web-tunnels that fluttered and contracted almost as though they were breathing. They passed more glowing fungi that threw their shadows out in alarming caricatures across walls and floor. More than once, Skutbad led them into dead ends where the tunnels funnelled down to nothing or met the bases of huge stone pillars. Several times they had to sprinkle unstikka onto masses of webbing that fouled their path, so that soon they had only the dregs of Zograt's own bottle left. At a wide intersection they were forced to cower behind a boulder, watching the gangling silhouette of a horse-sized spider as it picked its way along a tunnel separated from theirs by only a thin skein of web.

Zograt thought of Skrog in danger up above and felt the panicky need for haste.

At last, the monstrous silhouette was gone. Zograt hobbled out from behind the rock and found himself almost nose to nose with a surprised-looking Twitchleggz grot.

'Er,' said Zograt.

The Twitchleggz drew breath to shout. Running on pure instinct, Zograt headbutted him. His victim reeled, nose spurting, eyes wide with shock. Ignoring the blinding pain in his head, Zograt raised his magic stick and twitched his fingers. A green bolt shot out and hit the grot, who keeled over with a gurgle as fungus burst through his flesh in several dozen places.

Zograt turned to see his ladz staring at him with wary respect. He gestured in irritation, head still throbbing.

'Told yooz already, 'urry up!'

Skutbad hastened past him and led them along another tunnel. This one sloped down and widened out until it fed into a web-ceilinged cave. Other tunnels led into the space, not only at ground level but as sticky shafts from above. Zograt saw the signs of mass habitation here, from campfires and dirty bedding to loot and scrappy lean-to huts that reminded him of Badwater Drop.

'No more Twitchleggz about,' observed Wabber. 'Dey must all be chasin' Nuffgunk.'

Three large braziers illuminated the space, their smoke rising to vanish through web-funnels in the ceiling. At the middle of the chamber was a crude idol fashioned from rock and painted with bioluminescent goop. It was part grot, part spider, and looked to Zograt as though it had had an arm or two stuck back on with thick webbing.

'We tipped dat over last time we woz down 'ere, broke it good,' said Skutbad. Zograt gave him a withering glare.

''Ow impressive,' he said. His attention was captured not by the idol, but by the wide and noisome pit at its feet. Crude offerings of shiny gewgaws and old bones were heaped about the hole. Old stains that Zograt took to be blood also decorated its rim.

'Boss, is dat where she is?' asked Driggz, his voice shaking. Zograt looked to Skutbad, who nodded.

'So long as she ain't gone upstairs,' said the Spiker. 'But she ain't never left 'er lair when we done a raid before, don't see why she would now.'

Zograt contemplated the big dark hole in the floor. Had he imagined the subtle movement of something huge down there? he wondered. Was that the glint of firelight dancing in arachnid eyes bigger than his head?

'I ain't climbin' down dere,' said Wabber, folding his arms.

'Nah, that'd be stoopid,' said Zograt.

'So wot we gunna do?' asked Skutbad.

'Get her to come up 'ere,' Zograt replied.

'An' dat *ain't* stoopid?' asked Wabber.

Rather than reply, Zograt placed the tip of his magic stick against the ground, concentrated as hard as he could, then wiggled his fingers carefully. The power of the Bad Moon coursed through him, and this time he felt a modicum of real control. A heaving mass of mycelia erupted from the tip of his stick and raced away, growing rapidly thicker and glowing with a sickly green light as they burrowed towards the pit within a pit.

'Gunna squeeze her out, ain't I?' he said through gritted fangs. 'Wabber, get yer bogglerz ready. Rest of ya, keep 'im safe while he does 'is fing!'

Zograt felt the tips of his mycelial mass erupt from the walls of the spider's burrow as though they were his own fingers pushing through soil. He felt them blossom into grey-green fungi that ballooned to fill more and more of the space within the pit. He experienced a moment of triumph as he felt something huge press against them, squirm and thrash in increasing agitation, and finally heave itself into motion.

His elation was replaced by terror as Arghabigskuttla erupted from her lair with a furious screech.

Zograt had thought the spiders ridden by the Twitchleggz were big. They were utterly dwarfed by this arachnid demigod. Legs thicker than tree trunks scrabbled with terrifying speed, each sheathed in chitinous armour and ending in wicked talons. The Arachnarok spider's bulk was colossal, her bloated abdomen bristling with stiff hairs and coloured the yellow-green hue of vomit. Yet for all her enormity and power, it was Arghabigskuttla's head that held Zograt's gaze. Mandibular jaws yawned like a hungry chasm, ropes of venomous drool spilling from rows of jagged fangs. Eight bulbous eyes fixed upon him. He recognised all too well the monstrous intellect and outrage burning within them.

Every instinct Zograt possessed screamed at him to run away. Instead, he waved his magic stick wildly and shrieked.

'Dis is it, ladz! Stand ya ground an' stick to da plan!'

He was answered by the scuff and patter of fleeing grot feet. Zograt risked a glance and saw his followers dashing for any hiding place they could find. Even Driggz had abandoned him. The urge to join them was almost irresistible, yet in that moment it was eclipsed by a wild recklessness as the power of the Bad Moon waxed fat within his soul. Zograt turned back to Arghabigskuttla to see the vast spider had hauled her bulk from the pit and was coming straight for him.

'Zog it den, I'll do it m'self,' he snarled.

Zograt wiggled his fingers and sent a searing blast of green energy leaping from his stick right into the spider's maw. Shards of broken chitin flew. Sizzling ichor spattered the ground. Arghabigskuttla reared, squealing and beating the air with her forelegs.

'Don't like dat, do ya?' screeched Zograt, dancing madly on the spot and firing another green blast at the spider's exposed underbelly. Again, the bolt of energy hit home and Arghabigskuttla shrilled as foul purple fungus erupted through her gnarled hide.

Lunging with a speed nothing so huge should possess, the Arachnarok crossed the distance between herself and Zograt in seconds. She stabbed down at her tormentor with one huge leg. Zograt tried to throw himself aside. His twisted leg saved him, giving out under the sudden shift in his weight and spilling him sideways instead of backwards as he had planned. Arghabigskuttla's talon crunched into the ground precisely where he had planned to dive. Zograt had a split second to offer thanks to the Bad Moon for its protection before the spider's snapping jaws descended on him.

Zograt wiggled his fingers and conjured a tide of bugs that geysered up into Arghabigskuttla's maw. Mouth suddenly stuffed with wriggling and biting insects, the Arachnarok bit down hurriedly, gullet convulsing as she swallowed the mass of half-chewed insect matter.

Before Arghabigskuttla could focus on him again, Zograt scrambled away as fast as his twisted body could manage. He made for one of the blazing braziers, hoping the light and smoke might hide him from his attacker. Scrambling around the edge of the brazier, Zograt found himself faced by Wabber and one of Driggz's ladz, both cowering with their arms over their heads.

'Zog off, yoo'z da one wot made her cross!' hissed Wabber, trying and failing to catch Zograt's eye with his swirling orbs. The brazier suddenly whipped away from them, smashing over onto its side with a dreadful crash and spilling burning coals everywhere. Arghabigskuttla reared over them and gave a triumphant hiss.

She lunged at Zograt but recoiled, squealing, as she trod on burning coals. Instead of crushing him flat, the spider's massive head came down like a boulder on the cowering Bounder. The grot didn't even have time to scream as he was mashed into the ground then sucked into Arghabigskuttla's maw.

Scooting away on his backside, Zograt jabbed his stick into the ground and sent all his power surging through it. Bloated mycelial tendrils erupted around Arghabigskuttla like the tentacles of some monstrous sea beast and lashed about her. The colossal spider keened and strained, trying to rise. Zograt screamed with the effort of holding her in place.

'Now, Wabber!' he gasped. The Boggleye stared at him in mute terror and shook his head. 'Now or we'z all zoggin' dead!' howled Zograt, angry and desperate.

Shaking in terror, Wabber Spakklegit staggered to his feet and stared hard into Arghabigskuttla's eight bulging eyes. The grot's own eyes swirled with strains of purple and lurid green, and Zograt looked away as his own thoughts began to fog. If he lost focus now, he knew they really would all die and, more importantly, he would never be Loonking. Instead, he shut his eyes and poured all his strength into sustaining the fungal mesh that was just barely restraining the arachnid demigoddess. Arghabigskuttla strained against him, snapping one tendril after another. Zograt panted and wheezed as he sent more lashing up to replace them.

'Dat's right, yer majesty, look deep into me bogglerz,' crooned Wabber. His voice had taken on a weird resonance that made Zograt's skin crawl. 'Yoo don't wanna eat us,' said Wabber in a sing-song tone. 'Yoo fink we'z da best, dontcha? *Dontcha?* Now *look... at... meeee...*'

Despite his best efforts Zograt's eyes snapped open, and he glanced towards Wabber before he could stop himself. The little grot was inches from the spider's face, both of them underlit by the dying fires of the spilled coals. His eyes were lanterns of whirling colour that made Zograt's thoughts curdle and his gorge rise.

Those same indescribable colours spiralled within the moist depths of Arghabigskuttla's eyes and Zograt gasped in relief as he felt the spider stop fighting him.

'Yoo'z gunna do wot I sez now, aintcha, yer majesty?' said Wabber. 'Yoo'z gunna be under my control...'

The spider gave a rattling hiss and clicked her huge mandibles together.

Zograt rose warily to his feet, wincing and rubbing at his aching hip.

'I could 'ave her eat ya now, Zograt, yoo know dat, dontcha?' said Wabber, not looking away from Arghabigskuttla. The colours were dying in his eyes, but they remained as dancing motes in hers.

'Yoo could 'ave a go, but da Bad Moon wouldn't like it, an' neither would I,' Zograt replied. After what he had just been through, Wabber's threats felt small and hollow to him.

'She'd still eat ya,' said Wabber with a nasty smile.

'Yeah, and den da tribe would all get killed, an' we'd all be zogged. Wot's da point in dat?'

Wabber appeared to mull this over for a moment. Zograt kept the tip of his stick against the ground, surreptitiously seeding more mycelial roots around the spider's legs. He thought again of Skrog and Nuffgunk and all the rest of them.

'If yoo'z gunna zog up da tribe, best 'urry up an' do it, Wabber, cos uvverwise we got places to be,' spat Zograt.

Wabber sighed and nodded. 'All right, ya clammy git, yoo got a point. But don't ferget she's under *my* power, so don't muck me about.'

'When I'm Loonking, yoo can be da Spiderboss, 'ow'z dat?' asked Zograt, inventing the title on the spot. Wabber grinned with delight.

'Spiderboss Spakklegit, I'll 'old ya to dat, Zograt.'

'Yoo do dat,' said Zograt, releasing his fungal grip on

Arghabigskuttla at last. As his tendrils withered, so the Arachnarok rose back to its full height and stood, waiting patiently for Wabber's bidding. After a few moments more, Skutbad and Driggz emerged from their hiding place behind another brazier. Of the last Bounder there was no sign. Zograt presumed he had fled into the depths of Funnelsnare Pit, then dismissed him as irrelevant.

'See, me plan worked perfect!' he crowed. Skutbad looked suitably impressed, though Zograt noticed that Driggz just scowled, still shaking with the after-effects of his terror.

'Wot now den?' asked Skutbad.

'Well, we got eight of 'em now, so I reckon we legz it!' said Zograt with a self-satisfied grin. Wabber, Skutbad and Driggz stared at him. '*Legz* it, cos… da spider… got eight…'

They continued to stare.

'Oh, zog da lot of ya, just get on da spider an' 'ang on,' he said with a scowl. 'Wabber, get us back up dere, we got a tribe to boss.'

The ride up and out of Funnelsnare Pit was terrifying. Until he clambered onto Arghabigskuttla, Zograt hadn't given much thought to where they would sit or indeed how they would hang on to ride her. He had been vaguely aware that the Twitchleggz tribe rode on spiders, so had reasoned it couldn't be all that difficult. Only as the leviathan arachnid lurched into motion and began to clamber up into the webs above did it strike him that they probably used saddles or harnesses of some sort to avoid falling off.

Somehow, he and his surviving comrades all managed to hang on. Zograt kept a death grip on a clump of the spider's hairs as she hauled her vast bulk relentlessly upward, tearing through webs and dislodging dead tree trunks as she went.

Zograt blew out a breath as Arghabigskuttla finally crested the lip of the pit, but his relief faded as he saw dead grots and discarded weapons scattered across the clearing.

'More of deres than ours,' observed Skutbad.

'Yeah, but still,' Zograt replied. 'Wabber, get us to 'em!'

'Where?' asked Wabber, looking panicked. Zograt's mind spun, exhaustion clouding his thoughts. Sudden inspiration struck.

'Everyone, shut up and stay still,' he commanded. 'Wabber, keep da spider quiet.'

'Hush up a mo, yer majesty,' crooned Wabber, and Arghabigskuttla froze in place. Zograt strained his ears, praying to the Bad Moon that someone was still hitting a gong or shouting a battle cry. Relief flooded through him as he heard both sounds, dimly audible from some way into the forest.

'Dat way, follow da battle noise,' he said. At Wabber's urging, Arghabigskuttla set off at a ground-eating pace. Zograt was impressed by the way she simply shouldered aside the trees in her path, though the din meant they had to pause several times to listen for the sounds of fighting. Each halt ground on Zograt's nerves. How many of his tribe would be left by the time he got there? Had Nuffgunk stuck to the plan? Was Skrog all right?

'Zog's sakes, 'urry!' he hissed at Wabber as they paused yet again. This time the clang of gongs and the screech of grot war cries were clearly audible just ahead.

'Gettin' dere, boss,' Wabber replied and sent Arghabigskuttla lumbering forward again. A final grove of saplings crumpled before the Arachnarok's vast bulk and suddenly the Twitchleggz tribe and the last of the Badwater Boyz hove into view. Dozens of spider-riding grots swarmed around the broad clearing, some waving spears and screeching, others shooting arrows at a narrow cave mouth set into a humped grassy mound. It was the same cave the tribe had herded their squigs into before setting their plan in motion, the very one Nuffgunk had planned to retreat to then set the squigs on their pursuers to buy time.

Zograt saw dead squigs, slaughtered Spider Riders and a few

arrow-feathered Moonclan strewn about the cave mouth, not to mention the veritable forest of brightly fletched arrows sticking out all around the cave's entrance. Yet he was relieved to see his ladz still crouched in the cave's depths, huddled behind shields liberally festooned with even more arrows. And there, lurking in the shadows, head scraping the roof of the cave, stood Skrog. Zograt felt something unclench in his chest, allowing elation and relief to flood through.

'Zog me, we actually did it,' he breathed.

The effect of Arghabigskuttla's entrance was instant and electrifying. Every Twitchleggz grot in the clearing turned and wailed at the sight of her, before scrambling off their steeds and throwing themselves face first against the ground. Even their spiders hunched down and swayed as though in worship to their bloated brood mother. A shaman in a cape of web, feathers and bones fell to his knees and sent up a ululating cry. A hulking grot clad in chitinous armour wheeled his arachnid steed and stood up in his stirrups, raising his blades and howling out a challenge.

Wabber brought Arghabigskuttla to a halt, looming directly over the chieftain. Recognising his moment had come, Zograt hauled himself to his feet and stood precariously astride the huge spider's back. He willed his legs not to give out and pitch him off his perch at the worst possible moment as he stared imperiously down at his rival.

'Oo is yoo?' shouted Zograt. The Skuttleboss slammed one blade hilt against his chitinous breastplate and replied in a surprisingly deep voice for a grot.

'I'z Chief Kreepzogga. Oo is yoo, and wotcha doin' wiv our big skuttla?'

'I'z Loonking Zograt,' Zograt announced, realising that for the first time he genuinely felt worthy of the title. 'I'z got da Clammy Hand on me, an' Arghabigskuttla knows it. Yoo gunna fight me?'

Kreepzogga looked around at his tribe, then up at his spider-goddess, seemingly content to bear Zograt upon her bristling back. He lowered his blades.

'Nah, yoo da boss sez Arghabigskuttla, den yoo da boss!'

'Dat's right,' replied Zograt, brandishing his magic stick and grinning. 'I'z da boss!'

CHAPTER TWELVE

Gobfang Gorge

Closer now they sink their talons into the yielding flesh of the over-ripe world and feel its tainted juices spurt across their neverthere bodies as they drag themselves hungry eager wanting hating tasting between and through and around the shadows of the trees that wither at their touch and rot and fall to ruin in their wake and they are growing closer...

'I seez a dust cloud,' said Nuffgunk, squinting north over the plains. The daylight was a piebald fluttering of light and shade thrown by the ever-changing clouds, but it was glaring by Moonclan standards. Zograt and his enlarged war council had hidden themselves amidst the shadows of a rocky outcropping atop the slopes of Gobfang Gorge. From here they had a good view of proceedings but were partially sheltered from the terrors of the open sky. Zograt's horde skulked in hiding places amid the jagged rocks and cracks lining the deep valley.

'Ploddit's lot are coming,' said Zograt. He pulled his hood further down over his face and squirmed back into the shadows. ''Bout zoggin' time.'

'Everyfing's ready, her majesty done her bit,' said Wabber proudly. Bigg Leggzgit rattled the bones and feathers in his cape and ground his mandibles together. This, Zograt had learned, was a sign of the shaman's annoyance. Leggzgit was a disturbing sight, boasting extra arachnid eyes, vestigial spider limbs, and a malformed mess of mandibles growing inside his mouth. These rendered his speech into a mess of wet clicks with words mangled between them.

'Sh'kk'ee izz kk'not maaji'kk'sty, izz kk'Arghabigskuttla!'

'She's a zoggin' big spider, and she makes zoggin' big webz,' Zograt interjected before Leggzgit and Wabber could get into another row. 'Dat's wot I care about right now. Gunna 'elp us clobber Ploddit's lot.'

'I sed we should clobber Ploddit's lot,' muttered Driggz, who had slunk in Zograt's wake in the days since Funnelsnare Pit. Zograt supposed this was because Driggz no longer had any ladz to be the boss of, but he didn't have time to worry about it. If the spiders had spun their webs thick enough and his plan worked out, his horde was about to grow again. Zograt couldn't afford distractions.

'Right, Driggzy, an' now we'z gunna,' he said distractedly.

'Yoo sed I was stoopid,' said Driggz. Zograt shot him a glare.

'Yeah well, yoo *is* stoopid, but dat woz Naffs sed dat, not me.' Zograt was surprised at the glimmer of rebellion from his scrawny lieutenant. Driggz was growing a spine at last, he thought.

'I can see Big Limpy,' called Nuffgunk. 'Boss, he's zoggin' hooge. Makes Skrog look like a runt!'

Skrog had squatted down in the lee of the largest rocks and was shielding his collection of bugs from the daylight. He gave a growl that sounded like two slime-coated boulders grating together.

'Sorry, big lad, no offence,' said Nuffgunk.

'I see 'im too, 'e really is a biggun,' said Stragwit. The Brewgit distractedly fumbled at a spigot on his still, holding up a battered tin beaker to the resultant dribble then swigging while never taking his eyes from the approaching colossus. Zograt could see the Troggboss now too. The sight took his breath away.

'I thought Skrog woz big...' he gasped. Skrog grumbled again, and there was no mistaking his note of hurt pride. Zograt rolled his eyes. 'Easy, lad, not all about size, is it?' Skrog grunted and ever-so-gently patted the insects huddled in his shadow.

'Fink dis is gunna work, boss?' asked Nuffgunk.

'Betta do,' said Zograt. 'We put enuff zoggin' work in. Days o' marchin' through all dem caves an' tunnels t'get to da Glareface Plainz, bullyin' all da local grots an' dat 'til we found out when Ploddit would be comin' past an' where we could ambush da git.'

'Don't ferget me scarin' 'em all into joinin' da horde, den bossin' 'em to tell us wot tunnels would get us to Gobfang Gorge,' put in Naffs Gabrot. Despite spending his days embodying Glareface Frazzlegit, the Scaremonger had hidden from the daylight as much as the rest of them over the past days. Even now, he and his lugger Gobzit were cowering in the shade of Naffs' upturned mask.

'Yoo done da scarin', but it woz me wot bossed 'em,' Zograt reminded him.

'Don't ferget all da work her majesty done webbin' up da gorge,' said Wabber. 'All to catch a buncha dumb troggs.'

'Sh'kk'ee izz kk'not maaji'kk'sty!' exclaimed Leggzgit, brandishing his staff at Wabber.

'Where'd yoo leave 'er?' asked Zograt.

'Lurkin' in a big crack past all da webz,' said Wabber fondly. 'If everyfing goes a bit spattlethwapperz she can always pop out an' give da troggs a scare.'

'Good finkin',' said Zograt, staring north at the gargantuan Dankhold troggoth growing closer. Big Limpy was craggy and sun-bleached, so tall that Zograt guessed the top of his head would pass within feet of their hiding place. He did indeed walk with a perceptible limp, and Zograt found himself feeling an odd kinship for the towering troggoth. In his wake came dozens more troggoths. Most were lumbering Dankhold beasts, many nearly the size of Skrog. Zograt saw packs of Rockguts tramping along amidst the dust, scooping up handfuls of stone and dirt to chew as they marched. Here and there he even made out Fellwater troggoths, though these latter were few and looked, to Zograt's eye, rather dried out and unwell.

'Ain't just about catchin' some troggs,' said Nuffgunk.

'Course it is, wot else we doin' 'ere?' demanded Wabber.

'It's about da boss bein' da new Loonking!' announced Nuffgunk.

'I'nt dere already a Loonking…?' asked Da Fung, looking up from the little mushroom-monsters he'd conjured to fight one another in a ring of stones.

'Go back to yer 'shroomz, Fung,' said Stragwit, pouring himself another beaker of whatever concoction he was brewing.

''Shroomz,' said Da Fung happily and returned to poking his hallucinations with a stick.

'Shut yer gobz, da lot of ya,' said Zograt. 'Dey's comin'.'

He could see metallic glints amidst the dust cloud. Within moments a convoy of ramshackle wagons appeared. They were lashed together from scrap metal, splintered wood, gaudy canvas and shiny gubbinz, and they travelled on mismatched wheels or crude sled-runners. Each was pulled by mugger beetles. Big and glossy black with chitinous shields protecting their antlered heads, the huge insects raised their legs high as they scuttled along. Zograt could just see robe-swaddled figures hunched under awnings or in makeshift shelters atop the wagons. Ploddit and his ladz, he assumed, goading their beetles with prods of their sharp sticks to the creatures' soft abdomens.

'Here dey come,' he said. 'Leggzgit, Fung, spread da word fer everygrot to be ready. Da signul is Kreepzogga screechin'.'

Bigg Leggzgit stomped in a circle, swirling his cape with one arm and thumping his staff on the ground with the other. He chittered and clicked into the spider-skull set atop his staff. Zograt had seen the shaman do this several times over the past days and knew that by some magical contrivance, he was communicating with his tribe.

Da Fung snapped his fingers, causing his mushroom-monsters to disappear in a puff of reasserted reality. He rummaged in a belt pouch, eyes slowly rolling in opposite directions and his tongue poking out as he searched. The Shroomancer grunted in triumph as he plucked a tiny scorpisquig from the pouch. Flushed purple and clearly furious, the small creature snapped its jaws and flailed with its stinger. Da Fung dangled the scorpisquig over his face. Quick as a flash it stung him, first in one eyeball then the other. Zograt winced, but Da Fung just sighed with obvious pleasure and stuffed the scorpisquig back in his pouch. With bloody tears tracking his cheeks and strange colours dancing in his eyes, Da Fung stared into the heavens and hummed a little tune. As he did so, yellow-and-green mushrooms popped into being above him, beating veiny little bat's wings to stay aloft. Each had a wet mouth hole in its stalk, studded with teeth. Each trailed roots like insects' antennae.

'Off ya go, flappy flap, spread da word,' sang Da Fung. Drooling, muttering and sucking at their stubby teeth, his conjurations set off to do his bidding.

'Well. Dat woz 'orrible,' said Nuffgunk.

'Dere's a reezun we usually let 'im play wiv 'is 'shroomz,' said Stragwit, slurring slightly through his third drink.

''Shroomz,' echoed Da Fung happily, scratching his swollen eyeballs.

'Never mind dat, dey's nearly 'ere,' said Nuffgunk. Zograt leaned into the daylight and peered over the lip of the gorge. Ploddit's wagons were getting close, mobs of Squig Hoppers bounding between them as they came. The wagons slowed as they approached the shadowy defile and the Hoppers attempted to rein in their steeds.

Zograt glanced back along the gorge to where yard upon yard of webbing clogged it. Then he looked back in time to see a large grot clambering atop the biggest and spikiest of the wagons. He wore thick black robes, scavenged armour and a floppy 'shroom-brim hat, and brandished a three-spiked prodda that glowed green. Zograt presumed this must be Loonboss Ploddit.

The big grot gesticulated with his prodda, first at the gorge, then at Big Limpy and his approaching herd. Zograt could see his mouth moving, but Ploddit was too far away to be heard. The troggoths advanced relentlessly.

'Come on, ya big zogger, just a bit closer,' hissed Zograt. He felt powerless, his magic no use in this situation. He could only watch and hope everything went to plan. He sagged with relief as, after haranguing his truculent minions, Ploddit dropped back into his seat and gave his mugger beetle a jab in the nethers.

The wagons rumbled forward, Ploddit allowing several to rattle in front of his own as they bunched up and entered the gorge.

'They're gunna try to clear da webz before da troggs arrive,' said Nuffgunk. Wabber and Leggzgit snorted in derision, then glared at each other.

'Not gunna get da chance,' said Zograt, hoping it was true. He was relying on Kreepzogga now, not even a member of his own tribe. He wondered whether he should have orchestrated the ambush himself, whether putting his faith in the boss of the Twitchleggz tribe was asking for trouble, if–

'*Grrrrrrotagrotaspidaspida! Reeeeeeeeeeee!*'

Kreepzogga's shrill war cry echoed along the gorge, bouncing from the walls and causing Ploddit's ladz to jump with fright. Squig Hoppers fell off their steeds and were devoured by gnashing jaws, while a pair of wagons collided and ground to a halt. Zograt's grots emerged from every ledge, cave and crevice. Dozens of drawn bows were suddenly aimed at the wagons. Spider Riders and Moonclan grot mobs spilled out onto the valley floor, waving their blades in a menacing fashion. Kreepzogga himself rode his huge spider, a beast Zograt had learned was called Bitebite, out atop the mass of webbing spanning the gorge.

Determined not to be outdone, Zograt stepped out from the shadows of the rocks and slammed his magic stick against the ground. A fungal mass erupted under his feet, sending broken stone and earth tumbling as it swelled into a wide platform. Hobbling to its edge and doing his best to ignore its alarming swaying motion, Zograt pointed his stick at the wagons. He wiggled his fingers and performed what he now thought of as his Voice of Da Bad Moon trick. His words boomed out, underlaid by a tectonic rumble.

'Oi! Yooz lot down dere! I'z Loonking Zograt, an' yoo work fer me now!'

He watched the wagon-grots gesticulating at one another. A few Squig Hoppers made a break for it, bounding towards freedom. Arrows scythed them down.

Loonboss Ploddit clambered onto the roof of his wagon, casting a glance back at the approaching troggoths. They were getting near. Zograt could hear the thump-thump-thu-thump of Big Limpy's footfalls.

'Why?' shouted Ploddit, voice barely carrying up to Zograt's lofty perch.

'Cos we'z pointin' arrerz at ya, an' cos I'm da Loonking an' I sez so!'

'Yoo ain't da Loonking, yoo'z a scrawny git on a big mushroom! I should stikk yoo wiv dis!' yelled Ploddit, brandishing his prodda.

'I'z Loonking if I sez. Got da Clammy Hand on me!' Zograt retorted.

'I'll set Big Limpy on ya, cheeky git!'

'Yoo don't boss over dem troggs, yoo just follow 'em about an' pick up da bitz!' accused Zograt. 'Yoo'd just take da troggs underground if yoo woz in charge, so yoo ain't settin' Limpy on no grot! An' if yoo don't do wot I sez, dem troggs is gunna trample ya.'

Zograt watched as a swift and furious row broke out between Ploddit and his ladz. He glanced at the approaching troggoths, calculating the grots below were cutting it fine. Much longer and they would be trampled by the herd.

It appeared Ploddit had come to the same conclusion. He threw down his prodda in disgust then peered up at Zograt, goggles reflecting the daylight.

'Fine! Yoo'z da boss!'

'Good lad, now get out da zoggin' way before yoo get stomped!'

Ploddit and his ladz hastily backed out of the gorge, still under armed guard by a throng of Spider Riders and spear-grots. They abandoned the crashed wagons, one of which had lost a wheel and embedded itself firmly in the wall of the other.

Zograt watched imperiously, if not a little anxiously, as Big Limpy lumbered into the gorge and stepped over the wagons. The troggoths following him didn't slow for them either. The slow-motion stampede saw the wagons first upended then trampled into scrap. Zograt was awed; the troggoths had barely broken stride.

Suddenly anxious he watched Big Limpy pass under his platform, noting the birds' nests perched atop the troggoth's head and the landscape of fungi, rocky protrusions and insects carpeting his shoulders and back.

'All right, webz, don't let me down,' he muttered.

Big Limpy ploughed into Arghabigskuttla's snare without showing any signs of noticing it. Kreepzogga and Bitebite scuttled out the way as strand after silken strand snapped. Zograt watched aghast as the titanic creature strode on, webs giving way before him.

'He ain't gunna stop... It ain't gunna work!'

Zograt had been so sure. How often did Big Limpy come around, and what were the chances it would happen just as Zograt was gathering his horde to claim the mountain? He had been convinced that such providence must be the will of the Bad Moon. Yet there was Big Limpy, shoving forward through the webs, emitting subsonic growls as he forced a path. Zograt's eyes widened as he realised that Limpy was having to push.

The troggoth was slowing down.

Ropes of web clove to Limpy's legs and arms, and clung in bands about his chest. Lesser troggoths clustered behind him, stumbling to a halt as they bumped into his shins or one another. Big Limpy roared, and the sound was like thunder. He heaved. More strands snapped, but even more awaited him.

The titanic troggoth gave a last, irritable-sounding grunt, and halted.

Zograt blew out a breath and leaned on his stick. Amidst the rocks, and down in the gorge, his horde cheered and whooped.

'Now we just gotta work out how to herd ya,' he said to the mass of becalmed troggoths. And then, he thought, it would be time for the biggest challenge of the lot.

Zograt looked at his lieutenants: Nuffgunk sharing a celebratory drink with Stragwit, Naffs and Gobzit; Wabber and Leggzgit arguing; Skutbad lurking near Skrog and watching his bugs with interest; Driggz sulking in the shadow of a boulder; Da Fung, doing... unsettling things with mushrooms.

Their loyalty was his, but for how long?

'Proppa Loonking gotta have a proppa magikal hoozit,' he told himself, looking critically at Skram's glowing amulet and his magic stick. He was certain that neither would guarantee victory over all those human wizards guarding the mountain. There was only one artefact that would impress the Gobbapalooza enough to keep them in line and give him the raw magical firepower to blast a path into the mountain's heart.

'Dey're gunna be impossible to live wiv after I tell 'em,' he sighed, then hobbled off his platform back into the shade of the boulders.

CHAPTER THIRTEEN

Muttering Peak

When the Coven Unseen first reached Muttering Peak, they had found many chambers whose functions were opaque. Some they simply avoided, recognising their potential hazards. Others, Wilhomelda had assigned purposes to. Amongst these were the gloomy row of chambers she had designated holding cells. Rolling stone-slab doors on lockable metal tracks allowed them to be sealed from without. Narrow window-slits filled with thick transparent crystal ensured the cells' occupants could be kept in constant view. Silver veins criss-crossed the walls, illuminating each chamber and warding off malevolence.

Wilhomelda had ordered that sleeping pallets and buckets for ablutions be added to the chambers. At the time, she had vaguely envisioned needing to imprison engineers or alchemists if they became difficult, or perhaps locals if hostages were required to ensure compliance. Later she had wondered if she might have to put Lanette in a cell, at least until she saw reason.

How bitterly Wilhomelda wished she had obeyed that impulse.

'Never imagined our places would be reversed,' she muttered.

She paced from sleeping pallet to far wall then back, again and again. How long had she been confined? she wondered. Day and night lost meaning amidst the softly pulsing illumination. They had to open the door a quarter roll to slide food to her, and to retrieve and refresh her bucket. At first the mortifying indignity of such exchanges had been all Wilhomelda could think about, but soon she had started observing the rotation of guards on her cell.

There were always four: an officer, two soldiers armed with swords, shields and coglock pistols, and a wizard. This last precaution had made Wilhomelda contemptuous at first. Even her own coven appeared fearful of her powers, despite knowing no wizard of the Collegiate Arcane could conjure without foci and sorcerous accoutrements. Yet she had realised that the wizards' presence was a hallmark of Lanette's involvement. They were not there to counter spells Wilhomelda might attempt, but rather to provide a non-lethal counter to any escape attempts. How like Lanette to be thorough and considerate, Wilhomelda had reflected bitterly. If she made a dash for freedom she would not be shot or stabbed except as a last resort. Instead, she would be confounded by illusions or bound with sorcerous strands then thrown back into her cell.

Magic was not Wilhomelda's only talent, however. They could take away her locket, but not her mind. She had observed which of her guards watched her with cautious hostility and which treated her with the deference due to their Magister Princep. She had assayed conversations, memorising who spoke to her like a prisoner and who in awkward and apologetic tones.

As the hours ran into a turgid river she had slept, eaten, washed and relieved herself mechanically. Indignity and shame were forgotten. Wilhomelda's mind was elsewhere, analysing betrayals, identifying conspirators, determining a course of action she now saw she should have been brave enough to pursue weeks before.

Cold anger and indignation fuelled her contemplations, offering her a merciless clarity. She knew when the rot had set in. She knew who had caused it.

'Love and loyalty are for the lower orders,' she muttered as she touched one finger to the rough bedding of her pallet then began another circuit of her cell. 'To the great they are traps. Anchors that hold us down. Chains bound about us by those who hide their small jealousies beneath a cloak of concern.'

She cursed herself for acceding to be hobbled so. She saw now that guilt had been her undoing. Guilt at professing a love that had never equalled that held for her by the fierce young woman who had lit up her life like a firebrand. Guilt for the home together in Azyrheim that had always been Lanette's dream, and which had filled Wilhomelda with a slow species of suffocating panic. Guilt over the knowledge that, in the end, she would always choose herself.

'You sought to imprison me,' she sighed, pausing to press a palm to the cell wall.

'A star cannot be caged...'

Wilhomelda snorted. 'Yet you languish in your pillar,' she said. 'Can even godbeasts be so manipulated?'

'You think me imprisoned?'

Wilhomelda's skin prickled with gooseflesh.

'Are you not?'

Her only answer was a chuckle like dark water tumbling through Stygian depths.

'If you are not trapped then neither shall I be,' she hissed. 'I am your equal, spirit. I will be your master. Then they will all see.'

'She will not.'

Unwilling to rise to this bait, Wilhomelda resumed pacing. Her momentary pause had thrown out her count and she hastened to catch up. With no other means to measure time in her cell, she had determined how many circuits she could walk at a steady pace between one guard change and the next. Again, she tapped a finger against her bedding. Again, she began another circuit.

With the next changing of the guards, her chance would present itself. 'And then I will be unchained.'

Lanette sat around the guardroom table with Captain Gulde, the mages Kirithon and Norwhel, and a handful of Gulde's trusted soldiers. She hated feeling like a conspirator. It didn't help that they had armed guards at the chamber's entrances.

'I don't know how much longer we can wait, Mag'sec,' said Gulde.

'There's muttering, and worse,' said Norwhel, drumming his fingers on the tabletop. 'Even those who were on the fence to begin with are starting to question why we've got her locked up.'

'Gillighasp's doing, sure enough,' said Kirithon, expression disgusted. 'You can place bets he's been creepin' about, flappin' that tongue of his in the right ears.'

'Borster's hardly been quiet,' said Lanette. 'You'd think we'd clapped *him* in irons the way he and his engineers are complaining.'

'You ordered them to cease all work and hand over their tools,' said Gulde. 'For a lot of them, that's as bad.'

'They should welcome the bloody rest, not having to run around after that bully for a while,' muttered Lanette.

'The point stands. Things in the mountain feel hostile,' said Norwhel. 'One of the soldiers spat at me this morning!'

Gulde's eyebrows shot up. 'Unacceptable! Who, sir?'

Norwhel shrugged. 'One of Captain Rayth's. I took the matter to her. Do you know what she said? That I must have been mistaken, because her soldiers are loyal to those who fight for Sigmar. *Then* she had the nerve to ask if I was sure I was such a person!'

'This can't go on,' said Kirithon, running her hands through her hair then gripping the back of her neck. 'It's gettin' naught short o' dangerous. Coven's comin' apart at the seams.'

Lanette found herself the subject of expectant stares. She felt beleaguered and angry.

'What would you have me do?' she asked.

'Mag'sec, none of us doubts your loyalty to the Mag'prin, but it's been almost two weeks,' said Captain Gulde. Lanette found herself irritated by his gentle tone.

'I'm not an infant, captain. Speak your heart.'

Gulde nodded, frowning. 'As you say, then, sir. It's past time we left. Mag'prin needs to be took back to Azyrheim, in warded chains if needs be. She ain't in her right mind, and she's in danger of dragging us down with her. Trouble is, there's a fair few like Rayth amongst the ranks. Begging your pardon, Mag'sec, but there's doubtless more since you first moved against Borchase.'

'I didn't *move against* her.' Lanette was horrified. 'Is that what people think is happening? Throne of Sigmar, Wilhomelda has lost perspective. I've spoken to her five times since her... episode... She knows that she acted wrongly, I'm certain of it. Nobody wants to get her away from this toxic mountain more than me, captain, but it's not as simple as that! We can't drag her back and throw her to the witch hunters, and if we try to make her leave before she's ready I'm afraid she'll... do something unwise.'

'I fear we may have to *make* it that simple, and quickly,' said Norwhel.

'And go where?' asked Lanette. 'We are hardly welcome guests of the Tarembites. Drag the Magister Princep there in fetters and for all we know she'd end up on a pyre. We might have magic and soldiers on our side, but with the coven so divided and the casualties from the greenskin attack, I think their militia might overwhelm us.'

'Straight through the town, quick as we can, then on to the Howl Reach Realmgate,' said Kirithon. 'Astramar has a goodly garrison and a proper prison. Any who want to side with her ladyship can join her in the cells.'

'And then would come the questions, and the accusations,' said Lanette. 'How long before the Order of Azyr became involved? How long before this entire business reflected upon the Collegiate? How many covens are offered dispensation for extended requisition of Freeguild soldiery? I won't see this mess become another bloody excuse for fingers to be pointed at our order.'

Silence settled upon the chamber.

'Then what, sir?' asked one of Gulde's soldiers at length.

'Only other option is to strike first,' said Norwhel. 'Put people we trust into position through the mountain, move quickly, disarm those we know to be problem elements. Finish the job Magister Ezocheen started.'

'I didn't *start* anything of the sort,' exclaimed Lanette. Yet as she looked back on her actions of the past weeks, she couldn't deny she had crossed some lines. All for the right reasons, she told herself firmly.

All for Wilhomelda. To save her from herself. To keep her safe.

'Well,' said Captain Gulde, drawing the word out. 'If we were to do as you suggest, Wizard Norwhel, we could begin by–'

He paused as the sound of running feet echoed along the corridor outside. Lanette's hand dropped to her sword hilt. The focus stone in its pommel offered reassuring warmth to her palm, and Lanette readied a spell.

She heard a kerfuffle amongst the guards, then a Radiant appeared in the doorway. The novice was flushed from running.

'What is it?' she asked. The young Radiant leant on one of Gulde's guards for support as he gulped down breaths. Lanette fought her impatience. At last, he had recovered himself enough to speak.

'Magister... Borchase...' he gasped. Lanette was up and out of her seat in a heartbeat. Her comrades followed her lead, gripping staves and weapons.

'What about her?' asked Lanette.

'Escaped...' panted the Radiant. 'She's... escaped.'

Lanette ran as fast as she dared. She knew she couldn't risk out-pacing her comrades, or the handful of Radiants who accompanied them. Gulde had sent runners to rally those of the coven he knew to be loyal. Lanette hadn't waited for them to arrive. She couldn't.

Everything was going wrong, and she felt blame upon her con-science. Should she have acted more decisively? Had she let her feelings cloud her judgement? She knew that the answer was more complicated than that, that all she had said to her comrades in the guardroom was true. Yet the panic and guilt threatened to break her hard warrior's veneer. The worst of it, she reflected as she pelted up another flight of stairs with a Radiant clanking ahead of her, was that she was still more frightened for Wilho-melda than anyone else.

'Should have got her out of this place straight away, even if it meant camping in the bloody wilds,' she hissed. 'If this place has poisoned her mind, it's your bloody fault.'

She reached the top of the stairs with Gulde and his soldiers hard on her heels, then raced into the cell corridor. A gaggle of panicked-looking guards and several wizards awaited her. Lanette scowled at the way they straggled along the corridor, as though some had sought indecisively to go for help but never quite escaped the gravity of the awful moment. The door to Wilhomelda's cell had been rolled back. A silver glow swelled from within.

Lanette skidded to a halt in the entrance, but her angry ques-tions died on her lips.

She blinked in confusion.

Wilhomelda stood in the chamber, arms folded, wearing an expression of mingled sympathy and contempt. Lanette's eyes fastened on the locket hanging about Wilhomelda's neck.

'They said you were escaping,' said Lanette as her soldier's instincts fought the emotional turmoil that deadened her limbs and slowed her thoughts.

'Oh, Lanette. I am,' Wilhomelda replied.

Gunshots rang out. Lanette heard cries of pain, the steely rasp of drawn blades. Understanding caught up to her howling instincts. Dismay, anger and pain bloomed within her.

There was no time to ask why. No time to plead with Wilhomelda to see sense, to recognise how sick this place had made her, how it had preyed on her obsessions and fears. There was only time to draw her blade and fight.

Something moved in the corner of Lanette's eye. She ducked to one side. The clubbing blow meant for the base of her skull instead slammed into her shoulder, numbing her arm and almost making her drop her blade.

Lanette spun to see a soldier in a half-mask snarling as he raised his sword-pommel to strike again. She drove a punch into his jaw with her free hand and sent him reeling back.

A body thumped into her. A hand grabbed at her arm. Bloody fingers lost purchase and Norwhel slumped to the floor, soaked in gore from the ragged wound in his throat.

Lanette turned to see another soldier coming at her, sword wet with blood. Behind him, the corridor was a scene of anarchy as her outnumbered comrades fought to escape Wilhomelda's ambush. Lanette parried the soldier's first blow, cursing herself for leading them into such an obvious trap.

Yet again, her concern for Wilhomelda had clouded her judgement. Lanette vowed to herself that it would be the last time. Her sword met her attacker's again and this time she drove him back, his sneer becoming an ugly scowl of alarm. She saw no loyalty in the eyes behind his half-mask. She knew in that moment what her comrades had tried to tell her for days.

'I can't fix this, only end it,' she snarled and drew power from her pommel stone. Her enemy's eyes widened in fear as Lanette spat a hard incantation and unleashed sorcerous flames from her free hand. The blaze engulfed the soldier and sent him reeling back, screaming.

Lanette whirled as her first attacker came at her again, seeking to club her into unconsciousness. She ran him through then shoved his body off her blade, turning yet again to see Wilhomelda striding towards her with a face like thunder.

'Always must I contend with the failings of lesser minds,' snarled the Magister Princep. She stabbed outstretched fingers towards Lanette and hissed a string of un-words. Tendrils of purple light erupted from her fingertips and whipped like ropes about Lanette's body, seeking to bind her. Drawing again upon the power in her pommel stone and snarling a counter-curse, Lanette blew the tendrils apart in a cloud of cinders.

'Give this up, Wil, for Sigmar's sakes!' yelled Lanette. 'You know we have to stop you!'

'We?' asked Wilhomelda, pantomiming a look up and down the corridor. Lanette followed her gaze and saw she stood alone. More than half the ambushers were wounded or dead, but amidst their bodies lay Gulde, Kirithon and all the others who had followed Lanette to this bloody end. Wilhomelda's conspirators closed in warily.

She felt sick to her stomach. When she spoke, her words fell dead in the air.

'You said you were doing this to protect us.'

'I *am*,' shouted Wilhomelda in a tone Lanette recognised all too well.

'You only ever sound like that when you know you're wrong, and you just want me to stop questioning you,' she said.

'And *you* only ever sound so petulant when you know I'm right, but lack the wit to see how or why,' spat Wilhomelda. 'But none of that matters, Lanette, because you are taking my place in this cell. You will have plenty of time to reflect upon what a fool you have been, trying to usurp me and steal the mountain's power. Who knows, perhaps once you understand my purpose here, I might even deign to accept your apology and let you stand in my shadow again.'

Lanette's heart broke at the madness she heard in Wilhomelda's voice.

'I only wanted to save you,' she said.

'I don't need saving!' exclaimed Wilhomelda, reaching out to relieve Lanette of her blade.

'No. You need stopping,' breathed Lanette.

Drawing on her anger and sorrow and guilt, she screamed a word of power so potent that it scorched her throat. The ruby pommel of her blade blazed like a star. Wilhomelda recoiled as white-hot flames exploded from Lanette in all directions. The screams of Wilhomelda's conspirators were drowned by the draconic roar of Lanette's spell as their clothes, hair and flesh caught fire and their bodies were bludgeoned by the pressure wave.

Lanette saw Wilhomelda flung backwards into her cell by the blast. Even now, part of her wanted to rush to the older woman's side, to gasp apologies as she saw to her hurts.

Instead, Lanette turned and ran through flaming devastation and charred bodies. She dashed for the stairs at the end of the corridor, intent only upon escape. She knew there was no one left in the mountain she could trust. Even as her heart broke for the friends and allies she left cremated in her wake, Lanette knew her only chance was to reach Taremb. Jocundas loathed Wilhomelda. If Lanette could reach the Listener's Court, if she could impress on him the horrors unfolding in the mountain, she knew she could at least get a warning out.

Never mind the Order of Azyr or the damage to the Collegiate Arcane. All that mattered now was foiling whatever baleful influence lurked in the mountain. She promised herself it would not have its way. Wilhomelda would be avenged. Not the monster she had laid low with her spell, but the woman she had known, and idolised, and followed into perils uncounted.

For her, Lanette would do what she had to. She clattered down a long stairwell and on towards the main gate, angrily swiping away the tears that blurred her vision.

Wilhomelda hauled herself into a sitting position. Her ears rang. She tasted blood and smelled singed hair. If it had not been for the secret wards worked into her locket, she suspected Lanette's spell might have killed her. As it was, the skin of her face and arms prickled with pain and there were blisters rising on her reddened hands. Yet mostly what Wilhomelda felt in that moment was outrage.

'She tried to kill me,' she said wonderingly.

'If one cannot have that which one desires, does not one then seek instead to destroy it, that no other may possess it in one's stead?'

Wilhomelda spat blood and scrambled to her feet.

'No, one bloody well does not!'

'And yet...'

Wilhomelda lurched into the corridor, wincing as she put a steadying hand to the wall and burst a blister on her palm. She surveyed the heaped and blackened bodies. Burned limbs rose from the charred mass, fingers crooked into claws. A stench of roasting pork filled the air.

'What did you do?' groaned Wilhomelda as her eyes crawled over the dead.

'She, or you?'

'For once in the long millennia of your oh-so-godly existence will you *bloody well shut up?*' snarled Wilhomelda. She needed to gather her wits. Everything had gone wrong, even after her careful planning. She kicked the blackened corpse of a soldier, neither knowing nor caring if it was one of those who she had charged with subduing Lanette.

'If you had just done your damned jobs,' she snarled, then threw an arm across her mouth as smoke found the back of her throat and contorted her in a coughing fit. She took a few steps down the corridor before realising she had no idea where Lanette had gone. Wilhomelda picked her way through the devastation to an adjoining corridor where the air was clearer.

From here she could hear the echoes of shouts, running foot-steps, swords clashing against shields. Her plans had encompassed a great deal more than just her own escape and the capture of her former Magister Secundi. Wilhomelda had to hope that else-where in the mountain, at least, matters were progressing better than they had here.

'What if she rallies them against me?' she gasped, spitting to clear the taste of smoke and blood from her mouth. No, she thought, Lanette wouldn't try to do that. With Gulde dead, her most reliable ally amongst the soldiery was gone. Lanette was robbed of her link to the Freeguilders. Some of them liked her anyway, sharing a soldiers' bond Wilhomelda had always found distasteful and yes, she had to admit, perhaps a little threatening.

'But this is not a contest of popularity,' she told herself. 'This is a matter of loyalty, and if Gillighasp is to be believed then Rayth and VanJesp are both ours.'

The notion of loyalty snagged in Wilhomelda's mind. Despite evidence to the contrary, and for whatever other faults Lanette had, the Magister Secundi prized loyalty.

'Loyalty to Sigmar. Loyalty to the cause. Oh Lanette, are you running to tell tales, girl? That just will not do.'

It was one thing to threaten the coven, Wilhomelda thought, or to play out petty jealousies and seek to overthrow her. But if she

guessed right, Lanette was even now bent on a course that might
see the power of Muttering Peak squandered, even destroyed by
those without the wit or imagination to see its uses.

'You'll ally yourself with the witch-burners,' Wilhomelda sighed.
'She must be stopped.'

'Yes.'

*'I know where she is. She treads my domain. Nothing within
these tunnels escapes my sight.'*

Wilhomelda steeled herself, crushing her last sparks of sentiment as though grinding cinders beneath her heel.

'Show me, and I shall do what must be done.'

The silver filaments within the walls pulsed. Knowledge poured
into Wilhomelda's mind. She clutched her locket with one hand
and shadow-stepped.

A moment of rushing darkness. The feather-touch of sable shadows whirling about her, then Wilhomelda stepped out into what she
recognised as the lower third corridor between the west coil-stair
and the engineers' chambers. She could hear the ring of running
footsteps approaching from around the curve of the corridor.

Wilhomelda grasped her locket and muttered words of power.
Then she placed herself directly beneath a marble arch.

Lanette did not look surprised when she found her path blocked.
She wore what Wilhomelda had always considered her soldiering
face, features set hard and resigned. The Magister Secundi raised
her blade and adopted a fighting stance.

'Move, Wil,' she said. Her voice was flat and emotionless.

'Stop this,' said Wilhomelda, striving for a reasonable tone. 'You
know you cannot escape my mountain. There is nowhere you can
run I cannot see you. I am trying to save you!'

'*Your* mountain now, is it?' asked Lanette. Wilhomelda watched
her Magister Secundi moving the fingers of her left hand in delicate patterns. She recognised a spell being surreptitiously readied.

'It is mine, as is the power of the godbeast within it. Mine to use for the good of all. You would recognise that were you not so blinded by ambition and jealousy.'

Lanette's mask slipped. Wilhomelda saw a flash of anger and sorrow in the younger woman's eyes. Once it would have hurt her, made her want to relent and try to see things from Lanette's perspective. Now it stoked her certainty that hers was the righteous path. Anyone who had perpetrated the carnage Lanette had, and who still thought themselves the injured party, must be as deluded as they were dangerous.

'You have lost all reason,' said Lanette. 'You are not the woman I knew nor the captain I followed.'

'Your hands are hardly clean, Lanette,' Wilhomelda shot back. She expected denials or rhetoric, and so was surprised to see another spasm of pain cross Lanette's face.

'They aren't,' she said. 'I'm to blame for all of this. I failed you, Wil, and I'm sorry, but I have to make it right no matter what it costs us.'

'*Do it.*'

'I know,' said Wilhomelda.

Lanette faltered. 'You know?' she asked.

'*Matters elsewhere are critical. You waste time on weakness.*'

'Damnation, give me a moment!' shouted Wilhomelda. Lanette's face darkened with understanding and anger.

'Even now, you speak to that abomination instead of me,' she snarled. 'You really are lost.'

With a wordless shout, Lanette hurled a bolt of fire at Wilhomelda. Or rather, she hurled it at where she believed the Magister Princep stood.

Wilhomelda watched from further back down the corridor, trying to feel satisfaction as the blast of magical flame passed through the illusory self that she had projected to block Lanette's path. It struck the marble archway with all the force of Lanette's anger and blasted a glowing crater in it.

The silver filaments lacing the archway turned dark. That darkness raced out from the point of impact, light dying, black oblivion swelling to fill the tunnel. Wilhomelda and Lanette stood in the void. She could just see her Magister Secundi's silhouette, limned by the glimmer from around the bend in the corridor. Lanette appeared to have frozen in horror, but she started as a subsonic rumble ran through the rock.

'What have you done?' Lanette asked in a voice like brittle glass.

'*I* did nothing,' said Wilhomelda. She felt the passageway vibrating around her, a localised earth tremor gaining power as the malevolence of the mountain crept in.

'You've killed us,' cried Lanette, breaking into a stumbling run and reaching out for her. 'Do you hate me so much?'

'No,' whispered Wilhomelda, throat suddenly tight. She didn't close her eyes. She wouldn't. If she looked away now she knew she would never be able to convince herself this deed was righteous.

'Wil!' screamed Lanette as the stones around her closed in like a clenching fist. 'Wil, help!'

'No,' repeated Wilhomelda. Stone crashed together with a boom. Lanette's cries were cut off with brutal suddenness. The last light from the passage's far end vanished.

Wilhomelda stood in darkness and let out a shuddering breath. She felt neither triumph, nor loss. She just felt numb.

'Linger not here. Your work is not finished.'

'No,' she said a third time, realising her blistered hand was hurting from how tightly she clutched her locket. Carefully she released her grip, absently wiping a tear from one stinging cheek as she did so. 'No, it is not.'

Wilhomelda turned her back on the dark corridor and walked slowly away.

CHAPTER FOURTEEN

Rotgut Mere

*How long they have pursued their quarry back and forth and back
again doubling winding growing hungrier angrier more savage but
now at last they taste and sense and now they know as slitherslip
and dwimmerslink through rot and mire and marsh a-bubble their
prey is near at hand...*

The Flashbanditz dwelled in Rotgut Mere, a festering salt marsh of
curdled mangroves wedged between the Shudderwood's northern
fringes and the Umbralic Sea. Even the most lurk-in-the-cave of
the Badwater Boyz had heard stories of the Flashbanditz and their
treacherous realm, Zograt included.

'Never thought I'd be sneakin' in dere meself though,' he muttered
as he limped along a mud causeway between bubbling pools under
lambent boughs. 'Speshully not alone!'

He'd had no difficulty finding Rotgut Mere, so known and
feared was it. Zograt's challenge had instead been keeping the
horde moving in the same direction without infighting, cowardice

or shiny objects slowing the march. Again and again the rambling horde had halted while Zograt menaced some truculent under-boss, lent his magics to herding Big Limpy and his troggs back on course, or broke up the impromptu squig-fights that had cropped up ever since Boss Hoppit and his Squigalanche joined them on the fringe of the plains.

Zograt reflected, as he squirmed under a fallen tree trunk, that being out on his own for a bit was a relief. Then came a flurry of eruptions from the swamp, gas jets rasping skyward and igniting in furious blue and green. Zograt cowered until the blasts died away, his bugs clustering close.

'Den again, bein' out on yer own ain't great,' he said. The sound of his own voice bolstered his courage, and he clambered from under the fallen tree with his bugs chittering and squirming. Zograt stared into the mists and squared his shoulders. He forced himself to start hobbling again, ignoring the way the glowing trees leaned down towards him. He swatted away their fronds and scraped at the slimy residue they spattered on his robes.

Zograt wondered if the trees were curious.

Or hungry.

'None o' dat,' he told himself. 'Yoo got a job to do, an' if ya zog it up, da Bad Moon ain't gunna be 'appy'.

On through the murk they slip and they writhe twining over and through as the saltbitter curdles at their coming and the squirm-things float dead in their witherwake...

The rambling march had given Zograt's lieutenants time to air various concerns about his plan. He heard them again now, as he limped deeper into Flashbanditz territory with rot-mud squelching between his toes.

'Da Gobbapalooza should come too, 'elp against da shamans!'

This had been Skutbad's argument, eagerly backed by the rest of the Gobbapalooza.

'Yoo just want to grab da Spanglestikk before I can get me clawz on it,' he'd accused. Their denials had been half-hearted, and soon subsided altogether.

Kreepzogga had tried next, he and Bigg Leggzgit somehow slipping past Skrog as he protectively stood guard and cornering Zograt amidst the roots of a whispertree, where he had snatched a few hours' sleep.

'Why don't we just go in dere wiv everygrot an' give 'em a good kickin'?' Kreepzogga had demanded.

Zograt had rebuffed the idea. Much as he liked an army to hide behind, they had struggled enough steering mobs of grots, fractious squigs, spiders, lurching wagons and a herd of recalcitrant troggoths through the many miles of Shudderwood.

'If we all go in, we'z gunna sink in da swamp, or get eaten by wurrleeches,' he had explained. 'Even if we don't, da Flashbanditz would see da horde comin' an' fink dey woz bein' invaded, wouldn't dey?'

'But kkdat's… exactly… wot'skk happenin',' Bigg Leggzgit had said.

'But we don't want dem to *know* dat,' Zograt had said, before squirming out from beneath the roots and hastening off.

'But why d'yoo need to go in dere?' This from Driggz, sidling up to Zograt during a halt in a soggy river valley where the troggoths had been allowed a wallow, and hunting parties had been sent out to replenish the horde's dwindling supplies.

'Wot? Yoo worried 'bout me, Driggzy?' Zograt had asked.

Driggz had scowled at this. 'Nah, but no one else likes me, an' if yoo wasn't around I'd get skragged.'

'We need da Flashbanditz cos dey got all dem shamans,' Zograt had explained. 'An' I needz da Spanglestikk. We gotta 'ave everyfing we can get our clawz on before we 'ave anuvver go at da mountin, Driggzy. Gotta make da Bad Moon proud.'

Driggz had been taken aback.

'Yoo mean yoo'z draggin' us back to dat stoopid humie town again?'

'Course, ya daft git,' Zograt had replied. 'Wot did yoo fink all dis woz about?' Driggz hadn't replied, instead slinking off muttering and shaking his head. Zograt had wondered, not for the first time, why he had ever thought that grot would amount to anything. Then other matters had seized his attention as a mass of squigs hurtled into the Skrog-wallow and panicked grots ran everywhere.

Their maws stretch aquiver and their talons rend rotwood and bloat-body and waveweed and rattlereed and on they rush and on so much swifter now so much closer so near so desperately hungry...

'If whole tribes ain't been able to clobber da Flashbanditz, wot makes ya fink yoo can do it by yerself?' That had been Nuffgunk, last to try to dissuade Zograt from his plan just hours earlier. The horde had been camped on the fringe of the Shudderwood by then, peering out over the steaming tangle of vegetation and slime that was Rotgut Mere. The reek of festering plant life and salt had been almost overpowering. It had competed with the potent fumes wafting from behind them as Stragwit brewed a very special and unpleasant poison at Zograt's request.

'I don't look like a threat, do I?' Zograt had said. 'Runt like me hobblin' along, no ladz, no Skrog?'

'Won't dey just skrag ya?'

Zograt had hesitated. Nuffgunk had hit upon his greatest concern with the plan. Still, he'd known he had to show confidence.

'I got da Clammy Hand on me. Dey ain't gunna shiv me, cos I got da protekshun of da Bad Moon.' Nuffgunk had seemed torn between suspicion and superstitious awe.

'Is dat 'ow it works?'

'Er… yeah, course,' Zograt had replied. 'Yoo gunna be able to keep dis lot from killin' each uvver or wand'rin off 'til I get back?'

Nuffgunk had puffed out his chest.

'Don't worry 'bout dat, boss. I ain't gunna mess it up.'

'Yoo betta not,' Zograt spoke aloud, addressing the Nuffgunk in his memory as he trudged further into the swamp. 'I ain't goin' through all dis just to get back an' find yoo zogged it up while I woz away, ya git.'

Skrog hadn't liked him going off alone again, but Zograt thought he'd managed to get the troggoth to understand. He couldn't have stopped Skrog following him by force. The troggoth was finally recovering from the wounds he had taken while saving Zograt's life, aided by healing salves provided by the troggoth-herders of Ploddit's tribe. Skrog hadn't tried to pursue Zograt, merely loomed in the forest eaves and given a low and mournful cry, then watched Zograt solemnly until the swamp mists had drawn a veil between them.

Zograt had to admit to himself that he would be very glad to be back in Skrog's protective shadow again.

For now, he focused on the task at hand.

'Find da Flashbanditz. Tell 'em wot I'm about. Challenge da–' Zograt's monologue was interrupted as his foot squelched knee-deep into salty ooze. He snarled and dragged the limb free, swatting away biting things with ropey wet tentacles that had battened onto his shin. He stamped on those that were still wriggling, spat into the swamp for good measure, then hobbled on.

'Challenge da chief. Don't try magik cos he's got da Spanglestikk an' I ain't beatin' dat. Instead, stick 'im wiv dis.' Zograt reached into his robes and tapped a claw against the slender tube affixed under his left armpit with a knot of spiderweb. 'Only get one shot, so don't zog it up. Den grab da Spanglestikk an' tell 'em dere's a new chief.'

Zograt ducked as something buzzed overhead, its spindly black legs trailing. He crouched, heart thumping and magic stick raised until the buzzing receded. With a sound like a tribe of gargants breaking wind, more green-and-blue blasts lit the murk to the left. They silhouetted something that was all spindle-limbs and lamp-like eyes, picking its way through the marsh. Zograt wasn't sure if it had noticed him, but all the cautionary tales of Shudderwood monsters crowded his mind and he cowered a while longer.

At last, cautiously optimistic that he wasn't going to get eaten, Zograt rose and limped on.

'Zog me I 'ate dis place. Wot's wrong wiv dese Flashbanditz?'

He spun at a sound from behind him. Zograt narrowed his eyes. He was certain he had heard a swift slither and a squelch as of something moving through the swamp.

'Somegit followin' me?' he breathed. Marsh gas belched and burned. Something gave a croaking call from atop a hillock of rotting wood, cut off with a sudden squawk. There came a splash to his left, followed by a series of bubbling chirrups. Zograt stared into the mists until his eyes watered, but there was no further indication of movement on the path behind him.

He grunted, then turned and hobbled on in what he hoped was the right direction. Zograt was counting on the Bad Moon to help him with that part of the plan, too.

'Find da Flashbanditz. Tell 'em wot I'm about...' He began the mantra again, and hoped the Bad Moon would hurry up and point the way.

As he took his next step, Zograt's shin met resistance. He looked down to see a slim strand of fish-gut wire, stretched between two mossy boulders. He had walked right into it.

'Oh zog...'

The wire broke with a twang. Motion rushed around Zograt as a net of the same fine wire erupted from the mud and carried him high into the air to dangle beneath the glowing boughs of a tree.

Several strange figures emerged from the cover of the rocks. They were grots, Zograt realised, but their mouldy grey-green robes were festooned with clumps of marsh plant and smears of mud that confused their outlines. One shook a fish-bone staff at Zograt. Beneath the grot's ragged hood, Zograt could see his face was painted in swirling patterns with biolumin-escent goop.

'Wotchoo, introoda?' asked the grot in a high-pitched sing-song.

'Dat's me,' grunted Zograt, who was bundled uncomfortably in the net with its strands cutting into his skin. He could feel tree fronds fumbling at his ears and scalp, but couldn't get an arm free to swat them away.

'Whassadooin' in ourrrr swampeh?' asked the grot, who Zograt took to be a shaman. The other two had produced spindly spears from amidst the rocks and were jabbing at Zograt's rump.

'Uvver dan bein' prodded by gitz an' fondled by a zoggin' tree, I woz hopin' to—'

'Yoogunna shurrupnow! Dunmatta wotcha doin' 'ere,' screeched the shaman, waving his staff. Zograt's heart sank. He gritted his fangs, expecting to be impaled or zapped. Instead, he heard the shaman rap out swift commands. His cronies ceased prodding and dragged a lightweight raft from behind the rocks. They set it on the swamp's scummy surface then hopped aboard, reversing their spears to act as punting poles. The shaman drew a curved dagger and sawed through the taut wire keeping the net aloft.

The bottom dropped out of Zograt's stomach. He landed with a splat on the muddy path. The shaman poked him in the nose.

'Yoogunna comewivus, seedachief an' tell 'im wot yoo'zabout!'

Zograt unpicked the shaman's dialect as he regained the breath that had been smashed from his body. Wheezing, he struggled upright, holding a hand up to show he meant no harm.

'Yeah, all right, dat works,' he said as he was prodded onto the bobbing raft. Zograt reflected that the Bad Moon didn't mess about when called upon. He hoped all that dangling and dropping hadn't broken the nasty surprise tucked under his arm. He couldn't check, with the shaman watching him intently and jabbing him every few seconds. He would just have to trust to the Bad Moon's blessings again and hope.

As the raft wobbled out onto open water, Zograt thought he heard a splash and a slither from somewhere behind and caught the vaguest hint of movement in the murk. He wondered if something really was following him. Zograt narrowed his eyes, trying to pierce the mists and catch a glimpse. Then he was prodded in the nose. By the time he looked back into the murk again, whatever had made the sound was gone.

The taste so near now it slides across the tips of fangs and tongues that quiver with anticipation as the scent of spellsource draws near through the mists...

Being poled through the swamps for an interminable span didn't trouble Zograt overly, though the motion of the raft made him feel sick. Having a smelly wet sack dragged over his head wasn't pleasant, but it too was tolerable. He could handle being prodded off the raft and along a creaking wooden jetty, up what felt like a thousand slippery wooden steps, across a swaying bridge of rope and planks, then up yet more stairs. He even put up with it when, part way through the journey, he was roughly patted down and had his magic stick, his slittas and Skram's amulet snatched away amidst mean chuckles and prods.

However, when a door creaked, the sack was ripped off his

head, and he was shoved into a cramped wooden cell, Zograt lost his temper.

'Yoo woz takin' me to yer chief!'

He hit the back wall of the small room. The planks felt damp and swollen under his palms. The smell of salt was almost over-powering, and as the door slammed behind him Zograt was left in near-total darkness. Only a few cracks between the warped boards allowed illumination into his cell.

He limped to the door and thumped it.

'Oi! I wanna see yer chief!'

'Shutchoo gobhole!' came the response. 'Chiefbusy. Seeyou whenee'snot!'

Zograt thumped the door again, then limped off to slump in a corner. He had a furtive root about in his armpit and breathed a sigh of relief. The tube hadn't broken. Belatedly it occurred to him that if it had, things would have gone very badly for him.

'Still clammy,' he muttered. Yet as time dragged by and the day-light in the cracks faded, Zograt's nerves jangled. What were they doing out there? Was he going to be dragged in front of the chief, or had he been tossed in a hole to be forgotten? He thought of his horde, camped back in the forest. How long before they gave away their presence and tempted the wrath of the Flashbanditz? Perhaps without him to keep them in line, Nuffgunk would lose control and the horde would disintegrate before he, Zograt, could get back.

'Bad Moon don't want yoo hidin' in a hole,' he told himself as the last glimmers of daylight vanished. 'If it did, it woulda left ya back in Badwater Drop.'

Zograt was working up his courage to use his magic, smash his way out of his cell then and improvise, when a dull thump reverberated through the walls. Another thump came, then more, steady and relentless.

Zograt recognised the beat of what he reckoned must be a very large drum.

'Well. Dat means somefin', he muttered, rising and cracking his nobbly knuckles. 'Wonder wot?'

He felt the restive motion of his bugs squirming through his robes as though they too were readying for action.

The door slammed open. Zograt found himself staring at several spear points and a shaman's fish-bone staff. The shaman's face paint glowed about the green-white orbs of his eyes. Zograt could see more bioluminescence welling behind his captors, wild patterns daubed across a wooden wall and part of a ceiling.

'Comeyoo rightnowyeah,' sang the shaman. 'Bosschief 'eegunna-seeya goodgood.' Zograt didn't like the nasty cackle that followed, but allowed himself to be led from his cell at spear point. He was marched down rotting wooden corridors festooned with barnacles and fungi. Crude but vivid, glowing patterns decorated walls, floors and ceilings at random. Their glare bored into Zograt's eyes after his dark cell.

He was shoved through a sagging doorway onto a wide platform beneath the open sky. A mass of bioluminescent swirls covered most of the platform's surface and glowed so fiercely that their light competed with the stars and planets above. Beyond the platform's edge, Zograt had a sense of crude structures raised on stilts, sagging rope bridges and stairways, and more glowing patterns. There were grots packed in to right and left, many with their own glowing face paint, all adding to the disorienting psyche-delic spectacle. Zograt noticed none of them stepped onto the platform's daubed designs, instead clustering in dense masses around its edge.

At the far end of the platform stood a throne made from glowing fungus, scrap metal and wood. A fan of spindly spears rose behind it, festooned with skulls, bits of rusting wargear and other crude trophies. Clustered around its foot were a gaggle of shamans painted with glowing patterns and wielding staves, rods and blades.

Jutting from the side of the throne was a rickety platform, upon which sat the great drum Zograt had heard. Two diminutive grots clung to its sides and beat its skin with bone clubs.

Upon the throne sat a figure Zograt assumed must be the chief of the Flashbanditz. Though clearly a large and well-muscled grot, the figure looked to Zograt more like part of the marsh had got up and started walking. He was covered from the neck down in glowing swirls, which ran beneath his garb of woven fronds, clotted mud and fist-sized barnacles. He wore a robe with hood drawn up, open and pooling about him like mouldering green-black wings. The hood threw his face into shadow, so that Zograt could only see the tip of the chief's nose and his wide grin full of fangs. Across the chief's lap lay a staff so long that Zograt assumed it must originally have been fashioned for a human or aelf. It was mud-spattered and encrusted with barnacles and fungi, but through gaps in this second skin Zograt could see glints of gold. The head of the staff comprised golden bands, roughly a foot in diameter, that interlocked to form an open sphere. Floating in their middle was a chunk of crimson crystal the size of Zograt's fist.

'Da Spanglestikk,' he gasped.

His captors hustled him forward, pushing him to his knees before the throne. The shamans peered down their noses at Zograt. The drum thumped and the grots around the platform's edge stamped their feet in time with it until the structure shook. Half-blinded by the kaleidoscopic glow welling around him, Zograt squinted up at the chief of the Flashbanditz.

The chief held up the Spanglestikk.

The drum thumped twice, *boom boom*.

The grots stamped in answer, *whump whump*.

Silence fell. Something deep in the marshes gave a high-pitched cry.

'Oo'zyoo, comewandrin' inta me swampz?' demanded the chief. His voice was gruff and phlegmy. He sounded to Zograt like he was gargling through a throat full of mud.

'Me? I ain't no-grot,' Zograt replied. His mind worked furiously as he tried to figure out how to whip out his surprise and kill the chief without getting butchered. When he had concocted this plan, it had seemed simple. The main challenge, in his mind, had been getting an audience with the chief.

Now, Zograt began to doubt whether he could produce his nasty surprise before getting impaled. And even if he did, his confidence was waning that the Flashbanditz would simply fall in line. Could he really reach the Spanglestikk before one of the shamans did?

'No-grot?' demanded the chief. Zograt didn't like his knowing smirk. 'No-grot got dem bugsacrawlin? No-grot 'ave a boncefulla 'shrooms? No-grot carryin' rounda magikstikk an'a loonstoon?'

Zograt froze. So far, every rival he had beaten had been bigger and meaner than him, but he had been cleverer.

'Da chief of da Flashbanditz ain't stoopid,' he said. The chief's grin grew so wide Zograt thought it might split his head in two. He rose, fluids drizzling from his robes, and raised the Spanglestikk over his head.

'Chief Blastagit izzabigsmartgrot!' he roared.

Boom boom went the drum.

Whump whump went the grot-feet. The platform shuddered. Zograt thought furiously.

'All right, ya got me,' he said as inspiration struck. 'I ain't no-grot. I'z a proffit of da Bad Moon!'

Silence stretched as they all stared at him in bewilderment. Chief Blastagit cocked his head.

'Yoo'za proffit, bugsacrawlin?'

Zograt tried to rise. Spear points jabbed at him, but Blastagit made an irritated noise and waved them back. Zograt struggled to his feet and allowed his bugs to squirm free. He raised his arms in imitation of Blastagit's gesture and tried to look imposing.

'I'z da voice of da Bad Moon and I'z come to give yooz all its message!' shouted Zograt, wiggling his fingers to put some boom into his voice.

Flashbanditz recoiled, which led to several despairing wails and distant splashes as those nearest the back were jostled off the platform's edge. Even the shamans looked wary. Blastagit sneered.

'Littlerunt finkza bignoise, yeah?' he said. 'Wot'sa message den, eh? Wot'sa Badmoon gotta say?'

Zograt reached slowly into his robes. Spear points came towards him again. Chief Blastagit waved them back. From what little Zograt could see of the bigger grot's expression, he looked genuinely curious. Zograt's talons found the webbing under his armpit and clawed it free. The hollow tube fell into his palm.

Zograt's heart was hammering. He had one shot with the blowpipe. Succeed, and the dart would send Stragwit's virulent poison coursing through Blastagit's veins. The solution was part fungal spores, part regenerating troggoth blood, and part toxin from Arghabigskuttla's bulging sacs. Zograt was quite sure it would kill anything it struck, just as he was certain that, if he got this wrong, he would be dead before he had time to lament his poor aim.

'Lemme tell ya da message, chief,' he said. Zograt whipped the blowpipe from his robes, drew in a breath, and blew hard into it.

The dart spat from the pipe. Zograt felt a moment of triumph before it hit an invisible wall of force in mid-air and dropped harmlessly to the ground. He gaped, trying to work out what had happened. Blastagit hadn't moved, but his expression was now a moue of mock sympathy. Zograt looked down and saw shamans, their fish-bone staves raised as they projected the magical shield in front of their master.

Zograt blinked in bewilderment. There was no way they could have reacted so quickly, he thought. Even his Bad-Moon-sent sorcery wasn't that quick to conjure.

"Ow did yoo do dat?' he asked, shock momentarily overriding the knowledge that his life must now be measured in moments.

'Me liddlemate toldme yaplanz, Zograt Da Skwurm,' chuckled Blastagit. 'Cummon outtashadowz, showyaface, backstabba.'

The shamans, who now all had their staves and blades pointed at Zograt, parted to allow a figure to slink round from behind the throne.

'All right, *boss?*' said Driggz.

Zograt gaped.

"Ang on, yoo told 'em me plans?' he asked. Driggz looked defiant, and guilty, and pleased with himself all at once.

'Yoo woz gunna leave me wiv da tribe. Weren't no way I'd survive 'til yoo got back. I toldya, Zograt, but yoo didn't lissen.'

Despite everything, Zograt was impressed. He gave a bleak cackle.

'Zog me, picked yer time to get some smartz, didn't ya?'

'Dey's gunna let me be a Flashbandit,' said Driggz. 'Better'n bein' some stoopid Badwater git. Once we done yoo, we'z gunna sneak up on da rest an' zog dem up too!'

Zograt thought of Skrog, unsuspecting, backstabbed by Driggz. He found himself angry.

'Ya followed me through da swamp, didya? Den snuck ahead an' told dis git everyfing while I was stuck in a hole?'

Driggz looked confused. 'Nah, I didn't foller ya. Snuck in well before yoo did, Zograt.'

'We found stoopidzogger stuckinna mudpit, stopped 'im get eaten bya biglanky,' chuckled Blastagit, waving the Spanglestikk expansively. 'He toldus alldastuff, an' now I'z gunna zogyoo rightup.'

Zograt reached for his powers, fingers wiggling furiously. They might kill him, he thought, but he wasn't going without a fight. Moreover, impressed or not, he wasn't going to let Driggz live. Zograt saw the realisation bloom across Driggz's features as smugness curdled into terror. He saw the shamans' power gathering about them like a crackling green thunderstorm, and above them all the roiling might of the Spanglestikk swelled as Blastagit levelled it at his face. At least the Bad Moon would get a bit of a show as he died, Zograt thought.

Something dark and writhing erupted from the glowing floor of the platform. Zograt felt agony tear through his feet and legs as dozens of needle points ripped his flesh. He was borne upwards with a terrified shriek. Green and red light exploded about him, then Zograt fell from the air to land with a crack on the platform.

He lay bewildered, thoughts a jumble. A cacophony surrounded him: shrill screams; mad drumbeats; the zap and crackle of greenskin sorcery. A virulent hissing cut through the din. Groggy, Zograt thought of angry scorpisquigs, or maybe an upended basket of slitherscutts.

Pain brought clarity. Zograt groaned as the agony in his legs, shoulder and jaw ripped away the numbing blanket of near unconsciousness. He writhed and whimpered. He dragged himself into a sitting position, fumbling with one hand at his face while using the other to paw aside the tangle of his robes to expose his legs. Zograt felt sick. From the throb in his shoulder, he must have landed on it when he fell but, by the blessings of the Bad Moon, hadn't broken anything. His face had fared less well. Zograt's jaw was swelling on one side, and he was forced to spit out blood and broken shards of fang.

A horrible tingle crawled through his flesh as he surveyed the damage to his legs. Deep gouges tore the flesh of both calves amidst a mass of circular puncture wounds. All were bleeding freely.

Zograt looked up blearily, trying to understand what had happened. He took in the pandemonium on the platform. Flashbanditz grots scrambled in mad packs across swaying rope bridges, one of which snapped amidst shrieks of dismay even as Zograt watched. Others hurled themselves from the platform's edge, evidently too panicked to think further than immediate escape.

Three grotesque beings writhed upon the platform, their forms insubstantial as smoke yet horribly solid. The creatures had humanoid torsos and limbs, Zograt saw, while their elongated heads were leech-like tunnels ringed with thousands of needle fangs.

The things whirled towards him and Zograt felt what little strength he had dribble away. They had struck from below, he realised. One of those horrible maws had rent his flesh, likely would have torn him apart and swallowed him down had it not been for the magic bombardment unleashed by the Flashbanditz. It must have struck his attackers rather than him.

'All tryin' to kill me at once,' he said with a weak giggle that turned into a sob.

The monsters squirmed towards him. They tore at the ground with long taloned arms, scuttled on incorporeal legs, writhed like serpents over and around one another. Terrified grots were caught in their path. The monsters didn't stop, or even seem to notice them. Emitting dreadful hisses from their quivering mouth-pits, they passed right through the Flashbanditz. As they did, Zograt saw the grots convulse then collapse, flesh ripped open, skin withering to grey parchment.

He reached for his powers but couldn't get a grip on them. Patches of his own skin, he saw, had turned that awful grey shade. The creatures bore down upon him.

A fiery blast of magic hit their conjoined mass from behind. Clots of incorporeal flesh tattered away. Grey ectoplasm slopped across the platform. The monsters turned as one, their hiss rising to a furious rattle. Zograt stared past them to where Blastagit stood atop his throne with Spanglestikk in hand.

'Dat littlerunt is mine!' screeched the incensed chief. His hood had fallen back to reveal mad red eyes beneath a high forehead painted with a glowing Bad Moon glyph. 'Flashladz, zogup dem slitherwotsits!'

Those shamans who had not fled howled and shrieked, stamped their feet and rattled fish-bone fetishes. Zograt felt the storm of magic gathering anew, even more formidable than before. Instinct drove him to scramble away, gritting his fangs against the agony in his mangled legs. He squirmed into the shadows near the edge of the platform, narrowly avoiding the trampling feet of fleeing grots.

The Flashbanditz unleashed their sorcery. Zograt's ears popped with the force of the magical storm. A pyrotechnic tidal wave of green and crimson engulfed the three monsters as they slithered, fast as striking serpents, towards Blastagit's throne. Raw magical force tore at them. A gangling arm spun through the air and splattered into slime as it hit the platform. One of the monsters recoiled, torn away from its twins by ectoplasmic green fists and punched repeatedly in the maw until its head came apart like a sack of offal.

Keening with hate, the other two horrors reached the shamans and tore into them. Withered bodies flew, landing and rolling like discarded rag dolls or plummeting from the platform's edge. Zograt saw one shaman hoisted high and dropped head first into a monster's maw-pit. The unlucky grot vanished with a scream as though cast down a deep well. Blastagit screamed and raved, dancing a furious jig on his throne as he flung bolt after bolt of magic from the Spanglestikk. Zograt was impressed despite everything by the power of the weapon. It blew rents in the platform, atomised shamans unfortunate enough to be caught in its blasts and ripped another of the hissing monsters in half.

'Dat power'z wot yoo came for,' he snarled at himself. 'Wot ya doin' lyin' 'ere, ya git? Ain't ded yet, is ya? Is yoo just a worthless runt? Is yoo no-grot?'

He wasn't, he was certain of it. If it hadn't been for the Clammy Hand, Zograt thought he would have been torn apart by monsters or blasted to bits by magic.

'Still breathin', still got magik, still got a chance,' he told himself then wiggled his fingers and gritted his teeth. Stilt-legged spiders manifested at his bidding, their bodies bulbous sacs of glowing fungus. They scuttled over his mangled legs, and he muffled a shriek of pain as they sank their little fangs into his wounds. Working quickly, the fungus spiders scuttled back and forth, back and forth. Stringy ropes of 'shroom-silk and glowing spit stitched shut the worst of Zograt's wounds and staunched the flow of blood.

Cursing Driggz, and the Flashbanditz, and whatever those monsters were, and even himself for his overambitious plan, Zograt staggered to his feet and clenched his fists.

'Not ded yet,' he spat.

The same, he realised, could not be said of Chief Blastagit. He had been ripped apart like a fistful of wet rags and strewn across his throne, which now dripped with his blood. The Spanglestikk lay discarded at its feet, while Blastagit's surviving shamans fled in terror.

The chief had not died alone, however. Zograt saw that now only a single hissing monster remained, hunched over the throne as it swallowed down another shaman with convulsive motions.

As though sensing his presence, the creature whipped around. Its maw stretched wide. It gave a rattling hiss.

'Zog yoo too,' spat Zograt. The monster rushed towards him and in that moment, Zograt dredged up every cruel trick and act of violent bullying he had ever suffered. Each moment of torment at the hands of those who thought themselves stronger and better than him raced across his mind's eye. His fear melted away, replaced by the bitter fury of one pushed too far, by too many, for too long.

A guttural scream tore from the depths of Zograt's narrow chest as the full magical might bestowed upon him by the Bad Moon waxed fat. He threw both hands forward and spectral ropes of mycelium erupted from his fingertips. They stabbed through the air and punched deep into the body of the onrushing monster. One tendril plunged through the thing's chest with a wet ripping sound. Another dived down its pit of a throat.

The monster convulsed, its charge arrested by the ropes of magical mycelia. It writhed and clawed at the dozens of tendrils transfixing it. Zograt screamed again and the mycelial ropes swelled with obscene vitality. They expanded within the monster's body and its thrashing grew more panicked as its wounds stretched wider and its incorporeal body bulged. The monster's skin strained then split as glowing fungi shoved out through its hide.

Zograt gave a third scream and raised his arms. Transfixed on the pulsing tendrils, writhing and hissing, the last of the monsters that had hunted Zograt was borne aloft. Ectoplasmic filth drizzled from its wounds as the tendrils ballooned within it. Its throat ruptured and a swaying mass of fungi swelled through the wound. Still the creature thrashed and reached for Zograt, but it was flickering in and out of view now as the shadowy stuff of its body was burst apart from inside. Its hiss rattled at the edge of Zograt's hearing, near eclipsed by the blood thundering in his ears.

He gave his fingers a final wiggle and out from his robes flowed a seething tide of insects. Thousands of scuttling forms erupted from Zograt's sleeves, spilled from the baggy folds of fabric about his body, and scuttled from his hood to swarm over his face and up his arms. They poured along the pulsating mycelial mass. The monster thrashed but could not stop the insects from spilling over its body and squirming busily into its gaping wounds. Stingers stabbed; mandibles chewed with obscene vigour; scrabbling legs clawed out stringy clots of shadow stuff.

The monster gave a last, desperate convulsion, then came apart in tatters of shadow and was gone.

Zograt staggered and released the energies of his curse. A huge weight of glowing fungi thumped to the platform, where they began to take root amidst the corpses and dig tendrils into the warped wood. Insects pattered down like rain, squealing as they scattered in all directions.

Fangs gritted against exhaustion and pain, Zograt stumbled through the devastation towards the ruin of Blastagit's throne. He felt eyes on him as grots emerged from hiding places to stare. If any of them attacked, Zograt knew he wouldn't have the strength left to fight them off. None did. They only watched, wide-eyed as the strange runt from the swamps limped through the carnage and halted before the chief's throne.

Zograt took up the Spanglestikk. He wiped blood and ecto-plasm from it and felt its raw magical might course through him. He thumped one end of the Spanglestikk against the ground and leant on it for support. He turned wearily to glare at the Flash-banditz now gathering on every side.

Shamans eyed him. Mobs of grots with glow-paint smudged across their features stared at him in awe.

He saw furtive movement near the back of the crowd, a figure trying to dart away towards a set of stairs.

'Grab 'im,' Zograt shouted. There was a brief ruckus, then Driggz was hauled to the front of the gathering and flung at Zograt's feet. He looked up with a sickly attempt at a grin, apparently too scared to speak.

Zograt looked down at Driggz for a long moment. Weary thoughts limped one after another through his mind. Coming to a decision, he addressed the crowd.

'Yoo all seen wot I can do. Dat's cos I got da Clammy Hand on me! Da Bad Moon picked me, an' gave me its power. I'm da Loonking, an' yooz lot is gunna fight fer me!'

He was rewarded with a ragged cheer. Driggz cowered.

'Any of yooz fink I'm wrong? Wanna tell me dere's already a Loonking?' Zograt yelled, glaring around at the assembled shamans and grots. None could meet his gaze.

'Any of yooz wanna try stabbin' me in da back?' he shouted. Again, there was no answer but nervous shuffling and downcast eyes. Driggz grovelled lower still.

'Not even yoo, Driggzy?' Zograt asked, lowering the tip of the Spanglestikk until it hovered before Driggz's eyes. The scrawny grot stared at the glowing staff and shook with terror.

'P-p-pleez... Zograt... da uvvers p-p-put me up to it...'

Zograt smiled coldly. He was tempted to blast the little git there and then, but it was his own fault that things had come to this, wasn't it? Zograt knew he had to be smarter if he was going to be Loonking. He needed to see the angles others didn't, keep his subjects guessing, and that started with Driggz.

'Nah, Driggzy,' he said, wincing as his wounded legs throbbed. 'Yoo got me good, nearly 'ad me. If it wasn't fer dem monsters, an' da Clammy Hand, yoo woulda.'

Driggz whimpered and pressed his face into the fungi and gore about Zograt's feet.

'Pleez, we woz mates,' he whined. Zograt looked around the assembled Flashbanditz then reached down and grabbed Driggz's shoulder. It shook under his talons.

'We still is,' he said, pulling Driggz to his feet. The scrawny grot goggled at him in confusion. Zograt saw hope and wariness warring behind Driggz's eyes and knew he suspected some cruel trick. But Zograt was sure of his decision. He turned to address the crowd.

'I'm yer boss now so get dis through yer 'eads. If yooz try to mess me about, I'll zog yoo up. Da only reezun I ain't gunna kill dis one is 'e woz my mate while I was still a runt. Never shivved me or took me stuff. Driggz 'ere is gunna be my bannerboy an' carry my big boss flag into battle. Now yooz lot just fink about all dat. He's my mate, he's my bannerboy, and 'e looks dis scared o' me. I don't care 'bout none o' yooz lot nearly as much as 'im, so just fink 'ow scared of me *yooz* oughta be!'

A ripple of muttering spread through the crowd. Those at the front edged backwards.

'Besides,' he finished, grinning nastily at Driggz, 'yoo 'ad yer one chance, Driggzy. Yoo ever try anyfing like dat again an' wot I just did to Chief Blastagit an' dem monsters is gunna look like snuffing it peaceful-like in yer sleep!'

Driggz quailed. The crowd took another step back.

'Now get all yer clobber,' shouted Zograt. 'Everyfing valuable wot ya got, all da magik and zappy wotnots an' weaponz, an' all yer food an' supplies. We'z marchin' out of dis swamp and yoo'z gunna join my 'orde. Gottit?'

This time the cheer was deafening, though Zograt suspected it was motivated as much by fear and a desire by the Flashbanditz to ingratiate themselves, as much as any genuine excitement. They scattered in all directions to follow his commands. Driggz sank onto his haunches, still shaking, and let his head fall between his knees. Zograt sat down heavily upon the wrecked throne. The remains of its former occupant squelched under his backside.

Zograt cast a jaundiced eye up to the heavens, seeking amongst the glinting stars for a sign of the Bad Moon.

'I got dem for ya,' he said. 'Da big 'orde, all da gitz to clobber dem humies and get into da mountin. Just one more stop fer somefin' I forgot first time round, den I'll give ya a show worth bringin' da Gloomspite for.'

But first, he thought as he slumped back into the soiled throne and closed his eyes, he'd have a bit of a rest.

CHAPTER FIFTEEN

Muttering Peak

Wilhomelda stood at her chamber window. Her last bottle of wine sat empty on the sill. She had drunk only a little before tipping the rest out onto the mountainside. She hadn't tasted the wine. It had brought her no gratification.

Wilhomelda closed her eyes. She gripped the sill. She tried to feel something, be it satisfaction or remorse, even pain. All she felt was hollow, and very tired.

The door rumbled open behind her. Wilhomelda heard Borster's heavy footfalls pause just inside her chambers. She assumed the engineer was taking in the wreckage, the upended furniture and broken glass. She turned and saw shock on his face.

'Magister Princep?' He made her title a question. Wilhomelda shook her head.

'Just Magister, Vikram. The singular requires no differentiating title for there is nothing to compare it to.'

'I… The, uh, the circlet is finished.'

Wilhomelda offered him a hollow smile. 'Congratulations, Vikram.

Your name will be remembered, as will those of Ulke and Gillighasp. A device to harness the might of a godbeast. Imagine the lives we will save.' He continued to stare.

'It is as I warned you Magister Prin… er… Magister,' he said. 'Employing the circlet will be deeply unpleasant. Once you are… wearing… it, you'll not be able to remove it again. I cannot promise you it will work.'

'Come now, Vikram,' she said. 'Where is that confidence?'

He scowled. 'The principles are sound, Wilhomelda, and the engineering is exactly as you asked.'

'Then there is nothing more to say.' She cut him off before he could repeat his concerns. 'There is always a price to be paid for power, and I am willing to pay it.'

Stone crashed in her mind. A last beseeching cry was silenced. A hand reached through the darkness and was gone. She flinched and turned her back on Borster.

'Little do we realise how steep that price may be,' she sighed, setting her fingertips against the empty bottle. 'But once we have committed to our road, Vikram, we who are righteous cannot step aside. To do so would render worthless the sacrifices we have already made.'

'*The last of the rebels within the mountain are slain,*' intoned the voice in her mind. '*They chose the wrong hiding place. Your position is secure.*'

'You may leave me,' said Wilhomelda, giving the bottle a gentle push. It toppled from the windowsill and shattered on the slopes below. 'I have no further need of your advice. Soon I will be the master of this mountain's power, and then none will be able to harm me, nor those under my protection.'

She heard Borster leave. His footsteps mingled with the chuckle of the spirit as it retreated from her mind. It sounded like grinding stone.

* * *

They gathered again in the pillar chamber. The essence of the ritual was the same: the machines; the wire tether; the pulsing veins of light. For Wilhomelda, though, everything was different. The coven barely had the remaining numbers to form the circle and were forced to stand far closer to the pillar than she considered safe. Engineers and wizards alike bore scars from the days of internecine strife that had followed what Wilhomelda now thought of as Lanette's attempted coup. She had stationed guards at every entrance to the chamber. Captain Gulde's rebels had proven tenacious, and Wilhomelda would not put it past the thing in the pillar to have lied to her about their demise.

'Soon, you will hide nothing from me,' she breathed, eyes fixed on the glowing pillar.

The other great difference in this second ritual was the circlet. Wilhomelda held it as the engineers completed their final preparations and her fellow magi prepared themselves. It was an elegant thing, she thought, a simple circular band of precious metals about which wound wire filaments. Delicate internal cogwork could be seen through crystal apertures set into the circlet's inner facings, whirring and trembling. It reminded Wilhomelda of the workings of her father's fine duardin-made pocket watch.

Even the curved copper needles that swept inward from the front of the circlet were pretty to look upon. At least, thought Wilhomelda, if one did not know their purpose. She should have been frightened and revolted at the prospect of the twin needles piercing her tear ducts then sliding at painstakingly calculated angles into the inner workings of her skull. Again, the image of her father's pocket watch surfaced. She wondered why she should think of it now. Then it came to her that she had given that watch to–

Wilhomelda cut the thought off and turned briskly to inspect the preparations. To her left was a wizard named Laghmann, who had managed to bind the wire about his left wrist as required despite having one arm in a sling. To her right was Gillighasp. He offered a sickly smile that did nothing to compensate for the wrongness she felt at his being there.

'Let us be about our work,' she said, loud enough for her voice to carry around the chamber. The dark shape within the pillar stirred lazily.

Borster dropped his goggles into place and scanned the room.

'Ready, lads?' he shouted. His engineers returned salutes, though Wilhomelda noticed they had donned all the protective garb they could.

Wilhomelda raised the braided wires that led to Borster's refurbished machines, thence to the balcony atop the pillar. She hooked the braid into the back of the circlet and felt its weight. Once she donned it, the wires would flow across her shoulder and up the back of her neck, then outward from there to circumnavigate the surviving members of her coven. She beckoned Borster to her.

'The weight drags. You will have to help me slide the circlet into place, Vikram. I might hurt myself otherwise.'

Her attempted jest fell dead in the air.

'We knew that might happen,' said Borster. His jaw was tight, his hands steady as he took the circlet from her. That was good, thought Wilhomelda. Couldn't have those tines juddering as they slid home.

While Borster held the circlet, Wilhomelda swept the assembled coven with what she hoped was a resolute stare.

'Loyal friends, it has cost us much to reach this point,' she said. 'We have been wounded in body and soul. We have lost...' Her voice caught but she forged on, evading the numb pit inside herself. 'We have lost those dear to us and faced betrayal. But so do all who seek to drive the wheels of progress. So do all who take risks that others dare not, who recognise that to truly defeat the evils of our reality we must be willing to pay *any* price, to cross *every* line, and see always the lives we will save and the good that we will do. I see you, every last one of you, and I know you will all be remembered as heroes and liberators. Join me now in this final ritual. Help me to chain this godbeast to our collective will! Stand firm by my side no matter what comes, and together we will achieve the power we need to protect every innocent life throughout the Mortal Realms!'

Her followers cheered her words. They looked worn and frightened, she thought, but their eyes gleamed with shared purpose, and many stood straighter. That was good. For all Wilhomelda knew, there were more lives yet to sacrifice to subdue the beast; she could not risk her followers' nerve breaking at some crucial juncture.

'Ready?' she asked Borster. Her face reflected in the lenses of his goggles, and she barely recognised the haggard and hollow-eyed spectre she beheld. Only the fire behind its eyes felt familiar.

'Ready, Magister. And good luck.'

Borster nodded to Ulke, who lurked nearby, dabbing at his lips. The small alchemist hastened forward and daubed a foul-smelling salve under Wilhomelda's eyes.

'To, uh, prevent any, uh, corruption of the blood or the flesh in the wounds,' he said. Next, he proffered a small vial of purple liquid. She took it.

'Drink. It will, uh, numb the pain. Flinch at the wrong moment, Magister, and, uh...' He left the sentence unfinished, stepping back as Wilhomelda swallowed the contents of the vial. There was something ironic, she thought, about drinking such a deadening draught when one already felt so little.

'Begin!' she shouted, even as a cold tingle spread through the flesh of her face. She imagined a wax mask draped over her skull.

Engines rattled into life. Bottled lightning leapt, throwing distorted shadows of the coven around the spherical chamber. The coven began their chant.

'Luminus liminiaris,
Occlusus penumbraii verifarium vo.
Umbracalis, umbrasestus, umbrathae.
Oublis electum vo.'

Gillighasp led them. Wilhomelda couldn't. Her lips were too numbed to form words. She nodded to Borster, who grimaced. As Wilhomelda tilted her head back, and the greasy feel of sorcery crept through the air, he lowered the prongs of the circlet towards her eyes. The tines grew larger. Her nostrils flared and she fought the instinct to turn her head aside. Wilhomelda held steady and tried not to flinch as the tines lost focus, now too close to see.

'Soon...'

Unable to speak, Wilhomelda could only direct defiant thoughts towards the entity within the pillar. Soon she would prove who was master and who servant. Wilhomelda took pride that she had never been a servant in her life.

With a twist of his lips, Borster slid the needles home. Wilhomelda felt pressure at the corners of her eyes, then–

She stood atop a pinnacle of stone amidst a raging whirlwind. It tore at her hair, her clothes, her flesh. It sought to rip her from her perch, to dismember her and scatter all she was to the void. Wilhomelda clung to the rock and screamed defiance into the howling wind. She grasped her locket and spat words of power as she sought control. The scene wavered. The storm shuddered and broke apart...

And became a corridor of glowing crystal down which she ran as something huge and dark pursued her. Wilhomelda couldn't look back. Her limbs felt heavy, as though simply to drag herself along she would need to dig her fingertips into the floor and heave with all her might while the dark presence drew closer and closer at her back. Wilhomelda rounded a corner with painful slowness, then another, realising the presence was toying with her. That knowledge filled her with a strength born of anger. Somehow, she turned and as she did the dark shadow was torn to tatters even as the crystal walls exploded...

And became a thicket of creepers thick with barbed thorns. Wilhomelda was trapped amongst them, her thrashing movements causing the thorns to tear her robes and rip her flesh as they coiled tighter about her. Daylight fell in blinding splinters between the creepers and stabbed at her eyes. Agony flared in Wilhomelda's skull as though the light were kindling the very flesh of her mind. The vines bound her like a mummy's wrappings. The thorns sank deep, and her agonies redoubled. Wilhomelda could not reach her locket now, nor move her pierced jaw to form words. She had only her will with which to fight back and she feared it would not be enough. The thought of Lanette came to her then, seated in the antique bergère in their study, in their apartments in Azyrheim. She was laughing at something Wilhomelda had said, one hand placed lightly on Wilhomelda's arm.

'You killed her...'

No, *Wilhomelda thought.* We killed her. I did what I had to, and I felt the pain of it. I sacrificed. You, though. You swatted my Lanette as if she were an insect and you a wilful child. And I hate you for it.

The fire in Wilhomelda's mind flowed suddenly through her flesh, blazing out to burn away the vines. She contorted in agony even as she welcomed the pain. Her tears sizzled into steam, but Wilhomelda laughed to hear the beast howl in pain...

And she was on her knees in the pillar chamber. Her body shook. Her eyes were aflame, her vision blurred. She felt the bite of hot metal in a band around her scalp. The sensation of foreign objects lodged within her head was amongst the strangest and most unpleasant Wilhomelda had ever experienced. She fought the desperate need to reach up and drag the circlet free.

Dimly she was aware of shapes clustered around her. One, larger than the rest, bent over her.

'Magister? Wilhomelda? Are you all right? Can you hear me?'

The concern in Borster's voice could almost have been touching.

'I am–' she croaked, then stopped as images flurried across her vision. Wilhomelda saw a man walking down a cobbled alley, looking up in alarm as wood splintered and heavy barrels spilled from a balcony. She saw an army of duardin and humans pushing their assault into the heart of an orruk battle line, and the waving greenskin totems approaching unnoticed through the forest on their western flank.

Again, the chamber resolved and Wilhomelda found her vision had cleared a little. Borster's face swam before her, the image suffering slight fisheye distortion but at least comprehensible.

'The visions,' she gasped, trying to make him understand before she was bombarded again. 'I see... much...' Again her mind's eye overlaid her physical sight and she saw the pillar chamber as though from above as small, dark figures scurried through its arched entrances. The image changed and she watched a woman in a tavern pick the right card from a proffered hand. Another shift and Wilhomelda saw Muttering Peak, and the jagged shadows that gathered menacingly around its feet. Blades glinted in the dark.

She heard the spirit of the mountain snarl. She had always heard its voice within her mind, but this was louder, more immediate. She felt a stab of triumph. It sounded frustrated, perhaps even alarmed. Wilhomelda raised her head and tried to focus upon the pillar. The dark shape still drifted within its glow, but she thought that it looked limp, more formless than before.

'I think... we... have succeeded,' she gasped. She raised one shaking hand and swiped at the wetness she felt on her cheeks. Her fingertips came away dark red.

Cries of triumph and excitement greeted her words. They hit her mind like splinters, and she hissed in pain. Wilhomelda rose on shaky legs then almost fell. The spirit growled within her mind and more images flurried across her vision. A tall man leaned over a table, worried faces swimming around him in a crowd. He held a sword and a burning brand, and he turned suddenly towards her with a curse on his lips. The world spun and hands were gripping her arms and supporting her back.

'You need help, and rest,' said Gillighasp from somewhere nearby.

'The attentions of, er, our best healers,' added Ulke.

'Not yet,' she panted, trying to focus on her visions. 'We need to... I see danger from without. Something... threatens... Forces marshal against us.'

Her bruised thoughts whirled. Was it Lanette? But no, she had dealt with Lanette, Sigmar forgive her. And the greenskin would be long dead by now. The Brood would have seen to that. Then who? Had Lanette sent a warning after all? Was the Order of Azyr even now gathering its forces beyond the valley? But surely, they could not have arrived so swiftly. Even if word had got out, it would take longer than that for her detractors to marshal their strength.

'Stormcasts?' she croaked. She became aware she had spoken aloud only thanks to the gasps of horror from those around her. Weakly she shook her head. The weight of the circlet dragged disconcertingly at the corners of her eyes.

'No... no... I didn't see...' And then she had her answer. She snarled, disconcerted by how much the sound resembled those made by the godbeast.

'What is it?' asked Borster. 'What in the heavens are you trying to say?'

'Jocundas ParTaremb,' she spat. 'He knows. He must know...

Infighting... Weak. He's jealous, Vikram. He wants to take... We have to act... first.'

Jocundas ParTaremb leaned over the table in his throne room. On it were scattered unfurled parchments, maps of the local area and a plethora of empty goblets, crumb-littered platters and candles burned down to stubs.

His most trusted advisors stood around the table. All wore expressions of concern and Jocundas could well understand why.

'The entire cavern?' he asked.

'That's the right of it, your lordship,' replied Guildmaster Reffert. The rotund man lifted a corner of his apron and dabbed sweat from his neck with an embroidered corner as he spoke. 'The fungus farms have been getting more unstable for weeks, as my reports have warned. And not just tremors and cracks. There's been insects chewing through beams, damp and mould like you've never seen, and some of the mushrooms that have been growing down there...' He trailed off with a disgusted grimace.

'And today an entire cavern has collapsed?' prompted Jocundas. He could not keep the impatience from his voice.

'Just so, your lordship. We've no notion what caused it, though you'll take your pick of the above. Seventeen farmers killed or injured. 'Twill take us days to dig through the rubble and find the lost.'

Captain Oswen, leader of the Tarembite militia, shook his head. 'First the mutations amongst the cattle, then the water in Venator's Well turning bad–'

'Bad?' interrupted Quillmother Utembri with a mirthless laugh. 'It curdled like milk, Oswen! And the beetles!' She scrubbed at her puffed sleeves and shuddered.

'Granted, ma'am,' said Oswen. 'But that, and the earth tremors getting more violent by the day, and the nightmares–'

'*Claims* of nightmares,' put in Jocundas' seneschal with a sneer. 'Respectfully, m'lord, I'm not convinced all this hysteria is anything more than that.'

'*Claims* of nightmares, then,' Oswen persisted. 'And now this. My point, Lord Listener, is that we are worse beset than I can ever remember by disaster and ill omen. It cannot be a coincidence that this comes when outsiders meddle with the mountain. You ought never to have allowed them access.'

'Captain Oswen, we have been over this,' said Jocundas wearily. 'I have despatched riders to Astramar, with instructions to enquire in the strongest terms as to the validity of the coven's actions and to demand urgent assistance. In the meantime, it is not within my gift to deny the agents of almighty Sigmar access to Muttering Peak.'

Lady Dolvetta JalTaremb, who had walked away to stare moodily into the hearth, now snorted.

'No, cousin Jocundas, but it *is* within your gift to forehear such events, and to plan accordingly.' She fixed him with a venomous glare. 'Why haven't you?'

Jocundas took a gulp of water from a goblet, buying a few seconds to consider his response. He had never felt closer to exposure, nor to paralysing panic. Battles he could fight, with blade in hand and an enemy before him. But what was he to make of these bizarre omens and horrible signs? How could he possibly pretend that he had known what was to come, when any sane man would have done what he could to prevent such disasters? Was it truly worse at this point to admit his lies, or to have his people believe he had known what was coming and done nothing?

Jocundas slammed the goblet down on the table. It was those damned wizards, he thought. They had disturbed the mountain. They had ruined the status quo he had so carefully established over decades. It was all their fault.

'This is the coven's doing,' he said. 'Captain Oswen, I beg your pardon a thousand times. You had the right of it all along.'

'Eh?' asked Oswen and Lady Dolvetta at the same time.

'My forehearing has failed me since those sorcerers invaded the mountain. You are all thinking it, and I do you a grave dishonour by pretending it is not so. I throw myself upon your mercies, my honoured counsellors, but I hope you will understand. For weeks now the whispers have been unclear, but I did not wish to cause panic. I could still discern fragments, and I have done what I could with those while praying to great Sigmar for clarity.'

He looked around at them: Lady Dolvetta, wearing her scorn thinly veiled; Captain Oswen, stoic; Reffert, a pale and sweating bundle of nerves; Quillmother Utembri, one eyebrow raised, arms folded; his seneschal, devoted and trusting as always. Jocundas adopted his most penitent expression and pressed ahead.

'I did not wish to fail you, my friends. I could not bear the thought that the problem might lie with me, and I could not place the burden of such fears upon you all until I knew the truth. But now I see my own self-doubt and misplaced faith in those who claim to serve Sigmar has clouded my judgement. The problem is not mine to own. The problem is whatever the wizards have done to disrupt my abilities!'

Gasps greeted this pronouncement.

'Are you saying that they have deliberately deafened you, or interfered with the mountain's gift?' asked Utembri, sounding horrified.

'It is at their feet we should lay these ghastly goings-on!' exclaimed Reffert, jowls quivering indignantly.

'Not only that,' said Jocundas, thumping a clenched fist upon the tabletop. 'I am saying we'll have no more of it! Already they have fled our streets, doubtless frightened of what we would do when we discovered their perfidy. I say we seize the initiative and pursue them to their lair. Captain Oswen, muster the militia. You and I will lead them up the pass to the very gates of Muttering Peak. We will have answers, and if needs be we will drive these accursed wizards from our lands by force!'

Jocundas felt elated as he saw that he had them. Nothing unified like shared prejudice and fear, in his experience. And Sigmar knew there was enough of both directed towards the Coven Unseen. He was about to continue when he was interrupted by a dull crash from outside the throne room.

Several of his advisors jumped. Everyone exchanged glances.

'Was that inside the court?' asked Lady Dolvetta.

A scream rang out, muffled but distinct. The reverberation of running feet shuddered through the walls.

'It was,' replied Oswen. 'Wait here, everyone, if you please.' He beckoned to the two militiamen waiting nearby. Hands on hilts, the three soldiers made their way to the door and opened it.

They got no further. Gunfire cracked in the hallway. Oswen pitched backwards in a spray of blood. One of his guards spun, a hand flying to her wounded shoulder before another shot hit her in the back and threw her onto her face. Blood soaked into Jocundas' fine rug.

The third guard howled in frantic agony as his armour glowed white hot. Jocundas recoiled with a grunt of revulsion as the stink of cooking flesh reached his nostrils. The luckless guard toppled, his armour blackened and fused to his steaming flesh.

Guildmaster Reffert screamed and backed away towards the throne. Quillmother Utembri whipped out a dagger. The door swung wide to reveal a tall woman in the garb of a Freeguild officer, a half-mask veiling her face. In one hand she held a bloodied sword, in the other a smoking pistol. Jocundas' mind seized with fear as he saw the mass of soldiers and wizards packing the passage behind her.

'I am Captain Persepha Rayth of Sigmar's blessed Freeguild, here at the order of Magister Wilhomelda Borchase of the Coven Unseen,' the officer barked. Jocundas saw no mercy in her eyes. He thought of his sword, hanging useless in its scabbard on the back of his throne.

'I am ordered to dissolve the seditious leadership of this unsanctioned and unconsecrated human settlement,' Rayth continued. 'And to carry out immediate sentence upon all those held guilty of sedition against Sigmaron and its sovereign territories.'

'Wait just a moment,' began Jocundas.

'No, Listener, I don't think I shall,' replied Captain Rayth. She raised her pistol, and a gunshot boomed in Jocundas ParTaremb's throne room. It was the last sound the Listener ever heard.

CHAPTER SIXTEEN

Badwater Drop

'Has dis tunnel subsided or somefin'?' asked Zograt, ducking under a lump of stone that bulged from the tunnel's ceiling. Behind him, Skrog grunted as he squeezed through the gap.

'It ain't changed, boss,' came Driggz's muffled voice from behind the troggoth. Zograt spat and shook his head.

'Feels cramped,' he muttered. He had only a small band with him: Skrog; Driggz; a handful of Nuffgunk's hand-picked ladz. Zograt saw no sense in dragging anyone else back to Badwater Drop, but after Rotgut Mere he wasn't going alone.

He had left Nuffgunk to lead the march in his absence, certain that even with his detour he would be able to catch up to the horde again well before they reached the human town. Zograt didn't dare be absent long. Even with Nuffgunk eager to crack some heads, he was worried what manner of anarchy he would come back to. The Flashbanditz had been antagonising Ploddit's ladz, and he was quite sure his Gobbapalooza were still fermenting trouble simply out of spite.

Yet this was something he needed to do. And so, he led his little band deeper, wending along dripping tunnels and crossing fungus-lit caverns where things squirmed in the gloom. Zograt leant on the Spanglestikk as he walked; his leg wounds hadn't festered thanks to his sorcery and the unguents provided by Stragwit. They still hurt though. His body felt like one big bruise even days after the fight with the monsters.

Zograt wondered if those horrors had been native to the swamp, or if they had been sent after him. His instincts suggested the latter, and his pendant glowed every time he pondered it, which he took as a sign from the Bad Moon that he was right. However, he had no notion who had sent them or why. Zograt was sure he had either slain or beaten every potential enemy who knew he existed. The possibility of another rival out there who he didn't know about, and who feared him enough to send such horrible assassins, both unsettled him and stroked his ego.

'All da more reezun to scrape up every bit of power I can get me clawz on,' he told himself as they neared Badwater Drop.

'Wossat, boss?' asked Driggz, puffing and panting beside him.

The scrawny grot had fashioned a formidable bosspole the day they returned from the swamp. He had nailed bits of rusted weaponry, glinty bottles, impressive fungi, mugger beetle chitin and other shiny gewgaws to a bundle of Flashbanditz spears, and had refused to be parted from the unwieldy trophy pole since.

Driggz had even insisted on bringing the bosspole with him through the tunnels. They had been forced to halt several times as, cursing and sweating, the skinny bannerboy manoeuvred his pole through treacherous sections of tunnel. A few of Driggz's scavenged 'trophies' had been knocked loose during these efforts, which the other grots had watched with a mixture of exasperation and mean amusement. Zograt had ordered Nuffgunk's ladz to pick the scattered trophies up, reasoning Driggz would want to nail them back in place later. Zograt was impressed with Driggz's apparent transformation. He didn't want to do anything that would cause his newly appointed bannerboy to backslide.

He offered Driggz a toothy grin. 'Jus' finkin', we'z come a long way since dis grotty 'ole, ain't we?'

'S'pose, boss, yeah.' Driggz was still wary, as though expecting to walk into some verbal trap that would spell his demise. Zograt didn't mind; he preferred Driggz on his toes and eager to please. He contemplated the dark tunnel ahead, leading to the now abandoned Big Cave.

'Yoo remember da way Skram used to kick us about?' he said.

'Yeah, boss, 'e woz a git,' Driggz replied. The other ladz exchanged shifty glances. Zograt remembered more than a couple of them from Skram's bullying sessions. He wondered why they thought they were here, whether some were beginning to suspect they'd been dragged down to the deeps for a bit of revenge. His amulet gleamed.

Let them sweat, Zograt thought. He wasn't going to harm Nuffgunk's best boys, but he didn't mind putting the fear of Gorkamorka into them. And he wasn't worried about anything they might try, not while he stood in Skrog's shadow.

'All dem beatin's, all da bites an' kicks an' dirty jobs,' Zograt murmured.

'Boss?' asked Driggz, apparently unsure if he was still part of the conversation. Skrog rested one huge fingertip on Zograt's shoulder and gave a low rumble. Zograt, surprised and pleased, patted the troggoth's warty digit.

'Yer right, lad. Where's 'e now, eh? Just a nasty stain an' a nastier memory.' He rapped the butt of the Spanglestikk resolutely on the ground. The blow echoed along the tunnel. 'Come on yooz lot, we didn't come down 'ere to stand around gawpin.'

'Wot *did* we come down 'ere for, boss?' asked one of Nuffgunk's ladz. Zograt was already hobbling into the tunnel, desiccated bug carcasses crackling underfoot.

'Foller me an' yoo'll see.'

Crunching through the drifts of dead insects made Zograt think of how he'd watched some bugs grow inside a chrysalis, and of how, once they were done with it, they shed it without a backward look. Emerging into Da Big Cave and seeing now what a cramped and uninspiring space it was, the comparison felt appropriate.

Zograt made for the tunnel down to Da Soggy Cave. He paused as his old junk-throne came into view. Driggz nodded at it.

'Yer furst throne, boss! Just imagine wot kinda throne yoo'll 'ave when yoo'z Loonking!' To his immense irritation, Zograt heard an echo of Da Fung's dreamy voice.

'In't dere already a Loonking?'

Yes, he thought, there was already a Loonking abroad in the realms. For all Zograt knew, there were dozens of grot bosses who had felt the touch of the Clammy Hand, and who had appointed themselves Loonking.

'A Loonking don't sit on a grotty little throne like dat,' scowled Zograt. He levelled the Spanglestikk. Green lightning pulsed along the staff's length, causing fungi on its shaft to pulsate and grow before collecting in the crystal and blasting towards the throne. The sagging edifice blew apart as though a boom-squig had detonated inside it. Bits of smouldering junk and burning fungus rained in all directions. Skrog grunted and swayed as a dented lump of metal bounced off his forehead.

Driggz cowered behind his bosspole.

'Come on, zoggerz, let's get dis done,' said Zograt, limping deeper into Badwater Drop.

As they made their way down the sloping tunnel towards Da Soggy Cave, one of Nuffgunk's ladz spoke up.

'Boss? Blowin' up dat throne woz a bit noisy, weren't it?'

'Yeah?' prompted Zograt. He could almost feel the grots behind him exchanging nervous glances.

'Well, ain't been no-grot down 'ere to eat fer weeks,' said another. 'Ain't Da Lurk gunna be 'ungry?'

'Prob'ly is,' agreed Zograt.

'Boss, ain't it gunna eat *us*?' asked the first grot.

Zograt rounded on them. 'Yooz gitz believe I got da Clammy Hand?' he demanded. They nodded hurriedly. Even Skrog rumbled agreement.

'No way yoo coulda give all dem uvver tribes a kickin' if not, boss,' said Driggz. 'Yoo'z da clammyist!'

'So yooz know da Bad Moon chose me,' said Zograt. They nodded again, looking puzzled and scared.

'Da Lurk's gunna do wot I tell it, cos ain't nuffin' dat 'orrible weren't made by da Bad Moon. It ain't gunna eat us grots, ladz.'

They blinked at him. Driggz spoke, hesitantly.

'So… wossit gunna eat den, boss?'

'Humies,' said Zograt with a nasty grin. He turned and limped on into Da Soggy Cave. His grin widened as he heard the scuff and scrape of them following.

It brought Zograt a sense of nostalgia to look upon Da Soggy Cave again. Here, his memories of constant abuse were tempered by recollections of Skrog's boulder-like fist coming down upon Skram Badstabba with awful finality.

All the scrap-hovels around the lake's edge had been demolished and scattered as though hurled about by something in a fit of rage. Some of the glowing fungi that illuminated the space had been torn from the walls or looked to have been chewed. The lake rippled with each water droplet that fell from the stalactites above.

'Maybe Da Lurk ain't 'ere?' asked Driggz.

'Perhaps it's ded,' suggested one of Nuffgunk's ladz.

'It's still 'ere,' said Zograt. He felt the Clammy Hand on his shoulder, its touch firmer than ever before. He felt as though the Bad Moon loomed just over the horizon of his mind. He could feel its sickly light welling within, and it made him feel as though he could achieve anything.

'But I knows it now, don't I?' he said to himself. 'Just cos da Bad Moon put me on dis path, don't mean I ain't gotta walk it meself. Gotta earn a proppa throne.'

'Boss?' asked Driggz.

'Yooz lot stay 'ere,' said Zograt.

Staving off the treacherous worry that he might be making the last and most horrible mistake of his life, he limped down to the lake's edge. Zograt threw his arms wide. He drew a deep breath and cried out, his magically amplified voice booming around Da Soggy Cave.

''Ere I am, ya skwirmy great git! Come an' get me!'

The echoes died away. Water drip-dripped onto the surface of the lake. Zograt heard nervous shuffling behind him. Skrog belched into the silence.

Feeling foolish, Zograt picked up a stone and hurled it into the lake. It vanished with a dull plop.

'Come on! I got places to be!' he shouted. Still, nothing happened. Zograt scowled. 'All right, yoo wanna do it da 'ard way.'

Zograt had crept around Badwater Drop unnoticed for most of his life. He had learned early to stay out of the way when danger threatened, peering unnoticed from hidey-holes as other grots met various messy ends. He had seen Da Lurk surge up from the dark waters to snatch and devour prey. Zograt had watched the monster and worked out, amidst all the thrashing and splashing, what it was. Now, as he gathered his magics and wiggled his fingers, he offered up a prayer to the Bad Moon that he was right.

The first stirrings came almost at once, not from the lake as he'd intended but instead from cracks in the rock walls. Hairy legs twitched. Febrile antennae scented the air. Many-legged insects squirmed into the light, glowing with faint bioluminescence. Fat-bodied arachnids with legs as long as a grot's arm made their stately way from their lairs, placing each step with exaggerated care. Chitinous wings whirred as bloat-roaches took to the air to answer Zograt's silent summons.

He heard yelps of alarm from his grots as first hundreds, then thousands of insects and arachnids were drawn towards him. Some halted near Zograt, forming a mass of shiny bodies and gangly limbs that carpeted the cavern floor. Others scurried up his legs into his robes, clustered on the Spanglestikk, or alighted on his head and shoulders. Still Zograt wiggled his fingers and strained his magics in a mighty summons. He shook and sweated beneath his seething shroud of insects. He felt things squirming about his toes as grubs burrowed up through the rock to answer his call. He worried he might be drowned in bugs before his spell succeeded. He could no longer hear anything but the chitter and scritch of the living mound that was building around him.

Then the surface of the lake churned. Huge bubbles rose and broke. Waves rolled across the waters, snatching insects from the banks. Despite the power of Zograt's summons, many of the bugs drew back in fear.

'Da Lurk!' screeched Driggz.

It erupted from the depths with a deafening hiss. It was a rising column of chitin and glowing gristle. Its nightmarish mandibles clashed like swords as it beat the air with legs longer than Skrog was tall. A forest of antennae waved atop its head, water raining from them as they whipped about like tentacles. Digging talons into the shore to anchor itself, Da Lurk stared down at Zograt with a mutant assortment of eyes. Some were faceted orbs that glittered with a rainbow sheen. Others were sickly yellow slits or bulging black sacs. A few even resembled cunning red grots' eyes.

He glared back at Da Lurk as insects and spiders scurried across his face in a panic. Zograt felt the satisfaction of having been right. Segmapedes could grow really big, but still Da Lurk was the largest specimen he had ever seen. For all Zograt knew, it was the largest segmapede there had ever been. Something had turned it strange. It had mutated and grown to colossal size, perhaps thanks to the touch of the Bad Moon or a diet of magical fungi. Zograt didn't know or care. What mattered was that this terror that had long preyed upon his tribe was an insect, and the Bad Moon had gifted Zograt with the power to command insects.

Water and slimy ropes of drool splattered Zograt like rain, but Da Lurk did not attack. It swayed in time to the wiggling rhythm of his fingers.

'Dat's right, Lurk. Yoo'z mine now,' he crooned. The vast segmapede thrashed its legs and clashed its mandibles, and then began to heave its immense bulk from the waters.

Zograt backed off hurriedly, though he took care not to tread on too many insects as he went. He knew Skrog was his loyal protector, but it still wouldn't do to antagonise the troggoth.

'Wot did yoo do?' shrieked one of Nuffgunk's ladz.

'It's a miracle!' cried Driggz. 'A miracle of da Bad Moon! Da Clammy Hand! Da Gloomspite!'

'Da Gloomspite!' screeched the other grots, catching Driggz's fervour.

Zograt felt power tingling through his body as he watched more and more of Da Lurk emerging from the waters to fill the cavern. He sensed the pull of something from above, as though a force he couldn't see was calling to him just as he had called to Da Lurk. With insects scurrying in every direction and clinging in clots to his body, Zograt turned to his followers.

'Yoo'z right, ladz, Da Gloomspite's coming. I can zoggin' feel it! We need to get back to da 'orde!' They screeched and stamped in answer, and Zograt joined them. If he could feel the Gloom-spite building then it meant that the Bad Moon would surely rise over his exploits, and soon. He limped across the cavern, plotting which tunnels would be wide enough to allow Da Lurk to follow him up to the surface.

It was time to go back to the mountain…

CHAPTER SEVENTEEN

Muttering Peak

Wilhomelda roamed the mountain. She followed tunnels through silver light and dark malevolence and avoided only one. Her pacing carried her up to the highest galleries of Muttering Peak, to where slender stone walkways passed through shafts of grey daylight falling through apertures above, and ancient wind chimes jingled somewhere out of sight. She walked down to the mountain gates to look out upon the pass, and Taremb smouldering at its mouth. She trod silent stairs and lightless chambers that no other member of her coven had even found. Her grasp of time slipped, not aided by the fact that she no longer seemed to require sleep or sustenance. All she needed was to walk, and listen, and see.

Sometimes she talked as she walked, addressing a shadow that kept pace with her in the corners of her wounded eyes.

'You see, Lanette? We become more coherent by the hour, the godbeast and I. We are a blurred image that slowly slides into focus. Axactiar, they called it. Did you know? The ones who worshipped it. You were wrong, dear Lanette. It is no daemon. They did not trap it in that pillar. They bound it there to preserve it, untainted, safe against the very touch of Chaos that you so feared. Together we will defy the gods and their tyranny.'

'Lanette, the visions clear! The whispers are whispers no more. Can you hear them? Do you see? So many possibilities, so many words of warning. They are jumbled still, and they come upon me without my bidding, but I know I can control them. I know I can see and hear. I just need time.'

Her feet always brought her back to the pillar chamber. It was never empty these days. Even when Lanette wasn't walking at her side, she passed knots of Borster's engineers and her own wizards, who frowned over whirring machines and performed obscure tests. Wilhomelda wasn't blind to the fear that crossed their faces when they saw her, the glances they thought they hid. She was under no illusion that she was changing in body as well as in mind, and supposed to those who did not understand, her transformation might seem alarming. Her footfalls were lighter than they had been, as though they barely brushed the ground. Her tattered robes did not fit as they should. Her eyesight, when it cleared of visions, had altered again just as she had been adjusting to the distortion caused by her circlet. Now it seemed as though she saw more, not just before her but all around. That seemed appropriate, she supposed. Axactiar gave her greater breadth of sight, and she was glad of it.

Each time she reached the pillar chamber she walked to its heart and pressed one long-fingered hand against the crystal. Each time it appeared to her that she reached a little higher up from the pillar's base. The dark shape within the crystal looked ever more diffuse and diminished.

Borster, Gillighasp, even Ulke had sought to arrest her wanderings. They spoke to her in half-heard voices about the need to perform tests, of her need to rest, of their desire to consult her on important matters. They spoke of strange tremors, spoiled food, damp and mould spreading through the lower chambers.

She brushed them away.

'They do not understand, Lanette. There is only one important matter, and that is the Leering Face.'

It interrupted her visions, waxing until it filled her mind's eye. Its smile was wide, filled with teeth like jagged rocks. Its eyes were craters, deep and dark and mocking.

Wilhomelda could tell that Axactiar was as frustrated and alarmed by the Leering Face as she. Its voice and hers were one now; it was a dominant strand within the weft and weave of her own inner monologue even when it whispered words of prophecy. Yet she heard Axactiar's anger, and something she worried might be fear.

'What can frighten a godbeast, Lanette? Whatever it is, we must be ready. Until it is dealt with, we cannot do all we said we would do. We cannot rival the might of the gods while the Leering Face looms before us.'

Instinct told her that whatever peril was gathering around the mountain, her attack against Taremb had not banished it. Wilhomelda needed to know more, but until she did her path seemed clear. She could tell her followers were confused and alarmed by her commands, but she insisted, and they obeyed. The mountain would be guarded night and day, the pass too. Taremb would be garrisoned and its walls held. Wilhomelda needed more time. For the sake of all she had sacrificed already, and all that she could do with this power, she was willing to pay whatever price she must.

A howdah had been lashed to Arghabigskuttla's back, to serve as transport for the warchiefs of the horde. Most rode in it: Zograt and Skrog, the latter of whom clung on uttering groans of displeasure; Bigg Leggzgit; the Gobbapalooza; Nuffgunk; Driggz with his bosspole; Boss Ploddit, having forsaken his wagon; even

Frazzdak, the newly appointed boss of the Flashbanditz. It had been Chief Kreepzogga's idea, though he eschewed the howdah himself in favour of riding Bitebite. At Zograt's insistence, Ploddit's ladz had been permitted to lend their aid in its construction. The result was a swaying contraption of chitin, scrap iron, webbing and ropes. Zograt thought it looked quite formidable.

He had been concerned that even the enormous spider might not be able to heft the weight of the armoured howdah. If Arghabigskuttla was struggling, however, she hid it well. The Arachnarok marched through the Shudderwood at such a relentless pace that the bulk of Zograt's horde had to scurry to keep up.

The ground shuddered in the grip of random tremors, and the forest canopy swished as though dragged hither and thither by a wind none could feel. Zograt felt the tug of the Gloomspite dancing through his limbs and filling him with savage vigour.

It was clear the rest of the horde felt it too. In previous days the punishing pace would have caused squabbles and desertion. Now, be it foot-slogging grots, spider riders scuttling through the treetops, bounding packs of squigs or lumbering troggoths, they all made tireless haste. Some of the bravest grots had scaled the chitinous flanks of Da Lurk and attempted to ride the colossal segmapede as it flowed through the forest like a river of shifting plates and rippling legs. Zograt had a good chuckle every time another would-be bug rider lost his grip and vanished beneath Da Lurk's talons.

'Ain't scared o' Shudderwood monsters no more!' cried Nuffgunk, shaking with excitement. 'Dey be scared of us!'

'Not jus' dem, neither,' said Wabber Spakklegit, from his perch above Arghabigskuttla's head. He'd almost come to blows with Bigg Leggzgit over that seating arrangement, with only Zograt's threatened intercession preventing blood being spilled. 'Da humies ain't gunna know wot 'it 'em!'

'Bad Moon'z on its way, ladz, ya can feel it!' screeched Ploddit, brandishing his prodda over his head.

'Bad Mooooooon,' echoed Da Fung, executing a clumsy twirl. Tiny scuttle-legged mushrooms popped into being as he spun and scurried madly about the howdah.

'We'z gunna smash 'em,' said Frazzdak, sounding keen to be included. The Flashbanditz boss had mostly lurked in a corner of the howdah and looked awkward since they had mounted up.

'Yoo ain't wrong,' Zograt replied. He was conscious that the Flashbanditz were mostly hated and feared by the rest of his horde and had done what he could to include them when he got the chance. 'Da Bad Moon'z coming–'

'Bad Mooooooon!' sang Da Fung again.

'And wiv da Bad Moon'z power I'z gunna show everygit I'm da Loonking!'

Da Fung stopped twirling and blinked his huge red eyes. He seemed to consider for a moment before blurting, 'Baaaaad Kiiiiing!'

This caused cackling to break out amongst the warchiefs.

'Give 'im a chance, Fung, 'e ain't zogged it up yet,' laughed Nuffgunk.

Zograt glared around with a jaundiced eye, then snorted in exasperated amusement. He would never be stupid enough to trust his lieutenants; most would likely still put a slitta in his back if he gave them the chance. But he was surprised to feel a strange sort of camaraderie. Putting it down to the intoxicating effect of the Bad Moon's approach, he pressed on with his speech.

'Da point is, ladz, yeah da Gloomspite'z comin', but dat means we *gotta* get dis right. Da Bad Moon'z gunna be up dere, an' we gotta make sure it enjoys da show!'

'So, wot we gunna do, boss?' asked Driggz, who Zograt had earlier primed to deliver this line and now did so with gusto.

'Glad ya asked, Driggzy, cos I gotta plan. But get dis in yer 'eads, ya gitz, it's gunna mean workin' togevver. Don't waste yer time backstabbin' each uvver, not while dere's humies to backstab furst! We start off by sendin' some o' da Twitchleggz to scuttle over da walls an' get a proppa eyeball of da humie defences...'

As Arghabigskuttla lurched on into the evening mists, Zograt outlined his plan.

In the dark of night, with lurid aurorae dancing across the skies and the ground quivering like a frightened beast, Zograt's horde launched their attack upon Taremb. There was no attempt at stealth. Zograt's scouts had warned him the humies were already manning their defences as though expecting a fight.

They had also revealed, however, that swathes of the town were fire-damaged, collapsed or beset by eruptions of glowing fungi and plagues of insects. Confidence bolstered by the scouts' words, Zograt Da Skwurm ordered an all-out attack.

Standing atop his war howdah, he watched his horde lurch into battle. His orders had spread by thumping signal drum, grotesque messenger fungi, and good old-fashioned yelling. Now Zograt felt a glow of satisfaction as he saw them being, for the most part, obeyed.

Boss Ploddit had returned to his wagons, which rattled up the slope on the horde's right flank. They followed Big Limpy and his Troggherd. Zograt was amused to see Ploddit's ladz still making a show of herding the troggoths.

'As though dey's followin' your orders,' he muttered.

On the left flank, Kreepzogga and his Twitchleggz were racing Boss Hoppit's Squigalanche towards the walls. Zograt saw they were rapidly outstripping the rest of the horde, but he had expected this. So long as Kreepzogga and Hoppit kept their mobs heading in the right direction, he reckoned they would spread enough mayhem to let the main horde advance virtually unmolested.

The centre of the line was where Zograt had marshalled his

Badwater Boyz, led by Nuffgunk. Their ranks were swollen by the Flashbanditz and various smaller bands of grots who had flocked to Zograt's bosspole during his march through the Shudderwood. All felt the pull of the Bad Moon. He doubted they could have resisted even had they wished to. Naffs Gabrot lurked about behind the grot masses, perched atop his Boingob skull as Gobzit lugged him back and forth. Naffs was waving his arms and doing his best Glareface dance. Zograt suspected his efforts would be largely irrelevant. The frothing horde needed little encouragement to charge in the right direction.

Scattered along the battle line were Flashbanditz shamans, easily visible thanks to their lurid glow-paint and the green corposant dancing about their staves. Zograt planned to get some payback on the humie wizards with his Spanglestikk, but he knew he couldn't be everywhere at once. He had thus entrusted his shamans with the task of countering the humies' magic.

Wabber had brought Arghabigskuttla in just behind the chanting masses of Badwater Boyz and Flashbanditz, where Zograt could drink in the gestalt power of so many greenskins on the warpath and enjoy the clangour of their drums, gongs and wailing squigpipes.

Da Lurk had not yet taken to the field. Zograt had used his powers to force the colossal segmapede to hide just inside the treeline. He knew when he wanted to unleash his secret weapon. It wasn't quite yet.

''Ere it comes,' he said.

'Wot?' asked Stragwit. Sudden gunfire crackled atop the translucent wood of the outer wall, causing the Brewgit to jump in fright and drop his tin mug.

'Dat,' said Zograt. He watched as bullets punched into the horde. Troggoths lurched as rounds burst from their backs. Grots fell, to be trampled by their comrades, or were shot off the backs of their squigs and spiders.

'Ain't as bad as last time, boss,' said Driggz.

'Didn't fink it would be,' replied Zograt. 'If dey's protectin' da inside wall an' da outside wall, an' dey been 'avin' fights while we woz away, dere's gunna be loads more of us dan last time but less o' dem. Gotta spread 'emselves out.'

Driggz frowned as he tried to keep up with Zograt's strategic appraisal.

'So... dey's da runt, and we'z da biggun dis time?'

'Ded right, Driggzy!' exclaimed Zograt. 'Dey's da runt!'

A stray bullet whipped past Zograt's ear. It ricocheted off a rusty helmet nailed to the bosspole before hitting Stragwit Skrab in the head. Blood sprayed across the surprised Gobbapalooza. The Brewgit was slapped face down into the deck of the howdah, the back of his skull a pulped mess. The contents of his still spilled everywhere, causing the assembled warchiefs to hop and curse as it scalded their feet. Arghabigskuttla squealed as runnels of brew spattered her back.

'Bang!' announced Da Fung, then fell on his face in imitation.

As Stragwit's former mates descended to pick his corpse clean of valuables, and Da Fung paddled happily, Zograt and Driggz stared at one another.

'Runtz is still dangerous, eh, boss?' said Driggz. Zograt scowled and turned back to the muzzle flashes and gun smoke atop the walls.

'Yeah, we is,' he snarled, raising the Spanglestikk. With a wiggle of his fingers, Zograt sent a bolt of green lightning arcing over the horde to slam into the wall top. There was a deafening crack and a blinding green flash. When the spots cleared from Zograt's eyes he saw he had blasted a crater wider than Big Limpy was tall. Any humies unlucky enough to have been standing on that section of the fire step were doubtless drifting ashes now. Green fire ate into the wood.

Zograt's horde gave a ragged cheer and redoubled their pace. Clouds of black-fletched arrows rose from the grot ranks to rattle down amongst the half-seen defenders. Greenskin magic blossomed as the Flashbanditz shamans chanted and stamped. Spectral green fists battered the translucent ramparts. Bolts of lurid ectoplasm splashed the wall, sizzling as they ate away at wood and screaming defenders alike.

To Zograt's left, the anarchic cavalry charge of Twitchleggz and Squig Hoppers crested the wall without slowing. Guns cracked, bones crunched, and human voices rose in suddenly silenced screams.

On the right, Big Limpy had also reached the wall. Zograt could see bullets punching into the huge troggoth. Gun smoke rolled thick along the wall top as the defenders poured everything they had into their towering attacker. Limpy considered the scene with ponderous curiosity. Then he swept one huge fist along the fire step and sent broken human bodies tumbling. The colossal troggoth tilted his head back and bellowed so loudly that, even at a distance, Zograt covered his ears and cowered. Big Limpy took a lurching step directly into the wall and, as lashed trunks and cross-beams splintered, just kept going. Grots cheered and gongs clanged as a wide section of the wall collapsed inwards before Limpy, and the huge troggoth led his herd through the breach.

By the time Arghabigskuttla reached the outer wall, every defender had been slain or had fled. Grots poured through a plethora of gaps. The outer gate had been flattened by Flashbanditz spells.

'Take 'er majesty through dere,' Zograt commanded Wabber. The Boggleye turned to the huge spider, which obediently scuttled through the sundered gateway and into the no man's land between the outer and inner walls.

The scene beyond caused Zograt to beam with malice and pride. Spectral figures had risen again from the churned ground to prey upon his grots, but this time they were having the worst of it.

'Dis time yoo'z da prey, ya spooky gitz,' he snarled. Flashbanditz shamans capered and cackled as they blasted spells into the apparitions. Shadow-creatures burst apart with indistinct wails. Here and there Zograt saw a gaggle of grots set upon one another as the spectres' powers took hold. Off to his left a geyser of green ectoplasm burst skyward as an unlucky shaman's head exploded amidst the tides of greenskin excitement. Despite these minor setbacks, it was evident that the shadow-creatures didn't stand a chance of panicking his horde this time around.

Zograt sent a blast of sorcery blazing down to erase two of the ghastly spirits as Arghabigskuttla stalked past. Grot mobs surged around the spider's legs, chanting praise to the Bad Moon and to Zograt as they hammered their gongs for all they were worth.

The inner wall still showed the scars of his previous attack, most notably around its gatehouse. Rubble and stonework had been piled into the breach where the gate had stood, but the barrier was nothing like as formidable as it had been. That said, Zograt could see lots of defenders, both lining the battlements and packed in behind their stone barricade. He spotted the blocky shapes of gun carriages dotted here and there. Braziers burned along the defence line, while above, the sickly aurorae danced and whirled faster than ever.

'Come on, ya gitz,' muttered Zograt. 'Wot else ya got? Bad Moon'z comin' an' yooz can't stop it.'

As though they had heard him, the defenders unleashed everything they had upon Zograt's horde. Bolts of sorcerous lightning leapt from the skies to explode amidst the greenskin ranks. Troggoths lurched to a halt, transformed into surprised-looking gold statues or frozen inside mounds of ice. Zograt snarled as he saw wildfire leaping amidst Ploddit's wagons. First one then another of the ramshackle constructions was consumed as the dancing flames raced over them with unnatural speed. Tongues of fire formed leering faces that devoured wagons, mugger beetles and scream-ing grots alike. Zograt was about to direct his own magics against the spell when a gaggle of Flashbanditz beat him to it. Under their combined assault the wildfire sputtered and shrieked before dying away to leave half a dozen blackened wrecks in its wake.

Bullets rained down on the horde. Artillery pieces whooshed and boomed as they spat rockets and hurtling metal balls into the greenskins. Big Limpy roared as a salvo of projectiles tore off one of his arms. The huge limb crashed to the ground as troggoth blood fell like rain around it. Limpy thrashed and stomped in agony, crushing several smaller troggoths. Then he reached down, picked up his severed arm like a club, and lumbered on.

Zograt's battle line wavered under the furious onslaught. Shamans and wizards duelled, conjuring and extinguishing spells. Bullets and arrows whipped back and forth. Naffs Gabrot thundered about, intercepting fleeing handfuls of grots and scaring them back into line.

'Zog me, dey ain't muckin' about!' shouted Skutbad Da Leg; he and the rest of the Gobbapalooza had ducked behind the howdah's armoured plates, along with Bigg Leggzgit. Skrog hauled himself to his feet and swayed forward, placing his bulk between Zograt and the firestorm.

'No need fer dat dis time, lad,' said Zograt. 'Fung, send dem message 'shroomz!'

Craning out from his hiding place, Da Fung willed a flock of winged fungi into being. They fluttered off into the darkness and dancing firelight. As they went, Zograt furrowed his brow, planted the Spanglestikk before him, and wiggled the fingers of both hands madly.

'Let's see ya deal wiv dis, ya gitz!' he screeched.

At first, the rumble was barely audible over the cacophony of battle. Then came a rending crash as Da Lurk slammed into a sagging section of the outer wall and flattened it. The monstrous insect didn't even slow, flowing like a rushing river of chitin and pistoning legs towards the inner wall. Screams rose from the battlements. Zograt saw humans pointing, gun barrels turned in the monster's direction as it raced across the open ground. Grots scattered from its path as it bore down upon the barricaded gap in the inner wall.

Gun crews swung artillery pieces to bear upon Da Lurk. Barely a handful of projectiles had flown its way when a ululating war cry rose from behind the wall. Zograt cackled with glee as Chief Kreepzogga and a tide of spider riders fell upon the gun crews from behind. They had followed Zograt's orders, not simply to attack the inner wall but to use their steeds' agility to bypass it and rush back along its inner face to attack the breach from behind. Boss Hoppit's ladz could still be seen in the distance, bounding madly along the wall top without a care for Zograt's plan, but it didn't matter. Even with Kreepzogga's diminished numbers, his assault had the desired effect.

The fire directed against Da Lurk slackened. Heedless of the craters blasted in its chitin, and the scattering of severed legs left in its wake, the colossal segmapede hit the rubble barricade and flowed right over it. A wizard screamed as he was snatched in the monster's mandibles and raised high before being bitten in half. Masked soldiers were crushed under Da Lurk's talons or fled for their lives back through the breach.

Zograt watched his secret weapon tear through the defenders then rush onward into the town. Raising the Spanglestikk and wiggling his fingers, he unleashed a fungal curse upon a trio of human wizards attempting to restore order. They howled as their bodies burst into swelling masses of glowing fungi. Down on the ground, Zograt saw Nuffgunk leading the charge through the breach with a great mass of Badwater Boyz all around him. Further off, Big Limpy was belabouring the battlements with his own severed arm while Rockgut troggoths tore through the stonework.

'We'z got 'em, boss!' screeched Driggz, waving the bosspole like a lunatic. As though in answer, the ground shuddered so violently that even Arghabigskuttla stumbled. Hanging on to the howdah, Zograt watched wide-eyed as cracks raced through the ground and up the wall. They yawned like jagged mouths. Grots and humans tumbled into the rents only to be vomited back out amidst masses of corpse-pale fungi. The strange blooms grew with incredible speed, swelling and thickening to veritable tree trunks in moments. Atop each bloomed a leering effigy of the Bad Moon. Within moments, a forest of hideous moon-fungi swayed around the inner wall. Great chunks of stonework fell, torn loose by burrowing mycelia, some taking screaming defenders with them in showers of rubble and dust.

Mad elation filled Zograt. He had never seen such a clear sign of the Bad Moon's favour. His warchiefs scrambled from cover to perform a wild war dance, kicking aside the pillaged corpse of Stragwit in their excitement. Bigg Leggzgit scrambled past Wabber and leapt down onto Arghabigskuttla's back, waving his staff and billowing his web-cloak like bat wings.

'Get stuck in, ladz!' yelled Zograt, his voice a thunderous boom. 'Kill 'em! Smash 'em! Stab 'em up an' grab dere shinies! Da Bad Moon'z comin'!'

Loon-tremors convulsed the ground as Arghabigskuttla bore Zograt and his lieutenants through the breach. Beyond the walls was bloody anarchy. Buildings had collapsed, strewing rubble across the streets. Cobbled roads were rent by dripping chasms above which fatted moon-fungi nodded. A trail of devastation showed where Da Lurk had ploughed headlong into the human settlement, levelling structures and spreading carnage as it went. Big Limpy loomed over the rooftops, clubbing at something out of sight with his dismembered arm.

Soldiers and wizards fought back where they could. They were joined by terrified-looking mobs of humans wielding burning torches, tools and farming implements. None could hold back Zograt's rampaging hordes, however. Grots fell upon the defenders in howling mobs, stabbing madly and looting their victims. Zograt saw a grot emerge from a scrum brandishing a bloodied pitchfork.

'It ain't bent, and look at da size o' it!' screeched the triumphant grot. 'Praise da Bad Moon!'

Zograt saw a human in elaborate armour leading a counter-charge up a side street beneath a fluttering banner. She shot a grot through the head point-blank then skewered another as her soldiers laid about with swords and shields. Zograt prepared to lob a spell their way when a bounding mass of squigs plummeted from the nearby rooftops with grots clinging on for dear life. Boss Hoppit slammed down atop the human officer, his huge squig crushing her into the cobbles in a spray of blood.

'Boss, look!' gasped Driggz, tugging at Zograt's sleeve and causing surprised bugs to fall from its folds. Zograt followed Driggz's pointing finger and his eyes grew wide.

Over the rooftops loomed the mountain. From behind its jagged peak a titanic shape was rising, rendering the mountain in sil-houette with its sickly yellow-green radiance. Zograt looked upon the leering features of his god as it waxed fat and the clouds fled from it as if in terror.

The aurorae were lost amidst the Bad Moon's glow, which swelled until it filled the entire sky. Where its light fell upon the settle-ment Zograt saw fungi bursting from wood, stone and even the flesh of the screaming defenders.

'Zog me...' breathed Zograt.

'Bad Mooooon! Bad Mooooon!' hollered Da Fung, hallucinatory fungi of every shape and size popping in and out of existence about his head.

'Praise da Bad Moon!' screeched Driggz. The horde took up the cry, many screaming and hollering until their eyes bulged and their jaws frothed.

Zograt felt their elation, yet as he stared up at the mountain, he saw again the vision of the staring eye within its dark chasm. He felt the dread power lurking within the peak and knew this battle was far from over.

'Da Bad Moon'z 'ere, but dat don't mean we won yet!' he said, rapping the Spanglestikk on the deck of the howdah to get his chiefs' attention. 'Bet yoo dere's still a buncha humies in dis town wot'll fight back if we give 'em a chance, speshully dem humie shamans. An' da horde'z gone loony, dey's all over da place!'

'Da humies is down, boss, we just gotta keep kickin', said Wabber with a nasty grin.

'Wotever is up in da mountin, it ain't beaten yet,' insisted Zograt. 'Dat's da power I came for, an' dis ain't done 'til I got it. A proppa grot wins a fight wiv a stab in da back. Dat's wot da Bad Moon came to see, an' dat's wot we'z gunna give it. Fung, send some more 'shroomz. Get dem to find Nuffgunk an' Kreepzogga and tell dem to keep da humies busy. If dey can, dey should push on through da town an' 'ave a crack at da mountin. Wabber, get 'er majesty movin'. We're gunna sneak up da side of da mountin, find a nice hole to crawl in through, an' finish this fight off proppa!'

'Gotcha, boss,' said Wabber before issuing sing-song instructions to his enormous pet. As Arghabigskuttla set off through the mayhem, Zograt whistled and pointed the Spanglestikk at a passing mob of grots.

'Oi, yooz lot, many as ya can 'op aboard. Yer Loonking needs ya. We got some stabbin' to do!'

CHAPTER EIGHTEEN

The Epicentre

Wilhomelda floated in a haze of visions. Scenes played out before her, one overlapping the next, manifesting as ghosts then solidifying until they seemed more real than her actual surroundings, only to break apart and flow into other possibilities, other futures. At times the flood was overwhelming. She guessed that had she still been wholly mortal with a mere human's mind, she would have been lucky just to be driven mad by the prophetic onslaught.

Axactiar's flowing monologue was as clear and relentless as the visions. Its voice was her voice, sometimes ringing in her mind, sometimes spilling from her lips.

'...but should the people of the Grey Vale choose instead to resist then the dead that walk shall be turned aside upon that battlefield providing only that the Smiling Prince can be prevailed upon first to change his allegiance, but before such time shall the fruit rot upon the vine of chances within the court of the Screaming Deeps where time and again those who fear to seize the hopes that once they had spiral ever downward unto the abyss in which their last redemption awaits like a glimmering star that burns the brighter for the darkness, and should the power be seized, yes, should we grasp that might before they see their hope then instead it will be turned to fire within our hand and set against the ones who stand in shadow beneath the comet's light, yet then will… will… rises again the Leering Face!'

Wilhomelda was jarred back to reality by the intrusion of the Leering Face. It took her time to grasp her surroundings, as though she sought to read words that were too large and too near. She realised she was hanging several feet off the ground amidst the wreckage of her chambers. As it always seemed to now, her presence bathed everything in silvery radiance that caused the shadows to shift in strange ways.

'The Leering Face,' she breathed. Cinders danced on her breath, blackening to ash as they drifted towards the ceiling and crumbled to nothing.

'Magister! Please! Can you hear me?'

Wilhomelda was surprised to find someone else in her chambers. She heard frustration in their voice, and was that anger? It was becoming more difficult for her to decipher such things. She already struggled to recall a time when she had been prone to such crude emotions. Had she really feared the powers of the gods? Had she really planned so base a use for Axactiar's might as simple prophecy, to shield the mortal creatures she considered under her protection? Had she sought to convince herself that such were her motivations?

At least, Wilhomelda reflected, the higher state to which she was ascending allowed her to see and to understand how self-deceiving and simplistic her ambitions had been. She had simply been frightened, and in her fear she had apportioned blame so she would not have to reflect upon her own failings.

Fear; resentment; arrogance; she saw it clearly now. She who had been so determined never to be the servant, never to be controlled or trapped. In the name of protecting those she held dear, she had sacrificed the very life that mattered the most to her and been blind to her self-deception.

At least now, she thought, she could–

'Magister, for Sigmar's sakes, *please!*'

Wilhomelda blinked, eyelids sliding around the metal barbs that had fused into the corners of her eyes. She had become distracted again, she realised. How easy it was to overlook mortals when one operated upon a higher plain. But she dimly recalled that she had a responsibility to the creatures whom she had led to this place.

With an effort of will she narrowed the focus of her mind to fully perceive the being before her. Its name fell from her lips in cinders.

'**Vikram.**'

The big engineer looked damaged, she realised. A livid burn marred his cheek. Soot blackened his skin and she noticed odd little welts on his flesh as though he had picked at many small round scabs. Even as she watched he scratched the back of his hand, breaking off a protrusion that was at once his own flesh and yet something delicate and fungal. Wilhomelda did not remember the man suffering such an affliction before. She focused harder on him and realised he was speaking to her.

'They're everywhere! Bloody everywhere! Taremb's completely overrun. We lost Sigmar knows how many good souls in the attack, and even more in the pullback down the pass. For the heavens' sakes, what's the bloody point of you turning into...' He choked on his words as he gestured wildly at her. 'Into whatever *this* is, if you don't help us? I thought you were going to use the godbeast to protect the coven?'

Wilhomelda watched curiously. He was clearly agitated. She realised something must be happening in the here and now that merited her attention.

'What is it, Vikram?' she asked. 'What has happened?'

He gaped at her, flushing such an ugly shade of red that she thought perhaps his strange ailment was going to kill him. He balled his fists and bit out strangled words.

'What use was all this if you don't even know what's bloody well happening? The greenskins, Wilhomelda! They came back! I told you this. They've attacked Taremb. Sigmar's throne, there's thousands of them, and they've got... monsters... And then... the moon...' Borster's words faltered. He crossed his arms across his chest and hugged himself in an almost childlike gesture of fear.

'Moon?' she asked, unable to determine whether she had simply lost the thread of his linear communication amidst the possible words he might have spoken, or whether he had ceased making sense. This seemed to anger him again.

'Yes, the bloody moon! Have you not seen? Did that... *thing*... in your head not warn you about that?'

She smiled. She could not help it. So limited an understanding of what was right before his eyes, and he had the temerity to call himself an engineer.

'It is not in my head, Vikram,' she explained, reaching for simplified concepts he would understand. 'Axactiar is me, now, and I am Axactiar. We are one. The ancients did not entrap us within the mountain. They enshrined us there, that we might remain safe and sheltered through all the long years of the Time of Dark Gods. To think, Wilhomelda-that-was deceived herself that we called her here, that she was special, chosen...'

Borster kicked a spar of broken wood across the chamber.

'What the bloody heavens are you rambling about?' he screamed at her. Wilhomelda was unperturbed. Mortals were given to strong emotions when they did not understand, or when they felt threatened by truths they did not wish to know. She remembered her own frailties in that regard all too well.

'It was a chrysalis, Vikram. The pillar. The mountain. A chrysalis must be hardened to protect the being transforming within,
do you see? We needed that confinement to refine. To distil.
We could touch upon the minds of mortals, and it is true that
it intrigued us and brought us amusement to toy with them. I
believe they called them Listeners, did they not? Poor Jocundas.'

Wilhomelda chuckled and was surprised to see Borster flinch.
She tried for a more solicitous tone. She had not meant to alarm
him.

'Try to comprehend, Vikram. To the I-that-was-Axactiar-alone,
the centuries of confinement were not long at all. Whispering
to the Listeners, choosing which to influence and which to shun,
this was merely the idle sport of one who drips water from a
fingertip to see which way each drop will trickle when it lands.
But then came the Leering Face, fatted and foul, looming over
all that I-that-was-Axactiar could foresee.'

To her surprise, this got Borster's attention.

'Yes! The bloody moon! So, you *did* see this coming, you just
didn't give a beggar's shit for the rest of us? Is that the way of it?'

'Why do you speak of the moon so? Which moon, Vikram?
There are many, that are, that have been, that could be.'

He pointed to the window. Intrigued, Wilhomelda turned her
gaze that way and realised as she focused that a sickly pale light
spilled through it. Where it fell, fungal blooms were colonising
the broken remains of her possessions. She was fascinated to see
that several strange growths had even emerged from glass shards
and the whorled stone of the floor.

'Just look,' he told her, voice shaking with emotion. 'But don't
let the light touch you.'

As Wilhomelda drifted across her chambers she realised she
had not completed her explanation to Borster.

'It was the Leering Face that made I-that-was-Axactiar realise that the mountain was no longer a safe haven. Something that could blot out all of our visions was anathema and to be avoided. Was it chance that brought I-that-was-Wilhomelda to this place then, Vikram? Fate? The machinations, perhaps, of some other deity as yet unseen? While the Leering Face continues to interfere, we cannot know. But you must understand that Axactiar's sphere of influence incorporates not only knowledge of all possible futures, but also mortals' lack of those insights and the fears and doubts that lack causes. Axactiar's pupation was not complete, Vikram. I-that-was-the-pupal-godbeast sought a host. I-that-was-Axactiar knew just how to tempt and to provoke I-that-was-Wilhomelda, whose power, and fear, and lust for control offered the perfect means by which escape could be effected from the–'

She halted as she reached the window. Wilhomelda ignored the poisonous light bathing her, the growths that burst from her flesh only to puff away as cinder and ash. She stared up into the sky at the grotesque celestial body filling it from horizon to horizon, whose unnatural luminosity seemed to curdle the waves of the Umbralic Sea. The moon's gaze was fixed on her. Its canyon maw was twisted into a mocking grin so wide it looked set to split the entire celestial body in two. As Wilhomelda watched, glowing shards plummeted from the moon, resolving into huge chunks of glowing stone that raised geysers as they splashed down in the ocean. She felt the mountain tremble around her and knew that more of the projectiles had slammed into its slopes.

'The Leering Face,' she breathed. She heard Vikram speaking again and realised that he was chanting a fragment of rhyme.

'Don't let him see you, little one, don't let him hear you cry, or down into the darksome depths, he'll bear you off to die.'

Wilhomelda swept across the chamber. She was dimly aware of Borster scrambling from her path, but he swiftly lost resolution as she allowed her visions to return. Images danced through her mind's eye. Threads of peril and potential slithered between her twitching fingers.

Soldiers, mages and engineers fight and die in the pass as greenskins press them back. The glass-smooth ground is awash with blood from which sprouts mutant fungi. Hails of sorcerous daggers and spectral tendrils stab and strangle. Diminutive attackers fall but the huge beasts that lumber in their midst cannot be stopped. War engines are smashed aside. Human lives are snuffed one after another. Insects squirm through open wounds and gnaw on the gelid flesh of eyes. Something dark and huge rushes through the midst of the battle and collides with the mountain gates...

Far to the south Tarembite messengers lean low on the necks of their mounts, urging them to greater speed. They know danger is all around them for these are hard and wild lands, yet their fear is not for that, but instead for the poisoned glow that taints the northern horizon. They cannot know what horrors transpire amidst the ruins of a home they still believe they can save. They know only that their message is more vital than ever, and that the realmgates lie ahead...

In one vision after another she soars into battle against the greenskin invaders and glories in unleashing her powers upon them. They burn and scatter as ashes. They writhe amidst fracturing possibilities until they are torn to temporal tatters. They are swallowed by shadow and seared by light. Yet in every vision there is something she does not see that creeps and slithers and she feels it suddenly like a questing worm boring through the meat of her mind and she looks up to see the Leering Face fill her vision...

And at last, she has it, the elusive strand that squirms like a parasite lodged deep in living flesh, writhing away from the clutching fingertips of one who seeks so desperately to tear it free. She sees an aperture in the mountainside, sees a bloated thing of legs and eyes and glittering malice that bears with it a brood that is a poison that is a dagger that if left unchecked will slide into her back and spread its taint through her and her mountain alike...

Wilhomelda refocused on the now. Borster cowered in the doorway to her chambers. She saw the smouldering trail she had left in her wake and wondered belatedly whether the engineer would have perished had he not moved aside. She dismissed the notion as irrelevant, not worth slipping backwards through possibilities to discern.

He lived.

He was present.

He was still of use.

'Vikram, there is danger,' she told him.

'There's worse than bloody danger, this is the end!' he cried. 'We're trapped in this damned mountain. We need a way out! You have to save us like you promised you would!'

'The mountain will endure. We have power enough to see it thus. But a threat unseen rises even as the lesser perils seek to seem the greater. We have guards still within the mountain, do we not?'

Borster gaped. Wilhomelda felt the tug of fate grow more insistent. She did not have the time to waste upon mortal frailties. She did not require his understanding, only his obedience. Aiding her was in his own interests also. She allowed a strand of her power to uncoil from her fingertips and ripple around him. Borster stiffened and cried out as patches of cloth and skin turned to cinders then drifting ash.

'Vikram, focus. There are still guards within the mountain, yes? They were not all sent to defend the gates?'

He cowered, accusation in his eyes, but when she raised her hand in threat a second time he replied.

'Yes, heavens curse you and send us back Ezocheen, yes there's guards in the bloody mountain. Why?'

'Rally them to the passageways around the third northern

gallery. The true threat approaches from that quarter. You, Ulke and Gillighasp will lead them.'

'Don't know everything, do you?' he panted, scowling. 'Ulke's dead. Took poison when we realised we were trapped. Last I knew Gillighasp was down at the gates, though Sigmar knows if he's still alive.'

'You will do this then,' she replied, mildly irritated that he could not grasp the important strand amongst irrelevant details.

'Half the passages around there are malevolent,' Borster said.

'The mountain holds no fears for us now, Vikram. It is ours to do with as we will, for are we not within and without?'

He seemed angered afresh by something she had said. Wilhomelda was glad when Borster shook his head and retreated. She knew with many overlapping certainties that he would follow her commands. The man was a fighter, for all his mortal faults, and that would make him useful for a little longer at least. She, meanwhile, had her own task in this moment. Vikram and a handful of soldiers alone would not be enough to stave off the blade of the Leering Face. Wilhomelda drifted into the corridor and extended her powers. Coiling ropes of silver light and dancing embers caressed the closest arches, pulsing in time with them then driving deep. She shuddered as the power of Muttering Peak flowed through her. She felt every tunnel and chamber like extensions of her own body. She extended her senses both in the present and the future, alive for the insect-leg tickle that would tell her where her enemies were, and where they soon would be.

There it was. She felt it, clambering up the northern slope some way below. She sensed a thrumming vibration of sorcerous power there, a thorn pricking her flesh that she knew bore poison.

'One of them carries a weapon,' she murmured. 'The weapon of the Leering Face. Prevent that, prevent it all.'

* * *

The journey up the mountainside had not been pleasant. The rock face had proved treacherous, even for a creature like Arghabigskuttla. Solid stone crumbled at the touch of her talons and slid away down the slopes. Cracks that offered purchase closed like mouths upon the spider's legs, while jutting spars were there one moment and gone the next amidst the thin mists of the higher slopes.

Worse, the howdah had not been built with climbing in mind. There were no restraints, as had rapidly become apparent when the overcrowded structure tilted from horizontal to near vertical. Zograt had hastily conjured a mycelial net that enmeshed Skrog and the grots, and had prevented most of them from tumbling to their deaths.

As the cords binding the howdah to Arghabigskuttla began to groan, Zograt had sent more fungal strands worming their way through its structure then looping about the Arachnarok's abdomen. All the same, the ascent had been a terrifying and drawn-out form of torture as Zograt waited for his magics to give out, the howdah to break apart and spill them into thin air, or Arghabigskuttla to lose her grip and fall.

Now he spotted a gaping aperture in the slopes above, a darker patch of shadow and unnaturally hard edges amidst the jagged rocks.

'Get us in dere,' he screeched at Wabber. The Boggleye crooned instructions to Arghabigskuttla. Legs scrabbling, flagging with exhaustion, the spider made a last lunge for the hole. Zograt's stomach did a backflip as straps snapped with gunshot cracks and the howdah lurched. Shrill screams of terror filled the air as Arghabigskuttla heaved herself up, and then into the gap.

It occurred to Zograt belatedly that they didn't know how wide the aperture was, hadn't been able to see from their angle of approach. He released a shaky breath as they swept through a wide gap and into the oddly curved chamber beyond.

Zograt had time to take in a huge space, lit by silver strands embedded in the walls, floor and ceiling. Then he spotted humans lurking in the tunnel mouths that led from the cave. They had guns.

'Look out, ladz!' he yelled, wiggling his fingers to disintegrate his fungal restraints. The howdah slid off the spider's back, tipped over entirely and crashed down on its side. Zograt and his followers were hurled through the air, tumbling to a stop amidst a rain of fungal slop.

Bullets whipped around Zograt as he staggered to his feet. Something huge moved in his peripheral vision, then Skrog was there, shielding him. Shock gave way to anger as Zograt heard him grunt with bullet impacts.

''Ow did dey know we woz comin'?' screeched Skutbad Da Leg. A bullet took him in the shoulder and spun him around in a tangle of limbs.

'Dunno, but dey's gunna wish dey hadn't,' snarled Zograt. He wiggled his fingers furiously. Screams erupted from the tunnel mouths as soldiers were engulfed in a tide of biting insects which flowed from within their clothes and burrowed into eyes, mouths, ears and nostrils. The gunfire slackened.

'Pull yerselves togevver,' yelled Zograt at his ladz. 'Driggzy, where'z dat bosspole?'

''Ere, boss!' said Driggz, who had extricated himself from the wreck of the howdah. He had a cut on his forehead and his hood had been torn off, but he brandished the bent bosspole proudly.

Zograt took a quick count of his surviving ladz. Wabber and Da Fung were in one piece, though wild-eyed with panic. Skutbad was injured but still alive, leaning on his stikka. Then there was Driggz, Skrog, Bigg Leggzgit and a large enough mob of grots that Zograt couldn't count them so assumed they must be plenty.

A huge shape rushed past him and pounced on the last handful of human soldiers. There were a few desultory gunshots, then the crunching, slurping sounds of feeding.

'And there's 'er majesty, of course,' said Zograt to himself.

Realising they were out of immediate danger, his ladz bombarded him with questions.

'Wot da zog's goin' on, boss? 'Ow did they know we woz comin' in 'ere?'

'Why'd we 'ave to come up dis way, we nearly fell off da zoggin' spider!'

'Wot's da plan, boss? Where we goin'?'

'Shut it!' Zograt yelled. He was still shaken himself from the terrifying ascent and didn't need to be second-guessed.

'It's da humies' mountin, innit? Maybe dey woz just 'ere. Don't matter cos I knows where we'z goin'. Da Clammy Hand is guidin' me.'

This much was true. Zograt felt an almost tidal pull towards the leftmost tunnel, which curved up and away into the mountain. Moreover, as he turned to face it his amulet glowed more brightly than it had before. If that wasn't a sign from the Bad Moon, Zograt wasn't sure what was.

'Wabber, yoo still got 'er majesty under control?' he asked.

'Yeah, boss,' Wabber replied.

'I'll tell ya where we'z goin' an' she can lead da way,' Zograt said. 'If we run into any more humies, dey's goin' to 'ave a zoggin' 'orrible day.'

This earned a cackle from everyone except Bigg Leggzgit, who scowled and rattled his staff. The Spiderfang shaman had evidently given up protesting the abuse of his tribe's deity, however, as he sloped along readily enough in Zograt's wake as they all set off.

One glowing tunnel wound into another then another, then into a domed chamber crowded with mechanical contraptions. Zograt drove his ladz relentlessly, shouting directions to Wabber, who kept the spider moving ahead while Skrog brought up the

rear. The troggoth's looming presence dissuaded Zograt's followers from sneaking off or getting distracted looting shiny objects.

'Yoo'll get first pick of da loot once we'z bossin' dis place,' Zograt
promised them. 'Fer now, we got backstabbin' to do.'

More guards attacked them as they were leaving the machinery
chamber. Zograt saw a big human with goggles yelling at a gang
of soldiers and wizards, just before Arghabigskuttla pounced on
them. Magic and bullets flew. A severed spider leg the size of a
sapling spun through the air, causing Bigg Leggzgit to shriek in
outrage. The little Spiderfang shaman hurled all his magical spite
at the humans, causing several to convulse and foam at the mouth
before collapsing with their flesh swelling and turning purple.

A blast of arcane fire shot from the melee and set Leggzgit
aflame. The shaman dashed in circles screeching before collapsing
in a smouldering heap.

One of Arghabigskuttla's legs slammed down on the wizard who
had hurled the fire spell, crushing her into the ground. The spider
caught the big man with the goggles, lifting him into the air in
her mandibles as he thrashed and screamed. Zograt couldn't help
an evil grin as the spider bit down and two halves of the human
thumped to the ground. His innards spilled as though emptied
from a sack. He gave a last gasp, then lay still.

'Right, come on, wastin' time wiv dis,' snapped Zograt. On
went the spider again, deeper into the mountain with the grots
following. Yet they had gone only another hundred yards or so
when Zograt felt an ominous premonition. He had almost been
trapped in a collapsing tunnel once, and he had never forgotten
the terrifying sense of bedrock shifting around him and closing
like a constricting throat. He had that same feeling now.

''Ang on, ladz,' he said.

The tunnel gave a heave. Glowing arches along its length twisted,
cracks shooting through them with sounds like gunshots. As each

broke, its light died and the glimmering veins radiating from it winked out in turn. Darkness, normally so welcome to the grots, engulfed them in a terrifying wave. The rumble of stone filled the air.

Zograt watched, appalled, as the tunnel constricted about Arghabigskuttla. The spider thrashed and tried to squirm forward, but within seconds she was pinned.

'Leg it!' he yelled as the groan of stressed chitin filled the air and Arghabigskuttla's screeches rose in pitch. Zograt was glad he didn't see the moment the spider's armour gave way beneath the relentless pressure. The loud, wet pop and the spray of stinging slime that chased him down the tunnel were more than enough.

'Majesty!' wailed Wabber, stumbling in horror as Zograt overtook him.

'Shift it, ya git!' yelled Zograt, hobbling as fast as he could. Suddenly he was swept up into Skrog's arms and cradled, the troggoth's loping strides carrying them back to the junction where the fight had happened. Zograt heard the rush and roar of rock closing in behind before stone met stone with a grinding crash.

Skrog halted at the junction and looked enquiringly down at Zograt, who glanced around. The collapse seemed to have stopped, halting at the end of the corridor where the nearest silver arch had held firm. A grot's arm protruded from between the slabs of rock that had sealed the passage. His fingers were still twitching.

Again, Zograt performed a quick headcount. Alongside he and Skrog, he still had Da Fung, Driggz, the distraught Wabber and those grots who had simply kept running as fast as they could.

'Wot woz dat?' asked Driggz.

'Somefin' bad, Driggzy, but we gotta keep goin',' said Zograt. The gravity pulling him was irresistible now. It was all he could think about. The pendant around his neck glowed as bright as the Bad

Moon. 'Skrog, dat way,' Zograt commanded, and the troggoth set off along the branching tunnel with the last of Zograt's followers scurrying behind.

They were barely halfway along this new tunnel when the sense of heaving rock came again.

'Keep goin', ladz, get through before it caves in!' yelled Zograt. Skrog broke into a loping run as the tunnel shook and cracks burst through the glowing arches. Zograt heard grots scream in fear and craned around to see the rest of his followers backing off as stone shards erupted from the walls.

'Boss!' yelled Driggz, then the stone closed with a crash. Zograt snarled. Skrog kept running, outdistancing the grinding stone spurs that overlapped and sealed the corridor behind them. Had his ladz been crushed, Zograt wondered, or had they managed to flee? What was he supposed to do now?

'No Gobbapalooza, no ladz,' he cried as Skrog lumbered on. 'It's gunna get us too, lad, if we ain't careful!'

Skrog grunted. Zograt pointed him up a flight of glowing stairs as his mind spun. Was the mountain itself attacking him? He recalled again the staring eye in his vision.

'Da mountin, or somefin' in da mountin,' he muttered, then gritted his fangs as the rumbling came again. Skrog turned and retreated down the steps as arches splintered and crushing stone tried to swallow them.

Zograt spat. ''Ow did dey know we woz comin?' he demanded as Skrog reached a stable junction and stopped again. ''Ow do dey know where we'z goin'?'

A thought struck him, a wild flash of inspiration that made him clutch the Spanglestikk with exhilaration and fear.

'Yoo trust me, lad?' asked Zograt. Skrog blinked at him then grunted. 'Good enough,' said Zograt. 'Head down dat way.'

He picked his route at random, resisting the pull of the correct direction with an effort. Skrog set off and barely moments later, Zograt heard the rumble of stone not from this tunnel but from the one down which the pull had tried to draw him.

'Bad Moon loves a bit of anarchy,' he shouted to Skrog as the troggoth loped onward. Bugs clung tight to Zograt's robes as he was borne along at a lurching pace. The rumbling abated, then began anew in the tunnel he and Skrog were dashing down.

'Dat one,' he yelled, jabbing a finger at a smaller side tunnel well off their route. Skrog ducked down it and kept loping as behind them came the sound of splintering stone. Zograt belatedly wondered if any of these tunnels were dead ends that might trap him and Skrog long enough for the mountain to find them again. He pushed the thought aside. You couldn't second-guess anarchy, he thought; that was rather the point.

Like the Bad Moon lurching through the heavens, Zograt directed Skrog down one passage then another. Up a winding stair, then right straight away into another side passage. Through a junction where humans in aprons and goggles ran hither and thither with armfuls of scrolls, only to vanish amidst grinding stone as the mountain tried again to crush the invaders.

At the next junction, Zograt thumped Skrog urgently on the arm.

'Now back, straight back da way we came!' he urged, praying to the Bad Moon that he was right. Skrog turned ponderously and thumped back down a corridor that was beginning to shudder and crack. The troggoth grunted and bent lower as the ceiling closed in. He stumbled as the floor convulsed underneath him, almost falling. Zograt saw silver light ahead amidst a narrowing chute of stone and realised that, if he flung himself from Skrog's arms, he could slip through the gap before it closed.

Instead, he brandished the Spanglestikk and drove all his power through it. Coloured lights danced before Zograt's eyes. The grinding of stone filled his ears. Green light flared and mycelia erupted on every side, chewing into the rock, turning it to rubble and then grit. Skrog groaned, heaved and squirmed free of the constricting tunnel in the instant before Zograt's spell sputtered out.

Stone crashed against stone, so close that the expelled air ruffled Zograt's robes.

Skrog grunted and lurched to his feet. Zograt staggered up from where the falling troggoth had spilled him onto the floor. He leant on the Spanglestikk and stared anxiously at the ceiling. Skrog was panting, lathered like a blown steed. Zograt knew that, if he had miscalculated, they wouldn't be able to escape another collapse.

Nothing came. Zograt blew out a sigh of relief. He felt the pull of the Bad Moon's gravity more keenly than ever, and knew his route snaked away up the passage to the left.

'Come on, lad,' he said, thumping Skrog on the leg. 'Da Bad Moon'z still got a job fer us.'

As they headed up the passageway, Zograt reached out with his powers and wiggled his fingers against his staff. He'd had enough of being hunted. It was time he got his own back.

Wilhomelda snarled with a frustration she scorned as all too mortal. She had lost the thread. The parasite had wriggled from her grasp, lost amidst the shifting possibilities of futures thrown into sudden chaos. The Leering Face obscured all.

'**But we know where it will go,**' she breathed, and cinders danced upon the air. '**It will chew its way into the heart of the mountain. It will seek power that does not belong to it. Very well, little maggot, let us meet. You have earned that honour, at least, before your end.**'

She set off, drifting through her mountain towards the pillar chamber, and the chrysalis from which she-that-was-Axactiar had not yet fully emerged. As she went, she barely noticed the shadowy suggestion of a figure that still paced alongside her in the furthest corner of her eye.

CHAPTER NINETEEN

Da Mountin

Zograt limped up a sloping passage with the Spanglestikk clutched ready. His heart thumped. His throat was tight with anticipation and his nerves jangling. The lunar gravity that had pulled him through the mountain was so strong now that he was certain his destination was close. It seemed his magic staff knew it too, for the crystal set into its head glowed with a fiery inner light.

'Reckon' we'z almost dere, lad,' he muttered to Skrog. 'Dunno wot we'z gunna find, but I don't reckon it'll be friendly. Yoo ready fer a scrap?'

Skrog grunted and patted Zograt upon the fungal strands that grew from his scalp. Zograt felt grateful for the troggoth's protective presence and wondered fleetingly what had become of Driggz and the last of his warband.

'Weren't much use dem ladz, but I 'ope dey ain't ded,' he said to Skrog. 'Be a zoggin' pain puttin' a new Gobbapalooza togevver, an' Driggzy just got useful.'

Zograt fell silent as he rounded a steeply sloping corner into a silver blaze of light. He squinted, eyes tearing, and saw that the illumination spilled from a circular doorway just ahead. Whatever destiny the Bad Moon had sent him to meet, Zograt sensed that it lay through that glowing doorway.

Every instinct beaten into him during Skram's reign told him to flee. Something terrible lurked ahead; he sensed it with the veteran survival instincts of the endlessly persecuted. He took an involuntary step back and his foot met that of Skrog, standing stolidly at his back. Zograt bared his fangs, squared his scrawny shoulders, and limped up the slope.

Vertigo seized him as he emerged into the spherical chamber. Walls became floor and up became across, making him stumble. Zograt was momentarily blinded by the silver fire burning from the crystal pillar at the chamber's heart and glowing within its walls. He dimly perceived a dark shadow at the pillar's heart, silhouetted by the blaze.

Skrog moaned in distress. Even the insects in Zograt's robes shrilled in alarm, some vanishing into his ears and nostrils in search of sanctuary.

Zograt saw strange machines dotted around the chamber. Strewn amongst them were burned human bodies. From his perspective, some sprawled upon the walls, others on the ceiling. Yet the strangeness of this could not long distract him from the chamber's only other living occupant. He forced himself not to cower as he gazed upon the entity at the mountain's heart.

Zograt saw that the crystal pillar was fitted with a spiralling staircase that ended in a railed balcony on which more weird machinery whirred. The monster stood on that balcony. Or rather, she hung in the air several feet above it, suspended amidst a corona of dancing silver light and whirling cinders.

The monster reminded him of a human, but her proportions

were wrong. Her legs and arms were too long. They hung strangely, as though an invisible force held her by the back of the neck and dangled her like a doll. Her fingers and toes seemed overlong, attenuated and ending in wicked-looking talons. The monster's skin shimmered like quicksilver; Zograt realised it was covered head to toe in iridescent scales that danced between shadow black and glaring silver as the light played across them. He was reminded forcibly of the Liar's Grass swaying beneath the canopy of the Shudderwood.

The monster's face was gaunt and stretched, pockmarked by dozens of eyes. Some blazed with inner fire. Some were black as opals. The central two were bloodied marbles, their corners pierced by the tines of a glowing circlet bound tightly about the monster's temples. Her hair swayed like a corona of white flame about her head, while embers and ashes billowed from her nostrils and needle-fanged maw to whirl away above her.

The monster fixed him with its myriad gaze and favoured him with a cold smile.

'There you are, little maggot,' it said. Zograt couldn't stop himself cringing this time. Her voice was painfully loud, an echoing clamour of overlaid whispers and shouts interspersed with a crackle like flame and the bass rumble of something ancient and terrible. 'For all the inconvenience that you have caused us, you are really such a little thing, are you not?'

Mastering his fear, Zograt stood firm, one hand clutching the Spanglestikk and the other wrapped around his fiercely glowing amulet.

'I ain't no maggot, I'm Zograt Da Skwurm!' he shouted. 'I got da Clammy Hand, and I'm da Loonking!'

'Loon-king?' The monster drew the word out and as she did, her mocking voice sounded like Skram and all of his bullying lackeys. Zograt heard Nuffgunk and his ladz laughing at him, felt again their kicks and blows. 'Is one who rules vermin amidst a dungheap now considered a king? King of maggots, perhaps. King of dregs.'

Zograt took a limping step forward, then another.

'King o' da grots! King o' da Gloomspite!'

The monster's outline flickered. She blurred, visual echoes overlaying one another. Her eyes blazed and her smile widened.

'Would it trouble you, maggot, to know that there are dozens who call themselves Loonking scattered throughout the Mortal Realms? Dozens of pretenders to a title held only by one.'

'So zoggers keep tellin' me,' he shot back. 'Yooz can all stick it up yer backsides.' Zograt wiggled his fingers, tugging at invisible strands of binding magic with all his mental might. The monster cocked her head and drifted towards Zograt. Her gaze bored into him.

'What are you doing, little maggot? Shall we look and see?'

Zograt had no idea if the monster could peer into his mind or decipher his magics, but he didn't want to give her the chance. He brandished the Spanglestikk and fed power into its glowing crystal. The monster's head snapped around and her eyes fixed on the staff.

'The threat…' she whispered.

'Fing about maggotz is, dey'll eat ya in da end,' said Zograt. With a wiggle of his fingers, he unleashed a blazing bolt of green fire at the monster. Her outline flickered and she was ten feet to the right of where she had been. Zograt's magical blast raced through the air and splashed from the crystal of the pillar without marking it. The dark shape within the marble shuddered as though in pain or excitement.

The monster looked at him pityingly. 'Perhaps not such a threat after all,' she said.

Zograt shrieked in anger and hurled another blast of green

flame, then another and another. Each time, the monster flickered in his vision and was elsewhere. His magics blasted a machine into glowing scrap that sprouted purple fungi, tore a section of the staircase away from the pillar, and struck the chamber wall with enough force to crack the surface and spread black tendrils of mould. Yet to Zograt's growing frustration and panic, he could not hit his mark. He backed up into Skrog's shadow and heaved again upon the sorcerous tether in his mind.

The monster floated closer, spreading her arms as she came. The bodies and machines over which she passed burst into flames before crumbling to glowing ash.

Desperate to keep her away, Zograt slammed the Spanglestikk into the ground and conjured a writhing mass of fungi that erupted through the crystal surface. They coiled towards the monster like the tentacles of some deep-sea leviathan. She turned her gaze upon them, and they deflagrated into cinders and burning matter.

Before Zograt could hurl another spell, the monster raised one taloned hand in a languid gesture. Searing sorcery burst towards Zograt, a roiling comet of liquid darkness and scorching silver flame. He screeched in panic and jabbed with the Spanglestikk, conjuring a counter-curse that hit the onrushing magics like Gorka-morka's own headbutt. The explosion threw him back, Zograt and Skrog tumbling across the spherical chamber and sliding to a halt.

Zograt's ears rang. His head felt like a pen full of squigs had been fighting inside it. He blinked through the blazing silver light and managed to focus. The moment he did, panic snatched him by the throat. He had clung on to the Spanglestikk, but to his horror the vaunted magical super-weapon of the Flashbanditz tribe was now a smouldering stump.

The monster hadn't even been slowed by their exchange. She was almost upon him, still wearing that pitying smile.

'Enough, little maggot. With your death will pass the Leering

Face, and then we shall ascend to greatness. May that offer you peace.'

She stretched her shimmering fingers towards his face. Zograt couldn't even recoil, paralysed by the panic and anger and self-loathing raging inside him. Had he been wrong all along? Had the Bad Moon blessed him, or had everything that happened simply been a product of luck and his own self-deception? There was already a Loonking, he thought. Who was he but another deluded pretender?

'Just a runt,' Zograt croaked. He felt the void-cold and the searing heat of her. His vision swam. His skin began to smoulder and rise as ashes from a pyre.

Skrog roared loudly enough to startle Zograt into motion. He threw himself backwards with a shriek. The huge Dankhold troggoth lunged past him and drove one boulder-like fist into the monster's chest.

Zograt saw her eyes fly wide with shock as she was hurled back. Cracked scales scattered from her body, pulverised by Skrog's blow. Zograt saw wild motion behind the monster and realised that whatever it was that lurked within the pillar, it was thrashing madly.

Skrog stood over his master, fists bunched, and let out another furious roar. Zograt seized his chance and wiggled his fingers, giving his mental tether another titanic heave.

'Come *on*, ya zogger,' he hissed through gritted fangs. Then came a rumble of anger that rose to a shriek like a choir being burned to death as they sang. Zograt looked up to see the monster ablaze with power, her brows furrowed over her mutilated eyes.

'You dare?' she roared.

The monster loomed over Skrog like a vengeful star. The troggoth swung his fist again, but she twisted her fingers in a gesture that made Zograt's head hurt to see. Fire leapt. Ashes exploded in a cloud. Skrog staggered back. The arm he had sought to punch with now ended in a smouldering stump at the elbow.

'Skrog!' yelled Zograt.

The monster struck again, then again.

Skrog bellowed in pain and misery as cinders erupted from his body. An ear was shorn away. One leg vanished, then a great swathe of the flesh from his back. Zograt watched in horror as his faithful troggoth fell, mutilated. Skrog groaned as crushed and blackened insects flaked away from his hide.

Fury raced through Zograt and he lurched to his feet, throwing both hands towards the monster and uttering a shrill scream. The power that raced through him threatened to burst from his flesh as uncontrollable fungal growth. It caused his forearms and fingers to bulge and squirm as though they were about to explode. It swept towards the monster in a wave of writhing mycelia, glowing fungi and squirming masses of insects.

She made a slashing gesture and Zograt's furious conjuration was torn to blazing tatters. It splattered the chamber wall in a slick of ectoplasm as the monster swept closer.

She was no longer smiling.

Zograt backed away, lips skinned back from his fangs, chest hollow with the magical force he had expended. He shook with impotent rage as she reached for him again. Suddenly, huge fingers wrapped around him and hoisted him off the ground. Propped on his mutilated arm, Skrog hefted Zograt like a stone and flung him from the monster's path.

Rushing air.

Whirling silver light.

Zograt hit something hard enough to break several fangs, then dropped like a sack of squig dung. He landed with a clang on something hard, and saw stars.

Dimly he heard another terrible shriek. Recovering his wits,

Zograt realised he was sprawled on the platform that ran around the top of the pillar. A mass of cogwork machinery chugged nearby, wires running from it to a metal spike driven into a crack in the pillar's surface.

Another choral scream rose, and Skrog howled. Zograt lurched to his feet in time to see the troggoth shudder as more geysers of flame and ash burst from his ruined body. The monster's back was to him in that moment, but Zograt had hurled so much power into his last spell that his magics had not recovered enough for a sorcerous backstabbing.

'Oi, glowy freek, I'm up 'ere!' he yelled, desperate to tear her attention away from whatever remained of Skrog. Zograt felt a moment's relief as she wheeled away from the troggoth, but it withered as he got a proper look at the blackened and truncated remains of his protector. Skrog showed no signs of life.

Zograt had no reference for the emotions he felt. He had never learned the words to interpret such feelings. Yet he gripped the railing of the balcony until his knuckles turned pale and ground his fangs until they threatened to snap.

The monster sailed serenely towards him. Her expression had changed again to a sort of mild disinterest. It was as though she saw past him, to the next task she needed to fulfil. Something thumped behind him and Zograt looked back. The shadow-shape within the pillar was pressed up against the inside of the crystal column as though avidly watching his last moments.

Zograt looked again at the strange machines, and the shadow, and then back at the monster, whose circlet burned with the same silver fire blazing from the pillar. He scowled as a thought tried to coalesce, but it was interrupted by a sudden drag within his mind. Zograt felt a malicious smile stretch the corners of his mouth. He spat over the railing at the approaching monster and wiggled his fingers furiously.

'Like I sed, yoo weird zogger, we'll eat ya alive.'

Da Lurk erupted through one of the entrance tunnels in a geyser of black chitin and thrashing legs, more and more of it surging into the chamber even as its head and fore-segments coiled around the walls.

The monster wheeled in the air and snarled.

'A curse upon the Leering Face! Still it clouds our eye!'

'Bad Moon take ya!' yelled Zograt and hauled on the magical tether one last time. His insects trilled with excitement as Da Lurk reared up and drove towards the monster like a battering ram. The segmapede squealed in pain as cinders geysered from its chitinous body, but the monster's attack came too late to stop it snatching her in its swordlike mandibles and slamming her into the wall of the chamber hard enough to crack crystal.

Zograt yelled in triumph. His cry was answered from below and he peered over the balcony to see Driggz, Wabber, Da Fung, Skutbad and several more grots staggering as they sought to get their bearings.

''Ow'd yoo get 'ere?' shouted Zograt.

'Followed Da Lurk,' Wabber yelled back. 'Figured wherever it woz 'eadin' in such an 'urry, we'd find yoo right in da middle of it.'

'Zog me, is dat Skrog? Is'e ded?' cried Driggz.

'Wot 'appened to da Spanglestikk?' wailed Skutbad, catching sight of the smouldering stump that lay near the fallen troggoth.

Before Zograt could reply, Da Lurk reared back and slammed the monster into the chamber wall a second time. Keening in a hundred furious voices, she grasped the segmapede's head with both hands and deflagrating chitin fountained from its head and body. Da Lurk thrashed and squealed, and Zograt's newly arrived followers cowered as the giant insect's convulsions threatened to crush them.

Zograt watched in mounting horror as the monster forced Da

Lurk back, blasting it with her powers again and again. She flickered and was above the blinded and agonised insect. She wrought her complex and mind-bending gesture anew, this time with both hands, and Da Lurk shuddered as gouts of fire erupted through its ravaged hide.

It was going to lose, Zograt realised. It was going to lose, and then the monster would turn upon him. She would probably kill his ladz, too, if they didn't have the sense to run. From the way they had started to sling arrows and hallucinatory fungi at the monster from below, he doubted they would be quick enough to make their escape.

Zograt felt trapped. Worse, he felt powerless. His Spanglestikk was destroyed. Skrog was likely dead. His magic wasn't enough.

'Why'd it 'ave to be right in da middle of da mountin where da Bad Moon can't see me?' he cried in frustration. He cast about for anything he could use to defeat this seemingly invincible monster. Something thumped against his chest as he turned, and Zograt remembered Skram's loonstone amulet still hanging about his neck.

'Loonstone,' he breathed. One by one, devious thoughts aligned themselves in his mind. The silver light in the pillar and the blaze around the monster's brow. The dark shape watching from within the pillar. His loonstone amulet, and the Bad Moon.

'Where yer god can see ya,' he said, looking from the shadow to the monster, then back to where the spike was driven into a single fault line in the crystal skin of the pillar.

Zograt tore the sickle-moon-shaped amulet from around his neck and clutched it like a dagger. He dashed across the platform towards the crack, but in that moment there came a thunderous series of detonations. From the corner of his eye, Zograt saw Da Lurk rear up, trailing smoke and ash, then crash down in smouldering ruin.

The air shimmered with heat haze and the monster hung above him, staring down with her many eyes. Her body was torn, oily darkness showing through the rents, and her mouth was set in a hard line of murderous anger.

'Enough,' she cried, and the force of the word almost drove Zograt to his knees.

Wilhomelda hung in the air above the greenskin and prepared to destroy him. He, and the Leering Face he served, had caused more than enough damage already. She had been forced to focus ever more upon the here and now, doubtless missing precious fragments of foresight and possibility as she narrowed her frame of reference ever further towards the merely mortal and the present moment. Yet the greenskins' anarchy demanded no less. Foresight, she had realised, would not avail her against so random and wilful a foe. She had to employ sheer might.

Her vessel damaged, her spawling intellect focused like a star's fury through a single lens, she turned her regard on her enemy.

'Enough,' she shouted.

'Yes, *it really is*,' replied a voice, flowing from thin air. Wilhomelda blinked in surprise as the shadowy shape that had walked so long at her side stepped into full view. She could not restrain a smile.

'Lanette, I did not lose you.'

She faltered. The apparition's features were vague, wisps of shadow drawn together to form the suggestion of a face, yet Wilhomelda could see they wore an expression of deepest sorrow.

'*You did not lose me, no. You threw me away. You sacrificed me for power.*'

Wilhomelda frowned. This was wrong. Lanette did not understand, that was all. Could she not see the greater good they had all served here, the nobility of her sacrifice?

'Sacrifice...' Wilhomelda repeated the thought aloud. She reached for her serene understanding, for the greater intellect and divine context in which all her decisions made inarguable sense. To her dismay, she found a hollow space where they should have been.

'Sacrifice, and for what?' asked Lanette's shade. 'To become this monster? Hollow host to a parasite-god that played on your fears and made you its puppet?'

'This is... wrong,' said Wilhomelda, her mind thrashing in search of escape from the accusations of a ghost. Yet even as part of her mind tried to reason out whether Lanette was a spirit, trapped within the chrysalis of the mountain by the nature of her death, or a memory rising from the remains of Wilhomelda's own mortal mind, or some phantasm conjured by a foe, another part of her consciousness heard her own fractured voice and the rumble of the godbeast's layered beneath it. She recoiled. She shook. Pain shot through her skull, radiating from her violated eyes.

'You failed everyone who trusted you,' said Lanette, calm and relentless. 'Do you really want to continue down this path? Do you really want to compound your evils, to complete the ruin of yourself, your friends, all our good work, by becoming the very monster you swore to protect us from?'

Wilhomelda's mind was an animal caught in a trap. She felt the wrongness of her altered form and squirmed with horror at the touch of her own scaled skin. She felt the agony of Lanette's death crash through her like an icy wave. She let out a sob that turned to ashes in the air.

'It is enough,' Lanette repeated. 'Please, Wil, I can linger but a moment more. The mists of Shyish gather before my eyes. You have one last chance. I beg you to take it. I forgive you, even now, but you must trust me.'

Lanette stretched out one spectral hand. Straining with every ounce of willpower left to her, Wilhomelda Borchase's ruined spirit reached out and took Lanette's hand in hers. Shadows swept around them. She heard the contented sigh of the woman she had loved for so many years, felt a flurry of regret, and shame, and inexpressible gratitude.

Then they both were gone.

Zograt saw something change in the monster's face. She reached out an arm, but not to him. Her features convulsed, then her eyes turned glassy.

'A mortal soul I need not,' the monster bellowed. 'A vessel was all I required, and that you have given!'

Zograt had no idea what the monster was yelling about, and in that moment he didn't care. He knew only that something had distracted it. He wouldn't waste his chance.

'Bad Moon, see dis backstabbin'!' he yelled, throwing himself down by the crack in the pillar. 'Bless me magiks an' 'elp me stick da Clammy Hand right down dis zogger's throat!'

Zograt grabbed the metal spike and heaved. For a horrible moment he thought that it was too firmly wedged, that his last grand gesture would amount to lying on his face and yelling at the Bad Moon in the instant before the monster slew him. Then, with a last mighty heave, he dragged the spike out of the pillar. Silver light blazed from the hole. Something like quicksilver mixed with blood spurted from it. The dark shadow thrashed wildly. He heard the monster roar.

Zograt stabbed Skram's loonstone amulet into the crystal pillar with all his strength, wiggling his fingers as he blasted into it every last spark of magical strength he had left.

Sickly light welled within the pendant. Cracks rippled along its length, moist mycelial filaments wriggling from them to plunge into the crystal pillar. Where they burrowed, so the glow of the pillar curdled into the Bad Moon's eerie loonlight.

Zograt saw the dark shape within the pillar recoil, then begin to twist and shudder. At the same time a ululating wail rose from behind him as many voices cried out in mounting horror.

The first fungal blooms swelled from the crack in the pillar, forcing it wider, sending fault lines leaping across its surface from which more damp fungi blossomed. The light of the Bad Moon swelled to fill the chamber and where it fell, the walls ran with damp and swiftly furred with mould and mushrooms. Human corpses twitched as insects chewed their way from their flesh, and fungi sprouted with grotesque ebullience from eye sockets and open mouths. The vast and ruptured corpse of Da Lurk stirred as countless tiny segmapedes wriggled from its innards. The pillar chamber was transformed into a pallid fungal grotto, dripping dank and squirming with countless bugs.

For all the Bad Moon's blessings manifesting around him, Zograt couldn't take his eyes from the monster. As corruption spread through the pillar at his back, so it blossomed from the circlet upon the monster's head. One blood-marble eye bulged grotesquely then popped with a wet splat, allowing a clot of fat worms to ooze from the socket. The other was pushed aside, and left dangling as glowing green mushrooms thrust their way from inside the monster's skull.

Clawing at the air, screaming in fury and pain, the monster rose amidst a column of whirling cinders. Its scaled flesh bulged, fungi bursting through only to flash to ashes and drift away.

'This cannot, this *cannot*,' it gurgled, and blood-wet beetles spilled from its lips. The monster's scales were tarnishing and flaking from its body, more and more fungi popping through its straining flesh to take their place. The monster wavered in the air, outline blurring and refocusing. Zograt felt a spiteful surge of triumph as he saw more skittering insects, each with a twisted little crescent-moon face, spilling from the widening rents in the monster's skin. They gnawed with fang and mandible as they trilled with delight.

'Toldya da bugs would eat ya,' sneered Zograt.

Distended by fungal growths, savaged by a swarming second skin of insects, the monster fell to land amidst a spongy mass of man-sized mushrooms. It retched, and instead of cinders a great cloud of glowing spores vomited from its jaws. Zograt felt the light of the Bad Moon on his skin, and the magical might of its blessings blossomed anew within him. He leaned over the railing. He pointed his fingers at the convulsing monster. He wiggled them.

The grotto came alive as insects beyond count converged upon Zograt's enemy. They came in numbers to dwarf the swarm already assailing the monster, piling higher and higher until they buried it entirely.

Zograt heard a muffled roar. One long-taloned hand thrust up through the drift of insects and clawed towards him. Two of its fingers had been gnawed off, and even as he watched, another, grossly swollen finger split down its middle as mushrooms bloomed from it.

The bugs surged back in.

The hand vanished.

The heap heaved.

Heaved.

Was still.

Zograt blew out a breath. He turned from the railing and hobbled painfully over to the pillar. Moisture and dirt smeared its surface, and its sickly glow showed through thick patches of fungal growth. Zograt fixed one beady eye on the shadowy form still floating in the pillar's depths. He couldn't be sure, hadn't really had a clear look at the thing before sticking the amulet into its pillar, but he thought it looked twisted now, as though deformed just as its avatar in the world outside had been. It twitched feebly.

'Yoo'z been mooned, mate,' he leered. He turned without thinking to see if the joke had penetrated Skrog's slow wits, and instead his eyes fell on the troggoth's broken body. Smile wilting, Zograt forgot his vanquished foe.

Limping painfully and missing his Spanglestikk to lean on, Zograt made his way down the stairs and through the fungus grotto to where the body of the troggoth lay amidst a glade of glowing mushrooms. Driggz and his companions flocked around him, but Zograt waved them away.

He looked down sadly at the burned ruin of what had once been his loyal troggoth companion. Skrog's body was blackened by fire, his hide burned away, his face awfully disfigured. White bone showed through in places, and he had only one arm left out of all his limbs.

'Oh lad, what did it do to ya?' asked Zograt. He limped up to the troggoth's head, which was cradled on a cushion of fungus. Zograt laid a hand on Skrog's burned brow and heaved a sigh.

'Yoo saved me life again. Yoo woz da best mate a weedy little runt ever 'ad,' said Zograt, then jumped as the troggoth opened one eye and rolled it towards him.

Skrog gave a faint grunt and tried to move his stumps.

'Zog me, wot is dat Skrog made of?' exclaimed Wabber, shaking his head. Zograt could only grin, patting Skrog gingerly on an unburned patch of scalp.

'Da Bad Moon made 'im to keep me safe,' he said. 'Don't yoo worry, lad, we'll getcha more o' dem healin' potions from Ploddit's ladz. Yoo'll be good as 'shroomz before ya know it.'

Skrog grunted again. Then, apparently untroubled by his ghastly injuries, he reached out with his remaining hand, plucked a fistful of glowing fungi, and shoved them into his mouth. The troggoth laid his head back and chewed, apparently content.

'Yoo done it, boss,' said Driggz. 'Yoo stabbed 'em in da back and brought da Gloomspite all da way into da mountin.'

'An' yooz lot showed up to 'elp instead o' leggin' it,' said Zograt, turning to survey the little gaggle of grots. 'Daft gitz.'

They shuffled and looked guilty, and Zograt had to stifle a chuckle. He was under no illusions. He knew that Driggz was here for the same reason Driggz did anything these days. Fear. That if he didn't live up to Zograt's expectations, the consequences of his disloyalty would catch up with him. The surviving members of the Gobbapalooza, meanwhile, made no pretence of their motivations, hunching over the burned remains of the Spanglestikk and muttering to one another. As for the handful of bewildered-looking ladz who had survived to this point, Zograt suspected they had just followed his warchiefs where they were told.

He squatted down next to Skrog and spoke so softly that only the troggoth would hear him.

'Don't matter. Dey woz 'ere, so dey seen wot we done, lad. Word'll spread. I couldn't keep 'em in line forever wiv just magic an' da frighteners. Kept 'em togevver long enough to clobber da humies, but it woulda fallen apart sooner or later.'

He looked around at his lieutenants again and grinned to himself. Skrog kept munching, giving no sign whether he'd heard or understood Zograt's whispers.

'Now, though,' Zograt continued. 'Now da story's gunna spread 'ow Zograt Da Skwurm beat da monster dat even Da Lurk couldn't kill.'

Skrog gave him a sideways look.

'Awright, Zograt and Skrog,' said Zograt. The troggoth went back to chewing.

Zograt knew grots, and he knew also that his deeds this day would earn him the closest thing to loyalty he was likely to get from anyone in his horde save Skrog. It would be the loyalty of bullies who gather behind the meanest and smartest of their gang through instinct and cowardice, but it would serve his purposes. It would cement his horde and his power.

'Who'z da Loonking?' he yelled. The startled grots jumped, exchanged looks, then turned back to him. Even Da Fung joined in their cry.

'Zograt da Loonking!'

'Just one more fing to do,' he said, wiggling his fingers. The drift of insects that had buried the monster flowed apart. Their retreat revealed a tangle of denuded bones. Amidst them lay a distorted skull with a rash of eye sockets, and with a fine cogwork circlet still secured to it by a pair of vicious metal barbs.

Zograt picked up the skull, gave a tug, and wrenched the tines of the circlet free with a gristly crunch. A fat spore-roach scurried from the left eye socket and up his sleeve before he cast the skull away. Zograt turned the circlet slowly in his fingers, admiring the way clots of fungus and cultures of mould had infested its fine workings.

'Yoo not gunna stick dat fing in yer eyes, is yoo, boss?' asked Driggz.

'Don't be daft, Driggzy, I'm not a complete loon,' said Zograt. One after the other he gripped the delicate tines and snapped them off, chucking them away.

Zograt set the circlet on his head. The fungal strands growing from his scalp twitched and writhed, and he felt them wind around the circlet and tug it tight about his brow. He felt the mind in the pillar briefly touch his own then recoil. That, he thought, was very interesting indeed.

Zograt grinned at his ladz.

'Loonking's gotta 'ave a crown, don't 'e?'

EPILOGUE

Zograt's lair

Zograt Da Skwurm reclined upon his throne. It was an imposing edifice, carved by the labour of many grots from cave-rock and living fungi, yet somehow, he never felt dwarfed by it. He was bathed in the sickly loonlight that had spread through the mountain after his victory, and which suffused his spherical throne-grotto most strongly of all. Behind him rose the fungus-thick crystal pillar, a prison for the entity that had once been the mountain's god. To one side of his throne stood Driggz with his bosspole. To the other stood Skrog, taller and more hulking than ever since Ploddit's ladz had helped him to regrow his mangled body. The troggoth wore a suit of armour fashioned from chitinous segments of Da Lurk. Zograt still felt as safe in the troggoth's presence as ever, but from the way his subjects quailed it was clear they thought Skrog now looked truly terrifying.

Upon Zograt's brow rested his crown, around which his cranial fungi had now grown so thick there was no way he would be able to remove it without considerable pain. Not that Zograt could think of any reason why he would want to remove his crown. Quite the contrary, with each day that passed he felt he was getting an ever-firmer grip upon the ruined entity still trapped within the crystal pillar.

The Bad Moon's power had ravaged it. Its avatar's gruesome end had driven it mad. Yet still it lived, in some fashion Zograt couldn't quite fathom, and it seemed to retain some flicker of its powers. At least, that was Zograt's assumption. Certainly, he had never heard mutters of another voice in his mind before donning the crown, and had never been able to conjure up sparks of silver flame with a click of his fingers either.

Zograt suspected that getting to grips with his new powers would be a slow process. In the meantime, he had the business of ruling to get on with. He stared imperiously down at Nuffgunk, who stood amidst a mob of Zograt's grot bosses. Of them all, only Nuffgunk didn't cower.

"Ow'z work goin' on me mountin?' asked Zograt.

'It's lookin' da business, boss,' said Nuffgunk, puffing out his chest. 'I got da ladz workin' 'ard. Won't be long 'til da whole fing's carved into one big loonshrine.'

'Zoggin' right. 'Ow many uvver gitz got a loonshrine da size of a mountin, eh?' said Zograt.

'Just yoo, boss!' Driggz piped up from beside his throne.

'Wot about...' Zograt waved a hand airily. 'Everyfin' else?'

Nuffgunk rolled his eyes.

'Da squig pens is overflowin' an' Big Limpy an' his troggs 'ave made a proppa trogg-wallow o' dat humie town. Da Gobbapalooza still can't get wot's left o' da Spanglestikk to work, but dat Flashbandit Bugscrut joined up as dere new Brewgit so maybe dey'll 'ave more luck soon.'

'Doubt, it, daft zoggers, dat stikk's wrecked,' chuckled Zograt. Nuffgunk smirked and continued his report.

'Kreepzogga's scouts say da clammydank is spreadin' good. No one's seen da Bad Moon again since we took da mountin, but everyfing's gone good an' manky all da way down into da south end o' da Shudderwood, so it's still spreadin'.'

'New recrootz?' asked Zograt.

'Couple more tribes turned up in da last few days an' swore da oathz. One of 'em woz orruks.'

There was a stirring amongst the bosses. Zograt crooked an eyebrow.

'Gunna 'ave t'make a few examples so dey don't start tryin' to take over, ain't I?'

'Reckon so, boss,' said Nuffgunk. Zograt leered and cracked his knuckles as insects squirmed through his robes.

'Sounds fun,' he said.

'It'll 'ave to wait though, boss,' said Nuffgunk. 'Got trouble on da way. Scoutz said dere's a lot o' humies comin' through da realmgates down south an' marchin' dis way.'

'Dat woz da first fing yoo should tell me!' said Zograt, leaning forward.

'Yoo said everyfing,' replied Nuffgunk with a scowl. Zograt scoffed and leaned back.

''Ow far away?' he asked.

'Few days, boss,' Nuffgunk said. Zograt nodded as though this were new information. In truth, his crown had whispered it to him already, and he had the rudiments of a battle plan figured out. However, if there was one thing Zograt had learned during his rise to power, it was that those who underestimated what you knew, or what you could do, were easier to beat into submission.

'Any word o' Skragrott?' he asked.

'Nuffin', boss. Or any uvver zoggerz calls demselves Loonking,' said Nuffgunk.

'Good, longer dat lasts da better,' said Zograt. He knew it could not last forever, though. It was in the nature of greenskins to conquer their rivals. He didn't believe he would remain unchallenged for long.

In the meantime, though, there was a battle to fight, and another chance to prove why a runt like him had been given the blessings of the Bad Moon.

'All right, Nuffgunk, put da word out. All da warchiefs to da Loonking's throne-grotto, quick as dey can. We got some humies to backstab, an' I reckon I knows 'ow we'll do it...'

ABOUT THE AUTHOR

Andy Clark has written the Warhammer 40,000 novels *Fist of the Imperium, Kingsblade, Knightsblade* and *Shroud of Night,* as well as the *Dawn of Fire* novel *The Gate of Bones* and the novella *Crusade.* He has also written the novels *Gloomspite, Bad Loon Rising* and *Blacktalon: First Mark* for Warhammer Age of Sigmar, and the Warhammer Quest Silver Tower novella *Labyrinth of the Lost.* He lives in Nottingham, UK.

YOUR NEXT READ

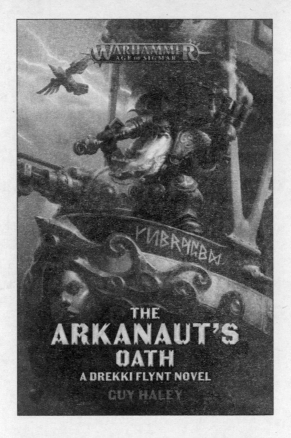

THE ARKANAUT'S OATH
by Guy Haley

In his first full-length novel, the swashbuckling Drekki Flynt finds himself at the mercy of his nemesis, Rogi Throkk, who sends him to find the fabled talisman of Achromia... or die trying.

An extract from
The Arkanaut's Oath
by Guy Haley

A poet spoke. This is what he said:

'Rain pounded. Cold gathered against the tops of the Fourth
Air. Bavardia suffered bad weather as a matter of course. For those
abroad on the street, atmosphere wrapped meagrely about the
body, failing to warm, failing to nourish labouring lungs. Everything was thin there – air, prospects, life, love. Only the rain was
thick, thicker than beards, thicker than oaths, thermals thrust up
from the lower airs, flattened by the chill into thunderheads that
lashed the town with oily, unpleasant waters.

'Drekki Flynt, Kharadron privateer, came into port. His crew
weathered the rain like rocks do, grey, silent and stoic. They were
grim. Nobody liked Bavardia.

'Bavardia was a young place, a lawless place, one of a dozen towns
budded off great Bastion, the last remnant of ancient, shattered
Achromia. If hope for the future had established Bavardia, despair
of the present ruled it. Heirs to a venerable empire, the citizens
brought ambitions with them that they could not fulfil. Their

dreams were beyond their grasp. A young place with an old soul, Bavardia was filthy as infants are, soiling itself, unsure of its limits, creeping up one crag, then up another, always on the verge of catastrophic tumbles, never settled, uncoordinated, wild with the potential and vulnerabilities of youth. Built upon ruins, reminders of what had been, sad, lost, and yet full of hope. Bavardia! A town of–'

'Oh put a sock in it, Evtorr Bjarnisson. On and on all the bloody time with the bloody poetry!' Drekki Flynt said.

The flamboyant ancestor face that fronted Drekki's helm was known across the Skyshoals. Then there was his drillbill, Trokwi, skulking head down on his shoulder. He usually gave the game away, and if the little automaton was still insufficient a clue, the massive axe Flynt carried on his shoulder was equally unmistakeable. For the truly unperceptive, the ogor plodding through the water in front of him cinched the deal. No one flew with Gord the Ogor but Drekki Flynt! Say Drekki's name aloud of a night and astound a bar. *'I've fared with Drekki Flynt!'* was a common enough boast. But just then, there was no one to see. No one to hail Drekki or to curse him.

To call the streets 'streets' was a generous lie; they were yellow streams pouring from the hills behind the town. The flood cut the earth of the unpaved roads, leaving hollows and rounded stones to take feet by surprise. Tall Gord was untroubled, the water foaming about his tree-trunk legs. For him this was fun. The others struggled on in his wake in varying levels of misery.

'Do we really need the running saga about how filthy this weather is in this filthy town, when it's all running down my bloody trouser leg?' Drekki went on. Rain rattled so hard off his closed helm that he had to shout over the noise.

'But, captain!' Evtorr protested. 'I'm chronicling your latest adventure. It helps to say the words out loud, so I'll remember.'

'Thanks, but no thanks. No amount of poet's polish is going to put a shine on this bilge pit, so stow it in your deepest hold, Evtorr, and keep it there,' said Drekki.

'I'm supposed to be *Unki-skold*,'[1] protested Evtorr. 'Couplets and rhymes is what I do, captain.'

'You're ship's signaller, too. Stick to that. You've more talent there,' chided Drekki.

The others in Drekki's party chuckled. Evtorr's verses were an acquired taste, one that no one had yet acquired. Evtorr's helm drooped. He had spent good money having its moustaches inlaid with silver, so all would know he was a poet. Never had his metal mask looked so woebegone.

'Yes, captain,' he said.

'Now now, don't sulk, write it down later, and torture us with it when it's finished,' said Drekki. 'You never know, you might pen a good one yet.'

'Doubt it,' piped up Evrokk Bjarnisson, ship's helmsduardin, and Evtorr's brother. 'He's been trying all his life. Not got there yet!'

'He left me out and all,' grumbled Gord. 'All stout duardin. I'm stout.' He slapped his massive ogor's gut. 'But I ain't no duardin!'

He laughed at his joke alone. The crew were too busy avoiding being swept away to find it funny. Being duardin meant being shorter than a human, broad across the shoulder, with powerful, stocky limbs and large hands and feet. Beards. All the usual physiognomy of the children of Grungni. Their form was suited to life underground, as ancient history attested, and surprisingly well fitted to life in the sky, as the more recent Kharadron nations had proven, but rather poor for swimming. Heavy-boned duardin sank and drowned more often than not, and a duardin weighed down by aeronautical equipment most certainly did. It was a fate they were at some risk of just then.

---

1 | Kharadrid: Ship's poet.

'Come on, stunties,' Gord said cheerily. 'Not that hard. Push on now.'

'Not that hard!' said Kedren Grunnsson, ship's runesmith. A unique appointment on a sky-ship. He was no Kharadron. You could tell by the way he moved. The crew wore aeronautical suits of design so similar they were virtually indistinguishable, but Kedren stuck out. He walked stiffly, as someone who had become accustomed to the gear rather than born to it.

'Over there! Way up's on that side,' said Gord. They waded to the side of the street.

'Look at this. Ropes!' Kedren said incredulously, tugging at the lines anchored to the buildings. They were at human height, for it was mostly humans who dwelled in Bavardia. 'What good are ropes? What about paving? What about drains? What about choosing a better site for their town rather than this piss-filled bathtub!' He grabbed hold just the same.

'You're no fun, ground pounder, too *grumbaki*[2] by half,' retorted Adrimm Adrimmsson, who was dragging himself along behind the smith.

'Is that me you're calling grumbaki, Adrimm? The grumbliest duardin alive? There's a cheek!'

'Now now, my lads,' said their captain, who had it a bit easier, being safe in the ogor's lee. 'We'll soon be out of the rain and into the dry. Ales all round. Some meat! That much I can promise.'

Adrimm didn't take the hint to shut up – he rarely did – and continued to moan at Kedren.

'I could have stayed on the ship,' said Adrimm.

'What, and miss all the fun in this sewer?' said Kedren. 'That's the fourth turd that's slapped into my gut.'

'I keep telling you aeronautical gear has its benefits, Kedren,' said Otherek Zhurafon, aether-khemist, and Kedren's long-standing friend. 'Sealed in. Turd proof.' He rapped a knuckle on his chestplate.

---

2 | Khazalid/Kharadrid: Old grumbling duardin.

'Proof? Pah! It will take forever to get the stink out,' said Kedren. 'I hate this place. I hate this *funti*[3] weather.'

'Listen to the oldbeard,' said Drekki. 'Evtorr was right about one thing, at least – *nobody* likes Bavardia.'

Offended, the rain redoubled its efforts to wash them out, and they were forced to cease their grumbling for a while.

'Keep on, stunties, keep on!' bellowed Gord. 'Nearly there.'

The crew reached a set of steps that led off the road to a raised pavement.

'I suppose we'll be dry now,' said 'Hrunki' Tordis, who would have had a monopoly on optimism in the crew, were it not for Drekki.

'Dry? Dry?! All this pavement is is a shoddy substitute for good civic planning,' said Kedren.

Gord stepped aside to let the duardin up. Buffeted by the flow yet untroubled by it, he shepherded his crewmates with care. A good job too. Although Drekki mounted the steps all right, Gord was obliged to catch Kedren to stop him being whirled away.

'Grungni-damned, Grimnir-cursed stupid *umgak*[4] city,' growled Kedren as Gord deposited him on the pavement. One after another the crew scrambled up, shedding filthy water. Buildings covered the pavement over, forming a sheltered area, though to duardin sensibilities it looked like it had been done by accident rather than by design. Buildings of stone leaned on buildings of wood, propped up over the pavement on wonky timber posts and rusty iron girders.

'This place was surely built by *grobi*,'[5] said Evrokk. There was a sense of wonder in his voice. 'You couldn't design a collapse better than this if you tried.'

---

3 | Kharadrid: A common Overlord curse. Best left untranslated.

4 | Khazalid/Kharadrid: Human-built. Also: shoddy.

5 | Khazalid/Kharadrid: The common species of grots.

'You say that every time we go to an *umgi*[6] town!' said Evtorr, still peevish at his brother.

'Worth saying, that's why. Unlike your verse, brother,' said Evrokk.

'Come on, come on, beards straight! Keep your aether shining,' said Drekki. 'Umgi build as they will, and bad weather we have, but good beer awaits.' Even Drekki didn't swallow his own bluster. His jollity was entirely forced.

There were a few folk around up above the flood but they hurried on by, heads down, eager to escape the weather, and not one recognised the captain, to his chagrin. The crew trudged into tottering alleys as water and shit surged down the streets below. A rat's maze to be sure, but it could not defeat their beer-sense. A duardin can find his way to a pub all turned about and blindfolded.

Drommsson's Refuge was the sole duardin-built place in town, with four square walls and a roof of precisely engineered bronze plates. Old Drommsson hadn't trusted human foundations and had cut his own right through the clay until he hit rock. Old Drommsson didn't like human beer, so served only the best duardin ales. Old Drommsson didn't like humans at all, but always seemed to find himself among them. Old Drommsson was a host of contradictions. Old Drommsson was a lot of things, but most of all Old Drommsson was dead.

'Fifty *raadfathoms*!'[7] Drekki said, recalling the old publican's words. 'Do you remember that?' He elbowed Kedren. 'He boasted long and hard about the depth of the pilings he had to put in. He always used to say that, remember? Fifty raadfathoms! Good old Drommsson. Eh, lads?'

He turned about. His duardin were subdued, aetherpacks steaming, rain plinking loudly from the brass.

---

6 | Khazalid/Kharadrid: Human.
7 | Kharadrid: Standard measurement of distance.

'Well, a more miserable line of skyfarers I never did see. Show some spirit! You're Drekki Flynt's swashbuckling crew, not a bunch of half-drowned skyrinx. I've got an image to think of!'

Nobody spoke.

Drekki sighed into his helm, a noise like a night wind teasing the rigging. For a moment, he wished he were back out at sky. 'All right, lads. First round's on me.'

The crew perked up remarkably.

Behind the Refuge's roof the great copper sphere of the brewery vat swelled invitingly, not dissimilar in appearance to a Kharadron aether-endrin globe.

'Now there's a promise of beers to be drunk, eh, lads?' said Drekki.

They reached the doors. They were sheathed in bronze, and decorated in beaten, geometric designs of the sort that once graced the gates of the ancient mountain karaks.[8] Very inviting, but Drekki stopped, and turned to face his crew.

'Hold it right there, lads,' Drekki said. 'Before we go in...'

'Can we at least get out of the rain before you give us one of your interminable pep talks?' Adrimm moaned.

'Eh? Interminable? Pep talks? You stow it, Fair-weather,' said Drekki, using the nickname Adrimm hated. 'This is important. We've got our rivals. We have our friends. There might be either in here tonight. We've a delicate job ahead of us. Our client does not want a fuss, of any sort. Keep yourselves below the aethergauge. I don't want a lot of notice. Certainly not like last time, right, Umherth? Umherth? Are you listening? That was embarrassing.'

'If you say so, captain,' said Umherth, not at all abashed. Hrunki, his constant companion, sniggered into her helm.

'A low profile, right?' said Drekki, wagging his finger. 'All of

---

8 | Khazalid/Kharadrid: The mountain fastnesses of the old Khazalid Empire. Most were overrun in the Age of Chaos, and remain ruined to this day.

you. Low profiles. So low, I don't want to see your heads over the bar. Got that?'

A rain-sodden chorus of 'aye, captain' came back.

'Right then,' said Drekki. He rubbed his hands together. 'Beer time.' He took a step, stopped, and looked up at Gord.

'Actually, you'd better go first, Gord. Just in case.'

'Right you are, captain,' said Gord. He covered three duardin strides in a single, decisive step, both hands out. They banged into the doors like battering rams, flinging them open with a metallic boom and revealing a big entrance hall, full of lockers for sky-farers' kit. From the atrium, inner doors led into the common room. Gord strode right in and pushed those open too.

Warmth, light and laughter streamed out. Someone was play-ing an aether-gurdy. Badly.

Gord stopped in the middle of the bar.

'Oi!' the ogor bellowed. 'Clear a table! Captain Drekki Flynt's in town!'

The noise faltered. When the hubbub returned, it had a dif-ferent flavour. Urgent, excited, somewhat annoyed.

Drekki grinned. 'Say what you like about our ogor,' he said, 'he certainly knows how to make an entrance.'

'I thought you said low profiles all round, captain?' said Evtorr sharply. He could nurse a sulk like no one else.

'Hush now,' said Drekki. 'You're spoiling it.'